The Huntress

Alterealm Series
Book 1

J. Risk

THE ALTEREALM SERIES
1 *The Huntress*
2 *The Seer*
3 *The Empath*
4 *The Witch*
5 *The Chronos*
6 *The Warrior*
7 *The Telepath*

Writing As: Jacqueline Paige

Dreams
Three steamy stories that started with a dream

Curses
Two tales of curses.

After the Silence
Volume 1 Bree

ANIMAL SENSES
1 *Heart*
2 *Scent*
3 *Passion*

MAGIC SEASONS ROMANCE
1 *Beltane Magic*
2 *Solstice Heat*
3 *Harvest Dreams*
4 *Autumn Dance*
5 *Winter Mist*

MYSTIC GIFTS TRILOGY
Re-release coming soon

ANCESTOR'S ENCHANTMENT TRILOGY
Coming soon

SINGLE TITLES
Solitary Witchling
Salvation

Published by FRP

Edited by Gaele Hince

ISBN: 978-1-7773723-0-9
ISBN (digital) : 978-1-7773723-1-6

ACKNOWLEDGEMENT:

Carsta – I've had many beta readers before, but never have they demanded I get to work and finish it so they can find out what happened! Thank you for making this one exhilarating and fun to work on.

CHAPTER ONE

I didn't even get both eyes opened and focused before I knew something was wrong. Where was the color? I was only seeing sepia? Everything was brown. Blinking rapidly, I tried to readjust my eyes to see if there was any other hue. It didn't change a thing and for the life of me I couldn't figure out why.

Sitting there, I tried to decipher what was going on and why I was sitting on the ground. Looking down I ran my hand over the dried dusty surface. Why was I on the ground? Craning my neck as far as I could in all directions, I looked around. Okay, where was the pavement and cement? The buildings and streets I called my natural turf?

The why's flying around in my brain suddenly decided the top question, was what the *hell* was going on?

Squeezing my eyes shut, I struggled to recall the last thing I remembered doing. I was hunting down a bounty—a nice one with a large dollar sign attached to her. I had tracked her ass down and…

I confronted her? Yes, I was minutes away from calling Frank and telling him to get out his shiny pen and sign my check.

So what happened between then and now? Not to sound repetitive, which is something that drives me nuts, but *what* the hell was going on?

Startled, I started to check for bullet holes or the deep crevices that knives leave behind in flesh. That had to be it, I'd taken a beating and this was that in between place you sit when you're near death's door, but not quite ready to see what lies on the other side.

Finding no critical injury, I slumped forward and rubbed my head. There was some rational explanation for this, there had to be. Had I been drugged? It could be some crazy hallucination. Any minute now I was going to either wake up in my bed at home or some hospital with a cheery nurse leaning over me, reassuring me we are going to be *just* fine. I only had to wait it out a little longer and all would be normal.

To kill time until I woke up, I looked around some more. Wherever this was it looked like a burnt out world. Not the charred kind of burn, but depleted and completely used up sort.

Vacant.

Sitting still wasn't really a strong trait of mine, so I figured I'd get up and take a look around, there had to be something to see around here. If my body was actually somewhere else for safekeeping, what harm could come to me, right?

I staggered like I'd never stood before, struggling to get my balance. Whatever was going on with me, my equilibrium was totally shot. Standing there swaying like grass in the breeze, I turned carefully trying to see if there was anything around me except rust tinted dirt and nothingness.

My heart stumbled around in my chest when I spotted someone coming in my direction. Yes! I wasn't the only one in this soulless place.

The closer it got to me made me the more I questioned my original conclusion. I didn't know, exactly, but it was not some*one* it was a some*thing*. No one label could describe it. Standing over six feet, it had the shape of a man dressed in jeans and a large, very out of fashion gingham snap up shirt. When I reached the face, I can only describe it as part wrinkle puppy dog with floppy skin crossed with Freddy and Jason after the slash scenes.

It stopped in front of me and instinct had me reach around behind me under my jean jacket for my raptor claw knife, which I put on as regular as underwear when dressing; and that would be everyday, by the way. Relief washed over me when I felt the small circular handle. At least while waiting to survive I got to bring my toys with me.

Big brown eyes assessed me slowly and I wanted to make the call that it was harmless, but yeah, having tracked down anything from a sicko killer to a card shark in the last three years, I knew better than to fall for sappy looks.

"Are you a magishian? You juisht appeared."

A male voice, even though he spoke with a heavy lisp that randomly inserted *ish* into his words. Then again if I had saggy lips like he did, I'd be happy to talk at all. I sized him up for a few more seconds, trying to gauge whether he was really in front of me, or if I was having some sort of psychotic episode. Was a magician good or bad? I decided the play dumb, being blonde did have *some* advantages. "A magician?"

Those brown eyes developed a nervous quiver. Magician equaled bad. "No..."

He looked relieved. "Oh good. I didn't want to have to bash you over the head."

I grasped my raptor tightly and shrugged. "Yeah, me either."

The sky brightened and began to glow a rust orange color. When I asked for some color, I'd hoped for something out of the orange family.

"We better go, they'll be coming soon."

"They?" I glanced around quickly, not wanting to take my eyes off him for long.

He nodded and pranced on the spot, the nervous movement had me on high alert. "The daywalkers." He whispered.

Daywalkers? Did I even want to know? I didn't think

so, but this bizarre nightmare wasn't going to be complete if I didn't ask.

Looking me over a few times, his eyes widened under the pressure of his drooping forehead; *that* was quite the expression. "You're not one of them, are you?"

I walked in the day, night and even at dusk, but I wasn't going to tell him that. I decided honesty might work, if not violence was always a good backup. Judging by his expression daywalker ranked on the bad list with magician. "I—I don't know what you'd call me."

Those sappy eyes looked me up and down a few times trying to figure me out. "You better come with me. It's not safe to leave you wandering around." He looked behind him and then motioned behind me and started walking.

I knew in my gut it was a mistake, but as I had no other real options… I didn't know where I was or what was going on and so far he knew more than I did. "Where are we going?"

Pausing he glanced over his shoulder and then lumbered along again. "I'll take you to Troy, he'll know what to do."

My eyes were starting to strain as the sky brightened. "This Troy, he's in charge?"

He stopped so suddenly I almost ploughed right into his back. When he turned, and looked at me, his eyes weren't a sad brown any more but were leaning more towards red. It had to be from the strange color of the sunrise. "You're not from Alterealm are you?"

"Is that where we are?"

He nodded.

"Nope."

That nervous jitter of his seemed to return all at one. "How did you get here?"

A reasonable question that I had nothing to offer that resembled an answer. "I don't know that either."

His red eyes darted to the sky. "We have to go."

Turning, he began jogging toward, well, nothing that I could see. Not wanting to find out what he was afraid of, I ran along behind him. All I could think was this Troy person, if he was a person, better have some answers.

He stopped again and dropped down onto his knees. Was he hurt? Surely that short jaunt hadn't winded him that much. He began tapping his hand on the ground. What was he doing? Looking all around us, I kept watch for anything really, not wanting to meet these daywalkers in the slightest. Just when I'd had about enough of his short break, he grasped something in the sand and pulled a door in the ground open.

"We're going to have to use the shortcut. We don't have time to get to the main gates."

Looking down into a hole with a ladder, I glanced around again and despite every muscle in my body telling me to run and get the hell out of here, I started down the metal rungs into a deep hole that would take me, hopefully back to friggin' reality.

CHAPTER TWO

I stood there at the bottom of the ladder and waited for him to come down. The floor was dirt, but the walls were something I knew and was happy to see, cement. The tunnel was at least eight feet wide and tall enough that I didn't feel closed in, but that could have had something to do with my height.

When the big guy stepped off the ladder and came to stand right in front of me, I realized I only came up to his chest and his clearance to the tunnel roof wasn't as spacious as my own.

"This way," he began a lazy jog down the tunnel.

Pulling my jacket tighter around me, I walked quickly behind him. I wasn't ready to run into the unknown. I'd had enough of that for one day.

The lights that lined the tunnel were shockingly bright and, no surprises here almost glowed orange. Would it be too much to ask for a little blue or green in this Alterealm place?

When he reached a door, he started to open it and then paused and waited for me. "Stay beside me, okay?"

I nodded. Did he really think I was going to wander off into God knows what on my own? Like it or not, he was my life-line in this screwed up adventure and I was sticking with him until the time came when I knew enough to get the hell out of here.

Placing a hand behind my back he ushered me though the door and closed it again. He turned and entered some numbers into a key pad and locks clicked into place.

If my tear ducts hadn't been filled with dust from the dried out place we'd just come from I may have shed a tear at the mere sight of advanced technology.

"Troy will still be awake. He likes everyone to report in just after sunrise."

I filed that information and kept silent. We walked though so many doors and rooms I knew there was no way I'd ever find my way out if I needed to. That left me feeling a little discomfited inside and wanting to hurry up and get some answers to get my weirded-out ass home.

When he paused in front of a huge wooden door, I felt like a dwarf lost in the giants' castle. If this Troy turned out to be an actual giant, I was taking the first tunnel I could find back out into the orange world.

Knocking once, he opened the door and went in. I stepped in behind him and used him for cover as I looked around to scope out what I was going into. There was no giant to be seen. There were half a dozen *really* big guys standing, leaning or lounging, all facing a man sitting behind a desk. The part that had me reach for the comfort of my raptor was that not one of them except the guy behind the desk seemed—human.

They weren't like my giant puppy guy with the sappy eyes, no that would be okay at this point. What they were, was, well I didn't know. They looked normal enough, yet their skin glowed and their eyes were bright colors; anything from green to lava red. I'd wanted new shades besides orange. Definitely a be-careful-what- you-wish-for moment.

"Troy." Puppy man clearly without a single *ish* that I noticed. "I found her in the wasteland, she just appeared."

My shaking hand grasped the handle tightly behind my back.

"Did you check her for weapons?" A large creature with neon green eyes and long white hair, that gave him a glow of white all over stalked toward me. He was dressed all in black leather like a biker and I found that to be the only normal thing about him.

"Back off Welsley." My finder stepped forward and blocked this other thing's path.

"Move aside *Quapple* or I'll have to move you. We can't let a stranger just walk in here."

My protector's shoulders slumped and that alone made me want to stick my blade into Welsley just for being a big glowy jerk. Glancing over his shoulder at me, his brown eyes apologizing, I gave him a little nod and stepped over so there was no one between the white guy and my path.

Neon green eyes moved over me and then paused on the arm still behind my back. He sneered and steeped towards me again.

Taking a nice wide stance, I braced myself for some action and pulled the raptor free. With a very practiced move, I flipped it from a hidden position to plain sight. I locked eyes with him. "You. Back off now or I *will* slice you a whole new lifestyle."

He stopped and there was no mistaking the shock on his face. I heard a few snickers, but wasn't about to look away from a pissy male that had just been put on pause by a woman half his size, even one that was having a bad day.

"Stand down." A voice of definite authority ended all motion and sound in the room.

My glowing aggressor stepped back and moved aside so I had a clear sight line to the man behind the desk. Nothing on him was glowing. To be honest, he was most likely the nicest-looking piece of man I'd ever seen. The am-I-drooling-on-myself kind of nice. He had long blonde hair that made my own look blunt and in need of some serious conditioning therapy. His face was taken right off some Greek god lineage of masculine beauty and slapped onto what looked like a body to match—at least the part I could see above the desk.

"Everyone move back and let our guest have a little breathing room."

Like soldiers marching, the six light-radiating beings stepped back as far as furniture and walls would allow. The Greek Adonis gave a small nod of approval and then looked at me. Hazel eyes with long lashes that made me jealous looked at me patiently. Feeling really awkward, I slid the blade back into the sheath on my back and stood up straight. Slowly his eyes moved to the only body that hadn't moved away from me.

"Quinton, I was beginning to worry. You've been gone three nights."

"I was safe enough." Again there was barely a trace of the lisp, as if he tried harder to conceal it then he had with me.

"I don't doubt it, but next time call or at least turn on your phone."

Phone? Music to my ears thank you very much for this weirdness, now call me a cab.

"Please take a seat."

Eyes widening, I looked back to see him looking at me. Glancing around at the others, I moved and sat on the edge of a chair closest to the door, trying to stay at an angle that let me see if one of the glow-brights made a move toward me.

Quinton came over and stood behind the chair, his sad eyes conveying he had my back. At this point I'd take what I could get.

The white haired one moved around to stand behind the desk. He crossed his arms, green eyes shooting darts at me. One of the others moved over and stood behind him. He wasn't as unearthly looking, with a dimmer shade of blue aura and red eyes.

"She's looking at us like she can *see* us." One of them said with fear in his voice.

Were my eyes supposed to be obscured? I could see them and I wasn't sure who but I could definitely smell one of them too and he was long overdue for a little personal hygiene. Slowly they moved to stand where I could see them, my first thought right after *you're screwed* was all those horror movie marathons were coming back to get me. All that was missing at this point was the screaming damsel —oh wait, I could play that part. I wasn't much of a screamer and rarely freaked out, but there's always a first time.

Glancing around the room again, hoping I'd missed the flashing exit sign I noticed the looks I was receiving ranged from shock to disdain. Except for the cutie behind the desk. Actually he fit more into the hottie category and leaned heavily to the sophisticated side of life with the way he just sat there observing everything.

Raising a hand, he waved off the others from speaking. "Do you know how you got here?"

Saving the lengthy explanations on my own personal theories I just shook my head in answer.

"What's the last thing you remember?"

He seemed like he was really trying to help me. I shrugged. "Not much, I was chasing down a bounty."

"You're a bounty hunter?"

I nodded and then froze when there were several gasps and sounds of shock in the room. Quinton sounded like he sighed in relief. I hoped that meant a bounty hunter was good thing in this place. "Where the hell am I?" I blurted out.

He leaned forward on the desk and looked like he was trying to think of a way to explain it to me. "This is Alterealm, which is more or less the same time, same place as you came from, just a slightly different reality." He smirked. "I believe we're what nightmares are based on."

Raising an eyebrow, I looked around at the guys with their own light systems built in and their pimped out eyes. "Are you seriously telling me that all those things that go bump in the night are true?"

The sexy one behind the desk flashed red eyes and I'm not kidding, *fangs* at me for a few seconds, just long enough to make sure I caught it all.

"Proof enough?"

"Yeah, that covers the next question too." Taking a deep breath, I reigned in that feeling you get when you want to run screaming. "So, why am I here and how the hell do I get home?"

Eyes all normal hazel again, he sat back and studied me. "First we must find out the why. Not just anyone can walk both worlds, it's very rare. Now tell me the last thing you remember."

My survival attitude kicked in, also known as sarcasm. "Should I be laying on a couch for this?" I heard Quinton chuckle behind me and fought the urge to smile. The others looked confused, but the man asking the questions did smirk, at least I think that's what those appealing lips were doing. Taking a deep breath, I sat back a little more. "Okay. I was taking down this chick, a bail jumper, Wanda something and I shit you not her alias is Glenda the Witch..."

He sat forward and held up his hand. "Wait. Black hair, two different colored eyes?"

I frowned, not liking he knew this. "Uh, yeah..."

"She belongs on this side," he said quietly.

Quinton stepped around the chair. "She's in trouble. Let me go help her, Troy."

The man sitting sighed. "Quinton, you know you can't cross over, right now...'

"You mean ever again." Quinton muttered.

"We don't know that and now is not the time to..."

I stood up. "Hello, can we get back to Wanda? I don't care where she belongs, she's a bounty and I don't ever lose a..."

The one with the blue aura stepped forward and pointed at me. "You're her!" He looked around at the others. "It's her!"

Hands on hips, I snarled at the hand pointing at me. "*Her* who?"

They converged on the desk like a swarm of flies and spoke quietly, all while giving me strange looks out of the corner of their eyes. Quinton remained where he was and I was half a second away from begging him to take me out to the daywalkers he feared. I'd like to wake up now. Promise never to eat fudge before bed again, I thought.

"Is your name Daxx? D.A.X.X?"

Please let this be a dream. "Yeah, how do you know my name?"

He motioned to the chair I'd been sitting in, I shook my head feeling a little better on my feet and ready to spring into action if I needed to. "An old prophet told of a woman hunter named Daxx that would cross between and serve justice." He looked up at Quinton. "You're right Wanda is in trouble if she sent Daxx here."

I backed up a few feet and lifted my hands to show I was emptied handed. "Look, as entertaining as all of this is, I really have to go."

"There are ways to prove what we say is true." The blonde behind the desk smiled suggestively.

My heart starting convulsing inside my chest. "Does it involve a stone alter and all of my blood?

He smiled, plainly to see this time. "No." He motioned once again to the chair. Quinton turned and gave me a little nod, he still had my back.

Sighing, I sat down and leaned back. Let them prove their crap and then go home, that was the plan.

"Do you have the mark of a sundial on your back?"

Lunging forward I glared at him. "Okay, how the *fuck* do you know about that? I don't even know how I got that!"

"You were born with it, but it wouldn't have become visible until you came into your power."

I snorted. "Power? Now I have power?"

He sat back looking amused at my reaction. "Shielding would be the best way to put it. Other supernatural powers won't work on you."

"Oh well, there ya go. Good to know." This guy was on crack for sure. I waved a hand around trying to appear calmer than I was inside. "So if what you're saying is true then how did the witch get me here?"

"She merely transported you, it's not a power it's a device."

I sat there and watched him for several seconds, waiting for him to crack a smile that told me he was just feeding me a line of bull. My theory of being in purgatory while my body was struggling to live seemed to be the more appealing one at this point. If what this guy said was true, I had no idea what I was going to do. Taking a deep breath I tried to keep my voice steady. "Whatever you say. Look, your story, while fun in the beginning is filled with a whole lot of gaping holes and you need to work on some serious rewrites. First you say a select few can *cross over* and presto now you have a device that does this…"

He flashed a brilliant smile. "I see where I left out a few pieces—anyone can cross over, only a few can do so without dying in the first minutes of doing it."

I closed my mouth that was hanging open. "Oh." Really, what could I say to that?

Quinton moved over to the desk. "We need to find Wanda."

Troy nodded and then looked back to me. "Why were you hunting her?"

Eyes wide, I sat forward. "She jumped bail. I'm a bounty hunter…"

He nodded. "Yes, but why was she arrested?"

"She beat the hell out of two guys, mind you I probably would have too, they were in serious need of some readjustments in the attitude department…"

"Troy…" Quinton said impatiently.

"I know." Leaning on his desk again he watched me. "She's in real trouble, Wanda doesn't have a violent bone in her body, if she…"

I got up, unable to sit still for a second longer. "Wait, are you saying she deliberately got herself arrested and then jumped bail?"

"Yes."

He offered nothing more. Sighing, I paced a few feet and then looked back at him. "Why?"

"To find you," he added with so much conviction I really believed him.

Could anything they were saying be true? Was I supposed to be here? I didn't know how the hell they knew about my *tattoo*, very few knew about it. Looking up from the floor I stared him down. "Okay, let's say I am starting to believe some of the crap you're shoveling, you said you could prove that I'm this hunter or whatever."

"I already believe." He added quietly. "I haven't been able to pick one single thought out of your head, and *that* I can swear has never happened before."

He could pick thoughts out of heads? Right. "Afraid I'm going to need a little more proof."

He smirked. "You haven't run screaming from the room, have you asked yourself why?"

"I've thought about it." I looked around at the others that had become very quiet and still. "Didn't think I'd get far to tell you the truth." I shrugged. "I'm more of a stay and fight kinda gal, not much of a runner." I glanced around at the others again, either I was getting used to it or they had dimmed the glow thing. "What else have you got?"

"Arius, can you *suggest* anything?"

A smaller one, and I mean he was less than seven feet tall smaller, stepped forward. "I've been trying, it's not working."

I frowned. "Trying what?" I watched Arius as he moved forward and stood in front of me. Had I thought smaller? He was just as big as Quinton was and perhaps his shoulders were even wider. He smiled at me and I couldn't help but think that was a definite player in front of me. Flipping back his long black hair he glanced around at the others.

"Pick one and tell me what you want him to do."

It took several seconds before it sunk in. "You can make them do whatever you want?"

"Yes." Another playboy grin flashed at me.

I hoped it was true. I looked around the room and then

zeroed in on the one with the white hair that still stood there and glared at me with disdain. Even without his eyes all bright green he still bugged me. "If I can't slice him a new life style, maybe he could be shown a little humility."

"Troy," The white haired one growled at me.

"Welsley, I will allow it." Troy uttered with that voice of authority again.

Sighing, Welsley moved around to stand a few feet away from Arius. "Don't think this gives you free reign to do this whenever the mood strikes."

"I only do what I am commanded to do." Arius stated drily and then turned to me. "What do you request?"

Studying the way Welsley sneered at me for a moment, I moved over and reached up to whisper my request so only Arius could hear me.

He straightened and looked down at me, a smirk playing at the corners of his mouth. "Not what I expected, but more than doable."

Crossing my arms, I stood there beside Quinton and watched Arius stand in front of Welsley. Welsley's eyes were locked onto Arius's as he stood there silently. I could tell when the suggestion, with his mind, had been made because Welsley's spine stiffened and even though I watched I wasn't sure if this was going to actually happen. With ridged movements, as if he was being pushed against his will, Welsley came over and stood in front of me. Dropping down to one knee, he looked up at me and I'm sure if he had the ability to kill with a look I would have fallen dead to the floor in that second. With his teeth clenched his eyes moved to Quinton.

"I—apologize for my rude behavior, Q-uinton." He clenched his jaw as if fighting what was happening. "I will..." he closed his eyes, "not call you Quapple again."

I hadn't known the end part, Arius must have added that little bit in for himself, but I still liked it.

Welsley stood up and glared down at me before moving to the other side of the room.

Quinton turned and looked at me. He didn't need to say it, I could see the surprise and look of thanks in his deep brown eyes.

I smiled and then turned to look at Troy. "Okay, so this could be fun." I shrugged. "What's next? You've got me on the fence. I just need to pick a side."

Everyone turned and looked at Troy with a mix of fear and excitement on their face. He pushed his chair back and stood up. "I don't have a witch handy or we'd try some magic and see if you can reflect it like Arius' suggestion."

I mentally checked to make sure my tongue wasn't hanging out as he stepped around the desk. My first thought of how he'd looked had been a slightly underestimated. He was huge, in size from height to well-toned width and leather pants had never looked so fine on a body before.

"I can't precisely prove that I have the ability to read one's thoughts…" he looked to Quinton. "Perhaps you could vouch for me?"

Quinton nodded and leaned closer to me. "He used to pick all those embarrassing thoughts you thought were your own and blurt them out when he was a young brat."

Troy raised an eyebrow at him and then looked down at me. "I've matured greatly since then." He glanced up and down me and I fought the little flutters that took flight in my entire system from his eyes moving over me. "May I?" He looked innocent enough in his gesture. "Sometimes if I'm closer I can pick up things from those that are more resistant to me."

My brain was thinking there was no one out there that would be able to resist him, I was struggling with it right now. Then I realized he meant to see if he could figure out what I was thinking, which might prove embarrassing on my side. "Give it your best shot." I wanted to cry uncle as he stepped close enough that I could feel the heat coming off his tall well-built body. I found out that he was not the one with the offensive smell, because he smelled of pure fantasy and sin.

He looked into my eyes as he rested one large warm

hand against my neck. I knew I was holding my breath, but I was afraid to breathe and tried to focus on clearing the naughty thoughts out of my head, just in case I wasn't impervious to his skill. He didn't need to know what I was thinking that involved his body and mine—naked. I couldn't do it one second longer. "Look, handsome—as much as the vibes from you rock me, if you get any closer I'm going to have to ask for some privacy…"

Hazel eyes moved over my mouth and then he looked back to my eyes. The look he gave me said he knew how I was feeling, but that he had not necessarily needed to look inside my mind to find that out. Dropping his hand, he stepped back giving me some air to suck back into my lungs.

"Mmm, not a thought to be had." Turning he looked around at the others and then moved back over and sat on the edge of his desk.

CHAPTER THREE

My whole body was humming still from him being that close. My brain was racing faster than my pulse as everything that had happened in the last hour of my life started to digest. "Okay. I need some space. Please, everyone just go find something else to be doing and let me think."

Troy nodded to all the inquisitive looks around the room and bodies started moving toward the door.

I pointed at him. "You. Stay. There will be questions."

Quinton looked hesitantly from his leader back to me. "I'll just be outside if you need me, Daxx."

My heart bonded with this gentle creature at that moment. Reaching out, I placed my hand on his arm. "Thank you, Quinton."

His brown eyes were shining when they looked up from my hand on his arm. Carefully, he patted it and then gave a brisk nod to Troy and left.

Troy's eyes were appraising me carefully. "If I didn't know better, I'd say you were some sort of miracle."

"What? I think you have prophecy and fairy tale mixed up there, big guy."

He grinned and shook his head. "Never mind, it's complicated." He continued to lean there and look at me.

Suddenly feeling warm, I shrugged out of my jacket and

then looked down when I remembered I was only wearing a thin spaghetti strap top that left a lot of skin bare and showing. Looking back over at him, I watched his eyes that were red again checking out the flesh that was exposed. "So, are you a vampire or something?"

His red eyes moved back to my face. "Not exactly, but we've been referred to as such for centuries."

Nightmare returning… "You drink *blood*?" I reached for the handle of my raptor, needing to feel its familiar handle in my grip.

"Worse," he whispered as he straightened up and moved back toward me.

I swallowed and thought long about what could possibly be worse than sucking the blood from a body. I had no suggestions to offer up.

"We drink your essence." He stopped in front of me.

Slowly looking up the large chest in front of my face, I searched his red eyes. "My what?"

He leaned down closer and I swallowed again.

"Your essence. Your spirit." He said slowly.

Looking down at me again I watched his eyes brighten and fangs lengthen. I curbed the insane thought of touching one with my finger tip to see if it was as sharp as it looked. I believed the worse part now, just looking at him.

"We bite…" he touched the side of my throat with the back of his hand, "right here and drink your essence."

"And I die." Where was the run reflex that should have gone with that statement?

"Only if we take it all quickly, which as it turns out is bad for both parties…" he touched my throat slowly again and then whispered. "You don't need to fear me, little Daxx, part of your power is I can't take a damn thing from you unless you consent."

I leaned back and looked up at him. "Really?" My heart didn't seem to slow down at the thought of being safe from his bite. "Good to know. Now back away so we can get down to playing twenty questions."

Reaching out, he touched my hair between two fingers and then backed up. He went over and sat down on the couch and motioned to the chair across from it.

With a lot of hesitation, I sat down and leaned back. There were questions and too many to narrow it down to the most important.

"You seem to be accepting all of this better than I thought you might when you first stepped in the door."

Looking around the room, I weighed what he was saying. "Looks can be deceiving. I don't know why I'm not screaming for you to send me home, but that doesn't mean I'm buying into all of this yet either."

"Understandable."

"So, you're what, King around here?"

"More or less." Leaning further down onto the couch, he tilted his head and watched me. I was trying not to notice how soft looking his hair was as it fell to the front of his shoulder. "Would you like a quick history lesson then, maybe it will clear up some of your questions."

I snorted. "The only thing that will clear up my head right now is a bottle of JD and a long nap."

He grinned. "That's more procrastination than clearing."

"Whatever works, right?" Closing my eyes, I tried to zero in on one single thought and couldn't find a way through the fog to focus. "Okay." Opening my eyes, I looked back at his patient ones, to see they were hazel again. "Start slow and we'll take it from there. Explain this place."

"I can explain my existence. Pure bloods are born to this side. Every five hundred years twins are birthed by the queen, one will rule day and the other night…"

"Wait, so they rule for five hundred years?" Seriously?

"Yes."

I blew out a loud breath. "Wow, that's some great longevity there."

Troy grinned.

"So, you're one of the twins aren't you?"

He inclined his head. "I am."

"You have a twin?" Two of them that looked like him…
that was, well, awesomeness in its purest form.

"I do."

"How long have you ruled?"

He smirked, like he knew how I was going to react to his
answer. "Close to one hundred and sixty years now." A
sober look crossed his brow. "To answer the next likely
question, I'm two hundred and sixty years old."

My jaw dropped and I knew it but didn't rush to close
my mouth. Slowly I looked over this fine specimen of male
stretched out across from me. There was barely a wrinkle on
his face. "I need to get the list of vitamins you take. You
have two hundred and thirty-four years on me but look like
your thirty."

"Your approval warms me," he stated with a hitch of
humor.

I rolled my eyes at him. "Don't be getting all warm
anything. You said pure bloods are born here, where does
everyone else come from?"

All traces of humor left his eyes. "Your side."

I frowned. "I don't understand."

He leaned forward onto his knees and made eye contact
with me. "There are those that want out, that aren't meant
for the reality they're born into." He paused briefly before
continuing. "For hundreds of years there has been
speculation that somewhere in the family tree a pure blood
bred with one of your kind, but we've never been able to
trace it back to substantiate is as fact."

I held up a hand. "So, what am I? Are you saying I've
got some ancestor that was from here?"

"Perhaps you are, but there's no record of it. For as long
as I can remember even for my father and his father, there
has been a prophecy of a huntress that is neither from one
side or the other. She, in fact, has a foot on each side—so to
speak. It is told that she and she alone will stand equal with
the throne and keep the balance." He shook his head when I

leaned forward. "Let me finish before your sultry lips spew something that will make me cringe."

I pouted by didn't say anything.

"*The* Cross Over Huntress will only come to be in a time lawlessness is prevailing and threatening the balance." He looked upset for a moment before shaking it off. "I can only surmise there is more going on than I am aware of, or you wouldn't be sitting in front of me now." Leaning back, he looked me over for a brief second. "The first thing we need to do is find Wanda and see her back here safely. For her to cross and do what she did and not return…"

"Her ass is in deep shit." I finished for him.

"Yes."

I sighed loudly and long, trying to take all of this in. "Can I ask a few questions before we go rescue your witch?"

"She's not my witch, but yes you may."

I didn't bother asking what he meant by that. "Back tracking here to the foot on either side part. Explain." He stretched out an arm along each side of the back of the couch. I had to mentally smack myself a few times to focus on what he was going to say to take it all in with him offered up like that in front of me.

"Like my brothers and I, you do not need a device to cross over between your realm and ours, once you're taught how you will be able to do it with little effort."

"Ah…kay, we'll come back to that one later. Next question, what do you mean I stand equal to the throne and keep the balance? What am I a princess or something?"

A serious look flashed in his eyes. "More a Queen."

I laughed. Loudly. "Have you got your prophecies and fairy tales mixed up."

"Were there any more questions?" His tone wasn't soft any longer. I'd offended him.

"Roughly a thousand."

He stood up. "There will be time to find all the answers you need. You should rest, we'll go over at dusk and locate Wanda."

Getting to my feet quickly, I looked around the room. "I'm staying here for the night? Day?"

"I think it best. Now let me take you to your room. If you want anything to eat or require any sort of assistance, I'll leave Quinton at your call. He knows as much as I do."

Grabbing my jacket, I hugged it and followed him. "Is he as old as you?"

Troy paused by the door, a sad look crossed his face. "Older actually. I believe he's in the neighborhood of four hundred and fifty. He's actually my big brother."

Closing my mouth, I looked down at the floor. "Oh."

CHAPTER FOUR

We stepped into a room, a bedroom that had more square footage than two of my overpriced two bedroom shacks back home. I felt like I'd stepped into some sort of antique, medieval room. Everything was dark polished wood with deep blue décor. I liked it.

I zeroed in on the bed and once again my loose jaw sagged open. The thing was the size of my living room at home. Turning, I looked over my shoulder at him. "The giant won't be offended that I crash in his bed tonight?"

Troy smirked and then cleared his throat. "This room belongs to no one. It's been lying in wait for the Huntress."

That's me... "I have my own room? For how long has it been waiting?"

"Centuries, roughly twenty I suppose. We've updated a little here and there along the way, but if you wish to change anything that is your choice."

I had a room that had been waiting for my arrival for a couple thousand years. It didn't get any more fantasy realm than that. Going over, I opened a door and almost whimpered to see the gleaming bathroom on the other side. The tub was also something straight from homes for the rich and famous it was marble and I'm pretty sure half my neighborhood could have fit in it. "Am I expected to stay here, on this side now?"

"You can do as you wish."

"I do have a life, you know."

Leaning against the huge desk that sat on what had to be a priceless antique carpet, he looked down at the floor before seeking my eyes again. "I do believe this would be one of those times where life as you know it has been altered."

"Troy!"

I almost fainted as a large man burst through the door scaring me half to death. He stopped and looked from Troy to me, and then back to Troy again. I was looking at the twin; there was no mistaking that, it could have been a mirror with the exception of the blonde goatee on his chin. There was enough alpha male standing in the room now that the world, any one, would never be lacking.

"Daxx, may I introduce my brother, the ruler of the daywalkers. Chase, meet our Huntress."

The big guy faced me, with his hands on his hips, his hazel eyes moving over me taking in every single inch of me to be sure. "So it's true? I thought Arius and Leone were just being dicks."

"Well, I can't vouch for that fact, you did pull some pretty nasty pranks on them when they were kids." Troy, turned and looked at me. "Brothers, you know how they can be."

Hugging my arms around my waist I shook my head. "No, not really. I didn't have family."

A sad look crossed Troy's face, but he cleared it quickly.

Chase moved in my direction slowly, his eyes assessing me as he did. "I can't believe it's true, you're here."

I shrugged. "Yeah well, that makes of two of us then." I stiffened when he stepped around behind me and clenched my teeth as his hand brushed aside my hair that hung just long enough to cover the tattoo between my shoulders. He touched the center of the tattoo and my spine went rigid. I clenched my teeth and reached around and rested my hand over the handle of my knife.

"Did you see this, brother?"

Troy exhaled loudly. "No, I thought it might be rude to paw at her." His eyes met mine and without words he apologized for his brother. "Might I suggest you move away from the Huntress, Chase. You may have been too distracted to notice what her hand now rests upon." His eyes sought mine and held me steady. "You also missed her threatening to slice Welsley a whole new life style."

Chase stepped in front of me again and looked down at me. "You did that?" He smirked.

"Yes and you're coming close to the same offer." My body reacted to his closeness, not in the same way it had to Troy, my knees weren't turning to mush but there was something in the way he watched me that sent conflicting emotions coursing through me. They may be twins, but the man I was looking at was nothing like his brother.

His eyes grew serious. "You could try, Huntress."

I looked him up and down in such a way that I might offend him and make him move away. "Do you drink a person's essence too?"

Those eyes flashed yellow at me. "No."

I looked at his mouth trying to see if there were fangs, but he kept it closed. "What then? If you tell me you live on cheese whiz and peanut butter I'm going to have to call you a liar."

The smile that reached his mouth was one of a predator. He leaned down so his face was level with my own. "Where my brother sustains life on your spirit from within, I keep my heart strong on all those humanly emotions you have inside you."

I knew he was trying to intimidate me with his size and nearness and it was pissing me off. "Really? Do you sense what emotions are coursing through my humanly body right now?"

Scowling, he straightened and tried to hold me with a stare. "No."

I offered a sarcastic grin. "Good, because it's not an all

together pleasant one where you are concerned."

Troy burst out laughing. "I believe the expression is *snap*." He continued to chuckle softly as he came over and glanced down at me with a look of approval.

Every nerve in my body was saying it was done, finished. With one towering over me laughing and the other one snarling at me, I'd had enough. "You did say this is my room."

Troy nodded. "Of course."

I batted my baby blues up at him in one of those pathetic feminine ploys I only reserved for last resort. "And I stand equal with the throne or rather the both of you?"

"Yes." Troy smiled.

I smiled back and batted some more. "Good. Just checking." I glared from one to the other. "Now get out. Both of you. I've had enough of fairy tales and nightmares for one day, thank you very much."

Chase smiled wide when Troy's jaw dropped. "You were saying, brother?"

Troy recovered and turned towards the door. "Quinton will be just outside if you need anything, Daxx."

Chase stopped him with a hand on his arm. "You're leaving her in Quint's care?"

Troy looked at me for a moment before answering. "He found her and is very protective of her."

Chase sent me a startled look but spoke to Troy. "He spoke to her?"

"Yes." Troy gave me that look again that was filled with a soft look.

"The Gods lay in shock," Chase whispered as he went out the door.

"Indeed." Troy nodded to me once and then left, closing the door behind him.

CHAPTER FIVE

You know I had to try the tub, and that's what I did after I stood there and looked around for oh, twenty minutes or so. It was like I'd stepped into some kind of dream, well, if you didn't take into account all the men around here that had flashing eyes like built in glow sticks.

Tucking my knife sheath into the pocket of the satin soft royal blue robe that I found hanging in the bathroom, I went back into the room. I had to lift the material so I could walk without tripping, apparently, the huntress was supposed to be taller than I was. I wandered around the room. There were two more doors I hadn't opened and I wasn't quite ready to do that. Turning, I realized there were no windows in this place, and then I remembered going down the long tunnel fifteen feet underground. It was daytime and I was in the hold of the night side, so windows were probably a bad juju to have.

A quiet knock on the door had me pulling the raptor from my pocket.

"Daxx? It's Quinton, I brought you something to eat."

My stomach kicked me, reminding me food would be a welcome thing. "Come in."

Quinton stepped in and assessed me briefly before closing the door. "I didn't know what you liked, so I had

Mitz put together an assortment."

His lisp was back, and that made me feel better to know that he didn't try to be all stiff with me. In this place he had become the only one I would call my ally, the vote was still out on the rest of them. "Thank you." He set it down and then turned back towards the door again. "Stay with me for a bit."

He turned and sent me a surprised look. "Are you sure?"

I nodded and went over and sat down in the large chair he'd set the food beside. Lifting the lid, I checked out what this Mitz had sent for me. I liked them already. It was like snack food heaven with cheese and crackers and some vegetables and dip.

"Oh." He reached into his back pocket and pulled out a bottle of Dr. Pepper. "Is this okay?"

"Perfect." There was Dr. Pepper in this realm, how bad could it be? "Thank you."

He stood there with his hands stuffed in his pockets. "You need anything else?"

"No, I'm good." I motioned to the chair on the other side of the small table. "Sit."

He glanced nervously at the door and then sat down. "I was told not to bother you."

Raising my eyebrows at him, I smirked. "By who?"

"Troy and Chase."

I noted the sad look in his eyes. "Really? I thought you were the older one? You still take orders from them."

Shrugging, he looked down at his hands. "They were born to rule, everyone must listen to them. Mostly."

"Mostly. Yeah, 'cuz I see you bowing before them and following orders."

His eyes glowed with humor. "I said mostly."

Tucking my feet up under me, I leaned on the arm of the huge chair and really looked at him. I didn't know what had happened to make him look the way he did, but I knew at one time there had been a handsome face where the wrinkles now hung. "They both seemed shocked that you talked to me."

He sat forward and leaned on his knees, still clasping his hands together and looking at them. "I don't talk to many outside of family."

"Why?"

Those brown eyes sent me a bewildered look. "Have you seen me?"

Squinting I held his stare. "I'm looking at you, aren't I?"

"Then you have your answer." He nodded and looked back to the floor.

"No, I don't." Picking up the bottle, I opened it and took a sip.

"No one wants to talk to the monster," he said so softly I wasn't sure if I heard him right.

"Monster? I hardly think you're a monster." I rolled my eyes trying to add that dramatic effect to what I said.

"The stories will never die out completely, I will always be the monster. It's been almost a hundred years and no one has forgotten. How could they, just looking at me is a reminder."

He kind of reminded me of a friend I used to have. Craig was good at being down on himself and then he met a woman and got married and now she was down on him instead. I missed Craig. "I may never get used to how around here a hundred years is mentioned like I'd say a year in my time."

"How old are you, Daxx? If it's okay for me to ask."

I shrugged. "Yeah I don't get hung up on age like most females do. I'm twenty-six, going on eighty some days."

He grinned and it reached his eyes. "I think I have a few years on you."

"Yeah, Troy told me. I'm still digesting all of that."

"At least I look my age."

I laughed. "No, even for someone over four centuries you do not look old enough."

"I have wrinkles unlike my brothers' baby faces."

I knew he was trying to make light of how he looked but

I wasn't going to play into the pity party he seemed haunted with. "Their faces are too pretty; at least I know I can trust yours." He looked up at me again and there was something in his eyes that was way too heavy for having just met the same day. I cleared my throat. "Do you have a royal job too?"

He sobered. "I did."

"Did? What did you retire at three hundred or something? Go pension?"

He shook his head, but there was no smile to be seen. "I stepped down when..." he motioned to his face, "*this* happened. I used to be the enforcer, I kept the laws held."

"Why did you step down?"

Quinton stood up and paced a few feet away. "It's a little hard to enforce when you're the shining example of why the laws exist."

Shaking my head, I dropped my feet to the floor and leaned forward. "I don't understand riddles very well, Quinton."

"You should get some rest. I'll be outside." He began to move over to the door.

"Do I really need a guard?" I got up and followed him.

He stopped at the door and turned to look down at me. "We're not taking any chances." Grasping the door handle he leaned on it. "If I'm not there when you wake up, Rafael will be. He's my youngest brother and will see you're safe."

"How many brothers do you have?"

He smirked. "There are eight of us."

"Eight? Good god, don't they have birth control here?" There were eight giants roaming around here? I wondered how many of them had been in the office earlier.

"Yes, but when you live for several centuries you can have many children without it becoming taxing."

"I suppose."

A pleasant look filled his eyes. "Personally, I think mother was trying for the rare female child the queen occasionally has."

It was obvious he loved his mother. "How old are your parents?"

Gentle brown eyes caressed over my face. "They passed on when Troy and Chase took the thrones."

"Oh, is that…"

"It was an accident."

Reaching out, I rested my hand on his arm. "I'm sorry. I didn't have parents that I knew, so I can only imagine how missed they are."

"Thank you. Get some rest."

Exhaling loudly, I nodded. "I'll try."

He paused again with the door knob in his hand. "Daxx?"

"Yes?"

"Is that your real name?"

I smirked and shook my head. "No."

Leaning back against the door, he tucked his hands back into his pockets. "What is?"

I bit my lip and then shrugged. "When you're ready to tell me your story, I'll tell you my name."

A big grin appeared on his face. "Fair enough, little *Queen*."

I bared my teeth at the title and pointed to the door. "Out." I couldn't help laughing with him.

He swung the door open and almost walked right into Troy.

The laughter stopped for both of us.

Troy looked from him back to me, his eyes pausing long enough to notice how I was dressed. "I was checking that everything was alright, I was concerned when I didn't see you out here."

Not even knowing the rules, I jumped into to save Quinton from having broken anything with consequence. "He was keeping me company while I ate."

"I had Mitz put a snack together for Daxx." Quinton offered as he stepped out into the hallway.

Troy nodded. "Good."

There was some sort of tension in Troy I didn't understand. He'd been so laid back earlier and now he was tense. "Did you need to see me for something?" I asked trying to keep him from staring at Quinton any longer.

Turning, his eyes ran over me again. "I had wanted to speak to you, but I see you're ready to retire, so it can keep until later."

I motioned with my hand for him to come in. "No. I'm wide awake." I smiled at Quinton. "Thanks again."

"My pleasure little…"

"Don't even." I snarled at him and made him smile and then closed the door in his face.

Turning, I watched as Troy looked around the room and noted the tray and pop on the table. His eyes strayed to the bed.

Apparently, some male traits were universal regardless of which side of the realm you lived on. "What are you looking for?"

Sighing, he shook his head. "Just pondering something Chase said."

"Oh? Was it something regarding me sleeping with Quinton? Because that's what's going through your head and you're lucky I'm in a good mood or I'd have him come in and pummel you."

Stuffing his hands in his pockets, he looked down at the floor. "It's just so out of character for Quinton to be open with someone."

"Did you think maybe it's because I don't step aside or look away? I don't see him as a monster."

Troy's head popped up. "Neither do I."

"But many do?"

He sighed. "Yes, I'm afraid they do." He motioned to the door his brother was on the other side of. "Did he tell you?"

I shook my head. "Not yet and don't you either. It's not your place to tell." A tired look appeared in his eyes and it showed me he was truly as old as he said. "You wanted to talk to me about something?"

Nodding, he rubbed a hand over the back of his neck. "Chase tried to reach one of Wanda's coven mates, Clairee. She's nowhere to be found. We're wondering if she crossed to go find Wanda."

"Or whatever is going down has sent her into hiding."

He raised his eyebrows. "I hadn't thought of that, it's possible, Clairee is also a witch, if she doesn't want to be found, she won't be."

That extra sense I had acquired seemed to kick in. There was definitely something going on here and somehow I'd landed right in the middle of it. "We'll find Wanda tonight and then see if she has any answers." His tired eyes flicked to mine. "Shouldn't you be sleeping or something by now?"

"Yes, normally, but today doesn't seem to be going as usual."

"Tell me about it." I went over and stood in front of him. "This has been the weirdest friggin' day in my life."

He inhaled deeply and nodded. "It's been interesting." When he looked back at me, his eyes were a brilliant red.

"Why do your eyes just change like that?"

He shrugged nonchalantly, or so he wanted me to think. "Just tired."

"B.S. I'm pretty sure a dude as old as you has all the control in the world, even when tired."

A smile flashed and I caught sight of those fangs again. "You would think. Since the moment you walked into my office it seems to be malfunctioning."

"I don't understand."

He stepped back and looked down at me. His eyes, even red drew me in as much as the pretty hazel ones did. "Your essence is taunting me."

Here was another moment where I didn't have a quirky comeback, which seemed to have happened too often for me today. "If you think I'm going to offer up a small taste, I don't foresee that happening."

"I know," he whispered.

Shivers went up and down my spine. My hormones kicked in and the mental image of his mouth on my neck, for any reason popped into my head. Not happening I told myself even as I stood there almost hypnotized by the red eyes looking into my own.

"I should go."

Nodding, I stepped back forgetting to lift the material from the floor, stumbled a few steps forward and came close to doing a very ungraceful face plant on the floor. Troy caught me and pulled me against him as I struggled to get the satin unwrapped from my ankle. "Apparently, I'm too short."

"No, you're the perfect size."

Stiffening, I looked up into those red eyes and then looked away quickly. "Thank you." Grasping the material, I hiked it up and stepped back.

Troy continued to stand there and look down at me. He had a strange look in his red eyes and the fact that I could tell was a bit odd.

"Is something wrong?" I finally asked once I had the material all straightened out.

Tucking his hands back in his pockets, he sighed. "I'm sorry. It's just unusual when I can't read what a person is thinking."

"I would think something like that is refreshing, it can't be fun to constantly know what's on other minds."

"It is taxing at times." He grinned, "or entertaining. It's just this one time when I'd actually like to know I get nothing."

I smirked. "It might be good, help you to work on your people skills."

"My people skills?" His eyebrows creased. "That it might." Turning he went over to the door. "I'll let you get some rest."

I nodded standing where I was, I wasn't going to try moving again until after he left. When he opened the door, Quinton and two other males were practically standing with their ears against the door.

They straightened up and stood there. Troy looked from one to the other. "Raf, were you looking for me?" The one with the short blonde hair shook his head and stepped back out of the way. Troy turned to the other man. "Leone?"

Looking at the floor while he spoke, his eyes glancing quickly to me the one with the short spiked red hair shrugged. "I was out tracking, I just got back and…"

"Found out our Huntress has arrived." Troy supplied for him.

He nodded briskly. "So it's true?"

Glancing over his shoulder at me, Troy raised his eyebrows and then turned back to the men. "It is." When he sent me a questioning glance, I gave a small nod. "Would you care to meet her?"

Quinton stepped past him and came over to me before the other two could make it through the door. "Is this alright with you? I can tell them to get stuffed and wait till breakfast." Sighing loudly, he ran a hand back over his long brown waves. "You're probably wishing I left you in the wasteland."

I smiled up at him and touched his arm. "No. I was completely freaked right out when I found myself sitting on dirt in the middle of nowhere." The two came over with Troy, both of them were staring at my hand on Quinton's arm. I wasn't sure if I was breaking some sort of rule or protocol, so I started to move it when Quinton placed his hand over top and held it there.

He winked at me and then motioned to the men with his head. "Daxx, these are my two youngest brothers." Quinton motioned to the one with the spiked-out hair. "Leone, our enforcer."

I started to extend my hand when the man covered in orange dust dropped to one knee. He bowed his head and I had to bite my lip to not laugh out loud.

"Huntress Queen, it is a pleasure to meet you."

When he continued to kneel there with his head down, I

looked up at Quinton who sighed. "Leone, she doesn't know…" shaking his head he leaned down to me and whispered in my ear. "Place your hand on his head so the fool will get up."

Feeling more than just a little out of my comfort zone, I reached over and gently touched the top of his head. He looked up at me and smiled before getting to his feet. My only thought was, were all these brothers good looking with killer smiles? The women in this realm were very lucky.

When the tallest one with the short blonde hair stepped forward, he was smiling at me like I was his biggest secret. "Daxx, this is our youngest and he will be your other guard, Rafael." Quinton said quietly.

Rafael dropped to one knee. "Little Queen, it's awesome that you're here."

With eyebrows raised, I quickly touched his head so he would get up. In less than a day I'd gone from a bounty hunter that people spit on to someone large men knelt in front of, life was definitely full of surprises.

When he stood, Troy started to say something that I didn't get a chance to hear when the giant Rafael grabbed me around the waist and lifted me up off the floor and hugged me so tightly I thought he might snap me in two. "I can't believe you're here."

Sending Quinton a panicked look, he shook his head and sighed loudly. Without a word, he pulled me out of Rafael's hold and set me on the floor. I was feeling a bit like a favorite rag doll at the moment.

Leone groaned. "Raf, I can't believe you just did that."

Troy was laughing and shaking his head. "So much for her personal space."

"What?" Rafael looked from one to the other. "Come on, you can't tell me you guys aren't screaming inside with joy because she's real and here."

"Daxx will be the one screaming soon if you baboons don't back off and stop crowding her." Chase stood leaning in the doorway. He sent Quinton a dark look. "I thought I'd stop over and see if she was getting some rest and here I find half my siblings towering over her like eager puppies with a new toy."

Quinton waved his hands around in exasperation. "No one said I had to protect her from my own family trying to squeeze the life out of her."

Strolling into the room, Chase gave Rafael a questioning glance.

Rafael threw his hands up. "What? I have been seeing her for years and the lot of you thought I was completely whacked and now that she's here you're all standing back saying 'oh we knew she'd come'."

I looked up at Quinton. "Seeing me?"

Quinton nodded, and reached down to straighten my robe that was falling off my shoulder. "Raf has the gift of sight, and he has seen you many times over the years."

"Well just the last five for sure," Rafael stated.

I looked up at the giant teddy bear that had just hugged the breath out of me. "My tattoo appeared five years ago, just after I turned twenty."

"My god, she's a child," Leone muttered.

I scowled over at him, my patience for everything that had happened today snapped. "Hey—I'm twenty-six, thank you very much and I've been living on my own since I was fifteen. In life experience, I'm a fucking *ancient* one!" I spat at him.

Troy reached over and cuffed Leone in the back of the head. "I apologize for my brother's insult."

Chase chuckled. "I was hoping that cute little knife was going to come out."

Leone, rubbed the back of his head. "What cute little knife?"

I wanted to go home, I decided. Now would be good. First I was a child and now they were calling my raptor a cute little knife. I couldn't deal with this, I was sure there was no way I could get used to stuff like this. Reaching into the pocket I pulled my raptor out and flicked the case to the floor. "This one." I spun the knife around my thumb and shifted it quickly from a defensive hold to offensive. I ended the little show with it clasped in my hand pointed at Leone.

He looked down at the curved jagged blade and stepped back.

"And she knows how to use it boys," Chase drawled with a chuckle.

Rafael came over and looked down at the blade in my hand, he smirked at me. "I still would have hugged you if I'd known you had it."

I wanted to growl, but it was hard to with those blue eyes smiling down at me.

"Everyone needs to get out and leave Daxx to rest." Quinton growled and went over to the door and held it open.

I sent him a look of thanks and then watched as the men moved slowly towards the door, all except Chase. He stood beside me with his hands tucked in his pockets and looking down at the floor. Troy stopped in the door and glanced back at his brother and then to me before he went out it.

Quinton sent me a look and then cleared his throat.

Chase looked over at his brother and nodded. "I got it." He looked down at me, his hazel eyes glowing with energy. "It's good to know you have claws you aren't afraid to use. I like them." He gave me a cheeky grin and inclined his head before sauntering toward the door.

Maybe it was the reference to a cat, or just maybe I'd had enough for one freakin weird day, but I spun the raptor, tossing it so I caught the tip of the blade and flicked my arm towards the door. It hit the frame, level with the height of his head just as he reached the doorway.

Pausing, Chase looked at the knife now sticking out of the wood. With a grin, he turned and looked me over from the floor up. "Keep them sharp, kitten, you're going to need them." With that he disappeared out the door.

Quinton moved over and pulled the knife from the frame and came to me, holding it out. "*That* was something." He said with a grin.

I took the knife back and heaved a loud sigh. "I want to go home."

The light in his eyes dimmed and he gave me a serious look. "I won't let anyone else bug you, I promise."

I sighed again hearing the sadness in his voice. "Thanks, I'm going to try to sleep." I shrugged. "Who knows maybe I'll wake up in my own bed." Turning I went over and picked up the case for my blade and headed to the giant bed.

"It will get better, Daxx."

I nodded but didn't turn to look at him. I just wanted my life back, it may not have been much but it was what I knew. As I sat on the soft cover on the bed, I ran my hand over the smooth material. Problem was, would my life be the same knowing there were other dimensions and realities?

Somehow, I didn't think it would be.

CHAPTER SIX

When I opened my eyes, I had one of those moments when I wasn't sure about what was going on. Then again those seemed to be all the moments I had for the last day. Looking around slowly I took in the dark furniture and high ceiling and everything came back to me. It hadn't been a dream, I was not waiting to wake up in a hospital. I was really in a place called Alterealm. What I was going to do about that, I still didn't know.

A light knock had me bolt up and stare at the door. "Come in."

I was expecting Quinton to look around the door, and was more than pleased to see a woman peek through the opened door. This was the first female I'd seen since coming here and part of me was very relieved to see her. Stepping into the room she smiled at me. If this was a normal place I would have said she was in her forties, but since no one I'd met so far seemed to look their age, which was a good thing considering the ages they were, I had no idea how old she was. She had strawberry blonde hair, all pulled up into a hairstyle that I was going to say as being from the nineteen fifties. Not only was she the first female, but she was also the first body that wasn't well over six feet in height. I pegged her as being a few inches taller than my petite five foot four.

"Hello. I'm Mitz. I take care of the boys and I can't tell you how thrilled I am to have a female here, finally." Moving over, she opened up one of the doors I hadn't looked behind. "We had no idea your size, so this will be like stepping into a fitting room I'm sure."

I sat there, just staring at the huge closet she'd opened. It made the two foot one at my place look like a cubbyhole. Inside clothes lined the walls and shoes the floor.

She looked back out at me. "I've told the boys to start without you, and then you don't have to hurry." Holding up a pair of slacks, she shook her head. "I expect you'll want to wear jeans or something similar for the practice session before you go over to find Wanda."

Adjusting the robe so I could get out of the bed without being all tangled up, I slid to the edge and stood up. "Practice session?"

She peeked out from behind the clothes she was holding up. "Mmmhmm, the Kings insist on all of the family training together." Shaking her head, she hung up the jeans and pulled another pair off the rod. "It's been a relatively peaceful time for the last century, but they don't want to be caught with their pants down if there's ever an uprising again."

I know she was speaking English, because I understood the words but once again I had no idea what she was saying. "I don't understand."

Giving me a sympathetic look, she came over and held a pair of jeans up against me. "These will work, I think." She looked down at the robe pooling around my feet. "I love that our huntress is a normal sized woman, by the way. I had nightmares seeing a seven-foot-tall Amazon queen." I smiled, not knowing what to say. "The boys, or the royal brothers all gather each day for at least one meal, sometimes two if I can wrangle them all together that long and then they go to the gym and practice hand to hand weaponry."

Now, she had my attention. If there was one thing I was good at in my messed-up life it was fighting. "Really? I'm allowed to join in?"

She laughed softly. "You, love, are allowed to do whatever your heart desires. You are after all our Huntress Queen and that title will only ever be given to you and you alone." She hustled off back to the closet and started going through tops. "I think you should wear something that displays your tattoo, don't you? So there are no questions about who and what you are."

"Sure," I whispered even though I felt like I'd just been hit upside the head with a baseball bat. I could do whatever I wanted in this realm? Maybe it wouldn't be such a bad place after all.

****

Mitz left me standing in the door of the dining room, which in my eyes seemed more hall than in the room category. The walls were lined with portraits of gorgeous men and beautiful women, relatives I imagined judging by the resemblance to the seven men sitting around the table. The *table* looked to be the length of a basketball court to me, with the men all sitting down at one end and at least fifteen more chairs sat empty at the end closest to me. How big was this family?

Honest to Gods, seven giant muscular men sat around the table, all but two I had seen up to this point. I didn't quite get how the day ruler and night ruler were so close; as far as I could tell they were on the opposite teams. Then again, I had no idea the rules of the game so maybe they were civil by dawn and dusk and tormented each other in between. I didn't see Quinton, which made me even more nervous as he was the only one I felt a small measure of comfort around. Yes, that struck me as odd too.

The talking stopped when everyone turned and looked at me. Seven chairs scraped back from the table as they all got to their feet. I suddenly felt like a dwarf again in this room full of tall people. Leone pushed his chair back further and turned to face me, I watched as he lowered his head. "If you bow or kneel, I will cut off your knee caps." I said in a shaking voice. Lifting his head, he looked at me with his eyes wide.

Chase chuckled and shook his head. "Good. Here I thought it was only the shock of arriving that gave you that kick ass attitude."

Troy glared at him and then motioned to the empty chair at the head of the table. "Please, take a seat, Daxx."

Feeling like I was walking to the other end with a big spotlight over my head, I moved quickly to the chair. Murmurs followed me; I glanced over my shoulder to see all eyes on my back. The tattoo. When I got to my seat, I turned my back to the men and brushed my hair out of the way making sure they would get a good look. When I turned back around I glanced around at them. "Everyone happy now?" There were several nods. Pulling the chair out, I sat down and waited.

As the men sat back down, Mitz came through the door carrying a plate. She smiled and set it in front of me. "I didn't know what you liked, so I've given you a little of everything."

I looked at the *plate* that was like a mini buffet on a silver platter. Eggs, toast, bacon and sausage along with fruit and potatoes sat before me. My stomach growled, reminding me my last meal had been a long time ago. "It's perfect, thank you." With a big grin on her face, she went back out the door.

The men, now all settled back in their chairs continued eating. I was just picking up the fork when Quinton came through the same door Mitz had. He was carrying a plate and with his eyes down, walked to the far end of the table and pulled out a chair. All movement in the room stopped as all eyes were on him.

Glancing around, noting the shocked looks I came to the conclusion that Quinton rarely joined his family at meal time. Why he had sat with half a dozen empty chairs between himself and the others, I wasn't sure. I also wasn't going to eat with him sitting down there like an outcast.

Grabbing my plate and fork, I stood up and then froze

as all the men at the table stood again, including Quinton. Their mama had beat some manners into them early on to be sure. Moving quickly, I went down the table and set my plate at the empty place beside Quinton. Smiling up at his shocked brown eyes I sat down again.

Feeling like I was in that damn spotlight again, I lowered my eyes to the plate and decided to eat and pretend I wasn't being watched. Chairs scrapping against the floor and dishes clanging made me look up as the entire group of men were lifting their plates and cups and moving down the table. It was kind of sweet and a little odd, but I was going with it. I looked up at Quinton and watched the humor fill his eyes. "Are we gonna eat, or what?" I asked him.

With a grin, he picked up his fork and dug into the pile of bacon on his plate.

"Amen," I whispered and did the same thing.

The others settled back into their meal. I looked around the table and realized there were two I didn't know, not that I was going to say anything about it just in case it involved kneeling and everyone stopping eating again.

Quinton nudged me with his elbow and brought my attention back to him. He leaned down and whispered. "The scowling red head is Victor, the eldest and the one with the black hair and scar on his face is Michael."

I smiled at him and mouthed 'thanks'.

"Two more last night." Chase said looking across the table at Troy.

Troy paused with his cup raised. "Really?"

Chase nodded. "Do you think Wanda knows why?"

Eyes turned to me. "Hey, I didn't exactly have a conversation with her."

"She knows something we don't." Rafael said before he stuffed more toast in his mouth.

"I'm coming with you." Leone informed Troy.

"We should take Welsley…"

Chase shook his head at Michael. "We won't need him on that side, we have Daxx now."

I swallowed and then waved my fork around. "Excuse me." All eyes turned back to me. "First, walking around on my side with two giant yummy's…" I motioned to the twins, "is going to make it really hard to blend and move unseen."

Quinton leaned down to me. "Yummy's?" He snorted.

Ignoring him, I continued. "Second, no one that has a built-in nightlight radiating from them is going back with me."

"She speaks as blunt as a Queen." Arius added.

"One without refinement." Victor said with a note of disdain in his voice.

"Watch your mouth." Quinton said loud enough I jumped.

I patted his arm to settle him again. "It's okay, Quinton, really I have had worse things said about me, trust me."

"That will change." He muttered and picked up his glass.

"Daxx, we don't look out of place in your realm. You'll see us for true, but no one else will unless they've crossed." Troy informed me.

"Really?"

He shrugged. "You could have had one of us for a roommate up until you came here yesterday and you never would have known."

Even though I found that oddly comforting, it still creeped me out as I thought about it. I waved the fork at all of them. "No more talking. Just let me pretend this is a normal day while I stuff my face." Pointing the fork at Troy and then Chase I lifted one eyebrow at them. "Letting me believe you lived only on emotion and whatnot was *bad*."

Chase smiled, but Troy gave me a serious look. "We're actually pretty normal, in a lot of ways, just that exception of a few abilities and sustenance requirements."

I took a sip of the coffee, Quinton had poured into my mug and almost moaned. Coffee was my necessary sustenance. "Not that I'll remember any of this when I wake up from this wild dream, but how many of you are daywalkers?"

Chase raised his hand with a smirk on his handsome face. "I guess mother's genes prevailed." He lowered it and motioned to his siblings around the table. "Any one from this family can come to my side; it's just safer if I come here."

More questions were filed for a later date. "I'll have to come check out *your* side sometime."

"It would be an honor to have you." He grinned.

"Is that really a good idea?" Rafael asked hesitantly.

Chase clicked his tongue and shook his head. "My dear boy, if you think Daxx's only weapon is her cute little blade and sounding pissed off, I have the feeling you're in for a big surprise." He flashed a smile at me. "I suspect she might just kick some ass when she's in full swing, even large royal ones. Isn't that right, kitten?"

It sounded like a compliment, until he added the cat reference to the end. "I guess we'll see." Setting the cup down I glanced around at the men watching my every single move. "Will you be staying on for practice, Chase, or are you needed on *your* side?"

He chuckled and raised his cups to me. "Oh, I think anything pending can wait this evening. I wouldn't miss the chance for you to kick my ass for anything."

Challenge accepted, I toasted him with my cup and took a sip.

"You will not hurt her." Quinton said with a deadly tone.

Patting his arm, again, I winked at him. "I won't hurt him either."

Serious brown eyes studied me for a minute and then they widened. "Oh." He reached into his pocket and held out a small cell phone. "This is for you. I put all of our numbers into it for you."

I took the phone and looked at it. Top of the line and something I would never have been able to buy for myself. "This will work on both sides?" He nodded. I turned it on and tried to navigate through the menu screen. "This is so great. Thank you. I lost mine last week in the river when I had to jump in and haul a runner to shore…"

"You what?" Michael inquired.

I glanced at him and then back to the phone. "Bail jumper. He thought he could just hop off the ferry and get away from me." I found the contacts section and opened it. "I hauled his shocked ass to the shore, which wasn't easy while he was trying to choke the life out me, let me tell you, if I hadn't broken his nose I might not have got it done."

"Please, no more." Michael held up his hand.

Chase was chuckling again and giving me a look of what I could only describe as pure adoration. Troy was studying the food left on his plate and smiling at it.

Reading what was on the screen, I looked up at Quinton who shrugged. Under Victor he had put *'Victor uptight head of justice'*. I scrolled to his number listing and glanced at him again when I read *'Quinton rescuer of damsels.'* I exited the screen and tucked it into my back pocket before anyone could see how their brother saw them. "Thanks." I added quietly.

"Of course." He said from behind his mug.

CHAPTER SEVEN

When I stepped into the practice room that looked was more the size of a coliseum, I stood there trying to take it all in. This is what heaven looked like to me. It was a gym, with all the usual equipment in it, large mats and all the necessary items. Except the wall on the far side was medieval meets guns and ammo—all types of weapons hung on it.

Chase brushed past me, chuckling and headed over to the wall. When he reached it, he looked back and studied me. Turning, he moved past the guns and went to the wall with blades, knives and batons hanging on it. Picking up a long thin sword, he turned and looked me up and down again and then shook his head and placed it back in the holder. Moving his hand over the wall as if the right weapon would speak to him, he paused with his hand over what looked like a police baton. Grinning at me over his shoulder he pulled it down and turned to watch me walk toward him. He waved it around, spinning it and showing it off. I shrugged; having one like it at home it was at least familiar to me. When he bent the handle, a four-inch blade popped out the end and I know my jaw hit the floor.

Wiping the imaginary drool off my chin, I held my hand out like a child would in a toy store, wanting to touch it. Retracting the blade, he tossed it to me while I was still five feet away. I caught it with ease and turned it over in my hands. The total length when held by the small handle to the side was no longer than my forearm. Reaching behind me, I measured it against the length of my spine. It was perfect.

Leone and Rafael were standing a few feet away giving me an odd look. I grinned. "It will fit the strap I have at home for my wand." I said excitedly.

Quinton came over and looked down at me, an odd look on his face. "You have your own tonfa and carry strap at home?"

I nodded, still excited.

Shaking his head, he started to move to the wall. "Maybe you should be guarding us."

Troy tossed his jacket to the side and rolled his shoulders. "I'd ask if we're doing this in some sort of organized fashion, but I think I'd be wasting my breath."

Chase picked up a Bo that had to be six feet long. He grinned at me and then sent his twin a serious look. "Maybe you should let our Huntress know we heal quickly? Wouldn't want her to hold back or anything."

I snorted, with their size I wouldn't be holding back anything.

Quinton came over and flipped the knife out of the holder at his side and held it out to Chase. "Why don't you show her?"

Chase shrugged and took the knife from him. Winking at me, he slid the blade along his forearm, leaving behind a bloody red mark. Tossing the knife back to Quinton, he held his arm up. I stood there, mouth probably hanging open and watched the slice fade away.

"That's handy," I said with quiet awe.

"It is." Chase agreed as he shrugged out of the vest he was wearing.

"No one uses a blade with Daxx." Quinton said in a loud voice. Turning to me he grinned. "Feel free to use yours, little Queen."

I bared my teeth at him for calling me that again and

turned to watch the brothers walk out into the middle of the room.   Quinton stayed beside me.   I looked up at him. "Aren't you going?"

He shook his head. "They won't spar full out with me anymore."

"Why not?"

"I don't heal like that anymore." I couldn't miss the sad note in his voice and for some reason I didn't think it was caused by the healing part.

Jabbing him with the end of my wand, I grinned at him. "I have no problem kicking your ass, Quinton."

His brown eyes searched mine for a second before he grinned. Undoing the sheath for his knife, he tossed it to the floor and reached around behind me and grabbed a thick wooden sword. The thing had to be wider than my arm around and at least the length of my legs. Motioning to the floor, he waited for me to lead the way.

I glanced around at the other men ducking and lunging at each other and decided this wasn't such a bad thing. Fighting was something I could do all day. When you grow up doing something to stay alive, it becomes second nature. When I was sure we were far enough away from the others, I turned and looked up at him. Tossing the wand to my left hand, I reached around and touched my raptor, just to make sure it was right where it should be in case I needed it. Widening my stance, he still stood there. "Make a move, big guy."

He took a deep breath, hesitating and my patience left as he exhaled. Shaking my head, I lunged forward and hooked his ankle with the handle on the wand and pulled hard, diving out of the way when he hit the mat.

In a real fight, I would have been all over him like paint on the wall, but this was sparing and pummeling your practice partner to a pulp was frowned on, no matter what realm you're in.

Quinton got up and rolled his shoulders, the hesitation in his eyes was now replaced with a glint that said he was over his fear of fighting me. He crouched down and swung the wooden sword up into a ready position.

Batting my eyelashes at him, I motioned with my free hand for his to come at me. With a big grin, he did just that. I blocked the sword with the wand, and rolled to the other side but before I could hook him again, he turned and was facing me with a look that said he wasn't going to fall for any repeat performance.

We continued on like this for several minutes, with each block of his sword, my arm stung and I knew I'd feel this later, but wasn't about to let up for a second. The adrenalin was pumping and I was a definite junky when it came to this. I gained the advantage again and had him back-stepping across the mat, while out of the corner of my eye I saw Troy and Arius move out of our way. Ducking his swing, I stepped forward and jumped into a spinning kick and sent him crashing to the mat.

Realizing I'd just managed to kick him in the head, I rushed over and dropped down beside him. "I'm sorry." I said quickly. He blinked a few times and then looked at me with humor shining from his eyes.

"Good move," he whispered between breaths. "I'm out." He rubbed the side of his head.

I stood up and looked around to see everyone had stopped and were looking at me. Did I apologize for knocking their sibling on his ass?

"My turn." Chase started walking in my direction with a grin on his face. Something told me he wasn't going to hesitate, so I side-stepped away from Quinton and watched him swing the bo around as he got closer. It dawned on me then that these men had been doing this for hundreds of years *that* made the ten years under my belt seem like a minute.

He wasn't going to be delicate about this at all is what the light in his eyes told me. I inhaled and readied when he was almost within reach with the weapon in his hands. He glanced at my feet at the last second and I knew where he was going to strike first. As he swung, I jumped and pushed off his shoulder with my feet, sending him completely off balance. Before he had time to recover I hooked his foot and sent him crashing to the mat.

Before I could mentally pat myself on the back, he rolled and came at me again. Between his height and the length of the Bo, he could reach me without being anywhere near me. I sneered at him. "Afraid to get to close, your highness?"

I heard a few snickers from behind us and watched as he looked over my shoulder and nodded. I wasn't about to turn and see who was there. Tossing the Bo to the ground, he caught a wand similar to the one I held that came flying through the air.

"Does this please you, kitten?" He grinned and waved the wand, flicking his wrist.

"Immensely," I whispered as I lunged at him. He came close to connecting with my head as I ducked out of the way and jabbed the end of mine into his stomach.

He grunted, but kept moving toward me. "You can use your cute little knife, I won't cry."

I debated on it for a split second, but decided if I was taking him down, I was doing it on a fair level. "Too easy." I said as I rolled away just before his wand connected with my flesh. Before I could get to my feet, he hooked my leg and I landed flat on my back. I saw the satisfaction in his eyes, as he was about to drop and pin me to the floor. Timing it right, I kicked up with both feet and hit him square in the chest, sending him flying onto his back with a loud whop when he hit the mat.

Rolling, I jumped up and dropped down with my knee across his throat, flipping the handle of wand, the blade flicked out the end an inch above his face.

Dropping his hands to his side, he smiled up at me. "I'm out."

Straightening away from him, I turned to see the rest of the brothers standing watching me. Apparently, we had been the main show. I looked around at them. "Anyone else?" I looked at Rafael.

He shook his head. "Hell no, I've seen you really fight in my visions and I like life."

"Are we too late to practice?"

I turned to watch the long white haired Welsley saunter into the room. Beside him walked a woman as tall as him. She had long black hair and looked like a runway model that snacked on steroids, judging by the size of her biceps. "Not at all." I said making eye contact with the neon green eyes of the man I wanted to stab when I first met him.

He stopped and looked at Chase lying on the floor. "I am not fighting a woman."

The tone in his voice immediately set me on edge. I looked over at Troy, who stood there glaring at him.

"Please." The tall woman pushed past him and came over and stood in front of me. "I have no problem fighting her. Look how small she is."

"Shelby." Troy said through clenched teeth.

The woman turned and gave Troy a once over look, obviously some history there. "I promise not to hurt your precious Huntress, Troy."

Well that did it for me, I didn't care who she was or thought she was supposed to be, *she* had just enough of the wrong attitude to piss me off. I sized her up while she was still glaring back at Troy. I'd fought bigger, at least I thought I probably had somewhere along the way.

Quinton stepped toward me. I shook my head and he stopped. "Shelby, is it?" She turned and gave me a look filled with hatred. "I wouldn't want you to break a nail or anything, and your hair might get a bit mussed…"

With a battle cry that would rival a Viking she came at me. I didn't see any weapon but just her size was dangerous enough. One thing I learned a long time ago, anger has no place in a fight. When she would have touched me with that large hand of hers, I dropped down to one knee and made myself small, causing her to stumble right over me onto the mat on the other side.

Jumping to my feet, I turned to face her and found myself lying flat on my back on the mat; clearly I hadn't gotten out of reach enough. She straddled me and grabbed my wrist, pissing me off further; this was supposed to be sparring not wrestling. Kicking my leg up, I caught it around her throat and pulled her down off me. Before she had time to recover this time I made sure there was enough distance between us that I could see her coming.

She grabbed the wand that Chase had dropped and came at me, swinging it like a golf club. This woman needed to be medicated. I didn't know where my own wand was and I didn't exactly have the time to look around for it. I started to reach for my raptor, but hesitated too long as the wand clipped the side of my cheek. The pain radiated right up into my eye, blinding me for a half a second.

Backing away, my foot hit something wooden, without taking my eyes off her I reached down and grabbed my wand. This bitch had a serious payback on its way. She came at me again like a mad woman; I blocked two swings and had to clench my jaw as the blow vibrated up into my shoulder.

With a jab, I shoved the end of mine into her ribs and was rewarded with a very satisfying feeling as she grunted and bent forward. With a quick step, I swung my foot and caught her in the side of the head, sending her sprawling on the mat.

Backing away, I kept as much distance between us as I could. Behind her I watched Chase hold Quinton where he was, shaking his head. Chase understood I was not going to lose this by interference.

"Shelby that's enough!" Troy bellowed.

Straightening up, she took one look at me and started to come at me again. I braced myself. I made brief eye contact with Chase. "Does she heal?" I more or less snarled at him.

Chase just grinned at me and nodded.

When she was close enough, I waited for her swing and blocked it with the wand. Lunging down to one knee, I hit her in the stomach with my shoulder and sent her onto her back. Dropping down I held her there with one knee on her chest and the wand across her throat, my raptor was already in my other hand and resting against her cheek before she could blink.

I looked into grey eyes that were wishing me dead. "I don't know what the *fuck* that was about, lady, but you ever come at me like that again you better hope to hell you take me out with one move." I took a ragged breath. "I may not have been here very long, but I sure as hell know that when your King speaks to you, you damn well better listen."

Hands reached under my arms and lifted me off her. Victor came over and pulled Shelby to her feet. "Doing my job for me?" He was actually smirking.

"Just helping where I can." Huffing out a breath, I dropped the wand and let Chase guide me away from them. Troy and Quinton were heading towards Shelby. Three of the others were having what looked like some serious words with Welsley. Stopping by the door, Chase turned me so my back was to everyone else in the room.

Leaning down, he lifted up my chin and looked at my cheek. "Jesus, kitten, that's got to be burning like a bitch."

"Only when I move," I added drily, "Who the *hell* was that?" I let him lift my left arm and look at it. I knew it was red from blocking so many hits without even looking down at it.

"Troy had a thing with her once, a long time ago." He muttered as he lifted my hair to look at my cheek again.

"I don't think she knows it's over."

He grunted. "She seems to think he'll come around, although you'd think after fifty years she'd give up."

I shook my head and then squinted and lowered it. "Yeah."

"Quinton is going to take one look at this bruised up mug of yours and demand justice." His hazel eyes were filled with almost as much pain as I was feeling.

"Well, I don't have presto healing like you guys so I'll have to suffer through it."

Reaching down he pulled my raptor out of my hand, I

hadn't even realized I still held. Leaning around me he put it back in the sheath and then dropped down onto one knee in front of me. His face was almost level with mine. "I can help you heal." His hazel eyes searched mine.

"What do you have the healing touch or something?"

He grinned. "No." He touched just below the throb in my cheek. "My blood, any of my brothers' blood would heal you."

"As in drink it?" I would have scrunched up my face but it hurt too much to move.

Giving me a nonchalant shrug, he nodded.

"Uck."

Grinning, he touched my jaw so I had to look at him. "It wouldn't be that bad."

Biting my lip, I wondered if I could do something like that. A pain shot into my eye as I looked at him. "Would it do anything else to me?"

"Like grow horns and a tail? No that's later on."

I smiled and then winced when it sent a lightning pain through my jaw.

"The small amount you'd need won't do anything else, you have my word."

Before I could answer, he stood up and looked over my head. I turned slowly to see Quinton, Troy and Rafael coming quickly towards us. "Crap." I muttered.

"Brace yourself for a lot of coddling." He gently held my shoulder and turned me to face them.

When all three of them stopped in their tracks, I wondered just how bad my face looked. Quinton stomped over and placed a shaking hand under my chin and tilted my head up. Turning, he shoved through the other two men and broke out into a run going to the door on the other side.

"Shit." Troy stopped and looked at my face and then to the door that was banging shut after Quinton's fast exit. "Take Daxx to her room, Chase." He turned and jogged in the direction his brother had gone.

Rafael stood there looking at my face, with pain in his

eyes.

"Go help Troy wrangle Quint." Chase said. Rafael nodded and ran after him.

"Come on, kitten let's get you to your room."

CHAPTER EIGHT

I had no choice but to follow, I'd never find my way on my own. "Shouldn't you be sleeping or something by now?"

Chase chuckled. "Are you trying to get rid of me?"

I looked up at him. "No. Yes." I sighed. "I have no idea anymore; my life has been flipped upside down and I don't know which way I'm supposed to be going."

"You're doing a great job if you want to know. I doubt many would accept any of this as easily as you have." He led me through the third door, confirming I never would have found my way.

"I'm still expecting to wake up and find out this was all a dream."

"Does that cheek feel dream like?" He grinned down at me.

"Not really, no."

Opening a door, he ushered me through it. I stopped and realized it was my room. "Thank you." I went into the bathroom and flipped on the light. Going over to the mirror I stood there with my mouth hanging open. Damn, with the way it was swelling I'd be lucky if I could see in a few hours.

"Not pretty is it?"

I shook my head and looked at him in the mirror as he leaned against the door, "and your blood would fix this?"

He nodded. "Yes."

"What's the catch?"

Grinning, he came over and stood behind me and spoke to my reflection. "Trusting soul, aren't you?"

I raised my eyebrows at him, even though it burned.

"There's no catch, Daxx. A small amount will just heal you."

"And a larger amount?"

He smirked. "With a small ceremony and larger amount, you'd live a lot longer than your human body is presently equipped to do."

"Well, we won't be doing that."

He chuckled. "No, my brothers would castrate me if I talked you into that right now."

I didn't ask, just by the answer I knew somehow there was sex in that scenario. "So no side effects from a small amount? Just healing?"

"Just healing. You may feel a slight connection to me, but it won't last more than a day or so."

"This sounds a lot like vampire stuff."

Throwing his head back, he laughed. "Kitten, vampires are mere amateurs compared to my lineage."

That didn't sound promising. I turned around and leaned against the sink and looked up at him. "I don't want to know. Anymore surprises with other races and realms and I might just run away screaming."

Chase stopped laughing and tilted my chin up so I was looking right into his eyes. They had turned yellow. "I doubt you've run away from anything in your life."

"You'd be surprised." The ache in my face was starting to amplify and move up into my head.

"Let me heal you."

He whispered it in a way, almost pleading and I knew this was not a tone he used often. I swallowed the lump in my throat and then nodded. I stood there clutching the counter as he pulled his shirt over his head. If my whole face wasn't burning I may have appreciated how he looked a bit longer. I'd never seen real six pack abs up close and having them a foot in front of me was fairly impressive viewing. His chest was well muscled and made me silently congratulate myself for being able to knock him down earlier.

With a smirk, he leaned close to me and reached around and pulled my raptor free. I just continued to stand there and stare at his chest. He held the knife against his chest, just above his heart and I reached out and stopped him. Looking up at him I studied his yellow eyes. "Troy told me why his eyes go red near me, but why do yours turn?"

"Your emotions are well guarded from me, but I still pick up hints of the strongest ones." His yellow eyes burned into mine. "Anger, when you're nervous—any sexual emotions you feel."

I swallowed and then exhaled slowly. I couldn't think of a thing to say to that, so I released his hand and nodded. Watching him pull the blade across his chest, I winced for him. He tossed it to the counter and then with a light touch he guided my head towards the dripping gash above his breast. Bracing my hands against his warm skin, I leaned closer and ran my tongue over it. He hissed out a breath and his hand clenched in my hair. I licked over it again, taking the time to taste the sweet salty taste on my tongue.

"Have mercy, kitten, stroking me with your tongue is killing me." He groaned.

I felt my cheeks flush and quickly moved closer to him and placed my lips around the small wound and sucked gently. He moaned quietly and pulled me into his body so all of me was tight against him. Chase held my head with one hand and stroked the other up and down my back slowly as I drew his blood into my mouth, swallowing it quickly before I had a chance to think about it.

He backed me up a step until I was against the counter and couldn't help but feel how arousing it was for him having me do this. Sucking again, I lifted my lips away and slid my tongue over the cut once more. I didn't know if it was enough but my mind was quickly moving past healing and into an area I wasn't ready to go to.

Leaning down, he nuzzled my hair as I continued to lean against his bare chest. "I'm sorry. I didn't realize I'd have *this* reaction." Lifting his head, he moved back enough that I could look up at him. His eyes were glowing much brighter now. He exhaled slowly and closed his eyes for a second.

My whole body felt different as I stood there leaning against his bare chest. I could feel his heart beat under my chest and it was almost as if our hearts were beating together. Lifting my face away from him, I curbed the urge to lick him again, and not for healing purposes.

Grinning, he opened his eyes, a look told me he was picking up on my thoughts or emotions or whatever it was I was having. Surprising me, he stepped away.

Footsteps came from my bedroom. "Daxx?"

Chase motioned for me to go out, taking a deep breath, I moved around him and did.

Troy stood in the doorway. Seeing me, he came in. "Quinton is under control now." He started to come over, his eyes moving over my face. A puzzled look appeared in his eyes, but he didn't say anything.

Turning, I watched Chase come out of the bathroom with his shirt in his hand. My cheeks flushed warm.

Troy came over and lifted my chin, turning my head to study my face. Releasing me, he looked at Chase, his eyes pausing on the red mark on his twins' chest my mouth had left behind.

Chase pulled his shirt over his head and sent his brother an annoyed look. "I wasn't going to leave it. Another few minutes and she wouldn't have been able to see out of one eye. Is Shelby being dealt with?"

Troy stepped back from me and inclined his head towards him briefly before looking back at me. "If you're up to it, I'd like to go see if we can find Wanda."

"I'm up to it." I glanced from one man to the other, noting both of them now stood ridged. Reaching up, I touched my cheek, it was still a bit sore, but nothing like it had been. "Thank you." I made eye contact with Chase.

The hard look in his eyes softened. "I'd say anytime, but I think I'd prefer you not getting beat on." His eyes moved over my face once more before he looked back at his brother. "I need to get home. Let me know how you make out."

Troy nodded but didn't say anything in reply.

CHAPTER NINE

"Okay, so I just take a deep breath, close my eyes and picture stepping, inside my mind only, to the place I want to go on the other side?"

Rafael nodded. "That's it."

I rolled my shoulders to relax. "Right." I started to take a deep breath and then stopped and looked at Troy, "and if nothing happens?"

Shrugging, Troy looked at Rafael and then back down at me. "If your tattoo is in fact the real sundial, it will work."

"If I've gone through all this shit for nothing it wouldn't surprise me."

Troy placed a hand on my shoulder. "You wouldn't have survived this long if you weren't the Huntress, trust me."

"Okay." I rolled my shoulders again and huffed out a breath. "Okay, here goes nothing." Closing my eyes, I thought of the first place that was close to my apartment, but not right in the middle of the street. Taking a deep breath, I pictured stepping from where we stood to there.

Grabbing Troy's arm, I steadied myself when my knees did that jello thing like when you ride an elevator. Opening my eyes to tell him it wasn't working, my mouth dropped open. I was home again.

"You get used to it," he whispered.

"I did it." I looked around at the trees. "I knew this place was here, how do you guys do it so you don't land in the middle of a crowd?"

He grinned and shook his head. "I've never in all the years wondered that. We can transport right to another Alterealm resident, if we have some sort of connection with them, but I've never come out near anyone from this side."

"You know with some of the weird shit that happens around here, I doubt most would even notice if you did." I looked around behind us. "Rafael didn't come?"

Moving toward the edge of the trees, he shook his head. "No. He will if we need him, but you said you wanted to blend, so I thought perhaps it would be easier with just one of us."

I looked him up and down. Even in regular jeans that fit him very nicely in all the right places and a normal t-shirt that hugged his buff physique, he looked larger than life. "How tall are you?"

"Six five, what does that have to do with it?"

I shrugged. "Nothing, it's just at your height you don't really blend anywhere."

Grinning, he continued until he was out of the trees. Stopping he looked around us. "Where have you brought us?"

I stood behind him and looked around my neighborhood. It was just before dusk and still fairly quiet at this point. The good ones were smart enough to be at home and the troublemakers hadn't come out yet. Overall this neighborhood had seen better days. We were at least at the end where most of the buildings were still whole, well for the most part anyway. "This used to be a big park near my place." I glanced over my shoulder at the ground with sparse patches of grass and only a half a dozen trees left standing in the middle. "It used to be much bigger."

"You live *here*?" There was a note of surprise in his voice.

"Yeah, it's not much to look at, but I know all the

players well enough to know where you can and shouldn't go."

"It's like the wasteland, only with buildings."

Glancing around again, I shrugged. "I suppose it does resemble it, except for the orange part." Patting his arm, I grinned up at him. "Don't worry, I'll keep you safe." I walked out to the sidewalk.

Snorting, he strode after me. "Where are we going first?"

"I'm going to go see Frank, see if he's heard anything further on Wanda, he keeps his nose in on anything going on at the police station."

****

Stopping to see Frank had gotten us nowhere, other than Frank giving Troy the eye and asking too many questions about him. We left and went to the first dingy club on my usual list.

That had yielded nothing.

Troy walked along beside me, glancing at me out of the corner of his eye as much as I was doing to him when he wasn't looking.

"That Frank, he is your boss?"

Rolling my eyes, I glanced at him. "No. I am my boss. He just sends the jobs no one else wants my way."

"Why would he do that?"

There was a hint of something in his voice I knew if I took the time to identify I'd end up pissed off. "I rock at what I do. I've never lost a runner—for long."

"I see," he added quietly.

Stopping, I placed a hand on that rock-hard chest to stop him and looked up at him. "Why else would he?"

His eyes moved over me, a surprised look in them. "I think he does it because he wants you."

I laughed, that was just too ridiculous and kind of gross to think about it.

Troy looked annoyed. "You don't see how you look do you? Not really." He ran his hand down over my hair.

"Your hair is actually a natural blond, with streaks that make it look like you're standing in the sunshine all the time. It's soft and flows around your face, it's beautiful." Skimming his hand down over my cheek, he cupped my chin. "Your skin is flawless and perfectly shaded so you have no need of makeup." Running his thumb over my bottom lip, I stood there mesmerized by him. "Your lips, even when cursing are the most appealing I've ever seen, they ask to be tasted."

I wanted him to back up that last part, but continued to stand there like a mute, not wanting to blurt out something stupid. It's not every day a girl hears stuff like this, at least not this girl.

"Your eyes are the truest blue I've ever seen and draw a man in, and you ask me why else would he?" Drawing in a deep breath, he closed his eyes and stood there with his hand on my shoulder, only a few inches between us. When he lifted his lashes a bit, I could see the red under his lids.

Knowing I'd somehow tempted this big King, I stepped back and let his hand drop. "I'm nothing special, Troy."

He grinned and opened his eyes. "Not admitting or flaunting it is exactly why you are as appealing to all males my little Huntress Queen."

There was nothing I could say to that without sounding stupid or conceited, so I decided getting back to the task at hand would probably be the best thing to do right now. "It's a long shot, but we can go back to where I caught up with her the last time and try to pick up her trail from there."

Troy looked down at me for a long silent moment. "Do you think you'll be able to find her?"

I shrugged. "I don't know but unless you have a better way to find her…"

"We still haven't located Clairee, there was some discussion about asking Marcus to come up with some sort of locator spell, but he is in one of his moods where he has secluded himself and it's usually best not to disturb him."

"Who is Marcus?" I motioned to the alley way we had to go down.

"A magician. *The* magician actually. Oh, there are others but he has been around longer than anyone can remember and is the best."

"Quinton doesn't like magicians, why?"

She noticed he moved closer to her and was walking like he was stalking something as the alley darkened. Being so used to this area, she hadn't even stopped to think how bad it must seem to someone that had never been in it.

"After…" He paused, placing a hand in front of her to stop her from going any further. A cat ran out from behind a pile of crates. "Marcus and a few of his students tried to heal Quint afterward. Let's just say it didn't go well for him and Marcus ended up with a broken nose." Stopping again, he checked behind us. "You're going to find Wanda here?"

I grinned. "Not in the alley, no, just up here there's a place where a lot of people that want to stay off the radar hideout."

"I can see why, no one in their right mind would want to come here," he mumbled and walked even closer to me.

Stepping to the side, I steered clear of a bunch of guys leaning near the corner. It was hard not to laugh when they saw me and that male predator look appeared on their faces—and then when Troy came around behind me their eyes went wide before they averted them to the ground.

When I stopped to go inside, Troy was looking back down the alley. I nudged him. "I'll keep you safe your majesty."

His eyes flicked to mine and I couldn't help noting he wasn't impressed. "*My* safety wasn't my worry."

Reaching out, I grabbed his hand and went inside. With reluctance, he followed me. I didn't hold his hand for long, not liking having either hand tied up when I was in this charming establishment.

The music assaulted my ears as soon as we stepped through the heavy inner doors, the odor was the next thing my body objected to. The smoke and drugs, combined with the smell of alcohol and sweat made my whole system want to stop functioning. The lack of lighting made it the perfect place to do anything you didn't want someone to see regardless of what side of the law it rested on.

We'd only gone about five feet when a really big sweaty body stepped in front of me. Looking up my brain started a chant of 'shit shit shit'. Just who I didn't want to run into right now. Carlo was his name and he had issues with me for running down his brother and taking him back to jail. Apparently, it was *my* fault his brother got life for shanking someone over a few hundred bucks.

Reaching behind me, I pulled Troy closer until he was right against my back. I don't know if he was picking up the smelly vibes the fat brother was having in front of me or not, but he wrapped one of his big arms around my waist and held me against him.

Maybe it was how much bigger Troy looked with my little shell in front of him, or maybe he was sending out some back off mojo, I wasn't sure, but Carlo looked from me to him and then stepped aside.

As I went to move forward, I found out Troy was not going to let me escape that easily and either I was moving with him still holding me or not at all. Sighing, I let him coddle me all the way to the bar.

Hovering near the end of it, I waited until the bartender spotted me. With a smirk, he headed to the end. Jorge reminded me of a giant teddy bear, but I'd seen him in action and he was one mean teddy bear when he needed to be.

"Daxx, you're a brave and astonishing woman to come in here."

I shrugged, "gotta get my kicks somehow, Jorge."

His eyes moved over Troy as he towered behind me. "Since when do you tote around muscle."

Turning I looked up at Troy, his hazel eyes boring into mine with a look that told me to behave. "He's not my muscle, he's my boyfriend." Troy's mouth quirked like he wanted to grin but didn't.

Jorge's eyebrows went up. "Always wondered who

would be brave enough to take on the hunter."

I snarled at him playfully. "Have you seen that chick I was tracking a few days ago? Really long black hair?"

"Daxx, you brought your boyfriend on a chase?" Jorge shook his head and leaned over the gouged-up bar. "Might have seen her, but I have to tell you that others are inquiring too."

I scanned the bar wondering who would be looking for her. "You tell them?"

He shook his head and moved away to serve the people pushing their way. "Tread carefully, hunter."

Turning, I almost stepped right into Troy's chest. Blending he didn't do. Tapping his chest, he looked down and then placed a hand on either side of me and leaned down so I could talk to him.

To anyone looking it wouldn't seem out of place to have me whispering in his ear, but it wasn't one night stand words we were having. "Who else would be looking for her?" I tried to ignore how good he smelled, even as welcome as it was in this place.

Rubbing his cheek against mine, he answered against my ear. "We have to find her."

I rolled my eyes, no kidding. "Can you tell if anyone here is from your side?"

He nodded and just kept crowding my body with his warm one. "So can you, Huntress," he whispered against my ear.

Ignoring the shivers that went through me, I pushed gently against him. "Let's take a look around."

There was reluctance in his eyes as he straightened away and motioned for me to lead the way.

As I pushed my way through the crowd that was filled with every type of low-life you could possibly think of, I couldn't help notice the way the females were raking their eyes up and down Troy. It made me want to bare my teeth at all of them for looking. Of course I'd thought the same thing they were when I'd seen him too, but this was different.

I wasn't sure whether it was the amount of pushy people in the crowd or not, but Troy found as many opportunities to touch me as possible. A hand on the back, the shoulder, his body brushing against mine, we needed to get out of here.

I was just about to give up and go start pounding the pavement in the bad district, yes there were other areas that were worse than this, when I thought I saw eyes that were close to glowing a lavender shade. Leaning closer to Troy, I pulled on his shirt sleeve so he'd bend down closer and would be able to hear me. "Does Wanda have the same eye problem the rest of you have?"

He smirked, "eye problem?" Nodding he leaned down to speak beside my ear. "If you mean they change color, then yes."

"What color?"

"Most witches are purple or some shade of."

I started shoving my way through the people leading down the back hallway. With any luck I would be chasing the right witch, not that I wanted to think there were a lot of those wandering around on my side.

Not bothering to take the time to see if Troy was following, I barreled through two people glued to each other's faces and bolted out the door. Stumbling through the it, I stopped and looked around the back alley. The first thing I noticed was the reek of an odor best described as slum, the second thing I noticed was the lights were out.

Why did half the people I chase down end up in dark places? Was I supposed to take that as an omen and find a new calling?

"Wanda?" I called out hoping it would be that easy. There was really only one way to go in this space, but getting to the end had about ten different spots someone could hide in and jump you. Wishing I'd brought a baton with me, I had to hope my reflexes were fast enough with the raptor to deflect any potential beatings coming my way.

Moving in almost slow motion I began working my way toward the first obstacle and possible jump spot. When I was a few feet from the dumpster I stopped. "Wanda, I came back to help."

A sound from the other side of the metal bin had me tense and get ready for some action. My hand was a hair width away from the handle of my knife.

"You're really her." A voice said from behind it.

"The Huntress?" I backed away a few feet, not taking any chances.

"When I sent you over, I wasn't even sure I had the right person."

I remembered what happened to those that crossed without a device. "Lucky for me I was."

She finally stepped around the corner of it, eyes still glowing the pale color. I had remembered right, she wasn't a giant like most of the others I'd seen from the other side, but she wasn't tiny either. Her long black hair almost down to her knees, she flicked it behind her and stepped out further.

"I can't believe you came back. I thought I would have to hide here forever." A look I knew all too well was still on her face, the way she held herself she was ready to run again if I didn't say the right thing.

"I brought back help."

Her eyes dimmed and began darting around the looking into the darkness. "Who did you bring?"

There was no mistaking the fear in her voice.

"Me." Troy's voice came out of the darkness behind me. With a few steps that echoed on the pavement he was standing beside me. He looked down at me for a second. "Don't do that again."

I shrugged. It wasn't my fault he couldn't keep up.

"Sire." Wanda dropped down to one knee and lowered her head.

These people really were into the whole monarchy thing, I thought as I watched him go over to her and touch the top of her head. She stood slowly and looked up at, the relief very evident on her face.

"I wasn't sure it was the true Huntress when I sent her."

She whispered in an apologetic tone.

"She is definitely our Huntress Queen, Wanda."

A noise from the other end of the alley had her jolt. Troy took her arm to stop her from running. "You are safe now."

With her head shaking, she looked up at him quickly and then back behind us. "No," she whispered. "I'm not. They are looking for me."

With that I was back on guard. I didn't know who the hell *they* were, but if it was someone from their side, I wasn't taking any chances. "Let's get back to my place and then we'll figure out what to do."

Nodding, Troy took Wanda's hand and motioned to the end of the alley. "Can we get there going this way? I don't think I want to go back inside."

Smirking, I started walking toward the end. "Yeah, I caught the looks some of the women in there were giving you. It must be a tough life to have them drool on you."

CHAPTER TEN

Wanda paced around the room without pause. If she didn't stop soon I was going to snap. This place wasn't exactly big enough to pace without being in plain view all the time. It was distracting as shit.

"Wanda, come and sit down and you need to answer some questions. We need to know what's going on." Troy told her from where he leaned against the wall.

From the moment we got here, his eyes skimmed the room like he was waiting for something to scurry out and bite him.

I stood near the window keeping an eye out for any movement in our direction.

"You said there was a way to transport right to someone if they have a connection?" I made eye contact with Troy, he nodded. Turning, I gave Wanda a look. "Do you have a connection with anyone like that?"

She finally perched on the edge of the couch. "No, but it won't matter."

"What do you mean? Troy straightened and came to stand in front of her.

"The person I'm hiding from has power." Her eyes darted around the room as if someone was watching. "He can find anyone without a connection to them."

Squatting down in front of her, Troy eyed her. "There is only one person aside from Chase and I that can do that…"

She nodded before he could finish. "Don't say his name," she pleaded.

Oh please, I thought, were we really going to do the he-who-shall-not-be-named thing? "Who?" I blurted out.

Glancing at me over his shoulder, I could see the doubt on his face. "Earlier when I told you we weren't going to disturb someone, that person."

I scrunched up my face trying to remember that conversation. "This Marcus *the* magician guy?"

Wanda squealed and squatted down in a corner, watching the ceiling.

"Wanda, Daxx is protected from all otherworldly powers, you are safe."

With huge eyes, she looked at me like I suddenly grew wings or something just as screwed up. "I have to get to Clairee."

"We can't find her." He stood up and moved over to stand beside me.

"I know, I told her where to go and not to come back until I contacted her." She huddled closer into the corner. "If I go where she is, we'll both be safe." Like a ping pong ball her eyes bounced between the two of us. "I was afraid to cross back alone."

Shrugging, I glanced out the window again. "We'll take you."

"No."

I turned to look at her. "Why not."

"The two of you can't be seen with me."

Troy made an exasperated noise. "She's right." He glanced down at me. "We're going to need a little help." Moving away he pulled his phone out of his pocket and headed into the kitchen.

Leaving me in the room with the freaked-out witch, I felt like I was supposed to do something I wasn't all the comfortable with. Sighing, I went over and sat down in front of her. "It's going to be okay."

She practically threw herself at me, sprawling across my legs. "I'm so glad I found you."

Not knowing what I could possibly say to that, I chose not to say anything and just placed my hand on her head and left it there. Glancing back to the kitchen I hoped Troy made fast work of his phone call so he could come back and get me out of this awkward position. I tracked and chased people, comforting them was not on my resume.

"Michael and Raf will be here shortly." Troy announced as he came back into the room. He stopped and gave me the oddest look. I shrugged and tried to send back one that said to get me out of this spot. His lips quirked like he was holding back a smile then he cleared his throat. "Wanda, get off the floor and tell me what's going on." He used that authority voice, so she responded immediately. I needed to find out how he did that, so I could start using it when needed.

Before I could pick myself up off the floor, Michael and Rafael were towering over me. Wanda turned and threw herself at Rafael, he held her and sent his ruler an inquisitive look.

Michael held out a hand to help me up. "Raf used to be one of the guards at the witch's temple." He offered in explanation to the hug.

I paused long enough to note that in their realm witches were allowed a temple, some things were *very* different indeed.

For the next hour, I stood by the window keeping watch and trying to figure out what was going on. They were all up to speed and apparently, I had some catching up to do. I found out that Michael was the equivalent of a detective, so having him present was a good idea. Rafael was a guard, so yeah escorting the witch back seemed logical for him.

This Marcus guy had been a very bad magician. Wanda and her buddy witch Clairee had stumbled on his latest creation, a device that any one from their side could wear to cross over. This was not just bad but life altering, in a chaotic kind of way, letting those cross that were confined for a reason. Just what my side didn't need, otherworld beings that were a cross between a serial killer and pedophile. So we had our work cut out for us.

When they got to why she came here and found me, I was thrilled to discover it had been hard to do. No one wants to think they're easy in any way. This was where things started to get less clear for me. If I was understanding this right, the three-way conversation, there was someone on the inside and that was the reason why Wanda had to track my ass down and then hide out. Things were starting to sound more like my homeland on the other side than they had in the last few days.

"She's going to have to die over here." Michael stated in a tone that made it sound like they were discussing the color of her shoes.

Pushing away from the window, I moved over and looked from one to the other. "What?"

Troy leaned back and then jumped forward again like the couch bit him. "Wanda will have to die on this side if there are others here tracking her they can report back that she's gone."

"So, you're going to kill her?" This I wasn't feeling easy with.

Rafael shrugged. "It's only on this side."

Holding my hands up, I shook my head. "Okay, back up. Won't she be dead on both sides?"

Michael rubbed a hand over his forehead like his head was starting to ache. "No. She will be alive on our side. She just won't be able to ever cross again." He scowled at Troy. "Will you please call Chase so he will stop trying to jump into my head?"

Troy grinned. "I blocked him."

"Me too." Rafael added with a smile.

Michael sighed. "Well apparently I've no skill in blocking *him* out. My head is going to explode shortly."

"You guys can talk in each other's head?" I forgot about

killing Wanda.

Standing up, Troy pulled out his phone again. "Not really talk, we just know when one of our brothers is trying to reach us or get our attention."

"That's handy," I mused.

Michael rubbed his temples. "Most times it's great. He's just being a little pushy with it tonight."

Moving over by the door, Troy spoke quietly into the phone. I couldn't quite hear what he was saying, he nodded a few times and then his eyes started moving all around my place as if he was describing it. I looked around trying to see how he'd see it, and then I remembered my bedroom on that side and the dining room and decided he was probably trying to explain that I lived in a shoe box that had seen better days.

Putting the phone back in his pocket, he glanced at me briefly and then looked at Michael. "As soon as you two make sure Wanda is safely tucked away, swing around to Chase's and fill him in on all the details."

Rafael nodded and then held out his hand to Wanda. "Let's go get this over with."

Hesitantly she took his hand.

"We'll see you when you get back." Rafael said to Troy.

Then Wanda, Michael and Rafael were gone.

I looked around quickly. "Where are they going?"

"To make sure Wanda's death is public."

Scowling at him, I went over and looked out the window. "Shouldn't we be in on this?" Because seriously I wanted to see how this was going to be accomplished.

"No." He spoke from right beside me, almost making me jump onto the window ledge. "We can't be seen with her."

With nowhere to move, I looked up at him. "I missed the part where someone explained why to me."

Reaching over, he pulled a small section of my hair forward, in the light from the weak street light outside; it looked like it was as blond as his. "Because whoever is helping by following Wanda will go back to Marcus and tell him that the Night King and Huntress are up to speed on what's going on."

It took a few seconds to click. "Oh and we don't want him to know we have any clue."

"Right." He leaned closer.

Leaning my head back against the wall I tried to keep a little distance between us, not because I didn't want to be near him but because I *did* want to be near him. Complications like that I didn't need at this messed up reality of my life. "Easier to apprehend when they think all the top people are clueless."

"Exactly. I don't know who is helping from the inside, but from now on the only ones to be trusted are my brothers."

With my head up like this I realized I was giving him my open neck as he moved closer and inhaled softly beside my skin. "And you're sure about your brothers?"

"Absolutely. That connection we have that allows us to get each other's attention is also a great way to monitor one another." His breath brushed over my throat as he spoke.

"That seems like invading each other's privacy."

He chuckled. "We don't pick up on everything, just serious mood shifts and stress."

"Oh." Swallowing, I craned my head around so I could look into his eyes, they were red. Pushing gently on his chest, until he backed up, I moved out of the corner and into the open room. "We should get back and see if we can track down this bad guy then."

"I'm making you uncomfortable, again." He stayed where I left him.

"A little. I'm still trying to figure everything out." *And being physically attracted to you and your twin are seriously messing with my head.* Maybe it was just because I'd been alone for a while. Actually, almost eight months if my math was right, yeah that had to be it.

"I'm sorry you were just tossed into this. I forget that I've had years to digest all of it."

"And wait for my arrival."

Grinning, he leaned back against the wall. "And wait to see if the prophecy was true.

"You didn't always believe it?" I sat down and studied the way he stood there, almost blending into the wall, not moving in the slightest. He'd had years to hone the predator gig too.

"Not always. When I was younger I didn't want to believe that my future was dictated by a prophecy."

"Don't you mean my future?"

Glancing out the window, he shook his head. "There's more than one prophecy, there's actually many."

That made me feel better. "And the others, have they come true?"

He moved away from the window and came over to sit on the arm of the couch. "I can't answer that entirely, things are progressing in a way that says they are infallible after all."

"It makes me feel a little better that it's not just my life being directed."

He looked around the apartment silently for several minutes. "Would it be hard to give up this up and take what is yours on my side?"

When I considered the stained ceiling, cracks in the wall and sloped, peeling floor, I had to admit it wasn't a hardship to accept what he offered. "Why can't I do both? I have a job here."

"You have a job there."

"They both seem to be tied together. You have runners, I track runners. Does it have to be one or the other?" I started to get that feeling I was missing something again.

"Not if you want to do both, no, at this time I don't see a problem with it."

I didn't ask more, figuring his answer would be more cryptic explanations. I was tired; it had been one hell of a day so far. He straightened suddenly like he'd heard something; I sat forward and reached for my raptor.

"We have to go back now." He stood up and held out

his hand.

"Spidey senses tingling?"

He smirked, "something like that."

CHAPTER ELEVEN

The next week of my life was a blur, filled with so much new information that I was close to a system crash, and needed a break from it soon. In that time, we had managed to find two runners with illegal devices and bring them to justice. Victor was justice on their side.

I would have liked to ask what became of them once they were caught, but that man wanted nothing to do with me. The only time he stayed put and didn't find a reason to be somewhere I wasn't, was during a meeting, at meal time or practice. I still found it hard to believe he was five hundred years old. His mannerism was dated but he looked to be in his thirties and moved like he was in his twenties. I hadn't found the chance to spar with him yet and didn't know if I wanted to take on someone that had been fighting since the fifteen hundreds.

Yet.

During the numerous trips around their side I found myself with either Michael, Rafael or Quinton. I was happy to find out, by the way that they didn't live entirely underground and that there was a top side that had life and buildings, not just an orange-hued wasteland. The buildings and towns actually resembled my side, only it was cleaner here and, for the most part, a more pleasant place to be. I hadn't been to Chase's domain yet, but if my intuition was right our hunt for wrong-doers was going to take me there at some point.

Michael, I had discovered, was one of those that never offered up information. The conversations when we were alone were minimal and never about anything I hadn't asked. I didn't see us bonding in a buddy sort of way, so I stopped trying and focused on learning the laws he explained and working on finding the offenders.

Rafael was just as he'd seemed that first time he'd grabbed me and tried to hug the breath right out of me. It wasn't hard to see he was the youngest in the large family, even if in this case that meant being one hundred and ninety years old. We talked about anything and everything when we were out following leads in the search for Marcus. I really didn't want to meet him after hearing some of the stories. I always thought mages were something from fantasy books and movies, he was a little all too powerful and scary for my taste.

When I was with Quinton I was the most comfortable, which considering the way the guy looked, was a little strange. I still didn't know what had happened to him, but after seeing a picture of him posing with all of his brothers, I couldn't help feeling sad that such a nice-looking guy had met with disfigurement, and no one spoke about it.

More than once I'd almost requested that he tell me what happened, but I sensed it was going to be hard for him and I didn't want to do anything that messed up my time with him. I'd seen the looks cast our way, the odd expressions on enough faces to know he didn't chum around with anyone, or he hadn't until I came along; and I wanted to keep it that way.

In all of the things I'd seen since finding out there was an alternate reality to my world, the thing I found the strangest was they weren't dependent on technology. Oh sure, they had phones and computers, but they lived without them as extra appendages. That was something I hadn't seen on my side for most of my life.

If you took away the modern clothes and technology there were times you would think you stepped into another era all together. Their weapons, for the most part were based on the medieval time period, just newer and improved. They preferred these because after that things became less useful. I still had questions and thoughts about that, but time would tell.

The one thing they did have, and I was very excited about, was a huge TV room and just about every movie I could possibly think of. It was odd to think that these people that could lived as long as they did liked to sit around and watch movies when they found the time, but it was also something that made me feel more connected.

Hurrying down the hall, proud that I hadn't got lost for two whole days now, I turned the corner and almost barreled right over Mitz. Skidding to a stop, I grabbed her arms so she wouldn't tip over with the box she was balancing in front of her. "Sorry, Mitz."

She smiled at me around the box. "No harm done. Where are you off to in such a hurry?"

"Another meeting."

She smiled in that motherly way. "I'm sure they won't start without you."

I shrugged, "I dunno, a few of them are getting really moody lately."

"Victor is always moody, Leone too it's part of their charm." She shifted the box so it balanced on her hip and she could see me.

I laughed. "I wasn't talking about them."

"Oh, is there a problem I don't know about?"

I wanted to get there, but there just wasn't a way to be rude or hurry Mitz, she had an aura that warned you'd be struck down if you tried. "Arius only growls lately and if Chase winds any tighter, he's going to explode."

"Hmm. Arius does that from time to time, I think it has to do with his telepathy skill sometimes he can't turn it off and it overwhelms him." She shifted the box again. "And I know Chase is having a few issues on his side that he thought were long settled, so he's going to be strung tight for a while until it's all resolved."

I studied her for a moment. "You just know every aspect of their lives, don't you? How have you managed to stay sane this long?"

Another maternal smile. "It's my job, but more than that I suppose. Those boys are like the ones I never had. My mate and I always wanted children, but fate didn't see it that way."

"I'm sorry."

Hugging the box, she patted my cheek softly. "Don't be, love. I'm just happy I finally have a daughter after too many male filled millennia."

I only smiled at her. I had no choice, my heart had jumped up into my chest and stayed there, blocking off my air so I couldn't speak.

"You run along now. I'll see you after dinner."

"After dinner?" What had I forgotten now?

"Mmm hmm, tonight's the night all of the ladies are getting together to pick our gowns for the party."

I didn't remember a party. "Party?"

She made that tsk sound older women love to make at you when you've done something silly. "The party to celebrate the arrival of our long-awaited Huntress."

"Oh, right, *that* party." I hadn't forgotten, just blocked it from my mind.

"Chase said it would have to wait a bit, with so much going on, but we can still have the gowns ready when we get the go ahead."

"Sure. Sounds great." I tried to sound happy about it. I failed. I stood there with a fake happy smile on my face as Mitz moved in the other way. Just by the way she shook her head, I knew she was onto me, at least she didn't say anything about it.

Turning, I hurried to the dining room that doubled as our meeting room. I'd asked Quinton why and he said it was the neutral ground. I wasn't sure why exactly, but I left it at that.

As soon as I stepped through the door, the dark aura hit me. Something was wrong. The men were all huddling to the one end of the room and too many were talking for me to pick up anything helpful. I looked for Quinton in the group, but as tall as he was a few of the others were taller and I couldn't see him.

"What's going on?" I began moving to the end of the table.

Chase spun around, a look on his face I could only describe as pure anger.

"Chase?"

He sighed and stepped back to let me see in the towering group of them, in the middle was Quinton and it looked like he'd had the hell beaten out of him. Rushing over, I stopped right in front of him.

"Quint? What the hell happened?" One eye was swollen with a big gash above it oozing blood down his face. The other side didn't look much better. When I leaned back and looked a little further, I spotted the blood dripping down his arm and the hand on the other side looked like it was crushed.

Quinton didn't answer, just stood there his deep brown eyes staring into mine. I could see the shame he felt and somehow pieced it together. If he were any one of his brothers he'd be healing by now.

I turned and looked a Chase. "Is someone going to help him?" Glaring up at them, I growled. "I'd open up a vein myself, but I doubt it's what he needs."

Chase looked at Quinton and tucked his hands in his pockets. "I'm afraid our blood on each other isn't effective."

"What?" I looked at Troy to confirm, the pained look in his hazel eyes did that. "So what, we just stand here and let him bleed on the floor?" I looked up at Quinton. "Get into the kitchen. Now." Shaking my head, I pushed my way through them and waited for him to limp along behind me.

Pointing to the stool by the counter I went over to the sink and turned on the tap. Opening a few doors, until I found a bowl and towel, I filled it and went over to him. "What happened?"

He still didn't answer. As gently as I could, I wiped the blood away to see how deep the gashes were. The one above his eye was the worst so far. I went and got some ice out of the freezer and put it in another towel, thinking only for a second that Mitz would forgive me for ruining her white kitchen linens.

Placing his hand in the towel, I moved to the blood on his arm. "Why doesn't blood work for you like it did on me?"

"Because I already have it in my veins," he mumbled with his fat lip.

"Oh, you can speak. Good. Now what will help you?"

He shook his head, so I took that as nothing.

"What happened?"

"Went into the wasteland, for some quiet to think—" he hissed when I moved the towel to look at his hand again. "It's usually empty at this time of night." Gritting his teeth, he allowed me to look at his ribs. Bruises were already visible. "Saw a bunch that seemed a little skittish so I went to see what they were doing…"

"How many is a bunch?" I asked peeling the shirt away from a slash on his chest.

"Four."

"And?" There was no way around getting his shirt off without hurting him, so I pulled it off his arm quickly and waited until he settled back down on the stool before I began dabbing at the cuts on his arm. "Obviously they had blades."

"Devices too," he said breathlessly. "I got two of them off their wrists."

"Where are they?"

"Victor."

"And the fucks that did this?" I couldn't get the bleeding to stop on his arm.

"Two crossed before I could get them, Raf and Michael are bringing the other two in."

I didn't like the way he rasped while talking. "Ever hear of calling for back up?"

"No time."

I couldn't say too much on that point, I'd been in the same place too many times myself. I'd also come home looking like he did more often than I was comfortable admitting.

Quinton coughed and grabbed his ribs. There were tears in his eyes before he managed to stop, then he wheezed while panting to regain his breath.

I was close to tears myself. Rushing over, I got him some water and brought it back. "Tell me what to do to help."

"You could donate a little of your essence that has all of my brothers panting."

Turning, I looked at Chase who now stood in the doorway. "Would that help?" I looked at Quinton to see him glaring at his brother. Tying the towel on his arm, I went over to Chase. "Would that help?" I asked in a louder voice.

His eyes flicked briefly to his injured brother behind me before looking down at me. "Yes. He won't though. He hasn't in all these years since..."

"Enough." Quinton boomed and then started coughing again.

Rushing back over to him, I held him while he coughed so he wouldn't fall on the floor. "So, you're taking yourself out of the game?" That cough means a few mandatory organs have been damaged, along with I'm guessing three, maybe four ribs. Your hand is now a useless paperweight..."

"I'll get better," he gasped, his brown eyes pleading with me to drop it.

Chase was beside me in a few strides. "Quint, we need you now, not in a few months after you recover."

"I said enough. I won't do it." He started to get up and then started coughing again. Doubling over, he lost his balance almost fell to the floor.

Chase grabbed him and got him back up on the stool. I stood there feeling helpless and frustrated. Not a good combination with me. "Help me get him back to my room, where he can at least lay down."

Chase's eyes skimmed over my face before he nodded and helped him to his feet. "Raf and Victor found the two that didn't get a chance to cross." He paused when Quinton stopped and looked at him through swollen eyes. "They're in more dire shape than you are." Quinton gave a satisfied nod and began to move again.

Moving closer, Chase supported most of his weight. "They were one of mine and one from your side."

I thought he was talking to Quinton until I looked at him and it was me he watched. "What does that mean?"

Quinton grunted and grabbed his ribs with his good hand. "That this is a bigger mess than we thought."

"Great," I murmured holding the door open.

CHAPTER TWELVE

It took Michael and Chase to get him back to my room. He was barely able to keep himself upright by the time we reached it.

Once they got him propped up in the bed, I dismissed them, assuring them I would call if I needed anyone.

I bathed his cuts again, they were starting to clot, iced a hand that looked no better and then sat on the bed staring at him. The time to wait had passed, my patience was depleted. "Tell me what happened."

Quinton lifted his eyes and looked at me. "I did."

Shaking my head, I crawled up the bed and sat closer to him. "Not that. Tell me what happened all those years ago."

"Oh that." He closed his eyes again.

"Damariss Maxx," I blurted out before I could change my mind.

His eyes opened again and he gave me an odd look.

"My real name," I whispered.

"Damariss," he said quietly, "I like it."

I rolled my eyes. "No one likes it." I smiled at him. "Now you have to tell me your secret."

He sighed. "I almost killed a woman. From your side." He panted to catch his breath, "in the early nineteen hundreds."

I didn't know what to say to any of that, so I just placed my hand on his waist and sat there without saying anything, hoping he'd continue.

"I'd go and see her. She was so pretty and knew what I was and she was okay with it. Human essence is…" He stopped suddenly like he wasn't sure what to say.

"Better?" I asked.

Nodding, he tried to straighten up on the bed, without moving much. "I didn't just like her for that." He took a shaky breath. "We fooled around."

I was a little surprised, but kept my mouth shut.

He cleared his throat. "I got carried away, mixing feeding and…" His eyes darted around the room like he was trying to figure out how to say something.

I bobbed my head. "Sex. I get it."

"It's dangerous. I took too much and before I came to my senses she was almost void." His sad eyes filled with pain. "I brought her back with me, breaking more laws than I should have gotten away with." His voice faded.

"What happened to her?"

"Blood didn't work, several of my brothers tried. It prolonged what was left of her time, but she never recovered." A tear rolled down his cheek and I froze not knowing what to do. "She existed, quiet and docile for a few more years, Mitz cared for her here."

I couldn't imagine having to live through something like that and then have to be reminded every day afterward for even a day, never mind a few years. "I'm sorry, Quinton."

He looked at me with so much hurt in his eyes. "I took her life, her vibrancy from her—"

"You got caught up in the moment and made a mistake." I reached over and touched his cheek gently. "I think you've paid your penance."

Quinton shook his head. "No amount of time will ever make it right."

Sitting back, I looked at him for a moment. "I didn't say it would make it right. But you need to look after yourself too."

He shook his head.

I panicked at the thought of being here in this reality without him. I couldn't do it. "Quinton, don't leave me to deal with all of this on my own."

I caught the annoyed look he gave me before he lowered his eyes so I couldn't see what he was thinking. "You're not alone, you will never be here."

"No. I have several giants that hover over me like I'm a prize possession. You're the only friend I have here."

His eyes moved back to mine quickly. "You think of me as a friend?"

I nodded, not sure why he was so surprised.

"I haven't been close to anyone in a hundred and fifty years."

I shrugged. "Well, your people skills are a little rusty, but I'm no social butterfly either, so we'll work on it."

"Damariss, I don't know what to say."

I grunted. "You can start by *not* saying my name."

"I like it." He tried to shrug nonchalantly but hissed out a breath when he was reminded of the state of his beaten body.

"Let me help you, Quinton."

His eyes skimmed my face and he shook his head. "I don't want to hurt you."

"You won't hurt me. You seem have developed this serious big brother thing with me and I know you would never do anything to hurt me." He shook his head. "Please, I need you to be okay." I'd never told anyone I needed them and it must have been clear to hear in the way my voice trembled because he looked at me with so many thoughts going through his eyes, I couldn't keep up.

"I don't know if I can." Wincing, he lifted his good hand and held my chin gently. "I'd be afraid of hurting you."

Shrugging out of his hold, I scrambled off the bed and went over and grabbed my phone. "Pick a brother then, we won't be alone so you don't have to worry."

He was quiet for a long time before he heaved a painful sigh and looked up at me as I hovered with the phone over him. "Troy."

Nodding, I hit the number to call him. When he answered with concern in his voice I quickly said. "Can you come to my room, now?" I waited for his short reply and then hung up the phone and set it on the table. "There." When I looked back down at him, his eyes were going red slowly. I swallowed the reality of what I was offering suddenly dawning on me. I'd just offered up my neck to a being from a race I still didn't quite understand and was giving my blessing for him to take a bite. Would it hurt?

"You don't have to do this," he said quietly as if he could read my thoughts. As far as I knew he couldn't.

"I want to." I sat down, hoping to convey that this wasn't a big deal, even though my heart was doing double-time inside my chest. Unable to sit I jumped up off the bed and took my raptor off my back and set it beside the phone. I didn't want a reflex reaction to make me stab the man I was trying to help.

The door opened and Troy towered in it. His eyes moved over me and then he looked at his brother sprawled on the bed. Coming in, he closed the door and went over to the bed quietly. "I had hoped it looked worse than it was, but now that you're all cleaned up I can see how bad it is."

Staying where I was, I quickly blurted out. "He's going to take some of my essence." There. Now I had to go through with it.

Troy straightened and looked over at me and then back down to his older brother lying there with glowing red eyes. He nodded his head once as if he knew the reason he was here. Leaning over Quinton, he spoke in a soft voice. "I won't let you hurt her."

Quinton took a deep breath and then jolted as pain flooded through him. "Get me on my feet."

I rushed over and stopped with one knee on the bed so I could see around the large King taking up too much space.

"You don't have to move, I can just…"

"I'll stand." His voice was loud, leaving me no room to ignore his wishes.

"Fine." I bounced back up and paced a few feet away. About a hundred questions flooded through my brain in the short time it took Troy to get him on his feet. Would it hurt was the first thing, which made me feel like a wuss for even thinking it. What would I feel while he did it? Clearly if people donated willingly it couldn't be a horrid experience, right?

Troy held Quinton for a few seconds to make sure he was steady enough and then he backed away slowly. He looked over at me and I don't know what the look was he was sending my way, but it let me know that I'd better follow through on this.

Before I could run out of the room, I went over and stood in front of Quinton, looking up at his battered face. It was just the reason I needed to move a little closer to him. He was my friend and I wanted to help him.

I stood there trying not to visibly shake. Quinton didn't move, he just continued to stand there and sway, his red eyes moving over my face. It was a good thing I was one of those aggressive females, because clearly I was going to have to make the first move. Stepping into his body, I placed my hands against his chest lightly enough that I wouldn't hurt any of his injuries. He placed a shaking hand on my shoulder.

Remembering where Troy had told me they bit, I brushed the hair back from my face and tilted my head to the side, hoping he did this quickly before I had time to really think about it.

Quinton pulled me gently by the back of my neck until I was cradled into him. His hand was shaking and breathing was uneven, I didn't know if it was from his injuries or the anticipation. Glancing over at Troy, he stood there with his arms crossed over his chest, his eyes as red as his brothers.

When Quinton leaned down, his face brushing over my neck I almost squeaked out a sound of fear, which was something this girl didn't do.

"Thank you, Damariss," he whispered against my skin.

When he bit into my neck, there was a little sting, but nothing like I was preparing for. I could barely feel his teeth in me. The only thing I felt was an odd tingling sensation that spread from the bite and strangely enough a sort of peace came over me. Seriously, I thought as Quinton pulled me tighter into his embrace, what's the big deal with this?

Without warning, he straightened away from me and released my shoulders. "You taste like my sister," he said under his breath before he walked over to Troy, panting like he was still trying to catch his breath. "Nothing *ever* happens to her!" He growled and then stumbled toward the door.

"Wow, he has the whole big brother thing down pat," I chuckled.

Rafael came flying through the door. "I just passed Quint, he was crying..." He looked at me. "Oh my god! Is she alright?" His eyes flicked to my neck.

Raising a hand, I touched it to feel it wet.

"She gave consent," Troy said before Rafael could say anymore.

"Are you just going to stand there and let her bleed out?"

Troy jerked me around in his arms and lifted my hair. A pained look crossed his face. The room began to spin, so I clutched his shirt to keep from dropping to the floor.

"Troy. Are you going to help her?"

I looked up to see his face blur before me, but I could still make out his red eyes.

"I don't know if..."

"For Christ sakes! Besotted! The whole lot of you." Rafael swung me up into his arms and I had to grab his neck to remain steady. "I don't know where your little blade is huntress, but I am only going to close the wound. Of that you have my word."

I felt myself nod and moved my floating head to the side so he could. He lowered his head and I could feel his breath on my skin.

"Stop!" Troy growled from somewhere near my head. Strong hands pulled me out of Rafael's arms and I found myself looking up into red eyes I knew.

Leaning into his warmth, I tilted my head and almost sighed to feel his lips brush over my skin. With each stroke of his tongue across the bite mark a shiver went through me.

CHAPTER THIRTEEN

"What in the name of all that's holy is going on?"

Opening my eyes, I looked over to see a very angry looking Chase filling the door. He looked from Rafael to Troy and then zeroed in on me sagging in his twin's arms. With loud steps, he moved toward us.

"I pass Quint sitting in the damn hall, crying—*crying* and holding his hands over his face. Then I come in here… Raf, you have fucking blood all over your mouth and I don't need to ask what the hell you're working on brother King." With a gentle grasp, he pulled me free from Troy's hold and cradled me into his arms. "Wipe the blood off your face, Troy."

Tipping my chin up as he walked to the bed, he shook his head. I stared into his yellow eyes.

"And you look like a kitten high on catnip, Miss fierce huntress."

I giggled, yes actually giggled and dropped my head down onto his chest. His big hand nestled it against his warmth. I felt when he sat on the bed, keeping me in his lap and only then did I peek from under my lashes at the other two men.

Rafael stood there with blood smeared across his face, his eyes were glowing and he was panting like he'd run a race. Troy was worse. Even with a fuzzy head and foggy vision I could see him shaking, his eyes still shining a hot red.

Chase sighed. "Would one of you care to get some juice or refreshment for our Huntress Queen before she passes out?" He sounded more exasperated then angry now.

Troy jolted and then briskly walked from the room.

"Raf, please go pick up Quinton off the hallway floor and get him to his room."

Rafael nodded and bolted out the door.

Bright yellow eyes roamed over my face slowly. "And you, silly kitten, I don't know what you did to my brothers but I'm jealous as *fuck* and just a little hurt."

Reaching up, I touched his cheek softly. "Sorry." I didn't know what I was sorry for, but it seemed to be the most appropriate thing to say.

He smiled, so I traced his mouth. "That's all I get? Not even a little taste then?"

His tone was teasing, but I wasn't sure if he was. Dropping my hand, I turned my head so my neck was open to him.

Chase chuckled and leaned down to place a soft kiss over the tender spot on my neck. "I almost wish I could that way sweetling, but that's not how it works for me." He whispered against my throat.

Lifting his lips away, he smiled down at me. "As stoned as you are, I'd probably pass out if I even touched your emotions." His yellow eyes caressed my face. "You could be mine, Huntress Queen. I hope I am your choice," he whispered so softly I wasn't sure if he'd said it at all.

I had no idea what he was talking about but the tone he used was so soft compared to the usual sarcasm tone, I smiled at him.

"I should be shot for even thinking this, but it may be a rare moment to have you alone." His face was close enough to my own now that I could feel his breath against my lips. "If I can't appease one taste, may I another?"

I grinned at him again and tugged gently on his goatee.

His mouth brushed against mine and my head that was

already spinning felt like it was floating. Through the fog I knew I shouldn't kiss him like this, but a small part of me didn't care.

Shifting me in his arms, he grasped the back of my head and deepened the kiss for several heartbeats. I clung to him like a starving woman, not feeling the least bit ashamed for my actions. I had never been one to play timid when I wanted something and I wanted this man with the yellow eyes to kiss me senseless. As it turned out it wasn't hard for him to do at all.

Breaking the kiss slowly, lingering over my mouth he licked my lower lip and then lifted his head. "Are you going to stand in the doorway all night, Leone, or are you going to bring Daxx her drink?"

Turning, I looked over to see Leone standing in the doorway blushing and holding a tray.

Chase stood up and set me down on the bed against the pillows. His eyes had returned to hazel when he smiled down at me. "You may be the ruin of both thrones, kitten, at the rate you're disarming the eight of us."

I watched his mouth smirk at me. "I haven't done anything."

He sighed loudly and sat down. "I don't think you need to."

Leone hadn't said a word, he set the tray beside the bed and then stood there looking down at the floor. I watched Chase look at him out of the corner of his eye. "How did you get elected to bring the juice?"

Leone cleared his throat, his eyes darting to me like I was going to jump on him and then back to the floor. "I passed Raf and Troy helping Quinton to his room."

"Is he alright?" I tried to shift upright in the bed, but the room spun.

"He's in shock mostly."

"Shock?" Would anything ever make sense again?

Chase chuckled. "You didn't realize he hasn't tasted essence again since, well almost a hundred years?"

My mouth dropped. "No. Yes. He said he didn't, but I thought it might help him."

Leone snorted. "I don't know if it helped, but you took out three of my brothers in one swing, so if it's all the same, please keep whatever you have as far from me as possible." With that, he turned and walked out of the room.

I gave Chase a shocked look. "What did I do?"

Chase laughed. "You managed to scare the hell out of our fierce enforcer." Grabbing my face, he kissed me hard on the mouth. "You amaze me."

"Daxx!" Quinton stumbled into the room.

Chase jumped up and just stood there not moving, his stance told me he was prepared for a fight.

Leaning around him, I looked over at Quinton. Only it wasn't the same Quinton that had left a few minutes earlier. Crawling to the end of the bed, I hit the floor and almost landed on my face. With shaking legs, I staggered toward him.

"I'm so sorry," he managed a few more steps in my direction.

A strong arm wrapped around my waist from behind and I found myself held against Chase's body instead of collapsing on the floor.

Quinton stumbled again and stopped in front of me, tipping my head to the side he looked at my neck. 'I'm sorry, Daxx, I don't know…"

"It's fine." I brushed his hand away and reached up to touch his smoother cheeks. "Look at you, you're healed and barely a wrinkle. You're as beautiful as your brothers again."

"Beautiful?" Chase inquired against my ear.

Troy and Rafael ran into the room and then stopped. "Jesus, Quint. You didn't have to deck us, we weren't trying to stop you from seeing her." Rafael rubbed his jaw.

"Sorry," Quinton said in a clear voice, with no trace of a lisp.

Troy huffed out a breath and turned him by placing a hand on his shoulder. "I can't believe all these years you only needed the one thing you avoided."

"Actually," Chase said, still holding me tight into his body. "I believe it was because it was Daxx and not just some sustenance."

Troy's eyes moved over me slowly, pausing briefly on the arm that held me up. "What are you saying?"

Chase chuckled against my hair, his other arm wrapping around me. I wasn't about to complain with my knees made of jello.

"I'm saying, Quinton, Rafael and you Troy, hell myself as well. She intoxicated the lot of us like we were all twenty-year-old virgins."

The room went silent.

"What is going on here?"

Everyone turned to see Mitz standing in the door looking like an angry den mother.

Her eyes narrowed, as she looked at Rafael and then Troy. "Out." Turning, she scowled at Quinton. Her eyes widened and then she squinted at him. "Do not think for one second that pretty smile will save your hide. Out." By this time, she was standing in front of me, her eyes softened. "A bunch of Neanderthals, you'd think they'd never been in the presence of a woman before." She brushed aside my hair and touched the side of my neck. "I imagine Quinton released a little too much glamour into your system to hide the pain of the bite, you're completely wasted—he's just a little out of practice."

Stopping she turned and looked at the three men still behind her. "What part of *out* didn't you understand?"

I leaned back against Chase's shoulder and closed my eyes, they were too heavy to hold open. I heard mumbles and footsteps on the floor as they left the room.

"Chase, help her to the bed."

He swung me up into his arms and nestled me into his chest. I sighed and relaxed into him. "Chase?"

"Yes."

"What did you mean when you said you hoped you were

my choice? Choice of what?" I struggled to open my eyes and look at him.

Mitz made a sound of exasperation. "You boys haven't told her?"

Chase sat down and kept me cuddled into him. "Troy felt she had enough to come to terms with right now."

I looked from Mitz to eyes that were starting to turn to yellow.

"You will control yourself, Chase." Mitz snapped.

He grinned, even though he didn't look away from me. "I'm fine, Mitz. I would never harm our Huntress Queen."

She sat down and held a glass of juice in front of my mouth. "You're as smitten as the rest of them, Chase."

I sipped slowly and couldn't believe how thirsty I was.

"Yes, Mitz, I am. With good reason too. For two hundred and sixty years I've had to wait and wonder if this huntress existed at all. Now she's here and turns out to be more than any of us could have imagined."

Mitz helped me take another drink. "She has a good heart and will be a just hunter, for sure."

Pushing the glass aside, I grasped Chase's goatee to get his attention. "Stop talking about me like I'm not here." I said in clipped words.

"Ah, damn, kitten, your head is clearing. I was starting to enjoy holding you so complacently in my arms."

The fog was lifting a bit but I still felt shaky. Keeping my hold on his goatee, I smiled. "Thank you, by the way for coming to my rescue."

He smiled a genuine smile, "any time."

"You need to drink the rest of this, love." Mitz held the juice in front of me again. "As soon as you're able to hold yourself up right, well send prince charming packing and you can soak in the tub while I tend to dinner."

"I can see to her if you need to be elsewhere, Mitz."

Mitz lowered the glass and studied Chase. With a curious look, she turned to me. "Did you let him at your emotions, Daxx?"

I shook my head. "No. He joked about it but said I was too high." I glanced at him; he was looking at my mouth as I spoke. I felt my face flush and couldn't help the smile that followed. "We only kissed, nothing otherworldly."

Mitz cleared her throat. "I see." She patted Chase's shoulder. "Let's sit her up and see if she's found her balance."

Chase hesitated and then nodded and shifted me off his lap to sit on the bed. With a firm hold on my shoulders, he squatted down in front of me.

I nodded and he slowly released me, but kept his hands ready in case I wasn't able to stay that way. "I'm good." My head was still a little fuzzy, but the room wasn't moving like a tilt-a-whirl now.

Chase signed. "If my chivalry is no longer required, I will remove myself before Mitz kicks me out too." He brushed a soft kiss over my lips and stood up. "I'll see you at dinner, kitten."

I watched him go out the door and close it behind him. Turning to Mitz, I shook my head. "Mitz, what the hell is going on I don't know about?"

She held out a hand to help me up. "They should have told you, love. It's not right to be a pawn in a game when you don't know the rules. Let's get you settled in the tub. While you're soaking, I'll go get the book."

With slow steps, I moved toward the bathroom. "I don't think I'm going to make the dress party." Her words sunk in. "Book?"

She made a soft worrisome noise. "The book of prophecies for the King with the sons numbering nine."

CHAPTER FOURTEEN

With anger flowing through my entire system like hot lava, I was good to go. The fog in my brain had burned off and I shook from the violence coursing through my veins.

Hugging the book to my chest, I stood in the dining room doorway and watched the men that hadn't realized I was there. All eight of them sat at the table, grinning and joking with each other. Stupid jerks, every last one of them.

Quinton turned and smiled when he saw me. "Daxx, it's about time, we're starving." He started to stand and then his eyes went to the book I was holding.

"Are all women as ..." Michael stopped talking, his eyes also spotting the book.

Slowly moving into the room, I held the book up for all of them to see. All movement stopped. It was so quiet an ant walking across the floor would have echoed.

Slamming the book down on the table, I leaned over it and glared at them.

Mitz came darting into the room and then stopped.

"Mitz could you hold dinner for a few minutes?"

Her head bobbed a few times. "Of course, just tell me when you're finished."

"Thank you." I waited until she left the room and then straightened up and stood with my hands on my hips. "Did all of you know?"

I looked around at each one, not one of them would make eye contact with me. "I'll take that as a yes."

"It's all hog spittle," Victor muttered.

"Hog spittle? Victor, you do know what century this is right?" His green eyes connected with my own.

"Yes."

"Good. Maybe you should update your vocabulary and say something a little more modern."

He looked away.

"Is it?" I looked around, waiting for one of them to answer.

Leone pushed his chair back and started to get up. Determined to have my say, the raptor was out of its case and spun into the air, catching it, I stabbed it into the table beside the book.

"Fuck me," one of them whispered.

"Fantastic." Chase's voice echoed the first one.

I zeroed in on him, the man that had held me with such tenderness an hour before. "Chase?"

His hazel eyes met mine, there was no hesitation. He raised a brow in query.

"The contents of this book, is it a pile of crap or is it true?"

Glancing around the table, he turned back and looked directly at me. "Do you see any wives at this table, kitten? We're everyone a bachelor waiting for that connection." He leaned back in his chair. "Doesn't it strike you that in the five hundred years that Victor's been around, or even Michael in three hundred and sixty that they'd have found mates to keep them in line?"

I looked back down at the book and then at his eyes. "It says there's a ninth brother, where is he?"

"Your side." Troy leaned forward on the table.

"Excuse me? What is he doing on my side?"

Quinton pushed his chair back and those brown eyes moved over me slowly. "Our father confessed his infidelity on his death bed."

Rafael nodded. "Up until that point we thought the book was pure fiction because there were only eight of us."

"Or the King to have nine sons hadn't come to pass yet." Troy said quietly.

"How old is this brother on my side?" I tried to remember what it had said, having only skimmed most of it except the part about the Cross Over Huntress Queen.

Rafael glanced to Chase, who nodded. "He'd be around three hundred."

Grabbing the knife out of the table, I twirled it in my hand, a motion I always did while processing. "Three hundred years old?" Rafael nodded. "Three hundred—" I spun the knife thumb hold so it went in a circle. "Do you have any idea what it must be like for him to live in my world for that long?" They didn't get it. Shaking my head, I flicked the motion of my wrist faster. "He doesn't age. Can you imagine what it's been like trying to hide for that long?" Leone was the only one that shook his head. "Why haven't you looked for him?"

Chase cleared his throat. "We've tried." His eyes nervously moved from the knife back to my face. "We don't have many connections there so it's very hard to find someone that doesn't want to be found."

"Damariss, could you please put the knife down?"

Snapping my neck around, I looked at Quinton and scowled at him for saying my name in front of the others. He glanced at the knife still rotating in my hand. Exhaling loudly, I put it back into its case behind me and leaned on the table. "Do you even know if this missing brother is alive?"

Victor nodded. "He is, or the symbol on the front of that book would be blackened."

I looked down at the book between my hands.

"The two blackened leaves turned when our parents passed. There are nine green leaves and nine yellow ones."

I glanced up at Troy for an answer. "What are they for?"

Tapping a silent rhythm with his finger on the table, his

eyes searched out his twins then looked at me. "One color is for us, one for our mates."

Which brought me back to where I started on all of this… "I will find your brother." A few skeptical looks passed between them. "Hey! It's what I do."

I reached for the handle of my knife again, needing the comfort of touching it. "When were you going to tell me the rest of the huntress prophecy?" I didn't look at any of them, just ran my finger over the leaves on the cover, wondering if one of them was meant for me.

"I made the decision to let you settle in and adjust before discussing it." Troy offered in his voice of authority.

"I see." I glanced from him to his twin, "and the part about choosing one from the throne for my mate?"

"I wanted to tell you," Quinton said quickly.

"You should have." He at least looked repentant. I moved around the table and then stopped behind Chase.

He turned and studied me. "Are you going to stab me, kitten?" Even though his voice was light and playful, the expression in his eyes was serious.

"I probably should." Moving down the table, I stopped and looked at Troy. His hazel eyes were filled with apology, but his mouth didn't say the words. Shaking my head, I continued on until I was back to the book. "What happens if *this* huntress doesn't choose?"

"You condemn us to bachelorhood for evermore." Rafael said as he looked around at his brothers.

"And the line to the throne stops." Troy added, still taping out the beat on the table.

Opening the book, I flipped to a random page. "Seriously, none of you will marry or have children until your two rulers have their mates?"

"Only one has to…" Quinton stated matter-of-factly. "—with you." He added quickly and then looked away.

I ignored wanting to growl and continued. "And children?" I looked around at their puzzled looks. "Surely you have sex." *That*, I found was the wrong thing to say to eight males.   All answered loudly and at the same time, I couldn't pick out any one answer, but knew sex was definitely happening.

"We can only impregnate our true mate." Victor offered with an uncomfortable expression on his face.

That the book hadn't mentioned or if it did I'd skimmed over that part.   There were other things flying around in my brain, like the fact that I wasn't like them, how could I mate with a man that would live forever? If I did for some reason live longer, would I be the one to have the next twin rulers in two hundred plus years? How did they know someone was their true mate?

I knew they'd have answers, which is why I didn't ask, I simply didn't want any more information to deal with right now. "I can't choose right now." I said looking at the leaves on the book again.

The sound of a chair being pushed back echoed through the room. I didn't glance up to see which one was walking over to me. A hand with the ring baring the symbol of a moon cupped my chin and tilted my face up to look at them.

I looked into Troy's eyes they were bordering on turning red and it kind of creeped me out to know I recognized this now.

"No one is asking you to choose right now or at all for that matter."

I nodded and closed my eyes, because I just couldn't look into his right now. His hand dropped away. A quiet ringing sounded in the room. Realizing it was my phone; I pulled it out of my pocket and answered it.

It was Frank and I was actually relieved to hear his voice, anything to get me out of here. He talked quickly about a job. "What's the charge?" It turned out to be minor in comparison to some of the more recent ones I'd done. "I'll pick up the file in the morning."

Hanging up, I turned and looked at all the eyes watching me. "Enjoy your dinner, gentlemen."

I brushed past Troy and went back out into the hallway.

I could hear someone following me, but didn't slow down.

"Daxx." Quinton caught up to and touched my arm to stop me. "You need to eat, after earlier..."

My eyes moved over his face, noting he seemed to look better than the last time. The skin had tightened and the man I'd thought was a thing at first sight had a sculpted jaw and high cheekbones now. "I will when I get home, promise."

"Home?" His brown eyes searched mine. "You're leaving?"

I nodded. "I have a job to do and I can't find any in possession of the device if I'm on this side."

He stepped back. "Okay. I can come with you and help now."

"Maybe another time, I just need some space right now, Quint. Okay?" Not waiting for a response, I walked to the hallway and leaned against the wall. Closing my eyes, I focused on home.

CHAPTER FIFTEEN

When I opened my eyes, I was standing in my dingy apartment. It looked even smaller the last time after wandering around the large nightwalker, I'd say palace, but it wasn't. Dwelling? Whatever it was called the bathroom was larger than my whole apartment. Then again, when a group of giants lived there, it made sense.

I didn't bother turning the lights as I navigated over to the wall that seemed to be my think spot in this tiny space. Sliding down, I looked outside at the street light.

My mind was mush. So many thoughts at the same time, I didn't know how to begin to sort them out. For as long as I could remember I didn't actually belong anywhere, not fitting into any one group for more than a few days. I'd always thought it was because I didn't have any sort of normal upbringing, but now I had to admit that was just an excuse I used to not fit in. I liked my life, for the most part. I looked around again, debated on turning on the lights, but it looked better in the dark so I left it that way.

If I hadn't witnessed and lived everything since that night I tracked Wanda, the first time, I wouldn't have believed it. Screenwriters had taken over my life and were tossing things at me from every direction. I was just a bounty hunter from the wrong side of life that had to fight every day of her existence just to stay in the game. Now suddenly I have a group of people, from some other realm to boot, telling me they've been waiting for me and that's where I belong. The part that was messing with my head the most was I liked being there. All the weirdness blended with who I was, I wasn't *normal* in any way and now I find out there's a whole race of beings that aren't normal at all.

I didn't even know about their way of life, on the outside they looked normal, when they weren't glowing with the flashy eyes at least, and that was good for me. I could always get to know more about them as my comfort zone expanded.

The words from the book kept coming back to me, that was a whole lot of 'I don't know what to make of this stuff', to put it simply. How in hell had I been selected to be the Huntress Queen that had the delightfully horrid task of choosing between two identical twins to mate with for all of eternity and then some? There had to be a typo or something everyone was missing. It was written a long, long time ago maybe a part was lost in the translation. Maybe I was just supposed to have a brief affair with one and then the other, and carry on my merry way. I groaned at the ridiculous thoughts randomly taking over my mind. Was I taking all of this too literally? The brothers all seemed serious about it, or the few that had actually said something.

Pieces were fitting together, little things here and there. The looks between Troy and Chase from the moment I'd first seen both of them in the same room. The way each of them watched when I was close to the other. Troy's cryptic conversation about prophecies and the separate parts appearing to come together— Did they really think I was the one that was going to control whether the eight, no make that nine men died alone in some distant century or if they lived their own happily-ever-after?

This internal discussion was getting me nowhere.

I scrolled through the numbers in my snazzy new phone. My popularity was skyrocketing with a shattering ten contacts entered. Aside from eight brothers, Frank was in there and

Crissy, a woman I was determined to get off the streets.

I dialed the one number on the list, the only one I was sure would tell me it straight.

He answered on the third ring.

"Victor, its Daxx."

There was a long pause. "Daxx, I can honestly say you've surprised me."

I grinned. "No doubt. Have you got a minute?"

I heard a female voice in the background.

"I haven't interrupted anything, have I?"

He cleared his throat. "No, I was…" More murmurs. "What can I do for you, Huntress?"

With that the other voice grew quiet. I had to give it to him; he could make a point without being rude. "I have questions."

"I am surprised you called me."

Dropping back against the wall, I stared at the stained ceiling. "Well, I figured with you being Mister Justice and all you'd tell me the truth."

"Of course." His tone was less ridged.

A mental pat on the back for me, I'd managed to compliment him without even trying. "It was either you or Leone—you're the only two that aren't treating me with kid gloves."

He sighed, "there's good reason for Leone's reaction.

"He doesn't like women?"

"What?" He chuckled softly. "No, I can assure you that is not the reason." There was another pause. "Leone's afraid you'll be his downfall."

"Downfall to what?"

"About thirty years ago Leone had an addiction." When he paused again I wasn't sure if he planned to continue and then I heard movement in the background and a door close.

"Leone was addicted to pure human essence. I believe he's afraid you will tempt him and send him back to that place he worked hard to climb out of."

I was shocked. Not because he was telling me, but that

the brothers had weaknesses like the flawed humans I knew. "I'll be sure to keep my essence far away from him."

Victor chuckled again, adding another surprise to my tally. "I'm afraid that's impossible my dear, you absolutely reek of it—in a very appealing manner of course."

"Of course." I repeated, not sure if I'd been insulted or complimented. "I'll still try to stay clear of him." Apparently, that was the end of the discussion when he didn't say anything further. "And why do you keep your distance and pretend I'm not there, Victor?"

"I'm not willing to change my life after five hundred years because of some words scribed in a book."

I grinned. "Not ready to give up bachelorhood?"

"Mmm, something like that. Now, Daxx, please tell me why you called."

Enough small talk. "Am I seriously expected to choose between Troy and Chase? Does everyone on your side expect this?"

There was a pause long enough to make me squirm. "Yes."

"What if I don't want either of them? Don't get me wrong, they're both hot and seem okay, but I don't know them and I really don't think I'm ready to settle down for an eternity with either of them."

"Then don't."

"Seriously? And what about the part where none of your brothers will ever have a mate if neither ruler does? Do you believe it?"

He cleared his throat, something I realized he did when he would rather not answer. "It's true."

"It's not just a psychological thing because they think it's true?" I could hope, right?

"No. Clearly I've never experienced it, but there is a *bonding* when mates find each other and not one of us have."

"Maybe you haven't found the right one."

"Daxx, you are aware of how old my brothers and I are, don't you think there have been a fair number of females in those years?"

It took a second to get what he was hinting at and then I almost broke out in a sweat trying to do the math. Even if Victor, for example had sex once a week multiplying that by what, we'll say four hundred and seventy-five years roughly—that would take the count into the thousands, more double digit thousands! "I get your point." I said quietly. "What if I'm not *the* one for either of them?"

"There's only one way to find out." He added dryly.

My eyebrows shot up. "Are you saying I should sleep with both of them to find out?"

There was a pause and then an exasperated sigh. "I said nothing about sex. I wouldn't suggest something like that. Nor would they agree to it. They may be fair rulers and twins, but they are still male and no man likes to share."

Frowning, I stood up. "Then what were you suggesting?"

"Get to know them. Perhaps spend some time with Chase on his side and then with Troy."

"Oh." It didn't seem as bad as the idea of sleeping with both of them. Not that having sex with either would be a hardship, but I wasn't ready to go there. "I suppose I could do that."

"Don't let their looks confuse you, Huntress Queen, they are not identical."

I nodded to my empty apartment. "I already know that much."

"Is there anything else I could assist you with?"

I had about a hundred more questions. "No. That's it."

Victor cleared his throat. "My brothers are all brooding now that you've left."

"But not you—"

"I'm talking to you they aren't"

"I do have a job here too."

"We are all well aware of that."

Wandering over, I looked out the window and stared at my reflection in the dark.

I didn't look like anything special, and certainly not a Queen, whatever that should look like I wasn't sure.

"Daxx?"

Victor's voice brought me back to the conversation. "I would like to thank you, while I have the opportunity."

"For what?"

"Quinton." His voice had softened. "For what you did for him, I will be eternally grateful and in your debt."

A lump formed in my throat. "I really didn't do much."

"You did what no other could have, and while his spirit isn't as it used to be, the man I once knew is closer than he has been all these years."

If he continued I would end up in tears and *that* I really didn't do with ease. "You don't have to thank me, I like Quinton and I was happy to help." By giving a little essence and ending up stoned, I thought to myself.

"He is quite distressed you left."

Sighing, I took the hint. "I'll call him before I turn in."

"Thank you." His voice was still soft.

I preferred the icy Victor to this warm version. "I'll let you go, Victor. Thanks for the assist."

"Anything you need my Queen."

Cringing at his tone and words I hung up the phone and looked outside.

Would anything in my life ever be simple?

Before I could change my mind, I hit the number for Quinton. He answered on the first ring.

"Daxx, are you alright?"

Victor hadn't been exaggerating.

"I'm fine."

I could hear voices in the back ground.

"Were you busy?"

"No, just a brainstorming session, trying to decide where to start looking for Marcus."

Which meant more than one of his siblings were present— "I'll let you go then."

"No. Wait." I heard the voices fading and then a door

closing. "I'd rather talk to you."

"Too many chiefs in the session?"

He laughed, "You know them too well."

"Not really, I just know what too many men in one room means."

He was silent. "Are you okay?"

I shrugged like he could see me. "I'll be fine, I just feel like I was dropkicked today."

"I wanted to tell you, but…"

"You didn't think I'd stay."

He snorted, "I was right, you left right after you found out."

"I have a job over here, Quint."

"We need you here more."

Really, he played that card? "I'm sure you boys will track down Marcus just fine without me."

Going into the kitchen, I looked in the fridge. The shelves were empty except for a plate with something green and fuzzy on it, I kind of missed Mitz at this moment.

"It's worse than we thought, Daxx. Michael figures he made around a hundred of those devices before Wanda found out."

Closing the fridge, I leaned my forehead against the cool surface. "How many did you recover?"

"Thirty."

That left seventy day or night walkers in possession of the device and free to enter my side anytime they wished to do anything they could get away with. Whether I wanted to be mated for eternity or not wasn't the issue now. Keeping a balance was. "It shouldn't take me long to find this guy tomorrow. I'll be back when I'm finished."

"I could come and help."

Opening a cupboard, I discovered it was empty too. "No, I doubt he'll be a challenge, I got it."

"Oh. Okay. Hang on."

He must have covered the mouth piece because all I could hear were muffled voices.

"Daxx, Chase would like to speak to you."

I bit my lip and held my breath for a few seconds. "I'll see him tomorrow."

He covered the mouth piece again.

"I'm supposed to tell you if you come back with so much as a scratch he's breaking someone's neck." Quinton snorted. "He'll have to get in line for that."

"I got this, okay? Just tell everyone I'll be back tomorrow sometime."

"Be careful, little Queen."

I smiled. "Will do."

Hanging up, I tucked the phone into my pocket. I looked around at the closed cupboards and then turned and went toward the bedroom. My stomach would just have to get over it; I was too tired to go get food right now.

CHAPTER SIXTEEN

When I opened my eyes this time I was really relieved to see I was in the giant dining room, the fear of ending up in the wasteland when doing this was never going to leave. I needed to ask for a map, so I could study everywhere and know how to get help if I needed it in the future if a cross over didn't end well.

"Daxx!"

Almost jumping on the table, I turned around to see Quinton striding in my direction, fast.

"I've been wandering around waiting for you to get back. He stopped moving and eyed me up and down.

Obviously, the remnants of the dumpster I had to dive into to drag that punk out were still visible. Wait until he gets closer and gets a whiff, I thought trying not to smirk.

"What did you do to yourself?"

Eyes wide I looked down at my stained, dirty jeans. "I didn't do this to myself."

Scowling he stepped closer and brushed my hair back from my face. "What happened to your lip?"

Running my tongue over my lip, that still throbbed like crazy, I tried to shrug it off. It was embarrassing. "The punk got in a lucky shot."

"Who got a lucky shot?" Arius wandered in carrying an

arm full of rolled up papers. He paused and frowned at me. "What happened?" Setting them down, he moved around the table and came over and tipped up my chin. "Do we need to buy you a face mask, my Queen?"

Rolling my eyes at him I pulled my face out of his hand. "It's nothing. He got one swing before I nailed him and had the cuffs on him."

"Him? A male hit you?" Quinton's tone sounded lethal.

Holding my arms out, I looked back down at my clothes. "Can we talk about this after I've had a shower? Maybe the smell isn't bothering you but I'm starting to get tired of the stink.

"Arius, I found more in the library…" Michael froze where he was as soon as he saw me standing between his brothers. "Huntress, you're back." He smiled and then frowned before his face had finished the smile. "And I see you've been busy blocking blows with your face again."

Before I could growl a response, Quinton took my elbow and guided me in the direction of the door. "She'll explain after she's gotten cleaned up."

As he wheeled me around the corner, I glanced back to see Michael dialing his phone. Great the gossip chain had begun. It was a fat lip and a little garbage residue. It could have been worse. It *had* been much worse in the past.

At the second door he led me through, we almost walked right into Victor and Leone. Leone spotted my swollen mouth, but didn't say anything, just squinted with a look I could only describe as annoyance. Whether it was at the fact my mouth had taken a blow or because he didn't want to notice, I wasn't sure. Victor managed to shock me by grasping my chin in his big hand and lifting my face to look at it closely. "Quinton told us you assured him this would be an easy task for you." His green eyes actually held concern.

"I was a little winded. The punk ran up an entire stairwell of a building, it had to have at least ten floors, and then went back down the fire escape. I caught up to him when he fell into the dumpster." I shrugged. "He got one good swing in before I took him down."

"Mmm, I see." He backed up and looked down at my clothes. "That also explains the odor."

"That I'm just going to scrub off."

Nodding he stepped back further. "We'll see you at the meeting then after you're finished."

"Meeting?" I looked up at the three of them, wishing for one moment that they were normal height. If I stayed around them too long my neck was going to get sore from lifting my head that high all the time.

"We're going to sit down and figure out how best to round up the devices and the people responsible."

Turning so I wouldn't take too long, I headed in the direction I was pretty sure was my room. "I'll be there in fifteen minutes."

Nodding in a regal way, Victor turned back to Leone.

"Can we just stick a bag over my head until I get to my room?" I asked Quinton who walked silently beside me.

"No need, they'll all know before you get to it."

"Great," I muttered and turned in the way he pointed. He just chuckled and kept moving forward.

We didn't even reach my room and Rafael came jogging up. When he stepped in front of me, I almost walked smack right into his chest. Lifting my chin with one finger, he frowned.

"Maybe I should just go with you on all your jobs."

I gave him a blank look that I hoped he caught.

"Just remember I will always get your back if you need a hand, little Huntress."

There was that word again. *Little.* I was almost preferring Chase calling me kitten to constantly being reminded I was not gigantic like they were. "I'll keep that in mind. I'm just going to get cleaned up and go to the meeting."

Releasing my chin, he nodded. "I have something to take care of then I'll be there, shouldn't take too long."

"Fine."

****

The only brothers I hadn't had to explain to were the two rulers, no doubt though one or more of their siblings had told them what happened. It didn't stop them from pausing in their conversation to give me a once over, identical expressions on their face and the same concern in their matching hazel eyes told me my fat lip had been noted and would be filed for future reference when it suited them.

I paced along the length of the table, wishing everyone would hurry up and get here. The last we waited on was Rafael. Maybe it was being back here that had me edgy or I was still pissed for letting that asshat get a shot at my face, but I was jonesing for some action and drawn out meetings weren't within my comfort zone.

Troy and Chase were off in the far corner, heads down, words I couldn't hear being spoken. At that moment, they looked every bit the rulers. There were lives at stake and laws had been broken, both Kings wanted swift resolution and justice.

I killed a few minutes trying to see if there was any sort of visible difference in them. The only thing I could see was Chase's goatee and that he wore his hair loose, where Troy bound his shoulder length hair behind his head. Other than that, if there were differences they had to be internal.

Spinning back to go over my footsteps again, I paused behind the chair Quinton lounged in. "Someone should have mentioned snacks—that would have brought everyone together faster." I said quietly so only he would hear.

He chuckled and lowered his head so no one would notice.

The door opened and I hoped for Rafael, but instead Welsley walked in and looked around. He nodded to Victor and then spotted me and I swear the room almost iced up from the look on his face.

Nudging Quinton's shoulder, he turned and looked up at me. "What is that guy's position around here?"

Quinton rubbed the side of his face and game me an odd

look. "He was our hunter."

"Well, shit. No wonder he wants a piece of me," I murmured.

Welsley waited until his rulers turned and then bowed his head gracefully. "I was told that perhaps my assistance would be needed."

Troy and Chase exchanged a look. Before they could answer, I went around the table. "I'd like Welsley in on this."

A shocked look appeared on the white haired one's face. When he started to bow to me, I quickly added. "Don't you dare bow to me when we're just here for a brainstorming session. Try it and your hair will be much shorter when you lift that head again."

Giving me a wary look, he nodded and moved around me to sit at the table.

Chase was grinning at me when I turned back to look at them.

Rafael walked through the door pulling a shirt over his head.

"God, I hope she was good to make us all wait this long." I drawled at him.

He froze. "I—what?"

Troy started laughing. "Go sit, Raf. Our Huntress is getting a little antsy."

"A little?" I snorted and walked toward the table.

With everyone finally sitting, the twin Kings took their seats and filled us in on how many subjects were missing from both sides. Apparently, this had been happening for a few weeks now and they hadn't been able to put it together until Wanda told us what was going on. At last count fifty were gone, which left twenty more, if Michael's count was right, waiting to cross over into my turf.

I listened to the plans, not adding much unless it was in reference to my side of the realms. Welsley I noticed also didn't contribute much more than I did, but I watched his eyes flare several times when he had something to say, then didn't speak it.

Holding my hand up, everyone paused and looked at me. "I think it's fair to say that this is a hell of a lot more than I signed up for." I grinned, "Okay, I didn't volunteer for any of it, but wonder woman I am not. There's no way I can track the fifty missing on my own."

There were several nods around the table. "I need a couple of captains to even the odds a bit."

A brief glance passed between Chase and Troy. "What do you have in mind, Daxx?" Troy asked leaning forward so his hands rested on the table, much like his brothers did when things were being discussed.

I glanced at Quinton. "I want Quinton and..." I looked directly at Welsley. "Welsley as my captains, or whatever you'd call them. Who knows the territory better on this side?" Welsley sat straighter. "I know the lay of the land and the natives on my side, but I know nothing about here. I can only take down one at a time, with their experience I think we could crack down and get this done before too much damage takes place."

"I would be honored to assist you, Huntress." Welsley said in a proud tone.

Chase winked at me and then glanced at Troy out of the corner of his eye, Troy was smiling.

"I'm in." Quinton stated without ceremony.

"Great." I sat back feeling like I had just built a huge bridge over troubled waters.

"What do you need from us, Daxx?" Victor offered up, again surprising me.

Pausing to smirk at him, I stood up and leaned on the back of my chair. "Give me some history on those missing, whatever you can dig up and pictures of the jumpers too." Moving down the table I stopped beside Michael and picked up the watch device. "They have to keep them on at all times?"

He nodded.

I turned it over and studied it. It looked unique enough that it would be hard to mistake. Raising my eyes, I looked from one pair of hazel eyes to the other. "This family of royalty accumulate any riches throughout the millenniums?"

Troy nodded slowly. "What are you thinking?"

Dangling the watch from two fingers, I waved it back and forth. "Someone sees this and they'll remember who was wearing it for forty or fifty bucks if you ask in the right neighborhoods, at least on my side."

"On ours too." Quinton confirmed.

Troy looked to Chase, who agreed. He shrugged at me. "Let's do it."

Michael and Victor both stood up. "With Leone and Rafael's help we'll have your lists and information by tomorrow."

I grinned. "Then I can go and kick some ass."

****

I was standing looking over maps of the day walker domains, trying to get a feel for the area when I suddenly had the feeling, I was being watched. Looking up, I glanced around to see everyone had gone, except the Kings who were standing across the room in almost the identical poses. Their arms were crossed the same way, they were leaning against the table in the same way and both were staring at me with the same expression on their face.

"Where's a camera when you need it." I joked.

When they both started walking toward me, my nerves zinged and told me to bolt now for my own safety. I ignored them and straightened up.

Troy spoke first. "We would like to apologize for not telling you everything."

I shrugged. "I'm over it. Mostly."

"It still wasn't right." Chase motioned to me. "You're not a pawn and this isn't a game."

"I didn't think it was." Moving away from them, I paced around to the end of the table. It was time to come clean. "Look, I'm a little, okay, that's a lie, I'm completely freaking overwhelmed with *all* of this. The whole other realm, other race of beings—finding out my tattoo just grew there and it wasn't the result of a bad acid trip." Troy raised his eyebrows but didn't interrupt me. "I'm a bounty hunter, so the easy part in all of this is that I'm the Huntress on this side, it fits, *that* works for me. As to being a Queen—have you seen where I'm from? Where I live?"

Moving back in their direction quickly I threw my hands up. "I've been alone—always, I never spoke to my foster parents as I bounced through the system. I bailed on that when I was fifteen and lived through the shit life tossed at me to get this far. *Now* all of a sudden I find myself constantly surrounded by people trying to look out for me." I pointed at each of them, I don't know why I did, just felt like I needed to. "To top it all off, suddenly I have seven *really* older than me, huge brothers that are all in my face and one lover I have to choose to spend eternity with." Throwing my hands up, I spun away from them. "Don't even get me started on having to have twins in two hundred and forty year's time."

Taking a deep breath, I tried to find some calm before I faced them again. When I turned around to look at them, I wanted to scream. They stood where I'd left them, one with red eyes, the other with yellow. "Great, now I've set the both of you off as a grand finale."

Troy moved in my direction first and then Chase. Neither reached for me, just moved closer.

"We're not going to push you, Daxx." Troy said quietly.

"We didn't make the rules, kitten, fate did that. We just follow them." Chase whispered.

Sighing I looked down at the floor, unable to deal with the whole eye color thing right now. "You don't get it, Chase." Feeling like a coward, I looked back up into two pairs of hazel eyes. "At some point in all of this someone is going to be hurt and it will be me causing it."

"What would you like to do?" Troy tucked his hands in his pockets and looked down at me with compassion almost bleeding from his eyes.

"I thought before I make any decisions I'd get to know

both of you first. Maybe spend some time with Chase on his side and some time with you here."

"Sounds reasonable." Troy agreed.

Taking a deep breath, I patted both of their chests. "Who knows I may loathe both of you in the end and choose just to go home."

Chase chuckled. "You won't take the easy way out, kitten, it's not in you."

I scowled at him, "maybe."

Reaching down, he tilted up my chin and touched his thumb to my lip. "I still don't like this, brother King, I think we should pay some retribution to the one that caused this."

Troy placed his hand under the other side of my chin and smiled. "I think your right day ruler, we should indeed."

Smacking both of their hands away, I turned back to the table. "Why don't you two go rule or do something *kingly*."

"Yes, my Huntress Queen." Troy joked as he moved away.

"I'll see you at dinner, kitten, try not to get beaten before then." Chase retreated as well.

CHAPTER SEVENTEEN

Promising I'd stay put while *they*, being Rafael, Victor, Michael and Quinton, went to check on *something*, I discovered I got bored really easy when left with nothing to do for long periods of time. Why hadn't I discovered this about myself before now?

To kill time, I'd gone to the library to take a look at that book of prophecies again. At the *library*, I found about a gazillion books and the very first old looking person I'd seen on this side. He reminded me of an old wizard, with the crazy long white beard and hair. He seemed to know what I wanted before I even asked him and handed me that book with the leaves on the cover.

After talking with him for a few minutes I discovered there were more than twenty books of prophecy and any time I wanted I could read those that had come true in the last ten thousand years or see what else the future held. It was hard to just walk out of there with the one book. I mean who wouldn't want to see what was going to happen a thousand years from now.

An hour later I was still in my room skimming through the book trying to find the part that would allow me to prove it was, well, hog spittle as Victor had so adequately put it. So far the book was winning.

It was divided into sections, each one pertaining to one of the nine brothers, but I just skimmed the start of all the others and didn't get into any of the details. I'd been told it had been translated into modern English only eighty years ago, like that was yesterday, but it still read cryptically to me. Not as difficult as Shakespeare had been for me in school, but it didn't give me much along the lines of hints as to how this was going to go down.

Pacing, I muttered again that this was all a dream and I needed to go home. I knew it wasn't a dream anymore, but I still wasn't feeling like the prophesized Huntress Queen. Shouldn't I be feeling all powerful or something?

Glaring at the book open on the desk I went back to it. Maybe if I broke it down it would make sense to me. The beginning was kind of boring, but I read it again.

For the King's sons numbering nine

Lives will change when new blood merges with those that reign.

Okay, so the new blood was human or at least some from my side. They had me there I couldn't find anything to argue with in this part.

Without mates shall all sons remain until the time of the Huntress Queen comes to be.

At a time with lawlessness and chaos, to be bred the huntress shall be born to keep the balance.

Hidden in another realm she hunts those lawbreakers and brings them to justice. Her destiny is concealed until the time of her need is upon Alterealm.

In an obscure way that sounded like me. I dragged runners back to jail, so again I couldn't argue with any of it. Why couldn't I just be this huntress person? Why did I have to be anyone's mate? It didn't sit right with me and I didn't see that changing at anytime in the future. Sighing loudly, I went back to the stupid fancy writing in the pretty book.

Neither of this world or her own, but of both.

When the marking unveils between her shoulders the sundial will validate she is true and waiting to be found.

Had I ever been waiting to be found? I don't know what

I was but waiting for something, maybe, but not being found I didn't think.

The sundial will protect her from all manner of trickery and evil force and shield her from powers of all.

Her beauty and skill of the hunt will win the hearts of the brothers nine.

Beauty? Now they were really stretching it. I wasn't a dog as far as looks went, but merely average, which was a good place to be.

The Huntress Queen Daxx will stand equal with the throne and none shall fail to notice her right to be there.

Nine brothers must lay in wait for her to choose her King.

From this point is where I didn't like what I read. The rest before it I could accept and other than a few minor details was okay with it, but the whole choosing one brother, one twin brother over the other didn't sit well with me at all.

True mate to either twin King if the bond be made, she must select one or the other that can hold her heart right.

See that part with being both true mates had me twitchy. Shouldn't it just be one only and the other couldn't be? So far, I liked both twins. Troy was a little more proper and standoffish than his twin, but then Chase was a little blunt at times for my taste. But overall, they both seemed like good choices, if one wanted to choose, which I didn't.

Leaning over the book, I forced myself to continue.

The Huntress's reign alongside her King will change the realms forever controlling the evil of both sides and bring peace to sun and moon.

And everyone lived happily-ever-after. I snorted and paced away again. It went on for pages and pages, describing the other eight sons and their true mates. All of it was cryptic. When they translated it, you think they would have made things a little clearer.

What was this bond that could be made? Was it something I'd know so I could stop it from happening? It said nothing more about it. How was I supposed to know which twin would hold my heart right?

A knock at the door made me spin around, eager for

anyone right now, anything to take me out of this deep thought mode. "Come in."

Troy came through the door. "I'm not interrupting you, am I?"

I shook my head. "No, just driving myself crazy with thinking."

"Ah, a dangerous thing to be sure," he smirked. "I heard you'd been left behind and thought you might be a little forlorn because of it."

Raising my eyebrows at him, I crossed my arms and studied him. "Are you aware your speech goes from normal to stuffy without warning?"

His lips quirked. "You *are* in an analytical mood, aren't you? I preferred old English when I was younger and sometimes I find myself switching back and forth." Moving further into the room, he glanced around and then paused when he spotted the book open on my desk. "Doing a little light reading, Huntress?"

"There's nothing light about that."

His lips quirked. "Unraveled all of its hidden meaning yet?"

Staring at the floor, I shook my head. "I haven't even gotten past the first few pages, but I'm thinking Victor's assessment is right on the money."

Going over, he ran his finger down the page left open. "What assessment was that?"

"It's all hog spittle."

Throwing his head back he laughed. "I'm sure Victor will be thrilled to know you agree with him now." Leaning back against the desk, he crossed his arms and looked at me. "Is it that bad, Daxx? To have my brother or I for a mate to dote on you and fill your every whim because when all is said or done, you know that's what will happen. We've been without true companionship for closer to thirty decades, would it be so rough to have a man that not only desires you but will go out of his way to please you?"

When he put it in those terms it didn't sound half bad,

but I wasn't going to admit it. I shrugged.

"It could be worse you could be me, I have two possible options in this book and to be truthful I'm not entirely sure which one I'd prefer." Turning he flipped the page and read the next part out loud. "For our King not chosen a mate lies in wait, born of human blood. She will rule over his compulsion as no other could and bring him life times of eternal peace." He lifted his head and turned around. "While that for the most part sounds intriguing and appeals, does it mean I would have to wait a few more hundred years for this mate to appear to me? And what of this compulsion she's to rule over? Is that a good or bad thing for the king that's hers?"

He started walking towards me and my nerves started doing that fluttering thing again. "I don't think you're getting the bad end of the deal Huntress." I'd had fair warning to move, but had stood my ground and now he was right in front of me standing so close I could feel the heat of his body.

Lifting my chin, he lowered his face closer to mine. "Would spending the rest of your existence with me be such a bad thing?"

I got lost in his eyes as they held mine. As much as I could I shook my head. "I don't want to be the one to choose."

Something went through his eyes so briefly I wasn't sure what. "It has to be you. My brother and I may be twins, but we are still very much male and look out for our own interests where a female is concerned. Would you rather we battle as they did years ago and the survivor gets the girl?"

I didn't reply, mostly because I couldn't focus on what he'd just said. I could feel his breath brushing over my lips and just his nearness made me forget what my problem had been. We stood like that for what felt like an eternity, his eyes, now red roamed my face, his lips only an inch from mine.

"I think you should go over and spend some time with

Chase," he whispered and then slowly released my chin and straightened back up but didn't move away.

I'd been so mesmerized by his closeness I almost swayed when he wasn't there. Placing my hands on his chest, I looked up at him. His hand played at the back of my head and I was waiting for more.

"Daxx…" Rafael burst through the door. "Oh— Shit, sorry," he mumbled and looked down at the floor. "I figured you were alone."

Troy's hand brushed down the back of my head once more before he stepped away. "Perhaps knocking to be sure would be a way to find out."

"Sorry I interrupted." Rafael sent his brother a hesitant look.

"It's of no matter, we were just discussing Daxx going over to Chase's kingdom tomorrow."

I turned and looked at him. We had? I didn't recall any sort of discussion taking place. Troy stood there looking at me, that look on his face I couldn't read was back in place. His eyes moved over my face once, pausing long enough on my mouth that in reflex I licked my lips.

With a soft word uttered under his breath, he nodded at Rafael. "Was there a reason you burst in here?"

Rafael nodded and then looked at me. "We found two more."

Troy cleared his throat. "I'll leave you to it then and will see you both at dinner."

I watched him walk out and had no clue what had just happened. Shaking it off, I turned to the man giving me strange looks. "Let's go see what Arius can get out of them."

CHAPTER EIGHTEEN

Quinton and Rafael still looked skeptical. Today was the first time I was going over to Chase's half of Alterealm. I'd only seen it on the miles of maps they had but hadn't once gone near 'the other side'. If the maps were correct, it wasn't that much different than the areas I'd been in over here.

I was finally led to a small room that had a door, with security lock on it. This was almost like the one Quinton had brought me in that first day, only I was told this one went to Chase's side.

Troy walked into the room. "Chase will be here shortly." He looked at his brothers with the same expression they had.

"Aren't you guys overreacting a bit?" All they were doing was making me nervous on what to expect.

"I have no doubt Chase will look after you. We're just a little apprehensive in letting you go." Troy offered a weak smile, but his eyes said he really wasn't happy with me going.

"It's not like this side, Daxx," Quinton said quietly.

"It's dangerous." Rafael added.

Rolling my eyes in their direction I shook my head. "Have you seen my neighborhood?"

Mitz came into the room carrying a small bag. "Oh for heaven's sake. She's only going over for a few days, you're all acting like it's an eternity." She set the bag down and smiled at me. "I packed you some of your favored outfits." Kissing my cheek, she turned and started back up the hallway. "Have a good time, love."

Sighing, Rafael came over and leaned down and kissed my cheek. "I'll call if we need you, little Huntress." I stood there and watched him leave, not at all sure where the kiss part had come from.

Quinton grasped my shoulders and spun me around so quickly, I almost tipped over. "You call me." He said with no leeway for discussion.

I nodded my head much like a child would when they're going off to summer camp. "I really don't know what you guys are so worried about."

"They're afraid I'm going to convince you to stay on my side." I turned to see Chase lounging in the open doorway. His grin reminded me of the big bad wolf.

Looking at Troy and then Quinton I picked up the bag. "I'm going over because, first I said I would and if I'm going to be the Huntress Queen of Alterealm shouldn't I know all of it?" Troy inclined his head but didn't answer me.

"Aw, kitten, I thought it was to spend time with me."

I smirked, "that too."

Chase held out his hand, the silver ring with the sun shining at me. I went over and placed mine in his. "I'll keep her close." He said to his twin, an odd look in his eyes when he did.

The tunnel was much like the one I'd come in on my arrival in this place, only it didn't go down, it was level. "What's with the tunnels?"

"It's faster, no traffic. Secure. This place wasn't always peaceful." He continued to hold my hand as we walked.

"Is it so those from night can cross without day?" I still wasn't sure of the difference between the sides.

Chase stopped and looked at me for a moment before we continued. "You've been so busy hunting down those with the devices; no one has thought to fill you in on a little history."

"It never seemed to be the right time to ask."

"Daylight won't hurt a nightwalker and the reverse is the same."

The tunnel seemed to go on for miles. "Then why have two distinct sides?"

"I won't go too deep into the history of Alterealm this time, but the distinction is mainly a different life style." He looked down at me. "That began as a way to separate and control offenders."

I mulled it over for a second. "I'm not getting it. Offenders?"

Nodding, he squeezed my hand. "Troy gets the do-gooders and I have to wrangle the bad lot." He shrugged. "In my great grandfather's time it was chaos, a daily blood bath my father used to say. It was during that time the King, and there was only one at that time ruled the two different sides to Alterealm." He sighed. "I'm afraid if you want all the details on our history you'll have to speak to Victor or Arius. I could never pay attention in that class..."

"You have schools here?"

Chase laughed. "Do we seem uneducated?"

I shook my head. "No, I didn't mean that. I have so much to learn."

He squeezed my hand again. "You have all the time in the world to learn whatever you want."

When he stopped, I realized we were standing in front of a door. "Let's get you settled and then you can decide what you want to do first." He entered some numbers into the keypad and the lock popped open.

When I stepped through the door, I was facing two very large, very scary looking men. They weren't scary in the way of gory; just their auras sent a chill up my spine. Before I could look to Chase, they both dropped down onto one knee and bowed their heads.

When I started to reach out, Chase took my hand and shook his head. "There's none of that touchy feely over here, that's a good way to lose a hand." My eyes widened but I didn't comment. "Sith, Bronx, may I introduce your huntress queen, Daxx."

Both men stood back up and nodded.

"These gentlemen will either be stationed at the door or outside your room."

Looking back up at the two men that looked more like pirates than anything else, I offered a small smile and inclined my head. I really needed to start taking notes on proper protocol around here.

Without saying anything further, Chase moved along the hallway. I glanced back around at the men who had moved back to stand in front of the door. "A little more security on this side."

His hazel eyes swept over my face. "A little more is needed on my side, kitten."

"Is Victor the justice on this side too?"

Chase nodded as he motioned down the hall we turned to go down. "Yes, all positions apply to both sides, I just have need of a few more over here. Leone is *the* enforcer and Rafael head of guards and so on, but I have to hold the reigns a bit tighter over here."

"You said you have the bad lot, what do you mean? Is this side like a prison?"

Opening a door, he led me into a large bedroom. "The prison is on this side, but I meant that I have the ones that don't like to follow the rules. If someone is judged or banished from Troy's territory this is where they are sent. "

"And the daylight part does what?"

He grinned. "It's easier to monitor behavior in the light. Both sides have a curfew that can only be broken for select special occasions. The wasteland has no law or curfew, so try to avoid that area if you're in the mood for a stroll."

Suddenly in just a short walk I'd learned more about this place than I had in all the time I'd been here. The only reason I could think was that on Troy's side, they didn't have to follow the rules with a rigid control where Chase had to all the time. It also told me why he chose to go over to nightwalker territory, most likely to get a break from constantly looking over his shoulder. I looked around and was surprised that there was a lot less antique furniture, without the ceiling to floor decorations of my other bedchamber.

"It's not designed for the Huntress; it's just a simple guest room if that's alright with you."

"It's fine. It's still a palace compared to my apartment."

He made an odd sound. "Yes, Troy described your apartment when you went to retrieve Wanda. It sounded tired."

I laughed. "Tired is one way to put it."

"Will you be keeping your apartment?"

I shrugged. "I think I should. I need somewhere that's just mine."

"I understand. Let us know if you need help with rent or fumigation, we seem to have monopolized all your time and without monetary compensation."

I turned and looked at him. "Chase?"

He raised his eyebrows.

"Why are you being so stiff with me?"

Flashing his charming smile, while his eyes caressed over my face. "I don't mean to be, I have to be a certain way when I'm home."

"It's just me, you can be yourself with me."

Moving closer, he leaned down so his face was level with mine. "Oh, I don't think I can completely be myself with you just yet, kitten, but I have hopes that someday I can." He brushed his finger over my lip and straightened away. "And if truth be told, I think I'm a little nervous to be alone with you."

My eyebrows shot up. "Really?"

"Yes and it's an odd feeling to have at my age."

I grinned. "No doubt, a guy as old as you, I thought you would have experienced it all."

His eyes flashed something I couldn't catch and wasn't sure if I wanted to. "Oh, not all, just my fair share."

Wandering away when that awkward feeling came over me, I peeked in the bathroom. Might be simple by his terms but it was several levels above the Ritz for me. "I don't think your brother feels the same, wanting me to himself."

He chuckled. "Which brother are we talking about, because in case you hadn't noticed I have more than a few."

Leaning against the door, I rolled my eyes at him. "The other King."

An odd look appeared on his face, lowering his lashes he hid it before I could figure it out. "I think you'd be mistaken on that note, kitten. I've never seen my twin lose control like he almost did when you helped Quinton heal."

"He didn't lose control." I tried to remember that clearly but there were a few foggy details.

"Didn't he?"

Frowning, I tried to recall but couldn't. "He sent me here."

Chase grinned. "That doesn't mean he doesn't want you there with him." He strolled toward me with that casual grace that seemed to be a part of him as much as breathing was to most. "I would wager that my brother King sent you here *because* he wants you."

"I don't see the logic." My heart started drumming a little faster as his pale eyes swept over me.

"That is not for me to explain." Touching my hair, he brushed it back from my face. "What would you like to do first now that you're here?"

I bit my lip trying to decide. This was the first time I'd been without two or more large brothers hovering around me. "I'd like to see the side you reign over."

Surprise filled his eyes before he smiled. "As you wish, kitten. Let me round up our guards."

"We're taking guards with us?"

Nodding he tucked his hand into his pockets. "I'm not taking a chance of anything happening to you." His lips quirked. "I may be a great fighter, but I don't think I'd stand a chance against all of my brothers if I were to let anything happen to their Huntress Queen." With that he turned toward the door.

Pausing with his hand on the handle, he looked back at me. "It's quite warm out today, so dress light and go nowhere on this side without your raptor."

I didn't want to tell him I never went anywhere without it. "Okay."

****

I don't know what I was expecting, but it wasn't what I thought as we spent an hour wandering around as Chase led the tour. This realm had all the technology my side did, maybe more with their devices to cross realities, but to walk around the village closest to where Chase lived it was like I'd stepped back into another era. The shops were quaint and filled with handmade wares, the people although dressed in today's clothes kept to their own space and were nothing but polite as we passed by.

"Not what you were expecting, kitten?"

I looked up at Chase and shook my head. "Not quite." We paused to look into a clothing store, where they actually made the clothing and it was like a step back in time if you didn't count the laptop sitting on the counter.

"The oldest families have kept the traditional feel of the village, I'm not sure if it's for novelty's sake or just to keep them busy." He motioned to cross the street. "The further away from here you travel the quaintness is lost and it bleeds into something more familiar to you."

"Pollution and mayhem?"

He chuckled. "And then some." He glanced over his shoulder. "I think you have a few followers."

Turning, I looked behind us to see a small group of teens following along behind us at a safe distance. At least they looked like teens. I needed to find out how the aging thing worked. One of them quickly came towards us and dropped to one knee. The two guards with us moved closer until Chase shook his head to tell them it was okay.

"Sire." He paused with his head bowed.

Chase stood there without moving or speaking until the boy raised his head again, then he nodded. The teen stood back up and I noted that he was almost a head taller than me. Was growing this large normal here?

"We noticed the marking of the Huntress... Is it true, sire?" He asked, his face flushing with excitement.

Looking down at me, Chase raised one eyebrow at me and then nodded. "It is." He stepped aside and motioned at me. "This is your Huntress Queen, son."

I stood there, not sure what to do as the look of fear and enthusiasm entered the boy's blue eyes. Before I could say anything, he dropped down in front of me. Here I was again not sure what I should or shouldn't do. Over the top of the boy's head, I asked for help from Chase with a look. He smirked and motioned with his head telling me a touch would be acceptable in this case.

I touched the top of the boy's head and thought for a moment he was going to pull a Rafael and grab me. I tensed, but he only stood up right in front of me grinning down at me.

"I can't believe you're finally here. Wait until I tell the others!" With that he backed up and bowed quickly and then took off back to his friends.

I stood there watching them all huddle, looks being cast my way.

"We better move on or you're going to have to be greeted by the whole gang."

Eyes wide, I nodded and turned to walk beside Chase again. He was grinning. "What?"

"By nightfall the whole daywalker side will know you're here."

"Is that good or bad?"

Chase looked around at the boys as they took off in the other direction. "A bit of both I'd imagine. The kids will fear your justice, some adults will challenge it."

I stiffened. "Great," I mumbled. That's what I needed people challenging me for no real reason other than the tattoo on my back.

I glanced down the street and was surprised to see Victor striding in our direction, with two large guards right on his heels. I'd never seen him in actual daylight and it was shocking how pale he really was. He sent me a brief nod and then went straight to Chase.

"We have a bit of a situation."

Chase gave him his full attention going from noticeably aware to very alert in a second without hesitation. "Explain quickly before you get a sunburn."

Victor's eyes held that annoyed look he often gave his siblings. "We've found a large compound that has at least a dozen involved with distributing the devices."

"Is the magician there?"

Victor shook his head. "No, but his right hand is."

Pausing only for a second, Chase glanced at the sky. "We'll have to move before dusk. Where are the others?"

Rubbing the back of his neck, Victor exhaled loudly. "Quinton, Rafael and Michael are on the other side with a possible lead," he glanced at me, "before they bring Daxx over. Arius has his hands full with the others from yesterday."

Chase nodded and looked at the two guards with Victor. I could see him doing the math and weighing the odds. He nodded to one of the men. "Go get Sith and Bronx, meet us at the stables." The large man took off at a run. Chase looked back to his brother. "Where's Leone?"

Victor dropped his head down. "I don't know. He went off the grid last night."

"He back there again?"

I wanted to ask what was off the grid, back where but with the tension radiating from the king and head of justice I decided now might not be the time for gossipy conversation.

Victor glanced up and then looked back to the ground. "Possibly."

"We'd better leave him be then." Chase looked at me, his eyes pondering something. With a look alone, I dared him to try and send me to my room to wait it out.

Turning to the other guard that had arrived with Victor, he motioned with his head in the direction we'd just come from. "Go get the Huntress a tonfa with blade and a dagger and strap. We'll be at the stables." Then he looked at the guard that stood nearest to me and straightened to his full height. With a low tone, he spoke softly. "Tim, you have one task to perform." His eyes moved over me. "You are not to let your Huntress Queen be out of your reach at any time." It wasn't his words but the way he said them that sent shivers up my spine. "She gets one scratch on her and I will hold you personally responsible."

Tim nodded once abruptly and then stepped behind me blocking the sun's rays from even touching me. I guess this was having a shadow in this realm.

Chase stepped in front of me. "You up for a take down?" His tone was light but the look in his eyes was dead serious.

I smiled. "I wouldn't miss it."

CHAPTER NINETEEN

When he had told the guards to meet at the stables, I thought we were talking about the old stables or what used to be the stables. As I stood outside watching the stable hands bring out the horses I didn't know what to do. They were real horses and like everything else in this realm, really large. When one of them stopped in front of me with a gigantic white horse I just stood there feeling like I should be asking for something I knew how to work, a motorcycle or even a bicycle. Riding and steering a horse wasn't something I had the slightest clue how to do.

"Never ridden, have you?"

I looked away from the huge beast to Chase as he walked up behind me. "City girl I'm afraid." Craning my neck, I looked up at the big blue eyes of the animal. "I don't think I've ever been this close to one."

"As much as I'd like to give you riding lessons, I don't think we have time right now." He motioned to the man holding the horse in front of me. "The Huntress will ride with me today."

I watched him lead the animal away again.

"She's yours by the way."

Looking down at the size of the print she had left behind I felt relieved I didn't have to ride something with feet that big. "What do you mean?"

"The horse. Angelica. She's yours."

With both eyebrows raised I looked back at the animal now running around in the yard again and then flicked my eyes to Chase. "She's mine?"

He nodded. "I've been breeding the same champion blood line for over a hundred years waiting, always selecting the white foal to groom for the Huntress. Angelica was born for you. I only let the female trainers ride and groom her."

"I don't know what to say."

Watching the guards come out of the stables, each leading two horses he shrugged. "Thank you works."

"Thank you." I fidgeted with the dagger strapped to my leg again, so I wouldn't have to look at him. "Why horses by the way? I know you have cars."

Accepting the biggest horse that had been led over, he patted its neck. "Easier to maneuver and quieter."

Sounded like a reasonable explanation to me. "Is it far?"

"Roughly twenty minutes." Grasping me around the waist he lifted me onto the back of the black animal. "Just stay up there until I get on."

I nodded, too nervous to say anything and clung to the animal with my knees while he climbed up behind me. There was no need to encourage me to lean back into him as he reached around me to get the reins. The animal pranced a few times, but stayed in one place.

"I've got you, kitten." He whispered in my ear, wrapping his arm around my waist. "Ready to go kick some ass?"

I was on the horse wasn't I? "Let's do this." I answered breathlessly.

****

The compound wasn't well guarded, so getting close enough to plan was the easy part. We watched a few people come and go, long enough to get a good idea of how many people we were dealing with. There were nine of us and we counted twenty of them, so far.

Victor pointed out a tall thin man in a blue jacket.

"That's him. He's mine." His voice had that ice-cold edge to it.

Chase nodded and moved back toward the horses. "We'll go in around the side of that small building to the left." He motioned to two of the men. "You two come in from the back of the middle building." They nodded and jogged off into the trees.

Victor started in the other direction, motioning for one of the men to come with him. "Fight well, brother."

Chase grinned. "Well enough to beat you, brother." The grin died when he turned to me, his eyes told me how much he wanted me to stay right where I was. "Do whatever you need to stay whole and alive."

"I always do." Pulling the tonfa from the strap on my back, I popped the blade out to check it. "Let's go."

Chase looked me up and down and then he turned dead serious eyes in Tim's direction in warning to remember what he'd said.

We didn't even reach the building before all hell broke loose. Apparently while we were watching them, they had been watching us. Before we could get around the building, two men jumped out of the trees, axes swinging. I had a holy shit that's a freaking battle axe moment, but I didn't actually stop to admire, I was too busy trying to avoid the blades of death.

Tim wasted no time inserting his body in the path between one of the attackers and myself. Usually I'd gripe over someone getting in the way, but in this case, I decided his broad sword outmatched my dagger against one of the metal axes trying to take a bite out of our flesh.

In a move that would have brought tears of pride to my eyes if I'd been standing back watching, he ducked and knocked the guy back just enough to make him pause with his onslaught. Never being one to stand on the side lines, I ducked under Tim's arm as he blocked a second swing and inserted the blade of my tonfa right into the guy's thigh. With a howl, he dropped the axe to the ground and grabbed hold of his leg. Two points for our team.

Turning, I watched as the other two guards disarmed the second assailant in a much more brutal manner. Tim quickly secured ours to the nearest tree and then came back to me.

As we headed around the building I heard the clang of metal on metal and turned the corner to see Chase in action. The moves he made during sparring were nothing compared to when he had his rage on. Actually, it wasn't rage, it was a methodical trouncing and it was beautiful to watch. He fought with twin blades, each were the length of my leg and probably the width of my arm. The sheer strength he put behind them staggered anyone that made contact.

I could have stood all day and watched him beat them down, one at a time, but the grunt that came from behind me made me remember this wasn't a weapons demonstration but the real deal. Liking my hide just the way it was, I spun around and ducked down ready to take on whatever was coming my way.

Not having time to look around and see if my shadow-slash-blocker was handy, I readied for the man heading my way. He at least brought a reasonable weapon to the game. I was almost happy to see a good 'ol pig sticker in his hand and not some medieval blade.

A few times he got too close for comfort, as fun as being able to fight full out without having to worry about cops dragging my ass in was, I decided it was time to get down to business and remind him it wasn't polite to stab a lady. Not that I felt I was a lady and above this sort of thing, in fact I might just travel all of Alterealm after this and seek out all the bad guys, I just wasn't in the mood for the pain of an injury.

His blade came so close to trimming my hair on one swing I could feel the air move beside my head. That was it for this one, I decided. Timing it right, I waited until he advanced again and let him think he had me on the run, so he'd loosen his stance just enough. With a quick spring up, I spun and landed a kick on his temple and down he went a satisfying yelp. Dropping down, I jabbed him in the stomach with the end of the wand just to make sure he stayed put before I looked around for back up to secure him.

Tim appeared out of nowhere and practically hogtied the guy to a nearby fence post. That man needed to enter a rodeo for sure, he had impressive speed and skill with those tie straps.

Surveying the action that seemed to be going on all around me now, I paused only long enough to make sure Tim was finished and had my back. I didn't want to get the guy in shit by taking off, and I felt a little more secure knowing he was nearby.

Chase was up against one of the biggest guys I'd seen since discovering there was another realm and for half a second I thought of going to aid him and even the odds a bit, but before I could decide how to do that a loud clang right by my ear brought me full circle. Tim had just blocked someone trying to take my head home as a souvenir. The lethal King was on his own as I set out to assist my shadow in taking out the S.O.B. after my head.

This dude with glowing eyes wasn't using a battle axe but he had a katana and the blade looked clean and sharp. When Tim took a blow to his hip, I didn't waste any time with drama, I grabbed my raptor and dropped to one knee and threw it. It embedded itself into the guy's side and down he went. Tim recovered and stumbled over to pounce on the guy and use a good portion of his large self to crush him into the ground. With a knock to the head, that one wouldn't be getting up any time soon. Sliding over, I pulled my raptor free and help Tim tie the unconscious attacker. "You good?" I asked him. He touched a hand over the gash on his hip and grunted as he got to his feet.

With a nod to me, we turned to see what other damage we could manage. There were fewer standing then when we started. With eyes wide I caught a bit of Victor's action as he took on the guy in the blue jacket. I understood now why he was justice. He was flawless in his execution and anyone that thought to try and escape him would be sorry. Tim bumping into me brought my attention back. He was holding his side and looking a little green now. Shit, my blocker wasn't going to make it at this rate.

Spotting a clear path, I pushed him in that direction so I could get both of us to someplace safe to assess his injury. Before we could reach safety, another maniac came at us with a saber, almost as long as I was tall, with crazy shining from his glowing eyes. At home my raptor was a serious weapon, if I planned on fighting here I think I needed to upgrade to something much larger.

Tim deflected the first swing from the new opponent and then dropped to one knee. I had to hustle around the downed guard to block the next swing with the tonfa. Thankful this wand was made of metal and not a wooden practice one, or the saber may have sliced right through it and my arm. There was no time for reflection on what he was going to do next, no time to get either my dagger or raptor ready as I danced in front of Tim trying to keep both of us in one piece.

I felt the sting of the blade in my thigh from a lucky upswing from the man wielding his blade like a scythe but I didn't look down to see how much flesh was missing. Tim managed to get back into a crouch and bought me the seconds I needed to get my dagger in hand. When the blade came towards me again I ducked down to roll but the slice out of my thigh muscle prevented me from completing it. I felt heat go through my side as the gleaming metal cut through me. Pain screamed from my nerves and I stumbled, trying to keep the attacker in sight as I collapsed onto the ground.

Dropping the dagger, I slapped my hand over the pulsing wound and raised my arm, hoping the metal wand would be enough to deflect any further strikes. I could see the crazed one hovering over me, the victory in his eyes pained me more than the bleeding flesh on my body. He had the advantage and I knew it as the blade came down, almost in slow motion I could see it. Just when I thought I'd be in more pieces than

I wanted, another blade intercepted the swing and Chase stepped over me, backing the attacker off with the skill of his actions.

I wanted to get up and help, but my body wasn't responding. A war cry sounded from someone and I turned to see Victor grasp the man from behind, his hand swiftly running a razor thin kukri blade across his throat. "The judgment is death for injury to the Huntress," Victor hissed. The saber fell from the man's hand and his body slid to the ground leaving a trail of red on the dirt.

Dropping his weapons, Chase fell to his knees on the ground beside me.

"Is Tim alright?" I panted and tried to push up to see the guard lying a few feet away from me.

Chase didn't even turn to look. "He'll live." Lifting my hand from my side, I watched the concern on his face turn to fear.

"Don't be mad at him…" I gasped trying to stay focused through the dizziness that suddenly hit me.

Victor appeared behind Chase and looked down at me. The same look of fear slid over his face. "Get her back. We'll clean up the mess here."

Chase nodded, without looking away from me.

I watched with blurred vision as he stood up and put his blades back into the straps on his back, then he looked around. "Find Leone and get him here now." There was ice in his tone.

All at once all my strength was gone and I dropped onto my back, squinting up at the King towering over me. I watched as he knelt down and felt even dizzier as he gathered me up into his arms.

"You're going to need help." Victor's voice came from somewhere, he sounded far away.

"Get Troy to my rooms as quickly as possible. I'll transport us there as soon as we reach the tree line." Chase's voice echoed in my ears.

I wondered for a second if I'd taken a blow to the head,

everyone sounded so strange. Closing my eyes, I tried to focus on how my body was feeling, nothing came back to me. The pain throbbed through me but it was like the rest of me wasn't there.

"Keep those eyes open, kitten, no napping right now." Chase's voice softly came to me in my dream.

Looking up, I could see his face, but it wasn't very clear. The motion of his walking felt like we were going up stairs. Through the fog that kept moving over me the first inkling of worry managed to grab me. I was really hurt this time. Steri-strips and some tape weren't going to do the trick this time out. I tried to lift my head and look around, had someone helped Tim or did they leave him lying in the dirt? I wanted to ask about him, but my tongue and brain couldn't coordinate to say it out loud.

Leaning into the warm body holding me, I closed my eyes again for a second as a wave of nausea threatened to take me. Breathing through I opened my eyes again slowly and then blinked, I was seeing a bedroom.

CHAPTER TWENTY

Chase leaned over me, his hazel eyes filled with determination. I was in a bed and had no idea how I ended up here. Had I blacked out?

"The King will be here in a moment." Mitz's voice filled the room. "He was dealing with a little uprising when Victor called."

Turning my head, I watched her almost run towards me.

"He sent me here to see if I could lend a hand…" She stopped beside the bed, her usual cheery faced blanching when she looked down at me. With a quick look to the man hovering over me, she turned and ran through a door. "Get those filthy clothes off her."

Now I was starting to worry. I felt Chase cut through the strap for my wand and then the one around my leg. When he reached around and pulled the case for my raptor off the back of my jeans, panic started to take over. Reaching out I aimed for his hand and ended up connecting with his wrist instead.

Grasping my hand lightly, he moved it and then used my own knife to cut away the leg of my jeans. Up until then I'd forgotten about the cut on my thigh and wanted to lift my head to look, but my muscles weren't obeying.

"We have to get you cleaned up, Daxx." Chase lowered

his head and worked the material away from my leg.

I'd only heard Chase call me by my name a few times and each time it was when things were serious. Hearing him say kitten right now would have been a comfort.

Mitz reappeared over me, the worry plainly etched into her usual smooth brow. "Go get yourself washed. I don't need you infecting her with the blood and dirt on you."

I hadn't even noticed if Chase was hurt, but from the sounds of it he was wearing the opponent's blood and not his own. Mitz continued to mutter under her breath as she wiped my side. With a frown on her face, she looked around and then grabbed something sitting beside me.

I heard the material of my shirt being ripped through with a blade, but couldn't summon the energy to look. A cool wetness moved over the burn on my side and oddly enough it felt better even though it hurt like a bitch.

Mitz looked over her shoulder and spoke to someone. "I can't stop the flow on this one."

Chase appeared in my limited view again. "Where the hell is Troy?"

"You have to give her blood." Mitz's voice wasn't gentle and that sent a new wave of fear through me.

I felt the bed move and then could see Chase beside me. "It won't do a damn thing if she bleeds it out as fast as I put it in." With a gentle touch, he brushed the hair out of my face. "I don't have healing saliva." He sounded frustrated.

Fighting to focus on his face, I tried to reach up to him and then pain shot through my entire left side. Grunting, I squeezed my eyes shut and tried not to make any noises I'd be embarrassed for later on.

When I opened my eyes, Chase was kneeling beside me stripping his shirt off. I knew I wasn't doing well when I couldn't even bring myself to look and appreciate.

"I got here as soon as I could." Troy's voice came from somewhere in the room.

When he came into my line of vision, I was surprised to see him streaked with blood and dirt. What had he been doing? He stopped abruptly beside the bed and looked down at me. "What the hell happened?" The ice in his voice surprised me.

"I'll explain later, right now we need to stop our Huntress from dying." Chase's voice echoed in my head.

Dying? Now I fought to stay awake. The bed moved again and I could feel someone lying against my side.

"Open your eyes, kitten, I need you to co-operate with me." Chase's soft plea made me look up at him. "There you are." I felt his arm move under me as he cradled me against his chest. My body felt like rubber and the only thing I could manage to do was blink. "You'll have to cut me, Mitz."

I didn't know what was happening when Mitz appeared over me again, but I could make out my raptor in her hand. She gave me a reassuring look. "You're going to be fine, love."

I wanted to ask why she was going to cut Chase, but he lifted my head closer to him before I could say anything. Licking my lips, I tried to grasp enough air to say something. A warm sweet taste filled my mouth. Vaguely through the haze I recognized it was Chase's blood on my tongue.

"Come on, kitten, try," his voice pleaded against my ear.

I licked my lips again and an understanding went through me. I was dying. The only thing I could think was at least I wasn't alone when it happened.

"It's healing before she can get enough." Mitz leaned over me again.

"Then cut deeper." Troy's voice came from beside me somewhere but I couldn't find the strength to turn my head and look at him.

"Do it." Chase said.

Closing my eyes, I thought maybe if I could just rest for a minute all of this would make sense. I could feel someone holding my chin but ignored that and left it to them to look out for me in this silent moment. My side still hurt and I wondered why in all of this I could feel that and nothing else. A warm stinging feeling moved along it and I could only surmise it was meant to feel that way.

"Stay with me, kitten, I need you to swallow."

Lifting my eye lids took a lot of concentration, but I managed to open them enough to see Chase's concerned face near my own. I wanted to thank him for picking me up out of the dirt but when I tried all I could do again was lick my lips and gasp to breathe.

"Cut me again." Chase's voice was shaking and it bothered me.

I tried to summon the willpower to reach up to him, but I couldn't feel my arm. Something ran down my throat and I almost gagged on it. When I tried to move my head the hold on my chin tightened.

"One more, love, then you can rest."

I couldn't see Mitz, but I felt comfort in her tone and tried to do whatever they were asking me to so I could close my eyes and rest finally.

"It's not enough," Chase growled from somewhere in the room.

"She's strong, Chase. We'll let her rest for a while and then rouse her and give her more."

I had to agree with Mitz, or would have if my body wasn't feeling like lead. I just wanted to sleep.

****

When I opened my eyes, the first thing I recognized was Chase's hazel eyes only inches from my own.

"Welcome back, kitten," he whispered.

My whole body throbbed and at this point I wasn't sure if it was a good or bad thing, but I was still here so maybe things hadn't been as bad as I'd thought. I could feel movement on the bed, but wasn't able to summon enough energy to turn and see why.

"I need you to stay awake for a few minutes, my Huntress and take more."

I blinked and wondered more what but before I could ask. Troy was leaning over me, the look in his eyes shadowed the same expression as his twin's.

154

"She's not going to stay conscious for long, stop dicking around."

It sounded like Quinton, but I couldn't see him. The bed shifted and I found my head being lifted again. This time I could feel the warmth of skin against my face and it was a comforting feeling. I felt the wet against my mouth and licked at it, knowing this time that it was Chase's blood that covered my tongue. If he was still trying to give me his blood maybe I wasn't doing as well as I thought.

It took every ounce of strength I had to swallow a few times.

"You should just cut your wrist." Quinton said from beside me.

"The closer to the heart the better her chances." Chase's voice drawled from above my head.

Understanding now that he was cradling me against his chest to give me his blood, I tried again to move and take what he was offering. I could feel his hand grasp the back of my head as he held me close to him and managed to stick my tongue out brush it over his skin.

"That's it, kitten, fight back." I could feel his breath against my cheek as I tried to swallow once more.

Feeling drained I closed my eyes and let my head fall back into his hold.

"You should go feed, Chase, keep up your own strength." Troy's voice said quietly.

"I will when I know she's resting."

I could feel Chase's arms lowering me back into the soft pillows.

"We'll stay with her. You go now."

Quinton was still here and he didn't sound pleased. For a brief second the fog lifted enough for me to wonder who exactly the *we* covered, but I didn't want to try to open my eyes to find out.

"You may have to give her more throughout the night, Chase. We can't contribute because then she's going to be really pissed if she wakes up and finds she's connected to more than one of us."

I wasn't sure, but that sounded like Rafael. How many of the royal brothers were hovering around me?

I felt the bed move and then the cool air hit me where Chase's warm body had been. "I'll be back in fifteen minutes, call me if she wakes." Chase's voice faded like he was walking away.

"You boys come home when he gets back, the Huntress will sleep through the night." Mitz told them in that motherly way. "Chase will need rest too if he has to keep giving to her."

I had questions but they were going to have to wait as my body lazed and peacefulness seemed to fill me from the inside. I embraced it and let myself go.

CHAPTER TWENTY-ONE

Feeling a warm body against mine, I knew without opening my eyes that it was Chase. I didn't know exactly how I could tell it was him but I could feel my heart synch with his. Lying there I listened to his breathing and knew he was sleeping. Opening my eyes, I looked around the dark room. I didn't know who this bedroom belonged to, but was thankful there was no one else in it. My arms were weak as I moved to flip the covers back.

"You shouldn't try to get up just yet." Chase's sleep filled voice was beside my ear.

"Where are we?" My own voice was hoarse.

The bed moved and Chase was leaning over me. "My room." He brushed the hair out of my face. "How do you feel?"

Sighing I took a quick assessment of my overall health. "Like I jumped off a cliff and survived. I did survive, didn't I?"

He smiled down at me. "The prognosis is leaning that way." Resting his forehead against mine, I watched his eyes shut. "I think I have grey hair now because of you."

I knew that was his way of saying I'd scared the shit out of him, but I wasn't ready for the details yet. "You're blond, no one will notice."

Lifting his head, he stared down at me. "You need to replace some fluids; I'll go get you something to drink." He was up off the bed and I was relieved to see it was only his shirt he was missing.

When he went out the door, I moved the covers down off my body and was a little shocked to discover find out I was wearing a large t-shirt. I didn't remember undressing in all of this, and hoped that it had been Mitz to assist me with the outfit change. I felt like I was eighty when I tried to move my body up enough to sit against the headboard of the bed. Grimacing I remembered where I was, maybe eighty wasn't quite high enough considering the circumstances.

Chase came back into the room and huffed. "What part of not trying to get up didn't you understand?" His voice was softer than the look he gave me.

"I ache from toe to scalp. I just wanted to change position." I continued pulling my body slowly up the sheet. A burning sensation jabbed in my left side and I stopped and froze trying to understand why.

"Let me do it." He set the glass down and moved over to slide his hands under me. In a slow movement, he had me up further on the bed then I could have managed on my own.

The burning let up a little bit, enough so I could breathe, but the worry that went with it was still there. "What did I miss? Last clear thought was Victor going all terminator on buddy with the sword."

Chase sat down and held the glass to my lips. "He bypassed the trial and went right to the sentencing when he saw you turning the ground red."

I remembered the guard. "How's Tim?"

"Drink." He moved the glass against my lips again. "He's recovering and alive thanks to you." He let me swallow before moving the glass to my mouth once more. "I saw him go down and you trying to cover him, but I couldn't get there fast enough."

I swallowed again and pushed the glass away. "You got there soon enough." More fog cleared from my brain and the burning in my side seemed to match the throb in my thigh. "How much damage did I sustain?" I tried to move my leg but my muscles refused the request. "I'm a little sore."

Chase snorted and set the glass down. "A little sore?" He stood up, hands on hips and looked down at me. "You were almost a little dead."

Trying to sit up further, I finally gave up and rested back against the pillows. "I caught that part as I faded in and out." Sighing I looked up at him, he looked tired and stressed and the reality hit me. "How many brothers will I have to put up with coddling me when I'm back on my feet?"

Sitting back down, he leaned toward me so he was right in my face. "All of them. I had to ask Quinton and Raf to guard the damn door so we could look after you."

"Great." I sighed and then groaned when even my chest ached.

"I'll go fill the bath so you can soak and then you should rest some more." He got up.

"Chase?"

Stopping he looked down at me. "Thank you."

"Don't thank me yet, when you're recovered I'm training you on how we fight on this side." His look softened. "You may not like me when I'm done."

I knew he was serious but I couldn't deal with anything more than a few sentences at this time. "I'm not sure if I like you now sometimes."

Grinning, he leaned down again and held my chin. "Be careful, kitten, until my blood connection wears off I can feel whatever your feeling. I may catch you lying to yourself."

When he released my face and strode to the bathroom, I laid there in the silence trying to figure out what he meant. He could feel what I was feeling? How did that work?

I could hear the running water and the light from the bathroom was bright enough that I could see things clearly. He stood in the doorway looking at me. "I'll do my best to shield you from my emotions, but I may not be able to block out everything."

Studying his large form shadowed with the light behind him, I nodded. "When my mind is functioning again, you can explain all of this to me."

"I will." He moved back to the bed and leaned down and scooped me up like I was a small child. "First, we'll get you back to your full strength and then we'll sort out the rest."

I squinted against the light as he stepped into the bathroom. Turning, he reached behind me and dimmed the lights until it was just a soft glow in the room. He set me on the counter across from the tub. My head was spinning and even though I didn't like feeling weak, I still clung to his arm to keep from sliding to the floor.

"I've got you." He straightened and took a hold of the hem of the shirt I was wearing.

Panic hit me and I moved to stop his hands.

With a glint in his eyes, he smirked. "Relax. Mitz made sure you were decent under here."

I released his hands and let him lift the shirt over my head. When he tossed it to the side I looked down to see Mitz had put me in a bra and underwear and was thankful they were plain white and nothing frilly or see through. I was shocked when I saw the red scar on that ran from my hip, across my waist and stopped just under my ribs. Reaching down, I touched it carefully and felt the raised ridge. I looked up at Chase to see he was looking at it as well.

Dropping down on his knees, he leaned forward and ran his finger along the edge of it before he looked into my eyes. I could see the pain in his. "With more blood, it will heal further."

I had almost died, for real. I could only nod, still trying to process that I'd almost been sliced in half by a sword. Not shanked by a pawn shop blade or beaten with a bat, which is how I always figured I go out, but cut down by a blade wielded by a being from another realm. My mind returned from its little side trip when I realized Chase was taking off his jeans.

He chuckled. "I'm decent too, kitten." I watched the jeans slide down his long legs and was almost relieved to see he had underwear on as well.

I wanted to commit this moment to my memory, so later on when I was feeling more alive I could ogle him in my mind standing before me in nothing but some form fitting black underwear. It was sad on my part to not even have the energy to stir up some appreciative emotion.

"Next time, kitten."

I didn't ask what he meant; I could actually feel his disappointment. We were both next to naked and the only thing we were going to do was sit in warm water together. My cheeks flushed.

He lowered us both into the large tub, and I knew it was much bigger than average when he fit completely with me resting in front of him, and there was still enough room to move around. The water felt like heaven. As my muscles relaxed I leaned back against his chest.

I felt myself nodding off and jolted, only to have pain streak through my side up into my chest.

"Relax, I won't let you drown." His breath brushed up against my cheek as he spoke softly to me.

Letting out a deep breath I leaned back against him again, resting my hand on his arm that was wrapped around my uninjured side. Everything faded into a warm comfortable place and I just went along with it.

****

"Daxx, I need you to take a bit more before you pass out completely."

Chases voice stirred me from a peaceful place. I was dry, so I knew we weren't in the water anymore. Soft material covered me and my head was rested on a plush surface. Somehow, I'd managed to doze through the bath and the return trip to bed.

My eye lids were heavy, but I was still able to turn my head toward his voice. With a gentle touch, he moved me so I was on my side lying against him. Reaching up, I touched his mouth with a weak hand and was rewarded with a kiss placed over my palm before he moved my hand to rest on his chest.

"Stay with me for a few more minutes."

I looked up at him and through tired eyes saw his were yellow. I didn't know why they were at this moment; surely it couldn't be my fault when I was this out of it.

"The cause is my own doing." He answered as if I'd said it out loud. With a gentle touch, he lifted my head toward his chest. "Drink," he coaxed in a rough voice.

I could feel his heart beat under my hand as my mouth touched the small wound on his chest and did the best I could to draw his blood into my mouth. He cuddled me closer to his body and through the heavy fog in my mind I could feel only one thing. Desire. It felt like my own, but not.

Warm lips brushed against my temple as I swallowed the warm liquid. "I can't shield when you're touching me," he whispered in a rough voice.

Licking slowly over the wound on his skin, I felt the incision sealing under my tongue. Leaning back into his hand, I looked up at the heavy yellow eyes watching me. I had no strength to move but at the same time I wanted to rub my body into his and had no idea how I could feel this when I was barely able to stay awake.

"These thoughts are not your own, kitten. Just ignore my weakness and get some rest."

It took a lot of concentration to reach up and grasp his goatee but after what felt like too long I had it and tugged his head down to mine. With a frustrated growl, his mouth touched mine in a gentle kiss and then he pulled his head away and moved his body back from mine.

"Sleep," he commanded in hoarse tone.

I felt the bed move and covers being lifted up over me and then darkness enveloped me.

CHAPTER TWENTY-TWO

I felt like I was whole again as sleep slowly lifted. There were hushed voices coming from the other side of the room and I stayed there with my eyes closed not sure if I wanted to see who was in here with me.

The bed moved beside me and I heard a soft chuckle I was beginning to recognize. "You may as well open your eyes. We're not going to go away."

Lifting my eye lids, I looked up at Chase. He was grinning and it didn't take me long to figure out he could feel the moment I had regained consciousness. "How do you feel?"

I moved slowly up on the pillow and then stopped when I could feel the air on my skin. Looking down, I watched as he pulled the sheet higher and realized I was naked under the bedding. Flicking my eyes to him, he lowered his lashes and to hide his thoughts from me.

"Daxx."

Chase sat up so I could see past him to where Quinton stood a few feet away. "Hey." I could barely manage more than a whisper. I wanted to sit up but due to my naked state I decided I would just have to stay put for a little longer.

Quinton strode over and knelt beside the bed. "How are you doing?"

I tried for a smile, but wasn't sure how it came out. "A

little rough, but better than I was."

"Quinton was wondering if you might be more comfortable in your own room on the other side of Alterealm." Chase's voice was casual but through the connection we now had I could feel frustration that was bordering on anger.

I looked from the hazel eyes that were watching my own carefully over to the brown ones that were filled with concern. "I think I'll just stay here for a little longer. Things might be sealed up, but I don't know how moving around is going to be just yet." I looked around the room. "How is it there's only you here, Quinton?"

He shrugged. "Chase has limited your visitors to one at a time for the day, so the others are home grabbing some rest before they come over." Motioning to the table beside the bed, he grinned. "Mitz volunteered me to bring you over some food."

"They don't cook here?"

Chase chuckled. "Yes we cook here. My guess is Quint was driving everyone crazy so Mitz sent him here to see with his own eyes that you were doing better."

"Oh." I tried to move up again without revealing that I had nothing on under the sheet. With a silent look to Chase, he stood up and went over to a dresser on the far side of the room. He pulled out a large white shirt and held it up.

Coming back over, he glanced at Quinton briefly and then to me. "She needs to drink more juice after the amount of blood she lost."

Quinton stood up. "I'll go get it." He looked down at me and then moved quickly out the door.

"He'll run the whole way," Chase whispered as he leaned over the bed. Reaching under me he sat me up slowly, watching my face the whole time. With one hand against my back, he held out the shirt to me. "I didn't want to put you in bed in wet clothes."

Doubting I would have noticed didn't seem to be the right thing to point out, so I just took the shirt and worked my arms into it. Every muscle in my side hurt as I raised my arms and lowered it over my head. When I was finished, he helped me sit up straighter on against the headboard. Taking a minute for the spinning to stop, I bunched up the blanket at my waist and moved it off of my left leg. I hadn't seen how it looked last night and the dull ache told me it must have been bad enough.

Bending my leg so it was out of the blanket I looked down to see a good four-inch red scar along the top of my thigh muscle. It didn't look as healed as I remembered the one across my side looking. Reaching down I ran my fingertips along it to feel it was still very sensitive.

"Troy focused on the other injury, figuring that one wasn't as life threatening."

I looked from the mark up at him. Certain pieces started to fit together. Chase saying his saliva didn't heal, the sensation along my side when he was trying to get me to take some of his blood. My cheeks warmed when the image of one twin over me without his shirt while the other one licked my side filled me head. I looked down at the blanket.

Chase sat down on the bed. "Don't even go there, kitten." He pulled the shirt down further on me and then slowly moved the sheet away so he could see the mark on my side. It looked less angry than the one on my leg, but in my opinion had a long way to go before I'd be wearing any belly baring tops.

Glancing up from the injury, I looked at Chase, his eyes were filled with regret and concern. In the same way he had figured out the twisted thought I'd just had I picked up on where his thoughts were going. "I would have gone regardless of what you had to say on the matter."

Nodding slowly, he lifted his eyes to mine. "I know." Clearing his throat, he leaned further away from me. "I have a few things to take care of. Will you be alright if I leave you with Quint when he gets back?" His tone was strained.

"Is everything okay?"

"Everything is fine."

I frowned at the clipped sound in his words. "I know you have *kingly* things to do. You don't have to babysit me. I'll be okay here by myself."

With a sound of frustration, he got up and tucked his hands in his pockets and glared at me. "There is no matter more important than your health. I will only be a few minutes."

I was swamped by emotions and couldn't tell where the ones from him started and my own left off. Chase dropped to one knee and leaned over me so his face was only a few inches from mine.

"I have to feed before I give you more blood and I am giving you more because your gashes do not please me in with the way they're healing. The one on your side went deep, we are not risking something inside not healing completely."

Grasping his goatee gently, I studied him for a moment. "I want to do it."

He gave me a puzzled look. "Do what?"

I swallowed. "Feed you," I whispered before I could change my mind. "You gave me your blood and saved my life, it's the least I could do."

The irises of his eyes started to turn a light-yellow shade. Taking hold of my hand that was keeping his face near he leaned closer. "I didn't do it so you owed me one."

"I didn't mean it that way."

In silence he watched me, our faces only inches apart. "When I do, it will be because you want me to, not to settle a debt."

A mix of relief and disappointment filled me, again I didn't know if they were my feelings or not. "Deal," I whispered and then moved closer and kissed his mouth lightly. I expected him to kiss me back, but he just stayed where he was his eyes moving over my face.

"I was hoping it had looked worse because of the blood everywhere." Quinton stood over us with a glass of juice in his hand and pain in his expression.

I realized the blanket was still leaving the marks visible.

"It's better than it was." I let go of Chase so he could sit up again.

"You need to give her more blood, Chase." Quinton held out the glass to me.

I took it and concentrated on drinking what was in it, avoiding looking at either brother at the moment. The emotions were making me dizzy.

"I have to go feed and then I will." Chase stood up and looked down at me as he spoke to Quinton. "Stay with her until I get back?"

"Of course."

****

After more blood and another nap I was sore and my leg was stiff, but it was like three weeks of healing had been fit into one day's time. If the royal fortune ever took a loss, the brothers could start their own pharmaceutical corporation and heal the sick and injured with a little injection of their blood. Of course, the fact that it had to come from their live veins might present a bit of a marketing issue, but it was still a thought.

Chase was off doing King stuff so I took this time of not being hovered over and tossed on some track pants and headed out to see if I could find my way around the tunnels and hallways. I'd only gotten ten feet down the hall from his bedroom door when I sensed I wasn't alone. Turning slowly, expecting a royal brother to be looming over me, I was pleased to see it was only Tim. He towered over me, but at least he couldn't send me back to rest. I looked him up and down, trying to find any sign of injury. There weren't any.

"You're alright now?"

He grinned down at me and I almost sighed in relief to see that it wasn't a perfect set of teeth and a charming smile, in fact he looked like he belonged in my neighborhood. "I have you to thank for my life, Huntress." He bowed his head in that way that was starting to get on my nerves.

I snorted. "Well you saved my ass about a dozen times, so I still owe you a few."

167

"I am sorry I allowed you to be injured."

"I'm pretty sure you didn't exactly *allow* that to happen." Was he crazy? Did he really think I was going to blame him for the psycho maniac that had tried to dice me up? I looked up and down the hall. "Does Chase have a workout room or something on this side?"

He bowed his head again; I stifled the urge to smack the top of it. "I'd be pleased to show you there."

Lifting my hand to motion for him to lead the way, he paused.

"I was surprised when the King placed me at your door to be your guard."

I shrugged, not sure why but wasn't about to admit it. "Maybe he thought we worked well together." Then I grinned, "we bleed very well together too."

He studied me for a long minute and then nodded abruptly and began to walk down the hall in the opposite direction. At least with my own personal escort I wouldn't get lost on this side.

Chase's workout space wasn't as elaborate as the one on Troy's half but it was still way beyond any gym I could ever afford to go to.

"You are well enough for a workout?"

I turned and gave Tim another shrug. "Sure. I just want to do some stretches and get things loosened up a bit."

I went through a few light moves, testing the resistance of my leg and side. It pulled but it wasn't anything unbearable. Looking around for a bar or something that was at least a reachable height for me, I spotted nothing remotely close enough to what I needed. Glancing over my shoulder to the man standing beside the door like he was part of the wall, I motioned him over. "I could use a hand."

His face was filled with a look of doubt, but he came over.

"Put out your hand." I watched as he extended his hand as if I was going to cut it off. I grinned. "I need you to be my bar. Hold my foot so I can lean into some stretches and get the blood flowing."

Relief washed over his expression. Nodding he opened his hand again so I could lift my foot into it.

"Much better." I worked on the leg that hadn't been injured but still noticed it pulled my side a lot more than I probably should have. "You'd think I had been in bed for weeks with the lazy feeling of my muscles."

"You almost died, my Queen" Tim offered quietly.

"But I didn't." I leaned forward over my leg again and ignored the way my side complained. "I can't afford too much downtime."

"I don't understand."

Ignoring the burning in my side I stretched up again. "I have a job in my realm too."

He grinned. "Yes, you are a hunter there as well."

Nodding, I put my foot back on the floor and squatted a few times. I hadn't heard from Frank in the last few days but there were always dry spells when it came to bail jumpers, so I wasn't worried yet.

Nodding to Tim, I kicked my sore leg a few times before placing my foot in his hand. This side was a little tighter and the stretching took me a few more times to get it to the point I was comfortable with it.

"Maybe you're pushing a little too soon," Tim offered in a quiet voice.

I leaned down again and grit my teeth against the burning sensation. His grip on my foot tightened making me pause and straighten. He eyes were locked on the door and I saw real fear in them. There was only one man on this side that would bring the large man to task. "Busted," I whispered before I pulled my foot free and turned to see Chase standing in the door.

"This doesn't look like resting." His eyes moved over me as if he was looking for a new injury.

"Just working out the stiffness." I watched as Tim moved quickly over to the door and exited without a word.

When I turned back, Chase was standing well inside my

personal bubble. "I left you to rest, Daxx."

Why did I feel like a child when he used my name? "I feel fine, better than fine." I offered what I hoped came across as a cheeky grin. "That blood of yours is quite the rejuvenator; you should bottle and sell it." He grunted his expression still serious. Moving away from him, I walked over to the weapon wall and pretended I was studying it. "I don't like lounging." I glanced over my shoulder to see him watching me. "And I don't like getting my ass kicked in any realm."

"You have an advantage on this side of the realms that most of your opponents do not have."

Turning I watched him move in my direction. "Really? And what is that?" If I had some advantage I really wanted to know what it was.

"Your size, I've watched you fight. The way you maneuver is something most over here could only dream of doing." He paused right in front of me. "And one other thing, you fight ambidextrously…"

"I what?"

"You seem to be able to use both arms equally well. I do the same, only it took me fifty years to master it."

I felt somewhat pleased that I'd done something in half the time. "Well, when you get injured as often as I do, having a backup arm is always good."

Reaching behind me, he pulled my weapon of choice off the wall. "So why do you fight with a small knife and tonfa?"

At least he hadn't called it a cute knife. "Because I'm good with them."

He nodded, like he was considering what I said. "Yes, but over here you are not limited to non-lethal weapons."

I snorted, remembering the battle axe trying to chop me in half. "So what do you suggest?"

Placing the tonfa back on the wall, he moved down it further. "I'm thinking something similar to what I use, only smaller than a katana." He reached up and pulled two Sais off the wall. "These, they are perfect for your size and can be both defensive and offensive." I watched him flip them from one position to the other. "There are multiple ways to score a hit with them…" He demonstrated some more.

They were a cool weapon. I'd never considered them before I suppose because walking around in my neighborhood with those on your back would be a good way to get arrested. But here, on this side, all was fair. "Okay let me try them on." I held out my hands and he shook his head.

"After, learning to move, your body's size and advantage comes first."

I shrugged. "Fine."

"And we take it slow today."

I really hated feeling like an invalid and the sooner we moved past that the happier I was going to be. "I feel great."

He smirked. "That's lovely to hear, but it's still slow."

My choices were his way or get my ass beat in the future. I didn't like having no real choice, but I sucked it up. "Fine."

CHAPTER TWENTY-THREE

Chase had warned me that I may not like him very much when he taught me how to fight in Alterealm. He had been right. The moves he made me do over and over and *over* again were starting to get on my nerves.

The secret was, or so he kept telling me, to do it so many times that it become reflex almost turning into a habit. I always thought habits were annoying.

He more or less said nothing other than one word each time I went through the series of moves, again. Saying it in every possible tone and volume didn't make it any better to hear, and it was the only response to any comment I had to make.

I understood the reasons behind the repetition but once I reached the stage where I didn't fall on my face or trip over those imaginary bumps in the floor, I was ready to move on.

I completed the sequence of steps, flips and lunges once more and then huffed out a breath and stood trying to catch it before he told me *again*. When he walked in my direction with a bottle of water I hoped it meant we were moving on to the next phase in this training. Not wanting to sound ungrateful, I say nothing as he came towards me. I mean seriously, how many people had the chance to learn how to fight from someone that had been doing it for two hundred years?

"I can't quite decide whether the emotions I'm feeling from you are good for me or bad for me." With a teasing glint in his eyes he handed me the bottle.

Uncapping it, I took a few small sips before answering. "That depends on how many more times you're going to make me do the same thing."

Reaching over, he brushed the hair back from my face. "I'm not making you do anything."

I shrugged. "You know what I mean." Wiping the sweat off my forehead, I took another sip and studied him. I didn't know if it was the adrenalin pumping or his blood in my system, but he looked good enough to lick right about now. When he grinned, baring all of his teeth, I knew he'd picked up on the direction my mind was wandering.

"How's your side doing?"

Bonus points for him by letting that slide by without comment. I stretched a little in both directions, side to side. "A little achy, nothing serious."

He nodded. "Do you want to continue or call it a day?"

"That depends on whether we're going to do the same thing or move on."

His hazel eyes skimmed over me from the floor up to my eyes, but he didn't say anything just turned around and walked over to the wall. Taking two flashy Sais off the wall he sent me an amused look. "Both." Coming back over, he stopped a few feet in front of me and flipped the Sais from a forward motion to resting along his forearm. With the flick of his wrist, he turned the handle in his palms again. "Same moves with an added motion." Tucking the weapons to his forearms again he looked from them to me. "When you're rolling, or flipping they stay at a resting position." He lunged forward, stepping with one long leg and moved the metal he held to a forward position. "When you stop, or change the flow of your direction, they are battle ready."

I nodded and took them from him when he held them out.

"Tomorrow we'll add a few more strenuous moves into the mix, but for today just work in feeling comfortable with them."

I flicked them much like he'd done, only without dozens of decades to practice it wasn't nearly as smooth.

"They should be used like an extension of your own arm, not in addition to it." His phone rang. With an annoyed look, he pulled it from his pocket and looked at it. "I have to go deal with some business. Do you want to practice some more?"

I stopped. "I wouldn't mind."

Tucking the phone back in his pocket, he came over and grasped my chin lightly. "*Don't* overdo it." His eyes caressed over my face, pausing more than once on my mouth. I thought he was going to kiss me, but he released my face and walked to the door. "I'll have Tim stay with you."

"Thanks." I said quickly before he was gone.

Without waiting for the guard, I turned around and walked to the other end of the mat once again. If I could pull this off, I may yet look graceful while doing it. Not that something like that matter in a fight, but I didn't like to be outdone by a bunch of aged men, so I had some catching up to do.

Chase didn't come back so I stayed there and performed the routine over and over with the odd applause from Tim when I managed to do it without dropping one or both Sais to the floor.

When just about every muscle in my body ached, I decided to call it a day. Tim walked me to my own room where I left a trail of sweaty clothes leading to the bathroom to soak in the tub.

As I sank into the steaming water, I glanced at the time and was shocked three hours had gone by since Chase had left. Worry set it, not about being left on my own *that* was well within in normal limits for me. I was a little concerned with being left alone so long. Three hours without seeing Chase, or even one of the brothers seemed a bit odd considering I rarely had a minute or more without one of the eight lurking nearby.

Getting out of the tub, I wrapped a lush towel around me. It was the size of a blanket and no doubt thicker than the one on my bed at home. There were just some things that no one would ever complain about in this life and a thick fluffy, larger than life towel was one of them.

I stared at my phone on the table wondering if I should call Chase and see if I had a reason to worry. After my almost departure from this and all other worlds, no one was telling me the progress in tracking down Marcus. Then again, in their defense, I hadn't been conscious much.

Gnawing on my lip, I walked over and looked down at the phone. What if they were involved in another battle right now? I didn't want to carry that train of thought any further. I wasn't a worrier, at least I never had been before.

A knock on the door had me spinning around so quickly I almost fell onto the table. Rushing over to the door, I opened it a crack and almost sighed in relief to see Chase standing there. Then I remembered what I was wearing. A big towel was still just a towel when it came to company.

"May I?" He motioned to the door.

Clutching the towel in one hand, I opened the door and let him in. His eyes took their time noting how I was dressed, the interest was plain to see but he didn't offer any verbal comment.

"Hi. I was soaking in the tub."

His lips quirked. "I know you haven't been back long. Tim just spent the last several minutes singing praises to your skill."

"Oh." Pulling the towel a little higher, I closed the door completely. "I think I've got the hang of it."

"Mmm." He tucked his hands in his pockets and just stood there looking at me. "You were worrying when I got here."

This blood connection needed to wear off soon, I was lucky if I knew what *I* was feeling most of the time, having someone else tuned in was not something I wanted to get used to. "I just realized how long it had been since one of your brothers checked up on me."

"Ah. I had hoped some of the concern was for me personally." He sent me a smoldering look and I couldn't have looked away if I wanted to.

"Some was."

He chuckled softly. "My brothers are resting at this very moment it is technically their night time. Early today they were all pursuing some very interesting leads."

"To finding Marcus?" Chase didn't flinch when I said his name, unlike almost everyone else.

"We believe we're getting closer. I should know more tomorrow."

Not caring if I wasn't entirely dressed, I moved over closer to him and craned my neck to look up at him. "I want in." I couldn't tell what he was thinking. How was it he could connect with me and know, but it didn't go the other way?

Without changing his expression, he looked me up and down and then stepped closer. Reaching out, he pressed his hand against my side hitting exactly where the wound had been a day before. "How's your side feeling?" His voice had dropped to a softer tone.

I didn't want to clutch at the towel like a shy school girl, but I still kept my hand in place. "Right now, all of my muscles are a little tender." I offered what I hoped came across as a cute little grin.

Raising one eyebrow, he glared down at me. "That's not what I asked."

I swallowed, trying to avoid inhaling how good he smelled. "It's tender, but nothing extreme. Now you can respond to what I said. I want in."

With his hand still pressed against my side, his eyes moved over my face. "Let's see how you feel tomorrow *and* if, in fact, there is anything conclusive to follow up on." With his other hand, he ran one finger along my collarbone to my shoulder.

I stood there not wanting to move away and watched his eyes change slightly as if they wanted to be yellow but he was controlling them. "If I'm equal to the throne, don't you have to do what I want?"

He smirked. "At the monarchy level, possibly, but on a male level…" His eyes burned into mine. "I'm still in charge and I will not allow you to run full steam into battle when you are not ready."

"Okay," I practically squeaked. What was it with this man towering over me that brought out the girly-girl part of me that I'd never *ever* been in touch with before?

We continued to stand there, his hand at my waist and the other one now fingering my hair that hung near my shoulder. His eyes were still trying to go yellow.

Taking a shaky breath, I stilled his hand near my face with my free hand. "Do you need to…" I swallowed again. "Feed again?"

At the mention of the word, his eyes leaned towards the brighter hue from the hazel. "I shouldn't, but I find the urge strong when I'm this close to you."

"I'd like to try it." *What?* My brain echoed inside my head.

Grasping my hand lightly, he lowered it to rest against his chest and looked down at me. "Not out of gratitude?"

I shook my head quickly, almost as if I didn't I would change my mind. "More out of curiosity than anything else I think."

It wasn't until he straightened to his full height that I realized how close his face had been to mine. "It's not the same as when you fed Quinton."

"I know." My nerves reminded me they were there once more.

He smirked. "It doesn't have to be unpleasant either." Lifting my chin, his eyes searched mine. "There is only one emotion I want to taste from you, kitten, and it would not be painful in any sort of way." His voice was soft and husky.

It took a few seconds for my brain to kick back in.

"Which one?" Did I sound needy? I hoped not because that was also something this girl didn't do gracefully.

Lowering his face close enough again, I could feel his breath on my lips. "I think you need to go get dressed before we discuss this further." He placed a gentle kiss on my cheek. "The emotion I'm after may not be the wisest to stir while you are wearing nothing but a towel."

Nodding, I clutched the towel to my chest, but didn't move. I understood what he was saying, but my body didn't care. At the moment feeling the heat from his body and his eyes holding mine captive, my mind wasn't objecting either.

A knock on the door barely registered.

"Yes?" Chase called out, still standing there holding my chin.

"It would save me time if you'd answer your damn..."

Chase released my chin and turned allowing me to see Troy standing in the door. He pulled his phone out and looked at it. "I didn't hear it."

Troy looked me up and down and I couldn't focus enough to figure out what the expression on his face conveyed.

"When you didn't answer I wondered if something was wrong." He glanced at me again before his brother. "I can see nothing is."

"I was telling Daxx we may be closer." Chase didn't let the look his brother was sending him make him move away from me, in fact I think he actually moved closer so our sides were touching.

"Were you telling her while she was bathing or drying?" There was no mistaking the sarcastic tone in Troy's voice.

I scowled. "Neither. I had just got out when he knocked; I didn't have time to get dressed yet." Pulling the towel up further, I looked from one King to the other. Not liking the territorial vibes they were emitting, I sighed. "I'll get dressed and then we can talk about what's been discovered." Moving quickly over to the closet, I pulled out the first top and bottom my hand connected with and then turned and went into the bathroom.

I don't think I've ever dressed as fast as I did and when I was finished I regretted not grabbing underwear to put on. Glancing at the one's I'd dropped on the floor earlier, I shook my head and went back out.

"Okay," I said softly even though I wasn't feeling very gentle inside. "What's going on?"

Chase stood leaning against the desk, his arms crossed over his chest. Troy stood by the closed door in the identical position. Both had their jaws locked and a distasteful expression in their eyes as they looked at each other.

Rolling my eyes when I wanted to groan out loud but didn't. "If you two are having some sort of internal argument I can't hear, you may as well say it out loud."

Chase turned and looked at me, his eyes softening as he looked me up and down. His lips twitched and I suddenly was blasted with a feeling of lust confirming two things, first that he did control this connection between us when he wanted to and second I should have put on the sweaty bra. "There's no discussion taking place." He shrugged, "I'm not sure what the issue is."

Troy sighed loud enough we both heard him and turned. Lowering his head, he looked at the floor. "I do apologize. The last day has been a bit trying." Lifting his head, he looked over at me, his eyes moving slowly over me. "First, we almost lose our Huntress, then we find out we're in some pretty serious shit and when I stepped through the door I..."

With the last part, Chase straightened away from the desk. "Raf's back?"

Troy nodded, the expression on his face looking bleak. "A short while ago. He's exhausted but managed to get in and out without detection."

"How bad?" Chase moved over to his brother in long strides.

"Bad," Troy said quietly.

I looked from one to the other. "Can we drop the cryptic speak and tell me what is going on?"

Chase turned, a hesitant look on his face. "With the help of another mage using a cloaking spell, Rafael has been undercover on your side of the realm tracking down some leads." He looked at Troy. "We have to tell her."

I didn't like where this was going. I reached behind me and then realized my raptor sat on the table. I suddenly felt more naked without it than I had in the towel. "Tell me what, guys?"

"We managed to find some leads on a few that have vanished from our side, the sort that should never be on *your* side," Chase motioned to me. "While you were recovering Raf, Michael, Victor and Quinton have been on your side locating them…"

"Them, as in the ones that should *never* be on my side?" I held my breath until he nodded. "Did they bring them back?" I didn't know what sort *they* were but if Chase felt they shouldn't be there then I was worried.

Troy straightened away from the wall and came in my direction. "It's not that simple. They're working with Marcus and Raf has discovered it's a lot worse than we first anticipated."

"What did he find out?" Chase asked in a lethal tone.

"There are close to two dozen in Daxx's realm. They meet the day after tomorrow."

"Two dozen?" I interrupted.

Troy nodded. "That we know of." His eyes flicked to Chase, who nodded before he looked back at me. "They are nightmares on your side. Cold blooded killers, mages and not the good kind and the rest are just crazy enough to think they can take over."

My spine stiffened. "Take over? What, my side?"

"That's the vibe Raf picked up." Troy confirmed.

"When are we going over?" Chase's voice sent shivers down my spine and they weren't at all good ones.

"Tomorrow night we're going to meet and get it set up so we're all over there long before they have a chance to do anything."

Chase ran a hand through his hair. "You're going to have to take more than one mage, possibly even a witch or two to keep the locals in the dark."

I processed this quickly. "You can block the humans from seeing?"

Sighing, Troy shrugged. "That's the plan."

Which meant it would be fighting like they were on this side of reality. "Where are they meeting?"

"Raf says it's a worse neighborhood then you live in." Troy stated with a note of surprise. "I find that hard to believe."

I snorted. "My neighborhood is a rose garden compared to the other side of the bridge." I chewed on my lip for a minute, doing some fast math. Eight brothers, plus me only made nine against way too many psychos. "We need more."

"More?" Chase came over and looked down at me. "More what?"

"Able bodies to fight." I ignored the look in his eyes that said he didn't think I should be involved. "If your witch or whatever can block out the rest of the world from knowing what's going on then I think we should take Tim and a few of the other guards with us, we're seriously outnumbered. "

His expression hardened. "I agree with the guards, but not to you going."

I could actually feel his concern for me; it was good, but bad. Good that I could feel it but bad because now I couldn't tear a piece off him for saying it. "My side, *my* territory."

Chase's jaw clenched and for thirty seconds he mulled it over before nodding abruptly and moving to the other side of the room.

I was suddenly swamped with emotion and couldn't even describe what kind of emotion. It was hot, but cold at the same time. Opening my mouth, I shut it just as quickly and looked over at Troy. "I'm going."

His lips quirked. "I didn't say otherwise. In fact, we

need you there because as you said it's your side. I believe you have to be present to keep the balance between the realms." With a quick glance to his brother, he rubbed the back of his neck and sighed. "I need to get some rest. We'll meet at breakfast and hammer out the details?"

"We'll be there." Chase answered before I could say a word.

Troy nodded and then looked down at me. There was a look on his face that he wanted to say something, but it vanished. "I'm glad you're recovered." He turned and left without waiting for a reply.

Mouth hanging open I stared at the door and then looked over at the man standing in the shadowed corner in my room. "What was that about?"

"I didn't shield my twin from the sudden urge to strangle you and kiss you; I'm not sure which I wanted more." The vulnerability was clear in his voice. "I'm afraid he didn't know what to make of it."

I didn't know what to make of it. "You know your life would be much simpler without all this connection stuff." I didn't move any closer, not sure if I really wanted to. "I have to be there, Chase, surely you know that."

Moving away from the corner, he walked over to the desk and sat on the edge of it. "I do but it doesn't mean I have to like it."

"I didn't ask you to like anything." Still reeling from the onslaught of his emotions moments earlier I kept my distance.

He sent me a heated look before he cloaked his expression with his long lashes and looked down at the floor. "I don't seem to be in control of that lately either."

I should have asked what he was talking about exactly, but that voice inside my head that keeps me from sticking my nose in things I really don't want to be in spoke up, so I brushed right over his comment. "I understand completely. I'm in another realm, who knew"

"Damariss, please come over here." His voice was soft

and it sent shivers all over me, the good kind.

Wary of why, I moved over to stand a few feet in front of him. His eyes, bordering on changing again moved over my face. "I'd like to have dinner with you and maybe for a few hours not have to debate fighting tactics or whether or not you should go to battle again, can we do that?"

In all the possible things he could say, that wasn't one of them, it wasn't even on the list of possibilities. "I think so."

Reaching out, he grabbed my hand and pulled me toward him. When I stood between his knees, close enough to see his chest rise and fall, he tipped my chin up and studied me. "Later, after we've had a chance to eat and relax, I'm going to ask if you're still willing."

I didn't have to ask what he was referring to, knowing that I had volunteered to be his next meal, or whatever he called it. "Okay."

Releasing my chin, he clenched his jaw a few times. "Could you please go put a bra on so Tim doesn't trip over his own feet?" His eyes dipped down to my chest.

Suddenly feeling like I had no shirt on, while my body responded to his stare, I nodded and backed away. "I'll be back in a minute."

CHAPTER TWENTY-FOUR

Laughing, I opened the door to my room and motioned for Chase to go in. "Please! If anyone actually fought in those boots they'd break their ankle in three places!"

Chase shrugged. "It's still sexy to watch a woman battle in high heeled boots. Although a real vampire is a lot harder to fight than that series makes it look."

I held up my hand, shaking my head. "Do not destroy my illusions that the scariest thing in any realm is you and your brothers, please." Really, vampires? I still couldn't deal with more info about otherworldly creatures. My world would be complete without knowing any more than I did right at this moment.

He cleared his throat. "I could be persuaded to omit some facts of truth, for a price." He gave me a teasing grin.

"What price?" I took off the case for my raptor and set it on the table.

"To see you fight in a skirt and heels."

Turning around, I glared at him. "Not in this life or the next."

"Aww, kitten, my fantasies are crushed." The easygoing stance he'd had for the last few hours seemed to slide away and in its place that predatory glide returned as he came over to me slowly.

I liked the playful Chase, much better than the one with the lethal tone that scared me, but the man walking toward me now sent goose bumps over me with that look. I didn't know if I liked this side of his personality, but my body did, as my heart beat kicked up a few speeds. "I enjoyed dinner and doing something relatively normal tonight." My voice sounded weak even to my own ears.

He paused in his step and stopped where I was just out of reach. "As opposed to the freakishly abnormal thing I'm about to ask of you?" Flexing his hands, he tucked them into the back pocket of his jeans.

"I don't think it's freakishly abnormal..." He raised one eyebrow at me. I shrugged, "okay, it hasn't been a part of my world up until now but all that's changed now, hasn't it?"

"I suppose that's up to you."

I gave him an easy smile, even though my heart was shuffling up my chest to the base of my throat. "Can I ask you a few things?" Trying to control the pounding of my heart, I took a deep breath. "I want to understand."

Chase inclined his head, suddenly taking on a more regal posture. "Of course."

"Do you only feed on humans?" It wasn't what I wanted to ask, but I thought I'd lead up to it.

"No. Others from this side work too. I just prefer the human emotions they're ... I find them more satisfying." He moved his hands and tucked them into the front pockets of his tight jeans.

"Does it hurt?"

He stepped forward and grasped my chin. "I would never hurt you." His tone was dead serious.

"I know."

Continuing to hold my face, he let out a slow breath. "It can hurt, depending on the emotion and the tactic used."

"The tactic?"

"Whether I ask or just take." He stood there, the look in his eyes told me he was waiting for me to judge him.

"What's it like? For you?"

"In most cases it's a rush, I feel it move through me like blood through your veins it warms me." He paused for a few seconds. "Depending on the emotion I'm tapping into it can exhilarate or even calm me."

"Too bad the doctors on my side didn't have that. They could calm the paranoid, recharge the drained..."

He grinned. "I don't think there's a way to mass market that part of me."

"Is everyone on your side this way?"

Leaning down, he brushed a soft kiss on my mouth. "That is too complex a question to answer in one night."

"Kind of like the history of here."

"Mmm, something like that." He rubbed his thumb lightly over my bottom lip. "If you prefer I can go elsewhere. You don't have to do this."

I swallowed. "I want to, but I think the emotions you're going to get from me right now are really uptight edgy ones." That's what we needed, a very large man running around uptight and strung out.

Smiling, he leaned down and spoke with his lips brushing against mine. "I think we can change that."

"Okay," I whispered with a voice I hardly recognized.

Taking my hand, he led me over to the two overstuffed chairs. Sitting down, he pulled my hand gently until I had no choice but to sit across his lap. My heart was thrumming a fast beat again.

Cupping the back of my head, he cradled it in his large hand. "Let's see if we can override those edgy feelings." He feathered soft kisses over my lips as his other hand moved to rest on my stomach.

Before I had a chance to adjust to the teasing movement of his mouth, he deepened the kiss, stealing my breath. Reaching up, I grabbed a handful of his hair deciding at that moment I didn't want him to move away. He lightened the kiss to a slow sensual one that took my breath away again.

Lowering his mouth to my throat, he slowly ran his tongue over my skin. When he reached the edge of my shirt, he pulled it off my shoulder and kept going. Moving back up to my jaw, he trailed light kisses until he reached my mouth again.

I expected more feather light kisses that made my head lighten but instead this time he crushed my mouth beneath his, leaning me back in the chair. Between the heat from his kiss and both of our emotions I felt like I was on fire from the inside out with just one kiss.

The longer the kiss went on the more I wanted to forget about feeding and just keep kissing. The man was the most sensual kisser I'd ever met. Then again if you have over two hundred years to practice it would give you a huge advantage in that and all areas.

He moved back to my neck and this time the teasing movement of his mouth became rougher as he traveled over my skin. Each time his lips touched me I was flooded with waves of lust so powerful I wanted much more than his mouth. The thoughts of what I really wanted from him should have shocked me but instead they made me hotter.

I pulled his shirt up so I could touch his bare skin. When I started running my hands down over his broad chest, he groaned deep in his throat and picked me up and set me down to straddle him in the wide chair. I could feel how turned on he was and the very idea made me want him even more.

Grasping the back of my head, he pulled my mouth back to his and kissed me with so much passion I squirmed against him. Chase lifted his head and looked at me, his eyes were glowing yellow and so intense I gasped as I remembered how to breathe.

Taking my chin in his hand, he ran his thumb over my bottom lip and did nothing but look at me. Another wave of lust hit me, making me rock my hips into him. The feeling kept growing and I wasn't sure if I could sit still much longer and let him do what he needed to do.

With a soft curse, he blinked and then pulled my head back down so he could crush my mouth beneath his.

Holding my thighs in his large hands, he stood up and began carrying me across the room. I couldn't have cared less where he was taking us, just as long as he continued to kiss me the way he was.

He lowered us to the bed without breaking the kiss. I was shaking with need when his body covered mine. Desire pounded at me as I wrapped my legs around him, not wanting him to move away. Lifting his head, he gasped for air much like I did, his yellow eyes were heavy from lust and it was the most erotic look I'd ever seen on a man's face.

Stretching my left arm over my head, he grasped my palm in his and lowered his mouth back to mine. Somewhere in the deep sensual kiss, I lost myself and clutched at his hair so he wouldn't stop again. Rocking his body into mine, I couldn't believe how good it felt despite our size difference we fit in all the right places. I moaned against his mouth and then gasped when he tore his mouth from mine and gently bit into the side of my neck. Even that felt good so I moved my head aside so he could do it again.

Another wave of lust hit me hard and I squirmed under him, wanting things to accelerate, now. As his mouth moved over that sensitive little spot on my neck I moaned again. His tongue stroked over it again, and then his teeth teased nipped at it, again heat burst into me and pooled where our bodies leaned into each other's.

Without warning, he was off the bed and standing five feet away panting. I just lay there spread out on the bed not knowing what the hell had just happened. "Chase?"

Holding up a hand he shook his head. "I need a minute." His blazing yellow eyes moved over me. There was a look of confusion on his face and panic started to cool the cravings I'd just been swamped with.

Sitting up on my elbows, I watched a thousand thoughts cross his face at lightning speed.

"I have to go," he panted while still trying to settle his breathing.

"What?" I jumped up off the bed and almost hit the

floor as my knees wobbled when my weight hit them. Moving over I grabbed his arm before he could make it to the door. "What's wrong?"

Emotions flooded into me, so many of them I couldn't process what they meant.

Stiffening under my touch, he turned and looked down at me. "I …" taking a deep breath he shook his head, "I was about to mark you."

I didn't know what he was talking about. "Mark me?" Something told me I wasn't going to like the explanation, but I held my ground and waited for an answer.

Closing his eyes, he opened them and then looked down at his hand. Reaching out he grabbed my wrist and looked at my hand and arm. Relief swept over his face. With a sigh, he moved away from me and went over and sat down in the chair we had started in. Leaning over his legs, he dropped his face into his hands.

I stood there, in shock from the sudden stop, confused by what he'd said and wanted to stomp my foot and scream. Would anything ever be simple again?

Lifting his head, he looked over at me, his eyes back to normal color but filled with a strained look. "I cannot feed from you."

I opened my mouth and then closed it. Going over, I perched on the edge of the table in front of him. "Did I do something wrong?"

He laughed in almost a sadistic way and leaned back in the chair to stare at me. "Oh, no. It wasn't anything you did, believe me." Sighing, he ran a shaky hand through his hair. "I have never felt that, *ever.*"

I sat there, having no friggin clue what we were even talking about.

"I started to and the emotion was so strong…" He waved a hand around like he was trying to find his next words. "So pure it hit me like nothing ever has."

Was that good or bad? Again, I had no idea.

"I have never…"

I jumped up and stepped back. "Yeah, never ever, we've covered this."

He stopped and looked me up and down and I didn't want to admit it but shivers traveled over each inch his eyes did. "I can't explain it, Daxx, it's not something that's happened before, but I do know that feeding from you is not going to happen for now." His voice was soft, almost pleading and my heart throbbed just hearing it.

"I really don't understand." Which was an understatement. "I thought…" I waved a hand at the bed. "We were…"

Getting up, he came over and stood in front of me, grasping my shoulders he leaned down so we were face to face. "Oh, we were and a few minutes more and we'd be having this conversation without our clothes on." He sighed, "and you'd be really pissed off with me." His look softened. "I almost marked you as my mate, kitten, and as much as I'd love that I think we should try to avoid that happening right now."

My eyes bulged. "What do you mean as your mate?" I looked at the bed like it had the answers. "I thought it was sex."

Releasing my shoulders, he straightened up. "That too." Shaking his head, he paced away from me. "My head is too full of you right now to explain it, but for now please accept that I cannot feed from you and we should avoid being too close until I understand what almost happened."

The fact that he wasn't quite sure made me feel a little better. A very little. "Fine."

Chase turned and looked at me. "Please don't be angry." He came back over and touched my chin so I had to look up at him. "If I didn't think you'd stab me with your knife afterward we'd be over there naked for the next twelve hours."

I pouted. Twelve hours? How would that be a bad thing?

Lowering his lips to mine, he kissed me softly. "And you

would stab me and hate me if I did what every instinct in my body is telling me to do."

Wave after wave of emotion poured into me, I knew they were what he was feeling and it made me a light headed. Then they were gone as quickly as they had been there. Taking a deep breath, I tried to stay calm and sensible. "So what now?"

Brushing my hair back from my face, he offered an unsure smile before dropping his hand and stepping back. "I leave. You rest. We've have a big day tomorrow and once we get through that, we'll talk and figure this out."

My jaw dropped. I'd forgotten all about it. Since when had I ever let hormones rule over me? Never had the prospect of sex erased logic. Needing to sort through the why and how, I nodded. "Okay. I won't say I understand but as I'm a little confused on what happened and you are as well, I think some time would help."

He grinned. "On one hand, it might." Stepping slowly backward toward the door, his eyes raked over me and those shivers returned. "On the other hand, no amount of time is going to stop me from wanting to hear you scream my name in pleasure, kitten."

My breath hitched at the images that flashed through my mind. His smile widened like he could see them as well. "I'll see you for breakfast."

I nodded, not even remembering how to form words.

CHAPTER TWENTY-FIVE

I watched as seven of the brothers checked weapons and joked with each other. For the dire situation we were facing, you'd think it was a game. Then again if you lived as long as they did even scrabble would lose its appeal after fifty or sixty years.

Quinton walked over and turned me to look at the Sais hanging all pretty in the straps on my back. I still had my raptor behind me and knife strapped to my hip, but I felt better prepared with the addition of the new blades I now felt comfortable. Chase had only let me practice for a few hours, but the movements came to me now without hesitation.

"Upgraded I see." He smiled down at me.

'I didn't want a repeat of the last time."

"No. That would be bad." He glanced over at Chase noticing, like I had, that his eyes strayed in my direction more than they did anywhere else. "Everything okay over with the day walkers?"

I looked slowly away from the hazel eyes holding me captive up into the curious brown ones. "Seems to be." Quinton's look of concern didn't change. I had to wonder if he was picking up on the vibes, or whatever it was between Chase and I, somehow. Leaning closer I lowered my voice. "When you have some time, I have about a gazillion questions."

He smirked. "Only a gazillion huh?" Shrugging, he patted my shoulder. "I'll see if I have enough answers for them."

Tim walked over grinning down at me. "I daresay this time out we're better prepared."

"Have you been ordered to stay with me again?" I glanced quickly at Chase.

Tim shook his head. "No, my Queen, I chose to be beside you." He grinned at Quinton. "What she can do with her new weapons is truly amazing."

Quinton looked from the burly man back down to me. "I have no doubt."

Victor walked into the room with a case in his hand and woman with red hair behind him. "Welsley and Clairee will be here shortly," he announced to the room.

Quinton leaned down and whispered. "As we take them down, that gadget in the case will send them back to holding cells until Victor gets back."

I was more than impressed. "I wouldn't mind one of those when I'm tracking jumpers."

He chuckled. "This one will only work to return to this side and for only two beings." He motioned to Victor. "The Justice and the Huntress."

My jaw dropped. "Really?"

Quinton nodded. "Vic will give you a quick rundown before we start."

I was still flabbergasted that I was allowed to use that device. "Okay." Turning my attention to the redheaded woman standing in the corner with her eyes closed, I nudged his arm. "Who's that?"

"A mage," he muttered with the distain clear in his tone. "Welsley will be bringing a witch with him. Clairee, because she can tap into Wanda's power on this side."

I was anxious to meet Clairee and hoped my message had reached her and Wanda. There hadn't been much time after the meeting to set the plans in motion.

When Chase, Troy and Victor all turned and started coming over Tim bowed quickly and muttered something and then moved in the other direction. I didn't blame him, those three were a force to reckon with, I wasn't sure if I was ready to take on all of them at once. Quinton started to move away as well until I grabbed his arm. "Stay," I demanded quietly. His only response was to chuckle softly.

Victor actually smiled at me when they stopped in front of me. "I am pleased you have selected more lethal weapons little Huntress." Troy nodded his approval as well.

I looked from one to the other before turning my gaze to Chase. His anxiety was very easy for me to pick up on. I sent him a knowing look, hoping he understood that he needed to tamp down on the excess emotions. Slowly I looked back to Victor. "I don't like being picked up off the ground."

He cleared his throat. "I daresay if you go down this time I will have a bloody massacre on my hands." His eyes moved between the two Kings before he sighed and held up the case. "I have your portable receiver to go with this." Pausing, he pulled out something that looked like an old-school pager and held it out. "A simple scan of the offender will suffice to send them back here to await justice."

The way he said the last part made my spine itch. I wouldn't ever want to be on his shit list. I took the device and turned it over in my hand. "I just push this and wave it over the *offender?*" He nodded abruptly. Clipping it to my waist, I shrugged. "Okay."

Welsley came into the room, a small dark haired woman right on his heels. She looked around at everyone in the room and then her gaze settled on me. With determined steps, she glided in my direction. Before I could do anything, the four men near me stepped in front of me creating a solid wall of backs and making it so I couldn't see a damn thing.

"Hey." I shoved between Chase and Troy until they moved and let me stand between them. "Seriously, you guys need to take this protective nature down several notches."

Troy leaned down so he could whisper right against my ear. "Someday you will understand how important *your* safety is to our kingdom, little Queen." He straightened and turned to look at his twin. A silent look of warning passed between them.

Shaking off the hostile emotions Chase dumped on me, I turned and smiled at the woman that stood in front of us waiting. "How is Wanda holding out?"

Brushing back her dark locks, she sighed. "Going stir crazy mostly," she bowed her head, "she sends her greetings, Huntress Queen." Lifting her chin, she looked at the two men crowding me. "And to you both as well."

I tried not to roll my eyes at all the regal crap. "Clairee, right?" She nodded. I held out my hand. "I need to speak with you for a quick minute before we leave." I could see the objection in Chase's eyes before he could voice it. "Girl talk, Chase." I winked at him and then took her hand and walked us to the furthest corner.

Glancing over my shoulder, I caught the curious looks from all the royal brothers. With a sweet grin, I turned back and leaned my head close to Clairee's, thankful she was close to my height. "Did Wanda get my message?"

She nodded her green eyes wide with excitement. "We worked on them for hours, but we only had time to complete four." Her expression was pained.

Four? I had hoped for eight, even ten. Four meant I had to actually choose who I wanted to protect. Talk about grueling choices. "But they'll work? Marcus won't be able to touch them?"

She nodded again and reached into her pocket. "How will you decide?"

I bit my lip and looked down at the four pendants she placed in my hand. "I have no idea." Clairee kept looking over at the woman in the corner. "Go if you have to plot your moves."

She nodded and then lowered her head. "I wish you a safe battle, my Queen."

I wanted to groan out loud, the titles were starting to make me feel just a little like a fraud. "Thank you."

I waited until she walked away and then turned and looked at the men in the room. How in the world was I supposed to give extra protection to just four of them? Who would be the most important here to ensure a safe return? All of them? Opening my hand, I looked down at the red pendants, they looked like dragons but I couldn't be sure.

For a few seconds I thought how much simpler my life had been before I even believed in things like magic. Funny how your whole world can change in the same amount of time it takes to blink.

Looking up at the men again, I noticed most were watching me warily. Victor would be plain offended if I gave him one, Leone and Rafael the same I imagined. Quinton got one whether he liked it or not, I needed him to keep me sane in all of this. Michael was staring at a spot on the wall, obviously doing a little psych prep of his own. I doubted he'd appreciate some girly notion that would protect him. Turning I studied Arius, I didn't know much about him but due to the fact he could grab his opponents mind and control them, my token would probably make him laugh.

Taking a deep breath, I made eye contact with Quinton and motioned with my head for him to come over. With a suspicious look, he did without bringing too much attention to the fact I had more or less summoned him.

When he stopped in front of me, I held out one of the charms. "Please take this and keep it on you tonight."

With his brows furrowed he took it and studied it. "What is it?"

I knew his opinion on magic and didn't want to tell him straight up that it was just that. "Just something I want you to have."

His eyes widened and then he smiled. "Thank you, Damariss."

I snarled at him showing my teeth. "You need to forget that's my name," I muttered.

"Never." He gave me a huge lopsided grin. Chase called him over. With another grin, he tucked the piece into his pocket and went back over.

Troy came toward me. "We're sending the first group over in a few minutes." He stopped and glanced at Quinton. "If he finds out you gave him something holding magic he won't be happy."

I didn't ask how he knew. "Then we won't tell him." I held one of the dragons out to him. "I have one for you as well."

He took it and studied it briefly before putting it in his pocket. "That's not saying much for your confidence in my fighting skills."

I looked at the huge broadsword hanging from his side. "It's for the fighting that doesn't involve brute strength."

Grinning, he stepped closer and then gave me a serious look. "Be safe, little one, we need you whole and healthy."

"I plan on staying that way this time." I looked up into his eyes and couldn't help notice that even though they were identical to his brothers, they were entirely different at the same time. He was nothing like his twin. This man in front of me went much deeper and hid more than all his siblings combined.

Straightening, he turned and walked over to Quinton and Tim. A warm feeling suddenly filled me and I didn't have to look far to find the source. Chase was coming to me, his eyes locked on mine. I waited until he was close enough that only he would hear what I had to say. "You need to get this connection thing under control, big guy, I can't be wondering what you're trying to convey in the middle of a fight."

With a burning look, he stopped close enough that I could feel the heat from his body. "Not to worry, kitten, when I want you to feel what I'm feeling you won't have to guess at it." He sighed. "I don't suppose you'd sit this one out and watch from the sidelines?"

Shaking my head, I scrunched up my face. "I'm not much of a spectator."

"I didn't think so." Leaning down he brushed a soft kiss against my cheek. "Hold nothing back, Daxx, I want you back without injury this time." Straightening he held out his hand. "Now give me my token of your affections and let's go kick some ass."

Frowning, I placed the charm in his hand. "How did you know?"

He grinned. "No one sneak's messages out of my realm without me knowing." He looked over at his twin still standing with Quinton. "You gave to them as well?"

"Yes, and I have one more for Tim."

Rubbing his jaw, a hesitant look crossed his face. "I don't think I like your attachment to my guard."

"You'll get over it." I patted him on the chest and started to move past him.

Grasping my arm gently he gave me a heated look. "Be safe."

A lump formed in my throat, so I nodded and then went over to Tim without looking behind me.

****

My first thought when I was suddenly back on my side was, this had better go down the way we planned it. There were only thirteen of us plus a witch and mage and we were headed to a battle with more bodies fighting against us. My second thought was why on earth had they landed us all on a roof? That part of the planning had been omitted when Quinton had brought me up to speed.

As soon as my legs felt steady again I moved over to the edge where Victor stood looking down. I didn't have to ask a thing when I looked over the edge and saw them gathering in an alley half a block away.

Chase appeared beside me and then Troy on the other side. Chase sighed loudly and then pointed to the others walking around the corner. "I don't care if he stands right in front of you, Kitten, the one wearing the red shirt you are to stay clear of."

I looked down at the guy, granted he was big,

enormously so but he didn't look any more dangerous than the king standing beside me. "Why?"

"Because he doesn't need to be touching you to feed." Troy supplied with abhorrence plain in his voice.

"Can he do that to me? I mean don't I have some sort of special mojo going on?"

Chase glanced down at me and then to his brother. "Let's just play it safe."

Victor cleared his throat. "Do you see the blur in the middle of the group gathering?"

All of us turned and looked again. I spotted the man in the middle of the group, he wasn't exactly a blur, but he seemed to be covered in something that made them look blurry, almost not there. "What is that?"

"Marcus," Victor growled.

Oh crap! Was the only thing my brain returned. "He's going to be right there out in the open?"

"We won't even be able to touch him." Victor turned and strode over to Clairee and the woman standing beside her.

I felt like I should have read the instructions to this game before jumping on board all of a sudden. "If Victor or I scan him will it work?"

Troy leaned on the break wall and studied the group. "It's doubtful."

"The plan is to take down his followers and then he'll be on his own again. He's gathering strength from all of them, making him more powerful."

"That's so cheating," I mumbled. Sighing I looked around at the others waiting on the other side. "How long are we waiting?"

Chase went over and looked over the edge at the other corner. "There are a few late arrivals coming from this side." He nodded over to Rafael. "Raf and Leone are going to follow them in, once they signal us we'll box them in."

I studied the alley they were all heading to. There was only one way out besides the way they'd come in, and unless they had wall scaling abilities they were screwed. Why would they pick somewhere with no escape? "Why would they pick somewhere boxed in like that?"

Chase came over and leaned beside his twin and studied it. "Because Marcus thinks he's outsmarted us and we're clueless."

I grinned. "I love crashing parties."

Troy pointed down the street to where Rafael and Leone walked along like they were just out for a nightly stroll. "Time to move."

"Let's party." Chase said next to my ear as he turned to follow his brother to the group waiting to start.

I followed the twin Kings down the fire escape, with Quinton and Tim right behind me. With a final glance to the witch and mage staying up top, I turned and looked around the group. There was a silent resolve hovering in the vibes, I decided at that moment if things went south during any of this, and any one of them got hurt I would personally hunt down this amazing magician that was the cause of all of this and beat him ten ways to dead.

Chase blew out a breath as he stood beside me. "I really hope those emotions are intended for the other side, kitten. They hurt just feeling the backlash from the energy."

I grinned. "We've got this."

"Amen," Michael whispered. He turned and looked around at his brothers for a long moment. "Fight well brothers." With a nod to me he turned and took off in a jog down the back alley that would lead to the gathering group. Arius saluted and then turned to follow him.

Victor paused in front of me and gave his brothers a quick glance before looking down at me. "Fight well, Huntress."

I was surprised to be included in this brotherly game they played. "Well enough to kick your ass, Victor."

His grin was wide as he turned and went in the opposite direction, taking only one guard with him.

Welsley didn't waste words, just nodded in our direction

and then motioned for the other remaining guard to follow him.

Turning around I looked up at the men all watching me. I was going in with more muscle than the entire body builders association. With the two Kings, Quinton and Tim I should have felt like the safest person on any planet, but I wasn't quite that cocksure just yet.

Troy patted Chase on the back. "Fight well, brother."

"Well enough to beat you, brother King." Chase replied as he turned and we started walking down the street.

To anyone watching, if they could see through the cloak, surrounding us, they would think Armageddon was about to rain down on them. The four towering men walked with long strides in synch with each other's step. In the middle was where I strode along beside them.

I mentally psyched myself up for what was to come and hoped I didn't get my ass handed to me. I had four objectives in this impending situation. First to get my ass out of it whole and second, to make sure all the men I were attached to did the same. The third priority was to avoid anyone wearing a red shirt, just to be on the safe side. And last, my own secret hope of getting close enough to *the* magician to knock him down a few pegs. If his magic or spells or whatever he did truly didn't work on me, I was the only one in all of this that had a chance to do something to stop him.

A bit much for my first multi-realm battle? Probably, but it kept me from running the other way screaming *we're all gonna die*. I detest cowardice and refused to give in to it. Then again, I could save that for the emergency exit, just in case.

When we reached the entrance of the alley, all of the others appeared alongside us. I looked into the alley at the unsuspecting group gathered closely at the far end. When I could see a tall man with black hair, streaked with white in the middle I turned to Chase and whispered. "I can see him clearly."

He gave me a quick glance and then nodded. "Then it's

true, he holds no power over you." Looking at his brother over my head, he gave him a glare. "He is a blur to us."

My nerves were zinging, if we stood here much longer I might back out of it all together. "Let's get this party started, boys." Not waiting for a cue from any of them, I started walking slowly into the alley. When I heard the hisses behind me I knew later on I was in for a lecture or two, probably eight.

CHAPTER TWENTY-SIX

"Hey!" I called out loud enough for the assortment of followers to hear. When they started to turn around, I stopped and lifted my arms in a vague gesture. "Can anyone join the club or do we have to buy the membership package?"

I didn't have to look behind me to know I had some large backup behind me when the expressions of fear, hatred and just plain shock appeared on Marcus's little collection of sleazeballs. A quick looksee told me there were probably only four of five that were all human like myself. Good thing to know I thought as I started walking cautiously toward them.

"Marcus," I said in a taunting tone. "You have been a very *very* bad boy."

The scary as hell guy in the middle glared at me. "So the Huntress has come to be after all."

"Bet your ass she has." Reaching behind me, I pulled the Sais free from their harness. I could hear blades clearing leather from all around me. Opening my arms, I held the Sais in the air. "Easy way or their way?" I motioned to the men behind me.

Marcus snarled, his eyes flashing an electric purple.

I took that as the latter and started walking toward them. I barely took two steps when four blocked my path to the magician. Before I could assess which one I wanted to beat on first, Tim and Chase flanked me, tipping the odds in my favor.

A rush of bodies went by us as we stood eyeing each other up. The sound of grunts and metal clashing came from behind us. I suddenly felt like I was in slow motion with everything moving but me.

That feeling lasted a whole of two seconds before a blonde chick wearing a really bad cat woman knock off with the scary glowing green eyes tried to take a slice out of me with the extra pointy knife she held. I had no problems getting out of her way, but wasn't about to back down. With a flick of the Sais I kicked into a spin that came so easily I almost went right past her. Ducking, I came up behind her and kicked out her knee to bring her down to my height. She growled and went down, her blade skittering across the pavement. I shifted the Sai to my other hand and pulled the scanner off my belt. Hoping it was just a simple push of a button, I held it over her and pushed. Her eyes widened and that was the last expression on her face before there was a light and an odd popping sound. All that remained of her now was her blade. I had to get one of these gadgets that worked for my side. Bounty hunting would so much simpler with one.

Clipping it back on my jeans, I spun back to the action and assessed how many bodies were between Marcus and me from the looks of it, all of them. Quinton and Rafael were double teaming an enormous man that looked like he belonged in a street fighter game. It was clear to see they had the advantage of fighting together for so many years. The big dude didn't stand a chance. When he went down, I ducked down and worked my way towards them, barely missing a blade that was intended to dice up someone else. With a scowl, I flipped around and got well out of reach.

Rafael was disarming the guy when I reached them, with a quick nod to me, he stepped back. The same bulging eye expression appeared on the downed man's face as I held the scanner over him. Pop, and he was no more.

A screeching made me turn quickly to see a woman with normal, non-glowing eyes charging for me. I didn't need to be psychic to know I'd just sent her boyfriend to a holding cell in another realm. She wielded a wooden baseball bat. I wanted to ask her if she was insane bringing that to a fight like this, but she swung it a few times and I decided questions would have to wait.

Putting one Sai back in the strap, I pulled my raptor out, surmising that if I got close enough she was going to have to go down fast before the wood connected with any part of my body. I hadn't asked Victor if I could scan humans, but she was wearing one of those devices on her wrist, so she was going to be my guinea pig. I jumped back out of her reach, only to have a thick arm wrap around my neck and squeeze. Breathing was barely possible.

Being confined in any way just happened to be one of those things that equally freaked me out and pissed me off. Without so much as a struggle I went lax in the hold and brought the hand holding the Sai across my body and stuck it right into the side of my captor. With a loud howl, I found myself free again but still facing the bat whooshing past my face. Scanning her was going to be a pleasure.

Glancing over my shoulder, I made sure there was no one on my team that was going to meet a stray swing when I ducked. As she raised the piece of wood to swing, I executed the new roll and duck I'd practiced and glided my raptor across her side. She grunted, but the bat still went up. Before she could turn, I was behind her and kicked out both her legs so she went down to her knees. She maintained her hold on the bat and I really had to give her bonus points for that; she was determined. In front of her the guy I'd stabbed was getting back to his feet. The sheer size of him down on one knee was enough to make me double take. Seriously someone on the Alterealm side had slept with an honest to Christ giant, they had to have.

Pulling the scanner off the clip again, I held it out to the woman and pressed the button, hoping I hadn't just sent her to Kansas instead of Alterealm. I'd have to ask about that later. She growled out a low gurgle just as the light flashed and I found myself with no one between me and the gothic Hercules, who was now on his feet again. In his massive hand was a battle axe that had to be almost as long as I was tall. Nothing short of a grenade launcher was going to take him out and one of those I didn't have.

Replacing the scanner, I grabbed my Sai again and backed up to assess how the hell I was going to survive this one. A quick glance over his shoulder allowed me to see how terribly thrilled Marcus was looking, and that pissed me off. Troy was suddenly at my side, and I wanted to bow at his feet and thank him, but before I could even make eye contact the hulk of a man came at us.

Normally I would baulk at someone stepping in to aid me when I was fighting but with the first deafening clash of Troy's broadsword blocking the axe, I decided maybe this one time would be allowable. Troy grunted, telling me just how much brute strength the other guy had. Admiring his ability was going to have to wait. I ducked and weaved out of the way, trying to find the right moment to help out as they met each other blow for blow. The first time I'd seen Chase fight I had thought it was beautiful, and Troy was no different as his moves were a masterpiece in action.

The battleaxe went up again and I noticed the wielder was favoring the side I had jabbed. Timing it for the next swing, I went down and flipped, coming up on my knees between the two large men. It wasn't the Sai in my hand this time, the scanner was held out and ready. Wasting no more than half a breath of time I pressed the button and then had to shuffle back before the axe came down on my head.

Troy scooped me up with a hand under my arm and gave me a quick nod before he turned to face a blade swinging past his head. I stood there, watching for all of a second, feeling like I was an ant in a horse race. Tall bodies and weapons were all around me and I couldn't see anything for the bodies that towered over me. Glancing at a dumpster against the wall, I moved over and climbed up on it so I could see where everyone was.

When I straightened up, I wished for a camcorder to capture what I was seeing. The brothers and guards were kicking some serious ass and it was so pretty to watch I wanted to weep. Shopping excited some females, not this one, a well-executed fight was better than a fifty percent off sale in my mind.

When I glanced in Marcus's direction I noticed he was waving his arms around like he was trying to do tai chi but just with his hands. I didn't know a thing about magic, but the intense look of concentration on his face told me he was whipping up something that wasn't good for us. I waited until he glanced in a direction and then jumped down and headed that way as fast as I could manage through the scuffling bodies.

Dodging a stray swing, or one that may have been aimed at me, I ducked around Arius and a man wearing a steel plated jacket as they tried to give each other a haircut with some sort of razor thin blades. I was in front of Victor laying a serious beat to yet another contestant for the scariest award. Turning to see Marcus looking at me and not at all pleased, I knew I had found the target he was after. Take out the justice and things would go to pot fast.

I couldn't exactly interrupt Victor to tell him he was in serious peril in the middle of a one on one, so I tried to stay in the direct path between him and the purple eyed psycho waving his hands in my direction. I really, really hoped all the talk of his powers being useless on me were true, because unless he was conducting an invisible orchestra I was about to find out.

When I heard a familiar pop behind me, I knew Victor had sent his tango partner to a holding cell. "Vic, get back. Marcus is targeting you." I didn't have time to turn around and see if he was listening.

Marcus raised his hands in the air, and everything around

him blew in a wind that only seemed to surround him. He glared at me and dropped both hands toward me. I don't know what he was supposed to be doing, I could feel pressure brushing over me but nothing that would make me worry too much.

A confused and then angry look flashed over the magician's face, telling me one thing. His mojo was useless against me. I'd breathe a sigh of relief later. "You didn't think we were going to make it easy for you, did you, Marcus?"

Out of nowhere the one with the red shirt stepped in front of me. Crap was the first thing that entered my mind. I was running on pure hearsay through all of this and wasn't in the mood to see if my huntress power was impervious to this guy. I didn't know how exactly this one fed and wasn't about to find out.

He advanced on me like I was a huge bug that needed terminating, stepping around him I ducked under his arm and tried to get behind him. My luck, the big guy had moves that were faster than the rest of the oversized Alterealm mutants.

Almost kissing the dagger he jabbed out toward my face, I dropped down to one knee and then kicked out trying in a poor attempt to take out his knee cap. My boot met solid leg that didn't budge at all. Double crap seemed the appropriate thought.

This time when he swung his arm in my direction, I reacted with an upper swing of my Sai, barely skimming it along his arm. His eyes turned this eerie washed out white and my brain said to run away but my damn body wasn't willing to throw in the towel. He lunged at me again and my foot caught something as I tried to step back. Landing on my side, I didn't stop to assess if any damage was done before I rolled and got to my feet.

Damn he was fast and I was running out of moves. I worked to stay out of his reach and not make eye contact with him long enough for him to see mine as I sheathed the one Sai and grabbed the knife at my side. For this I needed something I was comfortable with.

He came at me again and I tried a jump kick to his chest, but again it was like bouncing into a solid tree. When a new strength flooded into me, I almost stumbled in my step to stay out of his reach. My veins were suddenly over loaded with adrenalin and it took three more swipes and dodges for me to realize somehow Chase was using our connection to lend me some assistance. It also meant he could see the deep shit I was in but was a little on the busy side to lend any physical aid.

With sheer determination, I tried the kick again and actually made him stumble back a half step. It wasn't much but I'd take it. Changing tactics, I twisted around, jabbing at him with my knife to distract him so I could get beside him. Charging at him, I dropped down and attempted to take out his knee once more at the same time I poked at him with my knife. I connected with flesh, but not enough to even make him pause.

What did I have to do to give him a clue? There was no way in any life or realm he was taking a taste of anything me. Another wave of strength flooded into me and I soaked it up this time and did the exact move again hoping to catch him off guard with a repeat performance. The knife grabbed into some meatier flesh this time and he stumbled to the ground. Dropping my Sai, I pulled the scanner off my waist and aimed it at him. Before he could blink I sent him home. "We're going to need a medic for that one," I said mostly to myself.

Chase was standing over me when I looked up from retrieving my weapon off the ground. He glared at me and I wanted to laugh. "So sue me. He came to me I was trying to stay the hell out of his way."

He pulled me to my feet and gave me a quick once over. The pressure shoving at me was back and I knew that dick Marcus was at it again, this time he was hitting on Chase. Giving me an odd look, Chase looked over to where Marcus was and grinned. The wind burst through the alley sending garbage and anything not tied down scattering all around us.

"I think we pissed off magic boy up there," I said under my breath.

Before he could reply five guys came out of nowhere, swinging Bo's like they were nothing more than ribbons.

"Shit," Chase muttered.

"What?" I looked around at him.

"I think he just found a way around your charm."

I looked back to Marcus and then checked the guys moving slowly toward us, boxing us in. "What?

Chase put his back to me to cover behind us. "The guys are powered via Marcus magic and I'd bet my ass they're stronger than a freight train."

I groaned. "That is so cheating. I am going to kick his ass just for being a weenie."

The chatting was done as the first Bo was swung in my direction. What I wouldn't give for a taser right now, alfalfa with the bad hair-do and long stick needed a zap to adjust his personality. Ducking down, I slid and attempted to kick his legs out. It was like a fly kicking an elephant in the ass and less than effective.

Flipping, I came up practically under him and thrust up with both Sais, I connected and from the sound he made I was pretty sure he wouldn't be procreating any time soon, if ever. I actually had a very brief flash of guilt for that move; it was almost too low even in this fight.

When the next guy advanced on me, my weak moment was long gone and I hoped for the chance to try it again. He made this screeching sound and I paused long enough to wonder what the hell good a noise like that would be in the middle of the death dance. His Bo connected with my shoulder hard enough my teeth felt like they'd just come loose. Now I was pissed. Like the much larger otherworldly guys didn't already have enough of an advantage over me, they had to feed them freakin magic and then pummel me.

Gritting my teeth, I integrated my old street fight style with the new moves Chase had taught me and went completely Taz on his ass. It was one of those moments when I was glad no one had a camcorder or the time to use it. He obviously had seen what I did to my last opponent because there was no way he was going to let me get near that region of his anatomy.

While I took on one, I could hear the sounds behind me and knew Chase had his hands full with the rest, which meant sadly, I was on my own with this hopped-up villain. Moving to the side, I managed to avoid him, his Bo wasn't as slow as his feet though and it swiped past my head close enough to move my hair.

If I couldn't take him down, I was going to have to send him packing. With the Sai in one hand I grabbed the scanner and waited for the moment to use it. It didn't even phase him when I was all of a sudden fighting with one weapon and a little box in my hand. Clearly his IQ was no threat to anyone.

I had to abandon the other Sai and put it back in the strap when I came within an eyelash width of having my nose relocated on one swing. I really hated to lose a nice blade, but I needed something I could throw at this jerk while staying out of his reach. With a well-timed flick, I tossed the knife in his direction and did the mental happy dance when it embedded in his side and stopped him where he stood.

Not even caring if he was still breathing, I leaned over him and scanned without one ounce of remorse. As soon as he vanished from my sight, I turned and zeroed in on the guy holding his crotch and rolling around on the ground. That time I almost felt regret as I scanned his ass to Vic's jail.

Pulling my Sai back out, I spun around to help Chase. He was battling it out with two of them. I had no idea where the fifth guy went and really didn't care at this moment either. He could be found at a less crucial moment.

Chase took another swing and sent the one flying back on his ass. Knowing I wouldn't get another chance I lunged in his direction with the scanner aimed at him. When he went pop, I turned back to see the missing guy heading my way. What had he been observing and now decided I was the best target?

A swing of Chase's blade distracted him long enough for me to get closer. We worked as a team, with him blocking their swings and me trying to stab at any body part I could in hopes of striking a blow that would take them down.

It felt like it took us ten years to finally send one of them to the pavement. I scanned him, not even caring if he lived or not. Before I could even take a deep breath the last one took a wild swing in my direction and I stumbled back, landing on my ass and just barely missing a deadly smack upside my head with his Bo.

Tim appeared out of nowhere and snapped the guy's neck and then paused just long enough to raise one eyebrow at me.

"What, "I panted, "my boot was undone." A smile crossed his face before he turned to fend off another attacker.

Chase reached down and pulled me to my feet. "Rest later, kitten." He knocked back someone that stumbled toward us, "dire situation now."

Picking up the scanner, I glanced over to where Marcus was, only to find him gone. "I've had it with these jerks. You distract and I'll scan."

He nodded once and then headed back into the thick of it. There were only a half dozen left to take down, but it felt like thirty. Chase came at them from behind and assisted the brother or guard fighting them. When they were immobilized or distracted I rolled in and scanned.

After the last pop sound, it was silent. Looking around I checked to see if all of our guys were still standing. I wouldn't exactly say they were all on their feet and ready to go as they leaned, slumped and sat against anything. It was right about then my own legs decided that would be enough jumping around and I squatted down only to tip over.

Chase was beside me doing pretty much the same thing, so we leaned back to back while we tried to catch our breath. "I think," he hissed out a breath, "we need to stop Mitz from feeding us so damn much."

Quinton chuckled. "Maybe we're just getting old."

Leaning forward I found where he was sprawled on the pavement. "Speak for yourself gramps. This chick hasn't even seen thirty yet."

"You fight well for an infant." Quinton grinned at me.

"And you for a geriatric," I added still trying to catch my breath.

"Can we insult each other after a nap?" Rafael added to the banter.

Victor moved away from the wall and looked around at the few bodies lying motionless in the shadows of the alley. "I'll send these ones back to be disposed of." He looked around at everyone. "Leone, once I've got it cleaned up you go back up to the roof and take them back to our side."

Getting to his feet, Leone came over and looked down at me. "Caught some of your action, little Huntress." He grinned, "you can back me up anytime."

He may as well have just told me I was the most beautiful woman in the world, I felt pride fill me. "I'll keep your number on speed dial."

Grinning, he nodded and turned to leave the alley.

Michael, pulled Quinton to his feet and nodded down at me. "How are your interrogation skills?"

"I don't even know if I have any, but I can shake down scum for information." I moved to get to my feet, wobbling too much so I stayed kneeling.

"Good enough." He came over and pulled Chase to his feet. "Bring her to the cells."

Bending down Chase picked up his blades and put them back into the harness on his back. "We'll be there shortly."

I watched Victor lean over a body on the ground, he checked for a pulse and then did something with his scanner before he sent the body away. When I turned back, Troy towered over me holding out his hand. I let him pull me to my feet, keeping a hold on his hand until I checked to see if my legs were in working order again.

He stood there looking down at me with red eyes. "Are you alright?"

Exhaling loudly, I did a quick assessment of the aches starting. "Going to have some wicked bruises, but I think so."

I wiped at blood on his jaw and was pleased to find out it wasn't his. "Thanks for the assist by the way."

Grinning, he lowered his head. "You fought well, little Queen." Slowly he released my hand. "Are you still coming back tomorrow?" His eyes strayed to his twin standing a few feet away.

"Of course."

His expression relaxed. Clearing his throat, he straightened and turned to Chase. "I'll meet you at the holding cells."

Chase nodded and stepped over to brush something off my shoulder. I didn't want to know what I just figured I was better off not asking. "I don't know about Daxx, but I need a quick rinse before we start digging for answers."

The image of the large tubs on Alterealm came to my mind. "I could use a quick soak." Rolling my shoulders, I winced when the one the bat had clipped complained loudly. "And maybe an ice pack."

Both men hovered over me.

"You said you were alright." Troy's voice was filled with concern.

Holding up my hand to stop them from crowding me any further. "I am, just a little banged up in a few places."

Troy's eyes went to his brother. Chase nodded. "I'll take care of her then we'll meet you there."

Troy walked away without another word. Turning to Chase I looked up at him. "No more blood. This connection thing is freaking me out."

He shrugged. "You didn't mind it when I boosted you with a bit of motivation."

"That was different." I checked to make sure I had everything. "That wasn't an emotion I can't do anything with." Having nothing else to do to avoid looking back at him, I turned around and looked into yellow eyes. I wanted to think it was because he was hungry after all the energy, but my skin flushed with warmth letting me know it wasn't the only reason. "Like that, right there. Don't you believe in the element of surprise?"

He grinned. "I love the element of surprise, kitten and someday maybe I'll get to show you just how much." Taking my elbow, he moved away from the wall out into the open of the alley. "Had enough of your realm for tonight?"

Sighing, I glanced around the dismal space and then nodded. "Yeah, let's go."

CHAPTER TWENTY-SEVEN

Glaring at Chase, who continued to stand in the middle of my bedroom on his side of Alterealm, I growled. "Seriously? You want to check me over and make sure I'm okay?"

"Yes."

He didn't even crack a smile while he stood there, so I knew he was being dead serious. "I want to go to the cells and check out what's going on, can't we do this later?"

"I said I would look after you, and I intend on doing that."

The tone of his voice assured me that I wasn't going to get to clean up or do anything until I gave in. "It's just my shoulder that's hurting." A slight understatement, but I wasn't going to share that my whole back and arm was throbbing with pains shooting up and down it. When he continued to just stand there looking at me, I cursed many bad words inside my head and then started to take the harness off my back. As an afterthought, I turned my back on him when I went to move the aching arm, just in case I made one of those pained faces.

"I can feel the pain you're in, Daxx."

That definitely made the decision for me, there would be no more blood healing for this girl. I was willing to get used to being around others and having them in my face all the time, but my thoughts and feelings were my own and only shared if I wanted to.

Pulling the shirt over my head was pretty close to the most painful thing I'd ever done, except that time I had cracked three ribs or when my leg had been crushed when a jumper tried to back over me in his car. When the damn material finally cleared my head, I put my arms back down and stood there with my back to him. He hissed and I knew now I'd have to go look in the mirror and see how bad it was.

Not even sparing him a glance I walked into the bathroom and flicked on the light and turned my side toward the mirror. Well shit, my shoulder was the color of freshly ground up meat and looked like a giant blister wanting to burst.

"And *that* is you being okay?" He drawled from the doorway.

I looked at him in the mirror and made one of those dumb faces that you make when you know they're right but don't want to admit it out loud.

I heard his boots on the floor as he came over. "I can't just leave it like this, kitten, it breaks my heart just looking at you having something like that on you."

The soft aching tone of his voice made me look at him in the mirror again. He wasn't lying as he stood there looking at it he looked like he was hurting as much as I was. "The connection that goes with the blood healing..." How did I say this without sounding redundant? "I'm not comfortable with it."

He traced his finger over my tattoo, a look of fascination on his face. "I know." I shivered under his touch. "I find myself going through a lot of new territory lately as well, it's not just you."

Men rarely confessed things of this magnitude without prompt, so I turned and leaned back against the counter and looked up at him. "What do you mean?"

Running a hand through his already messed up hair, he

sighed loudly. "I almost marked you last night, Daxx." I nodded, I was there I knew this. He studied my face silently. "We would have been mated then, do you understand that? I almost took away your right to choose." His voice had a pained tone to it now.

"I got that part last night."

Shaking his head, he paced over to the other side of the room and then turned and looked at me. "I don't think you got all of it, sweetling, or we wouldn't be having this calm discussion right now." He moved back to me so quickly, I didn't have time to react before I found myself boxed in by his big arms with him leaning down in my face. "We would have been mated. Period. You can't undo that." His eyes, bordered on yellow so fast it was haunting. "You're not comfortable with the blood connection? A mated pair are connected in *all* ways. When one hurts, so does the other. When one is mad, the other feels it."

Well, when he put it that way it was a very good thing it hadn't happened. I was still coming to terms with this destined to be the mate of a king spiel, having no decision in it would have pissed me right off. I opened my mouth to say something, but the look he gave me made me close it again.

"Marking someone is no accident." He paused and leaned back a few inches. "It can't just happen with anyone." Nope, I still wasn't getting where he was headed. "I have never felt the inclination to mark someone, never mind almost lose my mind with the strongest emotions that filled me with need to do it."

The picture was getting a little clearer for me. "So what do we do then?"

Closing his eyes, he stood there with his arms still caging me in and took a few deep breaths. "Exactly what I said last night. Nothing. We take a little more time."

A thousand questions filled my mind. I asked the first one I could maintain. "Did you tell Troy what happened?"

Opening his eyes, he shook his head. "No, but I think he still knows." Pushing away, he straightened. "The connection between my brothers and I is mostly emotion based and there is no way he didn't feel a part of what I did last night."

I pointed at him. "Okay, that right there freaks me out." I crossed my arms over my chest and it dawned on me that I was standing in the bathroom having this discussion in my bra. "I'm not even used to be around others and now all of a sudden I'm supposed to share my emotions with others in a non-verbal sense."

The look on his face softened. "I know you're having a hard time with it, I can feel that and it is why I am fighting this constant battle to give you space."

Damn, he just racked up a few more points with that statement. "Thank you."

He glanced in the mirror at my back. "With that being said, it's killing me to see you hurt. Everything in me is telling me to look out for you, to heal you …" He sighed again and ran both hands through his hair in a frustrated move. "I will do everything possible to keep my emotions out of your head."

Even with his eyes more yellow than hazel I could see him pleading with me. Cursing my newfound weakness, I dropped my face into my hands and stood there. When I lifted it, I motioned around the bathroom. "Can I take a shower and think for a few minutes?"

Stepping back, he nodded. "I'll go get cleaned up and be back in fifteen minutes."

"Okay."

He stood without moving, just looking at me. "You were amazing tonight, by the way."

More flattery, a girl could get used to that sort of thing. "Mostly thanks to your teaching."

Chase shrugged. "I didn't do much, just guided you in a new direction. You did all the work."

"Go. I need some space for a few."

****

I barely got the zipper pulled up on my jeans when he

knocked on the door again. I knew it was Chase, without even opening it. "Come in."

He stepped through the door looking like a model for a sexy cologne ad. His hair was still wet, clothes hugged every muscle in all the right ways…

Raising an eyebrow, he stopped. "It might be a good idea to curb *those* thoughts for now."

That startled me out of the mental images I was mooning over. Clearing my throat, I tried to shrug it off and ended up wincing in pain instead. Okay, maybe a little help in healing wouldn't be so bad. I held up the arm that didn't want to die and fall off my body and opened my hand to stop him. "A minimal dose, nothing more. Just give the healing a little jump start."

He smirked. "I don't think I've ever been thought of as a dose before."

Rolling my eyes, I reached down and tried to pick up my boots, but the pain shot all the way up into my neck and I ended up dropping to one knee instead. Chase was beside me before I could try to recover. With gentle hands, he helped me to my feet.

"You are, by far the most stubborn woman I have ever crossed paths with." Without pause, he pulled the shirt, which had taken me more time to get on than I cared to admit, up my body and then he worked my arm back out of it. He groaned a painful sound. "Either you let me help you, now or I'll call Quinton to come see this."

"How is that fair?" I pictured Quinton's dark eyes bleeding with emotion and concern.

Chase shrugged. "It's not."

Growling, I stepped back and glared up at him. "Fine."

With a triumphant look that reminded me of a six-year-old getting his own way, he pulled his t-shirt off and tossed it into the chair. Without my permission, my eyes drank in the body he'd exposed and I had no problems placing my mouth against it, for any reason. With a slow appraising stare I kept going and moved to the waist of his jeans and then lower.

The evidence of him not minding my eyes caressing him was plain to see. I suddenly felt warm all over. Clearing my throat, I looked up at his face again. "Is it a good idea for me to take from your chest? Wouldn't a wrist or less appealing body part be better?"

"Probably, but I'm a glutton for punishment and it's a good excuse to hold you, I've spent most of the day wanting to drag you into my arms."

At least he was honest, I'd give him that. I looked at the smooth muscled chest again and my mouth dried up. "I repeat, is this a good idea?"

He took slow steps in my direction. "I've already fed, so that shouldn't be an issue."

I looked below his waist again and felt my cheeks flush. "I'm not sure that's the only issue…"

Grasping my chin, he lifted it so my eyes moved back up to his. "It's not, but I will behave." His eyes were so serious. "I will not mark you until you consent."

I didn't bring up the fact that he'd made it sound like I would chose him. At this point I didn't want to pick anyone, but I was starting to admit that in the end I may not have a lot of choice in the matter. Pulling my raptor out from behind me, I held it up to him.

With an intense look, he took it and pulled me gently until my face was a few inches from his chest. I looked up at him, so I wouldn't have to watch him cut into his own flesh again for my sake. His hazel eyes held mine with a look of such tenderness I almost backed away for fear it would take me over.

He scored his chest and rested his hand against the back of my head as I leaned into him and ran my tongue over it. He hissed out a breath and then wrapped his other arm around me and moved closer so my whole body was against his.

I let his emotions fill me, so I could drown out the pain and forget about the questions. As my mouth closed over the wound, I could feel it from his end and for him it was pure pleasure to have me do this.

He pressed a hand into the small of my back and held our hips together as his other hand kept my head in place. He made a soft growling sound as I felt his whole body shudder. I swallowed and started to pull away but his hand stopped me.

Leaning down he whispered, "Keep going, kitten, I won't lose control on you."

Trusting him to keep his word, I continued to take his blood into my system before the wound could seal and stop the flow. His lust flashed inside my mind for a brief second, just long enough to stir my own. Not wanting to torture the man that was trying to help me, I swallowed again and gently licked over the cut before moving my mouth away from him.

He stood there, holding me, his posture tense. With a soft curse, he reached down and lifted my chin so he could reach my mouth with his own. The kiss was deep and passionate but he remained in control.

With a groan, he released me and stepped back. I stood there feeling lightheaded and stared at his chest as he took deep breaths. Snapping out of it when he moved back over, I paused as he turned me slowly and looked at my shoulder. "You could use more, but we'll let that do its thing and see what happens." His voice was low and hoarse.

Nodding, I offered him a half smile. "Okay." I had to fight not to reach out and run my hand over his chest. "I think we should put our shirts back on and get to the cells."

He cleared his throat and went over and picked his up. "That's probably a good idea, I could use the distraction."

CHAPTER TWENTY-EIGHT

Now I was in awe, pure simple awe. The cells were nothing like I thought they'd be. I had pictured old bars and cement walls, you know, *cells*. This was way more than that. It was high-tech heaven for starters and just plain cool.

It was underground, so there were no windows anywhere and the security would make the Royal Mint weep with joy if they had anything close to the system here. If you didn't have the right handprint, not just thumb or finger the whole hand, you went nowhere.

Most of the area's I'd seen when we first arrived were clear walled rooms, like Plexiglas. There was only one door, which I had to assume was a bathroom for the unfortunate ones being held in the cell. Each cell had cameras aimed at it from all angles, it seemed redundant considering the cells were completely transparent, but then again, I just caught criminals I didn't study them.

Michael took great pleasure in walking me through and explaining things to me. Each prisoner had a wide red cuff like bracelet on and it stopped any *extra* abilities from being used. I mentally labeled those the magic jammers. They could only be taken off by a handheld scanner, locked up in a safe that only opened for the right handprints. High-tech indeed.

A few wore a second bracelet that was blue. Those ones prevented any close contact from anyone. I didn't ask what the offenders had done that wore them, it didn't take a great leap of genius to figure they were the ultra-dangerous ones.

My little tour concluded when we reached a door. Michael paused and looked like he wanted to say something, but then shook his head and pressed his hand against the panel on the door. "The ones we sent back are in here."

I looked behind me at the row of clear cells and wondered just how big this place was. As soon as we stepped through the door, he motioned me into a room right inside it. Stepping in there, I smiled to see most of the brothers gathered in front of some monitors.

Chase turned and smiled at me. "Impressed, kitten?"

I shrugged slightly. "A little."

He chuckled and motioned for me to come over.

I did.

On the monitors were the group we sent back home, I recognized a few that had tried to take me out of all worlds. Moving closer, I spotted the woman with that had tried to break me in half with her bat. She stood in the middle of the room with her arms crossed staring at the camera.

Victor came in and closed the door. "We're not getting very far."

Arius leaned back against the wall looking bored. "Why are you doing it the hard way?" He lifted his chin toward Troy. "We could go in and come out with everything you need."

Victor sighed. "That would be breaking about ten laws."

Quinton cursed under his breath. "After what they were trying to do, why should we give a shit?"

I had to agree with him there. I looked back at the woman. "What about the human ones? Have they said anything?"

Victor shook his head and pointed to the one I'd looked at. "She refuses to talk until she sees her boyfriend." He sighed. "She won't tell us who that is, so complying it rather difficult."

I looked at the screens, trying to spot him. "Quinton, where's the big guy you and Raf double teamed and I scanned?"

"That's her boyfriend?" Rafael leaned closed and looked at the monitors.

I squinted at one of the men on screen, trying to picture him in the dark. "Well it was after I scanned him that she went ape shit and tried to relocate my shoulder to Denver with a freakin baseball bat."

Chase leaned around me. "That's what happened to your shoulder?"

I glanced at him briefly and then nodded before I looked some more.

"Daxx, why didn't you say that? I thought it was a fall that did that." He sounded really annoyed.

Turning I gave him a confused look. "What difference does it make?"

Chase looked over at Troy, a look passed between them before he turned back to look at me. "There could be damage to the bone, I thought it was just flesh bruising."

"What's he talking about?" Quinton was now crowding me.

Glaring at Chase for a second, hoping he picked up on the thanks-for-nothing vibes, I sighed and looked up at the concerned brown eyes. "My shoulder was a little banged up, it's not bad now."

No one was looking at the monitors or plotting how to gain information, instead all eight brothers were looking at me. Rolling my head to the side, I sent Chase a look of annoyance, he had the good sense to look repentant for opening his big mouth.

"Guys, I'm fine." I lifted my arm, it only hurt a little bit compared to how it had. Putting it back down I rolled my shoulders. There was an ache, but again not as bad as it had been.

"You should get it x-rayed." Rafael said in a tone that

made the other men look more concerned.

"I'm fine." I looked up at Quinton. "Chase gave me some blood, it will be good as new in a few hours."

A surprised look appeared on Quinton's face, but he didn't voice why. "Let me take a look."

Glancing around at the men, I rubbed my hands over my face. There was no way I was going to take my shirt off with all of them standing there staring at me. Dropping my hands, I sighed again. "Its fine, Quinton, really." He didn't budge. I looked around at the faces watching me, hoping for some back up but not one of them were going to side with me on this.

With my hands on my hips, I glared up at Quinton. "Are you serious?"

He nodded, the determined look still on his face still.

"Unbelievable!" I threw my hands up in defeat and moved out of the group of them toward the corner of the room. Turning my back, I reached for the hem of my shirt but then stopped when I heard movement coming in my direction. Chase was suddenly standing in front of me, pulling me into his body.

"Just pull your arm out." He said quietly as he pulled the material out away from my skin.

I pulled my arm free and then angled my body into his so the only part that would be seen was a small amount of my back and one shoulder. I looked up at him, wanting to silently thank him, but he was sending out the look of death to all of his siblings. Why he hadn't spoken up before now, I didn't know.

Looking over my shoulder, I scanned over the faces in the room. A few pairs of eyes were on the protective man in front of me, the expressions were of shock and surprise. Troy's eyes were on my back, but flicked more than once to look at his twin, a pained look on his face. I didn't know what that was about and decided I didn't want to either.

Quinton came over and gently touched my shoulder. "Did it look this bad before you helped?" He asked Chase.

Chase leaned over me, pulling me tighter into his chest and looked. "It was ten times worse than that."

Quinton made some sort of noise, which I chose to ignore and just focused on the warmth of the body against mine to distract me from spitting at the audience behind me.

"You really have the tattoo." Rafael said with wonder.

Lifting my head away from Chase I looked over at him.

Troy shook his head, and then cuffed Raf in the back of his. "You had doubts?"

Rafael shrugged. "Well, no, but knowing and seeing are two different things."

"Are we done examining me?" I didn't try to hide the annoyance in my voice. Without waiting for an answer, Chase helped me get the shirt back on and pulled down. He ran his hands slowly down my back and looked at me, his apology was very plain to make out in his expression. I rubbed my hands over his chest in a forgiving motion and then turned around. "Now, can we find the slugger's man so I can go tell her he's just dandy?"

Arius turned from the screen. "You're going in?"

I grinned. "Oh yeah."

Chase chuckled. "The raptor stays on this side of the walls, kitten."

I shrugged. "Fine with me."

****

I was only half listening to the instructions Victor and Michael were giving me on interrogation, honestly if the woman had been from their side I would have paid closer attention, but as she was like me and fit the very familiar category of scum I generally chase down, I didn't think they could give me much to work with. That was only half of the reason I wasn't paying attention; the other half was Troy's behavior.

He stood on the other side of the room by himself, which in a room filled with his many siblings was odd to say the least. Every few seconds his eyes would move from his twin to me. From this distance, I couldn't make out the

227

expression on his face, but curiosity had me putting my instructors on hold and wandering in his direction.

He straightened away from the wall and uncrossed his arms as I got closer to him. There was no smile to greet me when I stopped in front of him.

"Is something wrong?" I asked quietly so everyone else present wouldn't stop to listen.

His eyes moved over my face slowly. "I don't believe so."

I hated the stiff proper tone he used, but let that slide by. "I know you do the strong silent observing thing more than the others, but you're taking it a bit further than usual."

His mouth quirked, like he wanted to smile but it didn't quite make it all the way. "I learn a lot from standing back and observing."

"I can't argue with that, but you seemed unsettled."

Both blonde eyebrows raised and he looked down at me. "You can sense what I'm feeling?"

I shook my head and then grinned. "Just an observation."

He almost looked relieved to hear that. "I see." His eyes moved away from me and in the direction of Chase again. "I've never seen him like this, or felt his emotions as I have been." When he looked back at me his expression softened.

"Are you blaming me or thanking me?"

"I'm not sure." His hazel eyes searched mine.

Feeling a little too much déjavu with the look he gave me, I glanced over my shoulder at Chase. "The blood healing is wreaking havoc on both of us these last few days." I turned back to him. "Maybe that's the reason."

Troy grinned down at me. "I'm sure you'd love to think that was the only reason."

Busted. "Yeah I would actually, can we leave it at that?"

He chuckled. "We could if you're feeling cowardly."

I rolled my eyes at him. "Okay then, the truth?" He nodded. "I have no idea what to think anymore. Nothing makes any sense to me."

Compassion filled his eyes. "I'm sorry, Daxx, I realize there's been a lot of changes to your world."

It was my turn to laugh. "My world, my beliefs, my everything..."

"We're trying not to push you." He sounded so sincere.

"I know, there's just so much—"

Chase appeared beside me and nodded to his brother. He placed a hand on my back and rubbed it gently. "Feel like partaking in a few interrogations with me, brother King?"

I watched Troy smile and nod at his twin, but noticed he looked at the hand that rested on my back and the look of what I could only say was envy in his eyes. Smiling up at Chase, I moved out of his touch. "I'm off to play some head games with the crazy chick."

Chase sent his brother a silent look before smiling back at me. "Take someone in with you."

"Yes, Sire." I winked at Troy and then moved back over to Victor. On the way past, I glanced at Arius who stood with his arms crossed and looking completely bored with the whole thing. I stopped in front of him and looked up in his grey eyes. "I have been instructed to take a chaperone in with me." He didn't say a word to that. "Wanna volunteer?"

A wide smile answered before his words. "Absolutely, my Huntress. Lead the way."

Victor sent both of us a warning look as we moved past him to the door. I don't know for sure what Arius thought, but I was pretending not to notice myself. I didn't have any funky extra ability to use, so as far as I was concerned anything I did was fair play.

We paused outside the clear door of the clear cell that held the scowling woman. I looked over my shoulder at Arius. "Does your hand print work?"

He gave me an odd look. "My hand print?" He smirked. "Huntress the scanner doesn't record hand prints, it looks for the balance of your Charma."

Turning I gave him my best *huh?* look.

Crossing his hands behind his back, he looked down at me with a light in his eyes that said he was laughing inside. "Your intentions—so to speak. It can measure the good or bad and if the balance is right it will open."

"Really?" I looked down at my hand like it was going to give me a preview of what my balance or whatever would be. "Think it will work for me?"

He snorted. "It better or we are in deep shit having the long-awaited huntress with a bad streak inside her."

I wasn't even sure if that was an answer to what I asked, but I shrugged and placed my hand on the scanner. A light passed under my palm making my hand look see through and then the lock snapped open. "Guess you're all safe with me."

"I didn't doubt it." He held open the door and let me go in first.

I walked in and wandered over to the other side, taking my time to look at the cot and small table near the top of it. When I was done there, I went over and pushed the door open and peaked into the bathroom. At least I'd been right about that.

When I turned around I expected the hostile female to be cowering away from Arius, she wasn't and in fact I don't even think she noticed he was there. So much for my intimidation ploy. Her murderous gaze was on me and me alone, she must have recognized me as the one that vanished her boyfriend. I gave her a quick once over, noting she had seen a bit of action before she tried to take me out with her sporty weapon, her clothes were dirty and had seen better days. "I see you remember me."

"Where is he?" Her voice shook with emotion.

I shrugged. "I might be willing to share information…"

"I'm not telling you anything until I see him." She crossed her arms over her chest.

Looking around her, I made eye contact with the hovering giant that still stood by the door, he looked bored again. Tucking my hands into my pockets, I studied the woman for a moment just to give that dramatic pause element into this game. "You do know my friend over there could just make you tell me, right?"

With a brief look at him she sent me a seething look. "I don't care if he beats me, I'm not saying anything."

I laughed, trying for a light carefree one, but failing. "Honey, he can get you to do anything his heart desires without ever laying a hand on you."

She looked at Arius again, who timed a flashy grin just perfect as she did. This time she checked him out just a bit longer before looking back at me. "Marcus warned us about the royal brothers ..." A quick look at him again. "It's true? They can do all sorts of freaky things?"

Remembering what her boyfriend looked like and the fact that his eyes had that whole neon flashy thing going on, I was a little surprised she thought the royal brothers were freaks. Clearing my throat, I swallowed the laugh. "Oh yeah, and more."

Stepping back, she looked me up and down like I held the answer to some sort of puzzle. "Your her." Her eyes filled with accusations. "You're from my side and a traitor."

My eyebrows shot up. "Excuse me?"

She paced over to the narrow cot and dropped down onto it. "You're the supposed mystical huntress, finally arriving to save the world." With her eyes looking at my feet she continued. "You should be on our side."

I checked with Arius before I commented, he shook his head having no clue what she was talking about. I met her eyes, seeing she believed what she was saying. "Who's side of what exactly?"

She sent me a look saying she thought I was a dunce. "The royals are going to take over *our* side." She snorted. "Some mystical savior you are."

Now I was just getting annoyed. "First, honey, I am not mystical anything. I am just as normal as you are."

Her glare called me a liar.

I continued. "I don't have any special abilities, unless you count survival. I do however know for a fact what

Marcus has been feeding you is a big pile of crap though."

"It can't be." She stood up again, suddenly agitated again.

"Let me explain a few facts that I know." I moved to stand back beside Arius and gave her the room to pace. She may not have held any sort of weapon, but I did know she wasn't restricted from taking any swipes at me and truthfully, I was feeling a little vulnerable without my raptor. "Marcus is handing out transporter bracelets to all the wrong players." She paused in her pacing to listen. "Half those that were on *your* side shouldn't be free to walk any realm, never mind handed the human population for snacks and entertainment…"

I watched her think through things, like a haze was lifting her expressions changed. When she came over and stopped right in front of me she looked like she was in a lot of pain. "I knew something wasn't right." She ran her hands through her tangled hair. "But I didn't want to see, not really, it was the only way Javis and I could be together *all* the time."

When she started to pull her shirt off, Arius straightened beside me. I looked to him and the look of confusion was clear on his face.

She revealed only her left arm and held it out. From the shoulder to wrist was an intricate tattoo, I'm not sure of what exactly but it was quite the piece of work. "We're mates. We completed the blood rite." She gave me a desperate look. "I have to know Javis is alright. He's not a monster, he's a guard from one of the daywalker villages. I can feel his pain…" She looked up at Arius. "Please?"

I looked from her pleading expression to her arm then up at Arius. He looked sympathetic now. Once again, I had no clue what was going on. "We'll be back shortly." Turning I motioned him to the door.

When we were standing back in the hallway, I looked in at her as she put her shirt back in place. Shaking my head, I stomped back to the room of monitors, Arius was right behind me.

As soon as we stepped back in the room, my mouth couldn't stay closed a second longer. I spun on Arius, who held up his hands like I was going to beat on him. Lifting my hands in the air I stepped back so I wouldn't take a swing just because he was convenient. "Find this Javis."

Nodding he moved over to the monitors where Quinton stood. He sent me a puzzled look. "What's going on?"

I sighed. "I have no idea." Leaning back against the wall, I gave him a serious look. "Marcus has them all believing the royal family plans to take over my side of the realms." His jaw dropped. "And as soon as we find her *mate* I'm sure we'll get a whole lot more information from her."

Quinton looked from me to Arius and then back again. "She's mated?"

"Tattoo and all." I held up a hand and moved over so I could see her in the monitor. "At some point was anyone planning on telling me this mating involved an arm of ink and pain if you're separated?"

He flushed with guilt.

"Yeah, that's what I figured."

Troy and Chase stepped through the door with Victor right on their heels. Turning I sent both Kings a look that would have wilted flowers. They both stopped so suddenly Victor walked into them.

Troy looked to Arius and Quinton. "Is there a problem?"

Arius tapped some keys to switch the cells the cameras viewed. "Other than we are holding a mated pair apart from each other and Daxx has just learned things about mating no one thought to explain to her? No, other than that all is well."

Matching hazel eyes flicked to me, both looking wary.

I grinned. "You know this just keeps getting better and better, boys." I pointed to one of the monitors. "That's him." Arius nodded and picked up a phone. I moved away from the monitors and walked slowly over to stand in front of the twins. Pointing up at Troy. "Was this another one of those things you thought to break to me gently, later on?" The guilt on his face answered without him having to speak. "I figured." Poking my finger into his chest I glared up at him. "Later, we're going to sit down and talk about all the things you've conveniently left out of my information pack."

Troy cleared his throat. "I believe you're aware of everything now."

"We'll see." Turning, I looked up at Chase, I wanted to be mad as hell at him too, but then remembered how he had stopped the night before and now understood why. Even with hormones running amok he had found the common sense to halt things before I ended up tied to him for the rest of my days. I pointed at him. "You could have explained a bit more."

Tucking his hands into his pockets, Chase looked down at me with a gentle expression in his eyes. "I planned to, as promised after this was dealt with."

My anger was completely deflated when I remembered he had said he would explain everything. Looking from his apologetic stare to his brother's hesitant one I hissed out a breath. "Fine but later, the three of us are sitting down and all the little details you didn't think I could handle are being tossed on the table."

CHAPTER TWENTY-NINE

I tried sitting and waiting which lasted about two minutes before I paced while waiting for Troy and Chase to get here. They were off giving orders or whatever, planning the next step.

Out of all the beings we sent back during the fight, not one of them could tell us where Marcus might be. When the few that were willing to co-operate tried to recall facts and information, they would suddenly be hit with jabbing pains through their skull. It wasn't that they didn't want to help; they couldn't.

After a quick looksee inside a few heads, Troy informed us that their minds were muddled and vague. Obviously, Marcus had thought of how to cover his ass in the event anyone was caught. So all we had were indistinct details that would take forever to piece together to create a list of places to look. Of course, having to cover two realms and not just one made it all that more tedious.

Stopping, I stared at the floor. The image of Javis and his crazy girlfriend kept coming back to me. They both settled down nicely once we had them in the same space. She clung to him and he held her gently like she was the most precious thing in his world. Their left arms wore matching tattoos from shoulder to palm, or so I saw when he was waving his hand around.

It wasn't the tattoo that was freaking me out, or even that no one had told me about it. The thing that had me ready to jump ship, or in my case realm, was that I knew there was a very real possibility it was going to happen to me. The mated part *and* the tattoo.

I stood there allowing myself three minutes of total honesty, then it was back to denial. I knew I was going to end up mated to one of the Kings. Never before in my life, in a sober state at least, had I been so drawn to a man. Or men and *that* right there wasn't going to happen.

Yes, I was attracted to both of them, they are identical twins, but there was no way in this or any other millennium I was doing the tag team scenario. I was a one on one kind of girl and planned to stay that way.

Which left me right back at a decision I was trying to avoid, having to pick one. What if I just stayed clear of the physical bits with both of them? Can't mate if we don't touch, even though all I think about when ever they're in the same room, or even not in sight was to touch ... and several other actions, none at all innocent.

Sitting down, my mind jumped on the train of thought and wandered further. Did I feel the exact same thing for both of them? I'd only been close to Troy a few times but each time, the heat between us had been instant and hot enough to boil water in less than a minute. With Chase, it was more of a smoldering flame that got hotter. So my choice was a slow simmer and then burn or just go up in flames.

Shaking my head, I stared at the door wishing they would hurry up so I could stop thinking about this. We had other things to do than mate. There was an uber bad magician to take down, and I wanted my piece of that ending. I had to find the missing brother; probably in some insane asylum on my side thinking he's completely wacko. Maybe I should just join him and take the easy way out of all this drama.

The door opened and I almost jumped up to hug Chase as he walked in. Yes, I wouldn't be stuck inside my head now.

Troy came in behind him and closed the door. Both of them looked grim and I wasn't sure if it was some new piece to the hunt, or if it was because we were going to *talk*. In my experience, there wasn't a male of any race that liked hearing that word.

"Sorry we took so long." Troy said quickly and then sat down on the couch across from me.

Chase settled on the arm and then looked me over once or twice. "You look more pissed off then you did earlier."

Of course, I do you left me alone with my thoughts. "I'm past the anger part."

He gave me a look that said he doubted that. "Again, Daxx, we're sorry you weren't told everything sooner."

Troy crossed his legs and leaned back. "Even though you've handled everything up to this point reasonably well, can you honestly say it would be the same if we'd dumped all of it in your lap that first day?"

I hated that he made sense. "I don't know, but I have dealt so far and think that maybe I should have been told more, long before now."

Chase flashed me smile. "In our defense, we've never had to deal with *the* Huntress, so you can't hold any mistakes we've made against us."

Troy looked at his brother for a moment and then back to me. "What would you like to know about being mated?"

"How come I haven't seen anyone with the tattoo until today?" It wasn't one of my original questions, but my mouth spewed it before I could ask any others.

"It's quite rare to find your mate," Chase supplied quietly.

I looked from one to the other. "But there are couples all over the place."

Troy smiled. "We are capable of falling in love and marrying someone else."

Frowning I quickly processed that information. "And if you come across your destined mate after you married another, then what?"

"Just because you find a mate doesn't mean you *have* to accept them. A heart wants what it wants despite fate's dictating."

I studied Troy for a minute, he was trying to answer but my brain was still stuck. Turning to Chase, I made a motion in the air with my hand. "How does it happen?"

He smirked. "Well, think about last night and I'm sure you can put the pieces together."

Troy straightened. "So it's true then? You almost marker her?"

Not even hesitating, Chase turned to his brother and nodded. "Yes and I had no control whatsoever for several minutes, I still don't know how I managed to stop."

Troy looked down at the floor, a hesitant expression on his face. "I wasn't sure when I felt something like I never have before."

"Imagine it from my end," Chase said a little too enthusiastically for my taste.

Feeling like I needed to remind them I was still in the room, I leaned forward in the chair. "What's the difference between marking and the blood rite?"

Slowly Troy looked away from his brother and directly at me again. "Marking is the tattoo, it marks you as mated, but without the blood rite it isn't completely binding."

Were there simple rules to this? "So, you don't have to stay with them?"

Thinking about it for a moment, Troy answered while Chase sat there looking at me. "I don't recall any that haven't, so I can't say for sure, but many have stayed together without the blood rite being done."

Did I really want to know? Yes. "And that's what it sounds like, exchanging blood?"

"Yes." There was no hesitation when he answered. I had to admit at least Troy was trying to be as up front as he said he would be.

"So how does this marking happen?" Chase sent me a heated look, I felt my cheeks flush slightly. "I got that part, Chase, but it has to be more than just sex for it to happen or there would be a lot more marked Alterealm inhabitants I'm sure."

Clearing his throat, Troy glanced down at his jeans and flicked some imaginary lint from them. "There's a release, outside the sexual pleasure, a complete trust and connection. I can't go into great detail because I've never experienced it, obviously." He held his left arm out and twisted it over like I wouldn't have noticed he didn't have a tattoo.

Despite them answering anything I asked, I still wasn't getting the answers I needed. Getting up, I paced over to the fireplace and turned to look back at them. "I still don't see *how* it happens." My voice held a whiny note I hoped they wouldn't pick up on.

Chase got up and was in front of me before I could say anything else. Stepping close enough that our bodies almost touched, he reached down and took my hand in his, our palms melded together. I tried to ignore the look in his eyes, the same one he always got before he kissed me. Leaning into me, he boxed me in by placing his other hand over my shoulder to brace against the wall. If his twin hadn't been sitting there watching us, I would have given into the urge to grab him and kiss him. My body started tingling when he was close to me, another few seconds and I knew I'd be in simmer mode. His eyes held mine with an intense gaze, then he looked down at our hands, squeezing mine lightly.

All the veils lifted in that moment and I understood how the connection was made for the marking to happen. I let go of his hand like it had just burned me and tucked both into the back pocket on my jeans. "I get it," I said softly, feeling a little silly.

Chase continued to stand close to me for a few more seconds, his eyes moving over my face and pausing on my mouth.

"May I ask if you felt it last… night?" Troy's voice interrupted our silent stares.

Moving away from Chase, I shrugged. "I can't say, honestly I have been feeling things I've never felt since I got here." Like wanting two men all the time, I thought.

"I've felt the pull since the time I walked in to find half my brothers crowding around her." Chase said softly as he moved around me and went back over to the couch.

Troy nodded. "Yes, I felt it the very second she stepped into my office and threatened to slice Welsley a whole new life-style." Again, he looked carefully at me before returning his gaze to his sibling. "What happened last night? I don't mean to pry, I am just trying to understand this beyond reading it in books."

Chase dropped down off the arm and sat on the cushion. "Daxx offered to let me feed from her, she was curious I suppose." I blushed, Troy's face filled with envy, but he didn't say anything. Chase continued. "It was like nothing I've ever experienced, I was damn near intoxicated in no more than the span of a few seconds."

When Troy looked at me, his expression had softened. "Yes I can relate quite well to that."

I remembered when I helped Quinton.

"And then I was consumed with her, every pore in my body drove me and I couldn't seem to stop myself. I still don't know how I did," Chase finished in an odd tone.

"Nor I," Troy replied.

Shaking my head, I went back over and stood behind the chair. "Well, I for one am very happy you managed it. I just thought it was …" My brain kicked in and I immediately stopped talking. Chase grinned, but Troy once again looked down at the floor, his jaw tense.

"Are there any other questions you need answered, my queen?" Looking weary, Troy got up.

I didn't know what to ask first. "Thousands, but I can't seem to find just one."

"Feel free to call me anytime you like if you need an

answer to anything. I have to go deal with a few matters." He looked around at Chase, who nodded his agreement.

A phone rang out, with a sigh, Chase pulled his out of his pocket and got up and moved to the far side of the room before he answered it.

When I looked back, Troy was standing only a few inches away from me. Several emotions crossed his face before he spoke. "Are you still planning to come back and see more of my realm?"

"Yeah, why wouldn't I?"

He looked over at Chase and then back down at me with a pained expression in his eyes. "I don't see my brother handling that well."

I couldn't say I hadn't thought of the blood bond being a factor when I went back, I was actually hoping it would wear off with a little space. "Hey, we had a deal. I spend time here with him and then with you."

His eyes held mine with a look so serious I couldn't look away, "And then what, little Huntress?" His voice was soft and low, making shivers crawl all over my skin. I wasn't sure if that was a good or bad thing.

I shook my head. "Honestly, I don't know, Troy. My head is all over the place, I'm not even sure if it's attached most of the time lately."

"I can assure you it's still exactly where it should be." He touched his finger under my chin for a moment, something soft but unreadable in his eyes. "I will see you tomorrow." With a final glance at his brother, he turned and left the office before I could say anything else.

The door closed as Chase hung up the phone. I didn't even have to ask if something was wrong, I could feel what he felt.

"I'm afraid I may have to leave you on your own for your last night here, kitten. It seems I have restless followers to calm."

The sad note in his voice made me feel like I should go over and comfort him, again not something I generally did.

"That's okay; you do have some pretty serious obligations attached to you."

With a grin, he leaned back against the desk. "Like a fungus at times." He sighed. "I had hoped for a few quiet hours with you before tomorrow."

"It's those quiet times that could get us into trouble." I tried to joke, but couldn't pull off the carefree tone as well as I had hoped.

Raising his eyebrows at me, he walked over toward me. "A little trouble can be a good thing." His gaze moved over my face.

Like a coward, I looked down at the carpet. "Until it turns into tattoos and blood rites." When I glanced back at him, he was only a foot away, the chair between us.

"I've promised to behave." There was a wounded tone in his voice.

"I know, but I think we should give ourselves a little space until this blood bond thing wears off, it could be the factor that's making things ..." I motioned between us, not sure how to say it.

Chase chuckled. "You think it's the bond that almost made me mark you?"

I nodded.

"Hmm, it could be a small factor, but let me assure you, kitten, with or without it I'll still want you."

Butterflies took flight in my stomach with the way he was looking at me. What could I say to that?

Tucking his hands in his pockets, he offered a small smile. "We'll put your theory to a test then? Keep our distance for a few days and see how it plays out after."

I wanted to breathe a huge sigh of relief, but thought it might somehow be an insult to him. "Okay."

Kissing his hand, he blew me a kiss and then motioned to the door. "I really must go. Tim will take you back to your room or to watch a movie, whatever you choose."

CHAPTER THIRTY

When I woke up, I was surprised that I felt at without with that 'where am I?' feeling. That made me feel a bit better, considering I seemed to be sleeping in a different place every other night. Now if my body could just get used to living with day as night and night as day, I'd probably have this other realm life licked.

Chase hadn't made it back before I almost fell asleep in front of the giant TV screen. The fighting movie suddenly didn't seem so action packed compared to the last few days of my life.

After showering and taking my time drinking the awesome coffee Tim brought, I started to feel anxious and could only surmise it was because I was going back to Troy's half of Alterealm. There was the possibility, I thought, that it was because I was leaving Chase's.

When I started just roaming the halls, with Tim trailing me of course, I didn't really have a destination in mind but realized when I took a definite left at the last option I was heading towards Chase's office. I wanted to see him suddenly. My stomach did this odd tightening, not in a bad way, in a totally good way, the way it did when Chase kissed me. Licking my lips, I thought of his sensual kisses; they melted me from the inside out. I guess that means the anxious feeling was from leaving him.

When I reached his door, it was open about an inch so I took that to mean he wasn't in some serious meeting if the door wasn't closed. Pushing it open I walked in. The tightening turned to heat coursing through me, and I knew then the feeling wasn't my own at all, it was Chase's and it was pure lust. I clutched at my stomach when my own feeling overrode the shared ones from him the second I saw him.

He was leaning against his desk with his shirt open as a tall red head in a *very* short, skin-tight blue dress was pressed up against him, her hands running up and down his chest as she straddled his leg. Their eyes were locked and his were a yellow that I knew well enough what was going on. My stomach flipped and that feeling that was purely my own became nausea.

The redhead gasped as Chase lifted his head and snapped around to look at me. I stood where I was, not moving. He straightened and pushed her away so she was no longer touching him. She looked at me and then sighed and quickly walked out the door on the other side of the room.

Chase stood there, his shirt hanging open, his eyes had gone back to normal and I could guilt filling them. A haze filled my head and I was lost, not even able to voice how I was feeling. Forcing myself to look away from him, I turned to go back out the way I'd come in.

"Damariss, please don't walk away and leave it like this."

I could hear his foot-steps behind me and his hand closed the door over my head before I could get out it. Taking a deep breath, I turned and looked up at him.

"My brother is a great man and true King," he said softly his voice heavy with emotion. "He's everything I can't be due to circumstance I can't change." He moved away from the door and put a few feet between us. "I would give him anything of this earth, except you," with a shaking hand he ran it through his hair, "not like this."

I leaned back against the door, not sure if my legs were

steady enough without something to support me. I moved my eyes over him as he stood watching me. His shirt still hung open, there was lipstick on his chest and I had to force my eyes to move past it. His cheeks were flushed and I honestly didn't know if it was from him feeding or the woman that had been manhandling him. A sadness filled me. "I can't do this, Chase." I shook my head so he wouldn't speak. "I understand you have to feed on emotion but I can't accept *that*." I pointed to the door the woman had gone out.

"I don't always feed off sexual emotions. I just prefer it when time is short because it is the safest one, the one that I can't take too much from the other person."

I wanted to believe him, but there was that little feeling in my gut that I got when things weren't what they seemed. "Do you ever feed off males?" He jolted like I'd poked him in the gut instead of asked a question. "That's answer enough."

He stepped towards me and then stopped. "If you were with me I would only come to you."

My heart throbbed, I wanted to believe him, I really did.

"What if I'm on the other side for more than a day? You'd starve yourself? I can't be responsible for that, you're a ruler, your subjects depend on you."

"I would wait. A day won't harm me."

He started to move toward me but I couldn't do this. Turning, I swung the door open before he had a chance to say anything else. Quinton was on the other side of the opening and I launched myself at him into his arms before he could move out of the way.

Cradling me into his large chest, his big hand holding my head tight against him, he turned so I was sheltered away from his brother. "What did you do?" His tone was serious and quiet.

"She came in while I was feeding off of Sabina."

Quinton stiffened. "Alterealm's whore? You feed off the *whore*?" His voice was filled with disbelief.

I cringed knowing it was worse than I had thought.

Quinton tried to squeeze me tighter, but I moved out of his arms unable to be here a second longer. Closing my eyes, I thought of my apartment.

When I opened them, I was in the dim living room. Turning, I stumbled to my bedroom and threw myself on the bed.

I don't know how long I lay there in the dark but when I opened my eyes I could see Chase leaning against the wall by the window.

He came over and squatted down beside the bed.

"I'm sorry, Chase."

"So am I, kitten. Return soon, my brothers need you." Leaning over he placed a kiss on my forehead.

I closed my eyes and when I opened them to say something he was gone. Rolling over, I decided to lay there and wallow in self-pity for a while before I kicked myself in the ass for being such a ninny and got on with life again.

It wasn't like I had any say in what he did, right? We had no commitment, we had nothing. There was no reason to sit in the dark and listen to *Air Supply*. Seriously he was a grown man, a few hundred years kind of grown, he could feed and get his kicks too if he wanted. I wasn't going to condemn him for that. I just couldn't imagine kissing him, and all the bits that went along with that while knowing he filled his cravings with other women.

Laying there, I looked at it that way, and ten other ways, all close to the same. When another thought invaded my brain, it was clear that I had other things to consider. If that was truly something I couldn't live with for, oh, let's say forever than where did that leave me with the choosing which King to be mated with?

The choice was Troy. I didn't know how I felt about him at all. Aside from the heat between us, he wasn't much like Chase. He didn't do sarcasm, which in case I haven't mentioned it, is my favorite language. Troy wasn't real big on sharing his thoughts either, at least never that I'd experienced. He may seem like he was all laid back and calm, but from what I'd seen he was stiff and all aloof, in a Victor way. Could I live with that?

I really didn't think so.

What now? Sitting up, I looked around my, to be honest, crap hole of an apartment and wished for a long second that I'd never taken the job of chasing down a jumper named Wanda the Witch. Guilt filled me, as I accepted that if I hadn't, then *the balance* may have been seriously screwed and apocalyptic style events would have occurred. Yeah, I didn't want to be the cause of all that.

End result of all this deep thinking? I was a living *snafu* no matter which way I looked at it. Uttering about twenty of the first curses I could come up with, I got up and wandered back out into the living room. It was dimly lit by a street light. I didn't bother turning on a light, because it looked better in the dark.

A knock on the door had me spinning with my raptor in my hand before I could take another breath. Careful to avoid the floor boards that groaned and would give away that I was here, I made my way to the door and looked out the peephole. My heart beat settled when I saw Quinton on the other side, looking very pissed off.

Slipping the blade back in the holster, I sighed and unlocked the door. He came in without so much as a word and closed the door behind him. When he looked around, I could see the shell-shocked look as he appraised *my* home.

"Yeah, it's not Alterealm," I said quietly trying to lighten the tension that seemed to vibrate off him.

"Did Chase come to see you?" He stepped further into the room.

"Yeah." I moved past him and sat on the couch.

"Did he apologize?"

I sighed. "Yeah." He still stood there radiating pure anger. "He didn't do anything wrong, really, I was just…"

"Repulsed?"

I considered that word. "Unprepared," I said quietly.

With a loud sigh, he came over and sat down on the arm

of the chair across from me. His eyes moved over my face. "Are you coming back?"

Inside my head I was saying no, but my conscience wasn't going to let me take the coward's way out of this. "In a few days."

He nodded and then sat there silently for a lot longer than I was comfortable with. "I want to say it's not what it seemed like and tell you that you jumped to the wrong conclusion, but I can't lie to you." Rubbing the back of his neck, he finally looked back at me. "He was just feeding off her, Daxx."

I nodded. "I know."

"But you also know that's how he rolls isn't it?"

"Yeah."

He stood up again and looked around. "This is…"

"Worse than the wasteland?" I offered up.

"Yeah," he shook his head. "What is that smell?"

I sniffed the air and then shrugged. "Normal for here." I was pretty sure he was smelling the mix of my multinational neighbors and their preferred seasonings. It took a strong stomach to get used to the scent of Asian and Mexican cuisines mixing on the same floor.

"It's horrible." Tucking his hands in his pockets, he looked back at the door and then to me, a look of hesitation was on his face. "Uh, I didn't come alone."

Straightening, I glared at him and then looked at the door. "Who came?"

He cleared his throat. "Troy." I must have looked like I wanted to bolt for the window because he raised his hand and shook his head. "He just wanted to make sure you were alright." Rubbing the back of his neck again, he squinted at me. "Can he come in for a minute before he gives me a migraine?"

I'd forgotten about the way the brothers could nag one another from a distance. "I suppose."

When he turned to open the door, I got up and put as much space between me and it.

Quinton held the door for Troy to come in. With a small smile, he looked back at me. "I'll be back in a little bit." He left and closed the door before I could object and ask him to stay.

Troy stood there in the shadows, but I could still feel his eyes on me.

"There's no need for you to check up on me, I'm okay." In any other reality, I could hope that would be enough and he'd agree and leave, but I wasn't in the land of make believe tonight.

"Maybe I was just in the neighborhood and wanted to drop by and say hello."

I came close to doing a double take at his quip. Troy was the last brother I would have thought would try to make light of the situation. "I didn't realize you liked to slum."

"Mmm, it's a first for me." He stepped softly in my direction.

"How do you like it?" His steps were careful, like he was afraid I'd bolt in the other direction. It wasn't a bad idea, come to think of it.

"It's a unique experience thus far."

He was only a foot away now and I was still undecided whether I should move or hold my ground. Crossing my arms over my chest, I leaned back against the window frame. My nerves were humming.

"I'd like to apologize for my brother's actions, but it would be insincere, I cannot make excuses for something that has been his way for so long."

He stopped when he was close enough I could smell him. It was one of those smells that make you want to sigh, it was that good. "It's fine, really." I studied a dark spot on the floor.

"No, little queen, it is not fine." Reaching over he placed one finger under my chin and tipped my head back so I had no choice but to maintain eye contact. "Chase should have discussed things with you. I thought he had actually with the way you were together, with the way he was behaving."

"Well, even if he'd wanted to, our time was a little hectic with near death experiences and battles."

A light came into his eyes. "Yet, here you are rock steady and strong."

"For the most part." I swallowed the lump in my throat.

With a soft look on his face as his eyes explored mine he smiled. "I can't speak for all of my brothers, but I am filled with a great pride in knowing you, and seeing how you handle everything so confidently."

I raised my eyebrows, wondering at what point I'd been confident in anything I'd done recently, but I kept that to myself.

"I would like to ask you to come back but I don't think that's what you need right now."

If his voice became any softer, I thought for sure I was going to melt into a puddle at his feet. "I just need a little space for now."

"Of course." With a light caress to my cheek, he lowered his hand and stood there looking down at me. "Truthfully, are you alright?"

I wouldn't be if he kept standing there looking at me with that pained look in his eyes. I was girl after all, even though I was raised a little rough, I still had a heart for crying out loud. "Yeah." I croaked with my mouth so dried out I could barely swallow. "I just need to regroup, nothing serious."

With a soft sigh, he looked away from me briefly before turning those hazel eyes back on me. "I would like to discuss something with you that I feel may be required."

His regal ruler tone had returned and my stomach tensed. I may not have known him for long but I did know enough to get that if he was back in monarchy mode, I wasn't going to like the topic. "What's that?"

Clearing his throat, he stepped to the window and stared out. "I have to consider your safety at all times, even when you are on your own side."

"I'm fine when I'm over here."

Turning, he tucked his hands into his jeans and paused to consider his next words. "I am not certain you will ever be until Marcus is brought to justice."

I squeezed my eyes shut for a second. Why hadn't I thought about that? I had challenged the big bad face to face, of course he was going to be jonesing for a piece of revenge. "What are you thinking?" My guts twisted, I knew what was coming before he even said it.

"I think it would be best if you weren't alone while you're over here."

I groaned inside my head, *really* loud. He was right, but that didn't mean I had to like it. "Who did you have in mind?" I held my breath.

He actually grinned. "I believe the decision was made for me on this matter. Quinton has gone home to collect a few things."

The idea of Quinton hovering over me was way better than any of the others. "Fine."

A look of surprise filled his eyes, but he didn't say anything about it. "It's a good thing you agree with Quinton, because Arius was the other volunteer."

I cringed at the thought of trying to go anywhere with him on my side. We could dress him down into the grubbiest clothes around but with his pale grey eyes and long black hair there was no way he'd ever blend in. "I'm a little more comfortable with Quinton."

"I've noticed." He paced over to the bedroom door and looked in for a moment before turning. "Why is that?"

His question shocked me. I shrugged. "I'm...I don't know I just am."

"He's very protective of you."

Rolling my eyes, I moved away from the window and went and stood behind the couch feeling more at ease with a piece of furniture between us. "I've noticed that." He didn't move or say anything to that. "I feel safe with him. He feels like the brother I always wished I'd had."

"Anyone of us would keep you safe, Daxx." He almost

sounded offended.

"I didn't say he keeps me safe, I said he feels safe, comfortable."

With slow predatory steps, he moved back in my direction, stopping on the other side of the couch. Suddenly the couch didn't seem big enough to me. "You only feel comfortable with Quint?"

The tone in his voice reminded me of a child. "Well, no, Rafael is okay except he always wants to hug me."

There was long silent pause before he spoke again. "I see." He squinted at me. "I find myself wanting to be able to read your thoughts, to understand."

I for one was glad he couldn't read them. "What don't you understand?"

"Have I done something to offend you? Is that why you're not comfortable with me?"

Oh, so it wasn't about the brothers, it was about him. "No. There's just this …" I waved my hand around like I could pull the words out of the air, "vibe between us, it's a little intense at times."

"Wasn't there a *vibe*," he paused on that word for a second, "between Chase and yourself?"

Glancing at the door, I wished for Quinton to return, now. "It wasn't the same." Brushing my hair back from my face, I studied him. "I can't explain it, it's just a feeling."

"You tense every time we're in the same space."

"I hadn't noticed." I lied.

"Mmm, perhaps it's my mistake then." He pulled his phone from his pocket and sighed. "Please give me a moment." Opening it, he strode to the other side of the room. "I was in the middle of a conversation." He said with an annoyed tone into the phone. "No."

I looked around the room, like I shouldn't stand there and watch him talk.

"She appears to be fine." He glanced at me again. "Most likely."

His whole posture had changed since he'd been standing

in front of me. Now he stood there rigid, his shoulders tensed.

"In a few days." Closing his eyes, he pinched the bridge of his nose. "Quint will be staying with her. I know. I will." He flipped the phone closed and put it back in his pocket.

I looked at the door, what was taking Quinton so long to get back?

"I'm sorry about that. Chase wanted to make sure you weren't over here alone."

I tried to shrug it off. "I really think you guys are overacting, I doubt Marcus will be looking for me here." I motioned around the room.

Shaking his head, he came back over to me in a few strides, this time stopping on the same side of the couch. "I won't take a chance. In this you have *no* choice," he growled at me.

I'd had men go all alpha on me before and I usually had to stifle a laugh, but with him there was nothing funny about it. Alpha was something he aced without even trying. My heart trotted inside my chest and I wanted to tell him this was the kind of vibe I'd been trying to explain. Of course, my brain and body weren't on the same page. "I don't take orders gracefully, Troy." It was meant as a warning, but he didn't see it that way when he grinned down at me, moving close enough I could smell him again.

He grasped my chin with a firm hold, his eyes burning into mine. I couldn't have looked away if I tried. "Gracefully or not, I will not let anything happen to you and you *will* keep someone with you at all times."

I wanted to buck against this overbearing side of him, but the way his eyes moved over my face, like I was something precious had me pause.

"*Nothing* can happen to you." His voice was gravely, but his hold was still unmovable. "I spent well over a hundred years awaiting your arrival, needing to see for myself that you existed." I watched his eyes turn red, expecting him to step back with they did. He leaned closer. "There is *nothing* in this world or any other that will prevent me from keeping you whole and well." His hand gentled against my jaw. "Please obey me in this, my little queen."

I wasn't sure if it was a question or not, but he had just successfully disarmed me. There was no way I could bring myself to verbally agree to obeying anyone, but I wouldn't argue with him on it.

We stood there, his red eyes holding my own with neither of us blinking.

CHAPTER THIRTY-ONE

"Sorry I took so long…"

Jumping apart Troy and I spun to look at Quinton standing in the door.

Glancing down at the floor, Quinton cleared his throat. "Sorry."

"I was afraid you were packing to move in permanently." I tried for a light playful tone, but failed miserably with my shaking voice.

Quinton looked from me to his brother and then back to me again. "Uh, I could come back in a bit…"

"No, I need to get back." Troy gave me a quick once over and then moved over quickly to the door. "Call if you need me."

He was out the door so fast neither of us had a chance to say anything. Setting his bag on the floor, Quinton looked at the closed door and sighed. "I hope I didn't interrupt anything important."

Did he? I wasn't sure. "You didn't. We were just talking."

I avoided the doubting look he gave me and moved out to the kitchen. Chances of there being any sort of food was slim to pretty much never, I knew, but looking in empty cupboards was a great way to avoid having to talk about any of his brothers. "We're going to have to get some groceries, or …" I opened the small freezer on the top of the fridge, "we'll be on an ice cube diet."

A chuckle came from behind me. "It's all taken care of. Raf is going to bring us at least one good meal a day while we're here."

I can't even describe how happy that made me. Turning around I squinted at him. "Didn't trust the food on my side?"

"Actually, I've had some pretty tasty things when I've been here lately, but Mitz cornered me when I was coming out of my room." He shrugged. "When she offered, I wasn't going to offend her and say no."

I paused for a moment to check out how much of the small doorway he filled, which brought the next thought, where was I going to put him to sleep? My couch was what they called a three quarters size, meaning there was no way he was going to fit on it. "Can't have an offended Mitz," I finally replied.

"So, are we staying in tonight?" He looked around slowly, the look of hesitation on his face.

I tried not to grin. "I need to go check up on someone." I hoped he would blend in a little better than Troy had when we'd gone to the club looking for Wanda.

Relief filled his face. "Lead the way."

Going over to the closet, I reached in a grabbed my knife off the shelf. Strapping the leg strap to my ankle, I tucked it in and pulled my pant leg down. When I turned around he was grinning. "What?"

With the silly grin still on his face, he pulled his pant leg up to show me the knife strapped to his.

I went over and opened the door. "Just goes to show we're both smart." Pulling my phone out of my pocket, I dialed Crissy. If she didn't answer it could turn out to be a long night tracking her down, the girl had no definite home address and randomly picked one hidden location after another to call home for no more than a week at a time.

I couldn't even begin to explain Crissy, she was either the most screwed up person I know or a friggin genius that knew things the rest of us wouldn't be able to live with. I'd met her about five years ago, when she was trapped in an alley with a bunch of punks harassing her. I *persuaded* the pukes to back off and leave her alone. For the record, I didn't mean to break that one guy's nose.

Since that day, we had spent a lot of time together, I'd even managed to get her to stay at my place a few times. There were times she seemed perfectly normal, then other times not so much. She could see things, or this is what she told me, I'd never been able to substantiate any of these things though. Each to their own, right?

Unfortunately, she had a knack for being in the wrong place at the worst possible time. At least ten times I'd had to go to her rescue when she found herself in some kind of predicament that would scar most people for life. Gang wars, robberies, hostage situations and trapped in automated buildings during power outages to name a few. For this reason, I always followed my gut feelings when I felt I needed to check up on her. It usually meant something was up.

After trying the third time, I was ready to give up and start going to every odd place I'd found her in the past, then my phone rang and her number came up. "Criss, I was just starting to worry."

"Daxx," she whispered into the phone.

I stopped walking, knowing that tone all too well. Quinton almost walked right over me. "What's wrong?"

"There are so many of them now. I don't know what happened to change the balance but I am freaked out totally and I just don't think I can do this anymore."

I could barely hear her by the end of the sentence. "Criss, hold the phone near your mouth." I constantly had to remind her of this. "Where are you?"

I could hear rustling and had to wonder where the hell she was crawling into this time. "I stopped by the club earlier, thought maybe you would be around. You've been missing a lot lately, Daxx." More rustling, like paper being crinkled. "I couldn't take it tonight. So many…"

"Crissy. Where are you?"

Quinton now stood in front of me and the concern on his face reflected what I was feeling.

"Safe for now. No one sane would look for me here." She giggled.

Taking a deep breath, I tried to stay calm, having learned a long time ago that if you raised your voice to her, she shut down. "I thought maybe we could hang at my place. I have so much to tell you about what's going on."

"Ohh, you know, don't you? That's why you've been hiding too."

I looked up into the deep brown eyes glaring at me to hurry up and tell him what was going on. "I haven't been hiding, I've been away."

"Where did you go? Somewhere…" She stopped talking and I couldn't hear any sounds for several seconds. "Daxx, could you maybe find a few minutes to come and get me? I think they're looking for me."

I cursed to myself. "Happy too. Where are you?"

"The recycling dumpster behind the old fish place."

I knew I shouldn't be surprised, but she had managed to do it to me again. "Stay exactly where you are, I'll be there in ten minutes."

"Okay. Bye."

She hung up before I could say anything else. Nodding down the street, I looked up at Quinton. "We need to hurry." I started walking, knowing he wouldn't have any problems keeping up to me.

"Who was on the phone?"

"A friend." I was close to jogging and he didn't even look like he was walking fast, some things just weren't fair. "She's a little unusual, but harmless." I didn't know if that was even the right word to describe her.

"Is she in trouble?"

I grinned. "Crissy is *always* in trouble, without even

doing anything." As I picked up the pace, I hoped that this time it was just one of her paranoid problems and not a real one. My plate was already close to over-flowing, I didn't know if I had time for anything else.

****

When we reached the back of the building that used to be an old cannery for various disgusting fish by-products, I slowed down and looked around. There were a few cars, but no one in sight. Anything that went down in this area, wasn't legal so I knew I had to get Crissy and get us out of here. I motioned to the corner of the building. "Can you keep watch? If she sees anyone she'll bolt and I hate chasing her down."

He raised an eyebrow, but didn't comment. With a nod, he went over to where I pointed and stood with his back to me looking around. I looked around again and then went to the dumpsters at the far end. They had been here for a few years, which made me wonder what was in them. Even if the devil himself were chasing me, I wouldn't have gotten in one of them.

"Crissy? It's Daxx. All's clear out here."

I listened to the motion inside as she most likely uncovered herself and moved to get out. When I saw fire engine red hair clear the top, I breathed a sigh of relief. Of course, her hair had been purple the last time I'd seen her. One more thing I'd never quite understood about her. If she wanted to stay below anyone's radar, why did she always pick the brightest hair colors she could find? "Nice hair."

Her pale face peaked over the edge. "Do you like it? It makes me feel so daring." She smiled, her amber eyes huge with excitement.

I didn't bring up that someone daring wouldn't be hiding in a dumpster. Then again, who knew what was in there. I reached to help her get up over the side, shaking my head when I saw the little bits of paper clinging to her. When her feet finally hit the ground, she turned and hugged me.

"It's so great to see you."

The exception to the touchy feely hug thing, was with Crissy. You really didn't have a choice, you were going to get hugged a lot when she was around. I hugged her back quickly, noting that hidden beneath her baggy black jumpsuit her bones were sticking out. Criss was only a few inches taller than I was, but when standing beside her I looked almost on the plump side, which I wasn't. One of these days I'd figure out a way to get her to settle down long enough to eat.

She stiffened suddenly and backed away. Turning, I spotted Quinton standing where I left him. "Hey, it's okay. He's with me."

Sigh sighed and began to brush the paper off. "I thought *they* found me."

I flicked a few stray pieces off her shoulder. "Who?"

Straightening up, she looked all around us, paranoia filling her eyes. "I don't know, but I don't think they're from *here*."

Oh I really didn't have time for the aliens delusion she had more often than any of her other ones. "What makes you say that?"

I followed her over to a heap of old bins and watched as she moved them around and pulled out her bag. Crissy traveled with her whole world in a large tote bag.

"Their eyes—they're not normal."

The hair on the back of my neck stood up. Had she seen some of the missing Alterealm runners? "Are they bulging or in the side of their head, what's not normal?" I took the one bag out of her hand and started walking toward Quinton.

She began digging in the big purse she always wore across her chest. "I tried to draw them, but it didn't turn out very well…" Pausing she gave me bored expression, "and no they are not bulging or in the side of their head. They're right where eyes should be they just do this gleaming thing."

That told me precisely nothing helpful. Quinton turned around and waited for us to reach him. I stopped a few feet away from him, hoping Criss wouldn't notice anything about his eyes.

She stumbled and came close to landing at his feet. With a little smile, she looked him up and down. "I thought maybe you just looked big from over there, but you really are."

Quinton glanced at me and then smiled down at her. "I'm average size for my family."

Crissy turned and gave me a wide-eyed look. I nodded. "Crissy, this is Quinton."

He held out his hand and to shake and scooped up the bag in her other hand and slung it over his shoulder.

She took his hand for a nanosecond and then stepped away and looked at me. "I'd like to go to your place please."

I handed Quinton the other bag and took her arm. "Let's go. Then you can tell me what's going on."

Nodding, she glanced behind us. "I really don't want to talk about it until we get there." She looked the other way. "You never know who is listening," she whispered.

I watched the odd look cross Quinton's face, but he just nodded and kept walking.

CHAPTER THIRTY-TWO

With sad understanding eyes, Quinton watched Crissy eat with barely taking the time to breathe between bites. Looking down into the carton of noodles in his hand, he sighed and set them in front of her on the table. "I'm done, you can finish these if you want."

Criss's red head popped up, she swallowed. "Oh no, I don't think I can eat another bite." Then she lowered her head back over the container in her hand and took another bite.

Glancing at me standing by the window, Quinton's expression asked many questions. None I could really answer. "Criss, explain who is looking for you."

She took a drink and then nodded. "I don't know their names or *what* they are. I was hanging at the club, you know that's where I find out a lot, right?" She continued after taking another bite. "He's probably the scariest man I've ever seen, if he even *is* a man." Setting down the empty container, she picked up the one Quinton had set down. "He has long dark hair with this white streak in it and is just freaky to look at." I made eye contact with Quinton who tensed at the description. "He's been at the club a lot and he's not alone." She shook her head. "He has these really creepy guys with him and their eyes…" Taking another drink, she set the carton down and turned to look at me. "At first I thought it was some weirdo club and they wore contacts or something, but they're not always one color and I really don't think they've invented contacts that change color…" Looking from Quinton then back to me she scrunched up her face. "Do they?"

I wasn't about to lie to her outright so I just shrugged. "Okay, so why do you think they're after you?"

"Oh." Looking down at her clasped hands she played with her fingers, stalling for a few seconds. "There were two of them talking to the black haired one and I couldn't hear, I mean really as loud as it was even if they yelled I wouldn't be able to hear." She sighed, "but I was staring, I mean jeeze who wouldn't? They turned and looked right at me and I ran…" She slumped back on the couch. "They followed."

Jumping up she wandered around the room without actually looking at anything or pausing. "I lost them, barely. The weirdest part was the dark haired one just appeared in the front of me at one point and was waving his hands around like he was conducting an orchestra, it made me feel kind of woozy but I kept going and they didn't catch up."

My heart skidded to a halt inside my chest. Marcus had tried magic on her and it didn't work and she could see their eyes. I looked at Quinton, who had the same thoughts going through his mind if the expression was any indication. "Crissy, just give us a second okay? I think maybe we'll get one of Quinton's brothers to keep an eye outside for us."

Her eyes grew huge. "*Oh*, that's a good idea. They could have followed us all along." She went over and looked out of the window.

Motioning to Quinton I walked into the kitchen. He was right behind me. I grabbed the front of his shirt so he'd lean down. "Should she be able to see their eyes?" He shook his head. "How can she?"

"I don't know. From the sounds of it Marcus tried to use a spell on her too and it didn't work." He glanced out to where she stood. "Is she always like this?"

My guts were tense; I wrapped my arms around my waist. "Yes. She's been seeing weird shit since she was a kid, things that sound so farfetched, but for some reason I believe she sees them."

"She seen Marcus and his crew."

I nodded. "Call Rafael and get him to find somewhere to hide out in this neighborhood and keep an eye out. I'm going to see if I can persuade her to take a shower and rest. Who knows when the last time was she's slept."

Quinton touched my arm. "Daxx, we need to fill in Troy and Chase or at the very least Victor."

I groaned inside. "I know, but I don't think she's going to deal very well with a room full of you guys right now."

We both looked out to see her peeking out the window again.

Quinton nodded. "You're right. I'll go meet Raf somewhere nearby and call Victor. We'll take it from there."

"Okay."

****

Getting Crissy to pause long enough to take a shower and lie down was a lot like trying to get a child with A.D.D. that was hyped up on sugar to sit down and be quiet. By the time Quinton returned I was ready for a nap.

He paused in front of the bedroom and raised his eyebrows when he looked in to see her lying on the floor with the bed between her and the window. I shrugged for an answer.

Going into the kitchen, I leaned back against the counter so I could keep an eye on the bedroom. "Where's Rafael?"

"Across the street near the roof." He rubbed the back of his neck. "Victor's working on getting someone on the inside with Marcus at the club so we can hopefully find out where he's hiding."

"That could take a few days." I glanced at the woman on my bedroom floor. "I don't know if I can keep her in one place that long."

"I had a hell of a time talking Victor and Michael out of

coming here to talk to her." He looked over his shoulder to where I was watching. "Is there any way we could explain to her about Alterealm that wouldn't send her over the edge?"

"I don't know," I whispered having thought the same thing a few times in the last few hours.

"Troy is pissed. He wants you back on our side. Now." He said it in a hesitant way.

Tucking my hands in my pockets, I gave him an amused look. "Did you tell him no?" He nodded. "Good. I'm not going back and leaving her here when Marcus is hanging out in my own neighborhood."

"Yeah I told him the same thing." He looked back at Crissy. "She's a little off, but I like her and don't want to see anything happen to her."

"I have an idea on how to get her to stay here for a while, but I have to go out to get some things."

He raised his eyebrows at me.

"I know, but I want you to stay here in case she wakes up so you can keep her here."

Shaking his head, he crossed his arms over his chest. "Write me a list, Raf can keep an eye on things from where he is."

I glared at him, even though I agreed with the idea that I shouldn't go wandering around alone right now. "Fine." Turning I dug around in a drawer for something to write on. Then all I had to accomplish was how to explain to Criss what was going on, without actually telling her what was going on.

****

It was just a little over an hour when Crissy came wandering back out, she looked sleepy still, I knew if she felt safer she'd probably sleep a lot longer. I'd been in that position more than once, so I couldn't say too much to her about it.

She dug around in her bag and pulled out a small container. Moving past me, she went out into the kitchen and put the kettle on.

Getting up, I tried to look relaxed when I followed her in, I was anything but. "Couldn't sleep any longer?"

Shaking her head, she shrugged. "I think I'm just programmed now to have short rests when I can."

Leaning on the doorframe I nodded. "Yeah, I get that." I watched her make her tea for a few minutes. "Quinton ran out to get some things for me." Clearing my throat, I tucked my hands into my pockets and stared at the floor. "I need to talk to you about everything that's going on."

She turned, her eyes searching my face. "You *know* something." There was accusation in her voice but not in a bad way. Sighing loudly, she picked up the cup and moved out into the living room. "Tell me." Sitting down, she turned and watched me with eager eyes.

I went out and perched on the arm of the chair across from her. "I don't know where to start really. I haven't been around for the last little bit because I've been with Quinton and his family…" I watched her closely, "where they live."

As she sipped the tea, I could see her processing what I'd said. If I knew her she would be analyzing my tone and what words I paused on. It was just one more thing she had going for her. "He's not from here either, is he?"

How did I explain that? "Not really." It seemed like a safe answer. "Neither are the guys you saw at the club."

Her eyes widened. "Oh, is Quinton here to get them? He's the good guy, right?"

I smiled. "Yes, he is."

There was a knock on the door and both of us almost hit the floor. Holding my hand up to her, telling her to stay put I went over, my raptor already in my hand. When I peeked out the hole, I was so relieved to see Rafael looking back at me. "It's okay, Criss, it's one of Quinton's brothers." Opening the door, I let him in and then closed and locked it again.

Rafael looked down at me and then past me to the red-head now kneeling on the couch staring at him. He smiled at her and honestly all I could think was the baby in the royal family was a real player.

Criss smiled back at him and stood up. She glanced at me briefly before she walked towards him. "Is Quinton like the guys at the club?"

Rafael gave me an uneasy look.

"In a way, at least they're from the same place."

She stopped right in front of Raf and stood on her tippy toes so her face was closer to his. "Can your eyes change too?"

He slid me a curious look and I nodded. "Yes, they do."

"Can I see?"

I was a little shocked she was being this forward, then again it was Rafael and when he wasn't in battle he was a real charmer with that lovable demeanor of his.

Rafael nodded and stared down at her. I didn't need to see his eyes to know they were now red because her gasp told me they were. She grabbed his face and pulled his head down closer.

Not used to that kind of reaction, Rafael smiled and Crissy gasped again. I stepped closer to see her run her finger over his fangs.

"Well," she looked at me, "it's sexy."

My jaw dropped right around the same time Raf looked over at me with a very pleased expression on his face. This was not the reaction I expected from Crissy, at all. Clearing my throat, I tried to redirect things back to something a little less strange. "Raf, was there a reason you came?"

He blinked and the red eyes were gone. Criss still stood there looking at him with awe on her face. Straightening away from her hold, he turned, with a goofy grin on his face. "Quint told me to meet him here." He shrugged, "so here I am."

"The eyes on those men were yellowish, some kind of green I suppose, well except the scary man, his were the coolest purple I've ever seen." Crissy touched her hair. "If I could find that shade for my hair I would do it." Shaking her head, she studied Rafael with a puzzled look on her face. "Does the eye color differentiate who is good and who is bad?"

With a serious look on his face now, Rafael turned to look back down at her. "No, it doesn't. Are all blue-eyed people on your side good looking?" She shook her head. "It's what's inside that makes us good or bad, not our eyes."

She smiled up at him. "Good to know." With slow steps, she walked around him, looking him up and down. "Is everyone from where you are from so big?"

He shrugged, that playful grin on his face once more. "Not everyone."

Criss spun around and looked at me with her hands on her hips. "It all ties into your tattoo, doesn't it?"

How she got from eyes and size to my tattoo, I will never understand, but then again that was how Criss's mind worked. "Yeah, actually as weird as it is, it does."

Criss jumped a few feet in the air and clapped her hands excitedly. "I *knew* it was destiny that placed it there." With a quiet chuckle, she turned again and then went into the bedroom to dig around in her bag.

Rafael looked at her for a moment and then over to me. "*Who* is she?" He asked quietly.

I leaned against the back of the couch and crossed my arms over my chest. "I don't know. She's always been different, but this is the first time what she's saying makes sense."

Standing with his hands on his hips, he studied her. "I've never seen her so I don't have any insight." He gave me an odd look. "Troy might be able to peek and see where it all stems from."

I wasn't sure I was comfortable with that idea at all. "I think for the time being keeping her safe is more important." I paused, wondering how the hell we were going to manage that. "Any idea why Quinton wanted you back here?"

Shaking his head, he wandered over to the window to look out over the street. "No. He didn't say."

Criss came bouncing back from the bedroom, a notebook in her hand. She almost tripped to land in front of

Rafael. "I just realized I didn't even introduce myself." She held out her hand. "I'm Crissy, well actually its Cristy but I am *so* not a Cristy type."

Another one of his soft grins appeared on his face as he took her hand in his. "Rafael."

She actually stood there and let him hold her hand for a minute before pulling it free. "You are filled with so much goodness, it's so nice for a change." With that, she turned and went over to the couch and dropped down, opening the book and began writing in it.

Sending me a curious look, he leaned back against the wall and watched her for a minute. "You can sense what's inside a person?"

At first I didn't think she heard him but then her red head popped up and she nodded. "Uh huh." She frowned. "I don't know how really, it's just been something I have done since I was a kid." A pained look crossed her face. "It's taxing at times, with the way the world is, so much bad out there…" Lowering her head, she went back to her notebook.

So many little pieces were clinking into place inside my mind. The reasons behind Criss and the way she was. If I could sense good and bad, I would lock myself up somewhere and never come back. What she must go through just to hang out anywhere public, I shuddered.

Going over, I sat on the table in front of her. "Criss, I need you to do something for me. It might take a few weeks of your time…"

Lifting her face from the book she smiled. "Anything for you, Daxx." She smiled. "I think I probably owe you a few."

I laughed. "Oh, maybe." Looking down at the notebook, I wondered what she was writing but focused my mind back on the topic I wanted to discuss with her. "If I set you up with my laptop, would you be able to do some serious research for me? It could go back hundreds of years actually."

She frowned and studied me for a minute. "You're looking for someone."

Surprised yet once more, I sighed. "Yeah."

"Does it have to do with the scary guy and what's going on there?" She held up a hand. "I don't want to know what he's up to by the way." She shuddered.

Shaking my head, I clasped my hands and leaned forward. "No it's not. I need you to find a certain type of story for me. Strange ones like a man never aging or being accused of oddities like being a vampire ..." I really didn't know how to explain it. So far she'd handled things pretty well, but saying I needed to find a three hundred year old man even sounded crazy to me.

Leaning forward, she considered what I was saying. "Vampires are real."

Rafael moved over and stood there with his arms crossed over his chest. "The man we're looking for isn't a vampire, but he may have been accused of being one over the years."

With a serious look on her face she studied Rafael for a moment. "This man is lost to you?" Raf nodded, a pained look on his face. "Do you know his name?"

With a sigh, he shook his head. "No. His mother's last name was Brown, that's all we know."

I rubbed my temples. With a last name like that it made the search a thousand times harder. Why couldn't it be an unusual last name? "It's going to be tedious."

She grinned. "I will have to clear my full schedule then." She turned sad brown eyes to Rafael. "I'll try to find him." She raised her eyebrows in an odd way. "How far back am I looking?"

I looked at the floor and spoke to it. "Three hundred years?"

She chuckled. "I don't want details. The more I know the more trouble finds me." Getting up she went back into the bedroom.

"Okay." Sighing I got up and went over to the window. "Quinton should have been back by now."

Rafael cleared his throat. "I believe he was summoned by our Kings for a little *talk*."

I held my breath waiting for him to tell me Troy or Chase were on their way here. Neither I wanted to see right now.

"I have Leone outside, if that's what you're worried about."

Turning to look out the window I shook my head. "No. I didn't think you'd leave us vulnerable." I felt him move up behind me.

"I'm sorry for the way things went, little huntress."

My shoulders slumped. "It's no one's fault, Raf, some things are just meant."

CHAPTER THIRTY-THREE

For three days, we stayed at my place. Raf and Quinton were the only Alterealm residents I had to face, but I was beginning to feel like a coward. I had to go back at some point and face things. I knew this.

Crissy was completely engrossed in hunting down the missing brother. In a few day's time she had lists and references and was on her way to actually finding out the mother's name. Modern technology was a very good thing, if you knew where to look and apparently she did. Keeping her busy also kept her in the apartment and safe. I wished I had of thought of finding something to do with her brain before. She didn't look as antsy either.

Somewhere along the way I decided I was going to let her continue to stay here when I was on the other side. If I let myself believe the prophecies I would be spending more time away than home in the future, and knowing she was looked after made me feel more settled with the idea.

We were no further ahead finding Marcus, and the longer we spent tracking him down the more I worried that something catastrophic was going to happen before we could do anything about it. Then again, tracking is what I did, and here I was hiding in my apartment so I was partially to blame for things idling.

I'd been forbidden to work for Frank. I wasn't all for the being ordered to do things, but in this case, I allowed it to slide by. Keeping Criss safe and finding Marcus was more important than a few bail jumpers. Of course, the fact that the brothers were footing my bills right now made me very uncomfortable, but again when things weren't so crazed I'd deal with that.

When Quinton and Rafael were ordered back to the other side, I knew my time was up, I'd have to go back. One of Troy's guards was placed on watch outside and Crissy was set up with enough food to feed three of her for a week. With Quinton and my numbers on speed dial.

Reluctantly, I said goodbye and told I'd be back soon and then went for a walk to the treed area in the park.

Thankful that I knew my way around a little better, I ducked into the kitchen hoping to grab some leftovers from Mitz. I was hooked on her cooking. She's replaced that soft spot in my heart that the little deli down my block had held for the last two years.

As I stepped in the door Mitz looked up long enough to see who it was and then pointed to the plate sitting heaped with food. It made me wonder if she had the gift of sight and just hid it from everyone.

I dug into the amazing eats and did a mental moan as I chewed. It was that good.

"He's a good man you know."

Pausing with the fork in front of my mouth, I glanced at her. "Who?"

"Chase. He'll be hurting that he upset you." She continued polishing the silver dish she held, barely glancing in my direction.

Setting the fork down, I watched her for a few minutes. "It wasn't meant to be. Some things can't be undone."

She nodded. "I know. He doesn't like to harm, that's why he selects women, for the most part."

"Mitz…"

Sighing, she waved a hand at me. "I know, love. I just

worry over him because he's on that side and his family is here. I think everyone does and that's why they silently hoped you'd choose him." She set the dish aside and studied me. "He was different with you here. I still can't believe he gave you his blood, he's never done that before." She smirked. "He swore he never would."

I swallowed down that bit of information for later. "I haven't chosen anyone."

Moving over to the fridge, she pulled out a Dr. Pepper and brought it over to me. "I know. Troy is going to be harder to get close to you know."

"Why do you say that?"

She smiled and it was one of those that meant she had secrets. "He keeps everything close to his heart, love. I just thought you should know."

"Well, thanks." I took a sip of the pop. "They all at practice now?"

Nodding, she moved back over to the counter.

"Maybe I'll go get a workout with them." I stood up.

"Don't hurt anyone."

With that puzzling conversation floating around in my head, I made my way to the gym. Next to Mitz's food this was my favorite thing, I had missed it. Horsing around with Quinton at the apartment wasn't the same at all. Watching eight men mix it up with each other was a sight to behold. I still hadn't fought them all, but today was a new day and maybe I'd get lucky and test out some of the things Chase has drilled into my moves.

When I opened the door, I stopped and just stood there. This was a little different then what I'd expected to see. The backs of six large men was all I could see. I could hear the grunts and clang of metal on metal. Maybe they were checking out something new and deadly.

Pushing my way between Quinton and Rafael, I froze when I finally found out why they were just standing there. It was new weapons, it was the real steel ones and they were being wielded by the twin kings—against each other. It only took me about ten seconds to know that they were dead serious about trying to slice and dice the other. From the looks of the sweat coating them, this had been going on for quite a while. Both had death in their eyes and guilt swamped me. Only a woman could come between two otherwise rational men. Me.

I elbowed Quinton, he looked down at me with worry in his eyes.

"Why are you guys just standing here watching?"

He clenched his jaw a few times before he answered. "We were ordered to stay out of it."

I shoved my way past him, heading to the wall of weapons. "They may be your rulers, but they're still your blood!"

Grabbing a real pair of Sais off the wall, I tested the weight of them in my hands and then stomped in the direction of the men three centuries old that were acting like they were twelve.

Troy had a cut on one arm that was deep enough that blood dripped onto the mat, from the looks of it his face had taken a few blows as well. Chase didn't seem to be fairing any better with a slice in the front of his shirt and fat lip. Both were so intent on the other that they had no idea what was going on around them. I watched the angle of the swings and blocks as I moved closer, if I screwed this up there would be two pieces of me.

Dropping below their swing level, I sprang up between them as they both rounded back for another swing. The tips of the Sais came to chest level on each chest, just below their collar bones. Both giant men paused in mid swing and looked down at me like they were shocked. "Can anyone join this party or is rampaging testosterone the prerequisite?"

Chase knocked the Sai away from his chest and tossed his broadsword to the floor. I watched him for a second until the shame filled his eyes before turning to the other man at the end of my blade.

Troy wasn't so quick to knock the threat away from his

body. He dropped the sword and then just stood there looking down at me, I wasn't sure what was going through his mind but there was no shame or embarrassment in those hazel eyes. When he placed his hands on his hips and took a deep breath trying to catch his breath, I lowered the weapon.

"What the hell are you two doing?" I looked from one to the other, still not sure if I should let them off that easy or bop them both with handle of the metal in my hands.

"It's an off day." Chase said breathlessly.

I snorted. "Yeah, well when I have an off day, I go take a nap and remove myself from having a tantrum on someone. I do not try to beat the bejeezus out of my brother."

"You don't have a brother." Troy said, still looking at the floor.

"A good thing for him that he doesn't exist if this is how I'm supposed to treat him then isn't it?" A snicker came from the pack of brothers hanging back. I turned and glared at them. "You aren't much better, standing here letting them beat on each other like you're all in a school-yard and took each other's favorite swing." The six men looked guilty enough so I turned back to the sweat covered kings, who still wouldn't look at each other.

Shaking my head, I went back over and put the Sais back on the wall. Trying to collect my thoughts, I stood there looking at it for a moment. When I spun around I glanced at the six brothers that were watching their rulers with wary looks. "You guys get out of here." Troy and Chase both looked at me. I grinned. "The two of you get to stay."

I waited until the door closed behind the slowly retreating siblings before I went back over to them. "What the hell happened?"

Chase's eyes moved over my face as if he was making sure I was okay. "He seems to think I did that with Sabina on purpose to send you running."

"That's ridiculous." I looked at Troy, he was glaring at his twin.

"You have *no* idea what you threw away." Troy growled

over my head.

Chase's entire composure changed. He looked at me, his angry, pain filled eyes moving over me before they flicked back to his brother. "I didn't *throw* her away! I God damned know what I lost!" Spinning on his heal, he strode from the room without looking back.

I stood there not sure what to do or say next. I was a little embarrassed that I'd come between two brothers, and a little pissed that they behaved that way *and* made speechless by Chase's comment. Sighing, I turned back to Troy and raised my hands in question. From Chase I expected impulsive behavior, but Troy always seemed so calm and methodical.

He blew out a long breath. "I didn't set out to beat the hell out of him," he admitted quietly.

Moving over I checked out the gash on his arm. "I think he got a few good swings in."

Glancing down at his arm he shrugged. "That he did." Turning on his heel he took a few steps toward the door and then stopped and looked back at me. "I didn't think you were coming back."

Tucking my hands in my pockets, I studied him for a moment. A sweat covered Troy was an appealing thing, or at least it was to me when my insides tightened. "I said I needed a bit of time. I didn't anticipate Crissy when we talked about it."

He nodded. "I would still like to meet her. The chance of her knowing the things she does make me curious."

"Me too, but she's a bit flighty. I don't want to put her before the overwhelming group of you and your brothers just yet."

He smirked. "You dealt with it fairly well."

I had to smile. "Well, my sanity has always been in question."

He didn't comment, just turned and walked out.

Turning, I looked around the empty space, an odd feeling coming over me. I had the strange feeling of home and yeah, my only thought to that was *crap*.

****

Shaking my head, I glanced away from the huge map of my neighborhood and looked over at Michael. "If you look at where the alley is that we beat them down in and follow it back to the club, there's a lot more places to look than just my neighborhood."

Moving away from the papers he'd been flipping through, he came over and crossed his arms and looked at the marked map. "We thought of that too, but so far no luck anywhere we check."

"Can Clairee or any mage do something? Like a seeking spell or… whatever?" I really had no idea if that was even possible, but hey it was worth a shot, right?

He rolled his eyes in my direction, looking bored. "Don't you think we haven't thought of that? They can find anything."

I bit my lip. "Is it possible a spell is hiding them?"

"More probable than possible."

I went over and leaned against the desk, scowling at the map on the wall. "So, someone that can see through Marcus's hoodoo needs to go looking."

Michael's back stiffened but he didn't turn. "It could be the reason we aren't finding anything."

Victor came into the room and just stood there looking from one of us to the other.

I took a deep breath and pushed away from the desk. "I can go start checking places out…"

Michael spun and glared at me. "Absolutely not." He ran a hand through his hair looking crazed. "Troy would have my ass if I allowed such a thing."

I shrugged. "As *the* huntress it's my call, not his."

Michael turned and looked at Victor, hoping for back up.

Victor looked down at his hand like he needed to examine something on it. "She is right," he said calmly.

Moving with stiff motion back to his desk, Michael sat down and shook his head. "I am so not telling him."

I glanced between the brothers for a moment, wondering what I'd missed while being away. "Isn't it my job to track him down? Why would Troy care how I have to do it?"

Michael snorted out a weird noise. "Oh, I don't know maybe the fact that you've turned from Chase narrows down the options to only him..."

Going over I slammed my hand on the desk. "First, I haven't decided a damn thing! Second if it's my choice I could choose neither in the end." I spun and looked at Victor. "I could choose Victor if my heart desired and no one can say a word." Victor looked like I'd just stabbed him in the chest rather than used him as an example.

He cleared his throat. "As interesting as all of this is..." He glared at Michael like it was his fault. "I was sent by Mitz to get you, my Queen." With a hesitant expression, he looked at me and then to the floor. "It seems you have a dress fitting."

Completely disarmed I straightened and gave him a wide-eyed look. "A dress fitting?"

He nodded quickly. "The kings have decided the welcoming dance is to happen in two days, before we go to battle again or some other incident postpones it and Mitz is in a huff because they aren't giving her enough time..."

They couldn't have shocked me more if he'd announced the Easter bunny was waiting in my room. "Really? We're putting Marcus on hold to play dress up?"

His lips quirked, but he didn't smile. "It seems so."

I looked from Michael, who was intently studying the floor, back to Victor who looked too amused for his own good. "We'll see about this."

I stomped all the way to Troy's office and went in without so much as a knock. Chase was standing beside his desk. They both turned, looking surprised to see me.

"Great, just the men I wanted to see." I paused long enough to check out Chase's face to see if his injuries were gone. They were. "What is this crap about having a dance when we should be out there tracking Marcus's ass down and locking him in a box in Timbuck-fucking-too?"

Chase gave his brother an odd look. "I told you she wasn't going to let it slide quietly. Although I expected time to escape before she got here."

Troy stood up, giving his brother an annoyed look. "Colorful description." He tucked his hands in pockets and stared at me. "Everyone from Alterealm is getting more restless by the minute, a dance in celebration of the arrival of the long-awaited Huntress may help to reassure and strengthen our subjects."

I stood there glaring at him, noticing Chase stepped back out of the path of our eyes locked together. I really, *really* didn't want to admit he had a point and could be right. That would have pissed me off more. "In two days?" He inclined his head in that aggravating regal way. "Fine. In the meantime, I'm going back to my side. Michael and I have figured Marcus is hiding their location with magic..." Troy visibly tensed. "...and because it doesn't work on me, I will be able to see through it."

Chase stepped back beside his brother. "What about your strange friend, I was told she can see through it too."

I sent him my best death look. "If you met Crissy, you wouldn't even suggest something like that."

Troy leaned over the desk. "I agree with that, bringing anyone else into this more than your friend already is, would be a mistake." He paused and took a deep breath. "What are you suggesting, Daxx? That we allow you to..."

I stepped over to the desk and leaned so my face was a few inches from his. "Allow? Did I miss something? Am I servant now? Or maybe you've adopted me and are my new dad?" Chase hissed out a breath and lowered his head without a word.

Troy looked confused. "No, you are neither a servant nor my *daughter*..." A lethal look appeared in his eyes as they bordered on turning red. "Your safety..."

"Is. Not. Your. Problem." I pushed away and paced, trying to resist the urge to smack him. Hard. "I am in charge of what I do and my own safety. Period." I spun back and glared before he could reply. "Stands *equal* with the thrones ring a bell here?" Glancing at Chase, I could see he sided with his brother on this, but he was apparently a lot smarter and knew when to keep his mouth shut.

Troy's jaw snapped shut and he straightened to study me for what felt like hours when it was probably just a few seconds. "We will…"

Shaking my head, I crossed my arms over my chest. "Not be coming with me. I'll take someone with me, but I am choosing who."

Troy looked to his brother, silent communication taking place. Turning he inclined his head again. "Very well. Who?"

I chewed on my lip, trying to decide who would be the easiest to work with. Any one of the royal brothers would drive me nuts right now. "Tim." I said with a nod.

Chase's eyebrows rose.

Troy frowned. "Who the *hell* is this Tim? Your first words while lying there bleeding out was concern for him." His eyes were red now.

Chase tucked his hands in his pockets and gave me an amused look. "Tim is the guard whose life she was protecting when she was hurt. He was her personal guard while she was on my side."

Troy's jaw clenched as he studied his brother for a moment. "Is he to be trusted to protect her if she almost died protecting *him*?"

Something close to being offended crossed Chase's face. He didn't like his brother doubting his decision making. "He is the most skilled of all my guards. When Daxx was hurt the circumstances were unpreventable." He looked at me for a second, regret filling his eyes. "They are very in sync with each other during a fight."

Troy stood there, looking down at his desk. "Very well. *Tim* will accompany you while you search out Marcus' location."

I wasn't entirely sure what just happened, but I'd take it.

"Great. Now apparently, I have to go have a friggin dress fitting ...whatever that is."

With an amused glint in his eyes Chase looked me up and down. "I'm sure Mitz will dress you in good taste."

I sighed. "Yeah, that's what I'm afraid of." With a cold glare at Troy, I turned and walked out of the room. I couldn't even remember when I'd been in a dress last, but it must have been when I was a child because I didn't even own a dress that I knew of.

CHAPTER THIRTY-FOUR

I resisted the urge to yank at the neckline of the dress, even though it took every ounce of willpower to not to. The dress that Mitz had gotten all teary eyed over, and guilted me into wearing, was *the* most uncomfortable contraption I'd ever worn in my life. I stood there, staring at the mirror wondering who the hell the chick was looking back at me. Okay, so I looked good, but that didn't mean I had to like it.

Mitz and her crazy friend had done something with my hair that made it look soft and wispy. I still doubted wispy was a real word. Of course, it had hurt like hell to have them both attack my head like it was a life or death quest. Now my hair had been curled, teased, pinned and sprayed and the end result was I looked…regal with curls hanging down and the rest all bunched up on top of my head. Who knew this was possible?

My shoulders were bare, hence the wanting to hike up the low neckline or bodice as I'd been corrected by Mittz. The *bodice* was too low. I was told it was entirely necessary to have my tattoo showing very plainly. Fine but what good shoving my boobs up did for my back I had no idea.

I was thankful that the color wasn't pink or this other peachy color Mitz's friend had tried to hoist off on me. It was a royal blue and that was the only thing I liked about it.

Well, okay I like that it wasn't poofy too. I had worried they were going to stick me in something that made me look like I was wearing a lampshade from the waist down. Instead it was gathered at my waist and fell straight down from there.

Lifting the edge, I looked down at the shoes again. I had refused the life threatening four inch heels that looked like nails with sparkly straps attached to them and insisted something that was dark blue and that actually covered my whole foot, explaining it would be more beneficial. Couldn't have the long-awaited huntress making her grand entrance by falling on her face, now could we?

Taking a deep breath, I held it and looked at the overall picture again. Yeah, I did look damn good. Even the earrings were kind of cool. Mitz had explained I was to wear one of Chase's emblems and one of Troy's so I had a moon dangling in one ear and sun in the other—which set things off balance just enough that I was comfortable with it. The necklace was a on a fine silver chain and had both emblems on it as well. I was informed they had been crafted for me and me alone hundreds of years ago. How did someone refuse something like that?

A knock on the door had me finally turning from the mirror. "Come in."

Quinton peaked in the door and then froze. He pushed the door open and just stood there staring at me. Taking a deep breath, he turned and spoke to someone in the hall. "We're going to need more guards."

I frowned, not sure why he would say that, but before I could question it, Rafael stuck his head in the door and whistled.

"Damn." He gave me his best player smile.

Okay that, I understood, especially coming from Alterealm's very own playboy. I smiled and looked down at myself. "It's not too much?"

Quinton finally stepped in, he looked really great in his black tux. "It's too much alright, but not in a bad way." Taking my hand, he spun me around slowly. "We're going to have to flank you through the whole thing so no one paws at you."

I patted my thigh and smirked. "Let them try."

Rafael shook his head. "Let me guess your cute little knife is strapped on?"

I snorted. "Only time I don't wear it is when I'm naked."

He cleared his throat. "Shall we go?"

I tensed. "If we have to. Walk slow dammit, these shoes are the dumbest idea yet."

As we headed into the hallway, Quinton tucked my hand in his and grinned at Rafael. "Our brothers are going to pass out when they see her."

Raf nodded. "Michael better have the camera handy."

I looked from one to the other. "What are you talking about? How did you two get elected to escort me?"

Quinton patted his chest. "I found you. First dibs was mine."

I rolled my eyes and looked at the other man, he smirked. "I won the toss."

"The toss? With who?" I decided men were still boys no matter how many hundreds of years old they grew to be.

"Arius." Rafael said with a big grin, "and he wasn't pleased."

Deciding there was too much testosterone suddenly choking me, I changed the subject. "So where is this being held and how many are going to be there?" I knew it was almost dusk, which mean both sides were up.

"At the big pavilion. It's not used much anymore, but back in the day it was for festivals and celebrations." Quinton glanced at Raf, they both had a longing look on their faces. "Everyone from both sides are invited, unless they're imprisoned or guarding those that are."

I swallowed. Everyone? Why had I thought it was only close family and friends? "Any protocol I need to be aware of?"

"Hey, little one, this is your night. If you want to dance

around naked and throw food that's your right." Quinton tensed and looked down at me. "You won't though, right?"

I swallowed the smile trying to come out. "Throw food? Never."

He raised one eyebrow at me and then stopped while Raf opened the outside door. When we stepped through the large arch I froze and stared. A large fancy carriage with four huge horses was waiting for us. Was I in a fairy tale and had been transformed into freaking Cinderella and no one had told me? Beside it stood Tim and Welsley all dressed up in tuxes as well.

Tim smirked and raised both eyebrows at me. "My queen," he said softly and bowed his head.

My stomach clenched, knowing I was going have to suffer through all the formality for the duration. The only thing to get me through was knowing when it was over I was off to hunt down a certain scum magician.

Welsley bowed his head and then straightened and gave me a curious look. "I am surprised you don't have a knife strapped to your waist."

I gave him a big grin and winked. "Nope, but that doesn't mean I don't have one somewhere."

He gave Quinton a strange look. Quinton laughed. "She *is* the huntress, remember?"

Shaking his head, Welsley opened the carriage door and motioned for us to get in.

By the time the carriage came to a stop my nerves were wound so tightly I wanted to tell them the whole thing was off. Wouldn't a mock battle or something be more appropriate to announce the arrival of their huntress? I thought so, of course Quinton had only laughed and hugged me when I suggested it.

Glancing out the window my heart jumped up to sit in my throat. The pavilion was an enormous covered area the size of a football field. And under it were hundreds of people. Just focus on the hunt afterward, I told myself as we stepped out onto the ground. Pasting on a phony smile, I nodded to Quinton and then looped my hand through his and Raf's elbows.

Talk about being put in the spotlight. We walked slowly down a path as the people parted on both sides of us. It was all a blur to me, one face after another. Looks of shock, admiration and amazement were on all the faces we walked by. I had never been so uncomfortable in my life as I was at this very moment.

At the end of the long wall of people was a platform with a long table. In front of the table stood the other six brothers, and the only thing that made me feel just a little bit better was they all looked like they'd been hit in the back of the head, shock very plain on all their handsome faces.

I looked slowly down the line and stopped at the two standing in the middle. Both wore the same blue I did, which made sense now on some fashion level I didn't quite get, but I got enough to know I wished I'd picked the peach just so they would be dressed in peach too.

On both of their faces was a look I would never forget either. Where the men standing beside them at least had half smiles on their face, neither twin did, instead they both had this shocked almost horrified look on their face.

I watched Victor elbow Troy, who jolted like he'd forgotten where he was. Turning his head, he said something to Chase, who gave him a blank look and then snapped out of it and nodded. Both stepped down the stairs together and started walking in my direction.

I must have tensed because both Raf and Quinton paused in step and looked down at me. I watched the kings carefully, both of their eyes had changed and for some reason I began to feel like prey instead of the honored guest.

"Is it safe to hand her over to them?" Rafael inquired quietly.

Quinton glanced from his brother to the two walking in our direction. "They'll behave in front of this half of the population."

I caught the half part and was happy the whole hadn't

shown up. "They'll behave or I'll beat them upside the head," I whispered as softly as I could.

Rafael chuckled and lowered his head. Quinton just sighed. The twins were right in front of us by then. Both bowed in only a way they could have pulled off in unison. When they raised their eyes up to mine, they were both still glowing.

Quinton and Rafael dropped my hands and stepped back so Troy and Chase could take their place. Glancing from one to the other I raised my eyebrows. "You guys look pretty good all cleaned up." We started walking again.

Chase squeezed my hand on his arm. "You look amazing, kitten, my heart still hasn't settled down."

I smiled, having no clue how to take a compliment like that. Troy didn't offer any words but he kept looking down at me more than anywhere else, so I took that as a compliment too.

"So can we go now?"

Chase grinned and nodded to some people we walked past. "Oh no, kitten you have to dance with all of us first."

I swallowed. "All of us who?" I said between my clenched teeth while still trying to smile.

Troy leaned down so his head was closer to mine. "The royal family," he whispered next to my ear.

I looked up and watched as Quinton and Rafael were taking their place in the lineup. I had to dance with all eight of them? Seriously?

We started up the steps. "What are you thinking, kitten?" Chase sounded suspicious.

I looked up at him out of the corner of my eye. "How painful it is to have a metaphysical tattoo removed."

Troy laughed and then looked over at his brother. "I think I'm insulted." He grinned.

Chase moved past me to stand beside Arius. "Well, it could be worse, we could have a huntress that *likes* all this stuff and wants to redecorate our homes."

I stepped to stand in the middle of them, smiling for real

this time.

Troy lowered his head long enough to answer. "Mitz would have us all in frills then for sure."

When he straightened, the whole crowd started clapping. Apparently, I'd just been accepted as the Cross Over Huntress of Alterealm. I looked right in the front row of people to see Mitz standing there with tears rolling down her face as she clapped. My heart jerked inside my chest, dammit, I *was* meant to be here.

****

The dancing with the royal family was spread out over the course of two hours. Yep, they made me wear this outfit and shoes for two hours. Some or all of them were getting beat downs during the next practice, that was for sure.

Dancing with Victor and Michael was kind of like dancing with my father, if I even had one it would have felt that way at least. They were both stiff and movements were precise. It was a good thing they knew what they were doing, because whatever dance we were doing I had no idea and just flitted along in my stupid heels like I knew what I was doing.

Quinton tried to crush me in that big brotherly way, but I laughed and breathed a little more when we did what could have loosely been called dancing. Of course, any turns made, he just picked me up off the floor so I didn't have to decipher which way we were turning next. We had barely stepped off the floor when he pulled me back out for a second dance. I didn't know if this was even allowed, but he was grinning the whole time.

I wasn't sure if there was a certain order things were meant to go in, but each time Troy or Chase had started toward me and one of the others had stepped between us and held out a hand. I had to wonder if the non-ruler siblings had conspired to keep me out of reach of their monarch brothers, if the grins passing from one to the other meant anything.

A few of the elders in the large crowd came up to speak with me after each dance. It was a bit of kick to have people speak to me with such respect, this sort of thing I'd never done but could get more than used to. Arius suddenly appeared in front of me with a huge grin on his face. I glanced around his shoulder to see Chase shooting darts with his eyes at his brother's back.

Taking Arius' hand I let him lead me to the dance floor. When we got there, he knelt down and held out his hand near the floor. It took a few seconds to understand what he was doing, but I lifted my foot. He took off my shoe and then the other one.

"I thought you might be a little more comfortable without them." He straightened and then twirled me out onto the floor.

When we stopped, I reached up to his shoulders and smiled at him. "You thought right." The music was slow and easy and he didn't try for any of the fancy steps his older brothers had. I looked over to see Raf and Michael grinning and looking over at Chase. "So, you boys haven't by any chance conspired to annoy your kings, have you?

He looked over my head to where most of his siblings stood. "There is that possibility." His eyes sparkled with humor.

I liked seeing him this way and not the stiff guy he usually was. "Why?"

Turning me with ease that made even me appear graceful, he smiled again. "We're brothers?"

I laughed. "Yeah that's a good enough reason." I smiled at Mitz as he whirled me past and then looked back up at him. "Leone and Rafael in on it too?"

"Of course." He looked down at me with serious eyes. "This may be the only time I get the chance to speak to you without an audience." His grey eyes moved all over my face. "Regardless of how all of this plays out, I for one will always be grateful for your existence."

I took a few seconds to digest that and then smiled up at him. "Thanks. Someday when I can look back and admit all of this really happened I'll probably laugh."

"You have far exceeded what all of us thought.

Remember that too." Before I could reply he whirled me around so many times I thought I might collapse if he stopped too suddenly.

Laughing as the music finished. I grasped his arm to stay steady. "Think it's acceptable if the huntress runs around shoeless?"

He bent down and scooped up the shoes as we walked off the floor. "I think it's perfectly acceptable."

People parted as we walked back to the tables. I noticed the look of fear and wariness on their faces as they looked at Arius. Glancing up at him, I noticed he was the cause of the looks with the glare on his face.

When we were back to the table, I stretched up and kissed him softly on the cheek. "You know you're not as badass as you make everyone think, right?"

He frowned at me. "Just don't tell anyone." With a wink, he dropped my shoes beside my chair and walked away.

Quinton leaned down and whispered over my shoulder. "The shoes are the only piece you're taking off, right?"

I smirked. "Have you ever worn a push up bra?"

His eyes widened. I laughed. "Relax, I don't even know how they got me in it, so I can't exactly take it off."

Rafael suddenly appeared in front of me. He looked over my head at Quinton and smiled. Turning I saw Troy and Chase standing near each other, annoyance clear on their faces. "The gig is almost up boys, Leone better meet us before we get off the dance floor."

Quinton laughed as Rafael grabbed my hand. "I'll tell him."

Rafael was the easiest to dance with so far. He didn't try to lead me around like a puppet, but adapted his moves to mine instead. Not that I needed any further evidence to know he was a ladies' man, but that summed it up for me.

Glancing around at the women as we went past them, I looked up at him. "So, is the royal family allowed to dance with others after the ceremony part?"

He gave me a curious look. "Why do you ask?"

I smirked. "I'm sensing a lot of females are envying me right now."

He laughed as his eyes darted around the audience. "Oh, well this dance is for us only I'm afraid."

"Poor Rafael, stuck with dancing with someone that is like his sister."

He snorted and then gave me a soft look. "Little huntress, you can be assured that I do not see you as a sister, in any way shape or form." His eyes raked over me, lingering on the fair amount of my front sticking up over the dress. He grinned, "but I do know which wells to drink from and which ones will get me shot for treason." He glanced over at his twin brothers standing talking to several older men. "Those two wouldn't give a damn if I was the baby brother or not."

I felt the color rise in my cheeks. "Oh." That's about all I could say to his confession.

Reaching down he tipped up my chin without us missing a step in the slightest. "If you by chance were to test the water and find neither to your taste, know I'm the first to step up next." He winked at me and then released my chin.

I only nodded, not that I would ever do it, but what else was I supposed to do. Looking as we went around the floor again, I caught Quinton's eye briefly. He was sending Rafael one of those looks that said he knew exactly what was being said and wasn't at all happy about it. Just what I needed in my new life, more brothers fighting.

As the song started to fade, Rafael leaned down and kissed my cheek. "Leone is on the other side waiting." He straightened and turned me once more so we were walking back across the floor, in the opposite direction from where the kings now stood.

When Leone stepped onto the floor as we neared him, I didn't have to ask if he really wanted to dance with me. He looked like he wanted to run the other way. "Is he alright with this?" I asked Rafael quietly.

Raf straightened and looked over at his brother. "Keep

him talking." His playful tone was gone.

I nodded and smiled as we stopped in front of Leone. "If we don't hurry, I may be tackled by one of those two." I motioned to where Troy and Chase were.

The pained look left his eyes when he glanced at them and then grinned. "Then we'll hurry." He grabbed my hand and pulled me out onto the floor.

The music was slow and easy, so I was thankful no special steps were going to be required, but with the way Leone tensed I wondered if it was such a good thing. "Are you going to be alright with this?"

He looked down at me, his blue eyes moving over my face. "They told you?"

I shrugged. "I was happy someone did, I thought I'd done something to offend you."

Swallowing, he shook his head. "No. Unless smelling so damn good is offensive."

I offered a small smile. "I'm trying to smell awful, but I don't think it's working."

He laughed and relaxed a little bit. "I have good days and bad ones. Your arrival just caught me off guard."

"Yeah well if it helps at all, it all caught me off guard too."

He hugged me tighter and moved us around the floor. "Just smack me if I start sniffing your neck."

"I can't smell *that* good." Of course, I had no idea what I was talking about, but Raf had said to keep the conversation going so I was trying.

"Daxx, you messed up three of my brothers when you fed Quinton ... I'm afraid you're like pure gold to me."

I sighed and gave him a puzzled look. "Is that a good or bad thing?"

"For most a good thing, for me a very bad thing." With a serious look, his eyes moved over my face again. "I would die to protect you though, never question that."

Closing my eyes for a moment, I opened them and sent him an exasperated look. "I think dancing with all of you is too much for me to cope with."

"Why?"

I shook my head and let him lead me wherever we were supposed to step next. "I'm finding out too many secrets." I frowned. "Which is bad for you guys I could turn bitch and use them all against you."

His jaw tensed as he stared down at me. "I don't think you'd do that."

I sighed. "Yeah, I won't and that just sucks to know this stuff and have to keep it quiet."

Laughing, he whirled me around and then pulled me tight against him again. We went past both Troy and Chase where they stood near the edge of the dance floor. The looks on their faces promised retribution. I waited until Leone turned me again and then spoke quietly. "I think your twin siblings are looking to beat on a few brothers."

Leone glanced around until he spotted them. He grinned wide at both of them and inclined his head. With a chuckle, he pulled me closer and whirled us right by them again. "They wouldn't harm their enforcer."

I rolled my eyes in an innocent way. "Maybe not but picking on one of their baby brothers, definitely."

He raised both eyebrows at me. "You could save us, you know."

The music started to fade. "I could, but why would I interfere with such matters?"

Stopping, he looked down at me and smiled. "Cruel," he whispered as he led us right in the very direction the kings stood waiting. "I'll leave you here, my huntress queen." With a formal bow, he turned and went quickly in the other direction.

I stopped a few feet from Troy and Chase and grinned at them. Chase bowed his head in a regal manner and held out his hand. Inclining mine in the way Troy always did, I went over.

Just as I went to place my hand in his, Troy grabbed it and twirled me away from his twin. "If you can't beat them…" He raised his eyebrows at his brother and twirled me further onto the dance floor.

When we settled into an easy movement, he looked down at me with a gentle expression on his face. "Were you in on it?"

I batted my eyelashes at him in an over dramatic way. "On what?"

He grinned slowly. "You were."

Shaking my head, I tried not to grin. "Not until I was dancing with Arius, then I figured it out."

"When Quinton did the second dance I was afraid all of them were going to."

"Oh, I would have put a halt to that."

He frowned. "You're not enjoying yourself?"

I wasn't sure how to answer him without offending him. "If I were in my jeans it would be a blast."

The tempo of the music slowed a little, he pulled me closer and then picked me up so my feet weren't on the floor. "If you're tired I could just carry you through this one."

I laughed. "It's not the dancing, it's this damn dress."

He set me down and turned us back into a smooth rhythm. "I think the damn dress looks incredible on you."

At his soft serious tone, I looked up at him. His eyes were bordering on changing and my cheeks flushed in reaction. "Thank you."

"Did Mitz get pictures?"

Rolling my eyes at him I dropped my head onto his chest. "Thousands at least," I groaned.

"Good because I think it might be a few millennia before we get you into another dress and I want to remember every detail of your beauty in it." His voice had lowered.

Lifting my head, I looked up at him. Even with red eyes I could tell he was being sincere, the way they moved over my face. I wasn't sure if we were still moving or not, I just fell into his eyes.

He rested his hand near my jaw and played with the moon pendant hanging from my ear. "This song is going to end far too soon," he whispered.

"Then dance with me again." I tried to look away from his face, but failed. This side of Troy I hadn't experienced before. He was almost vulnerable.

With a soft smile, he looked away from my eyes. "I'm afraid I wouldn't let you go even then and my brother king would be injured."

I blinked and tried to weed through his formal speak. Unless I was completely wrong he had just admitted something. Tonight *was* the night of secrets. "This is the same brother you tried to pummel into the mats two days ago right?"

A guilty look appeared in his now hazel eyes briefly before he looked back down at me. "The very same." With a smile, he pulled me closer and spun us around the floor.

It took until almost the end of the song before I noticed that not once had either of us hesitated in movement. We were in total sync with each other. Relaxing for the first time since I'd put the dress on, I let him guide me where ever he wanted to go. Even when he took us into a complicated move that ended with him dipping down slowly in front of him. The strangest part was I had let him, and managed it gracefully without having to think about it.

He smiled as he pulled me back up with a strong hand on my back. "I now have to hand you over to that man over there with the scowl on his face."

I glanced over as we moved apart. "The one that looks remarkably like you when you're in deep thought?"

Raising his eyebrows at me before looking back. "I look like that?"

Nodding, I stepped away from him and let him take my hand. We didn't go straight to Chase, he stopped and spoke quietly with the man in charge of cueing the songs before turning us back towards Chase. As we neared the edge of the floor, he looked down at me. "My Queen." He bowed his head regally and then placed my hand in Chase's held out one.

With a strange smirk on his face, he bowed his head to his brother and moved out of the way.

Chase walked us slowly to the middle of the dance floor. "Best for last, kitten?"

I smirked. "We'll say that."

When the music started it was a loud fast disco song. Sighing loudly, Chase glanced over to where his seven brothers stood grinning. "Bastards, every one of them."

Laughing I looked over at the man Troy had spoken to, he was smiling but had an apologetic look on his face. Reaching down he flipped a switch and a soft ballad started playing.

"I will die with a broken heart, kitten, after seeing you look like this tonight."

His words made my own heart ache. I knew what he was talking about and took a deep breath to say something to change the subject, but that wasn't what came out. "I'm sorry, Chase."

He shook his head, his eyes moving over my face with a soft look. "It wasn't you at all, sweetling. I am the way I am and until I change that, I will be alone."

"I wondered if maybe things were the way they were because of taking your blood."

He considered what I said for a moment. "It is possible, there were a lot of emotions bouncing between us." Smiling with that devil gleam in his eyes, he leaned closer and whispered against my ear. "I don't suppose I could get another chance without the blood bond?"

"Are you going to give up feeding from women?"

He sighed. "In some ways, I am addicted as Leone was." A sad look appeared on his face, "and as much as I want you, I don't think I could stop even then."

Reaching up I cupped his cheek in my palm. Turning, he kissed my palm and then whirled us around on the floor.

We didn't speak for the rest of the song. When it stopped, he smiled down at me and then leaned down and kissed my cheek softly. "Thank you."

With a formal step, he led me back off the floor and then disappeared into the crowd standing around the edges. Quinton appeared beside me and grinned at me. "I'm done dancing," I told him in a whiny tone.

He nodded. "I was going to say if you want I can sneak you out of here now."

"Really?" I grabbed the lapel on his jacket. He nodded. "Let's go then, what are you waiting for?"

Chuckling he lead me through the crowd to the waiting carriage. With it being dark and everyone mingling through the crowd, I thought we would make it without being seen but then Arius peeked from around the corner of the carriage. He grinned at me. "It's about time; I knew you'd bail as soon as the last dance was complete."

Pulling up my skirt so I could get in I gave him a bored look. "And what are you doing here?"

He shrugged. "Someone has to guard you."

Quinton elbowed him and climbed in. "That's what I'm here for."

"I'm helping. Just please take me back to the quiet and solitude." He got in and sat beside me, pulling his tie free from his neck.

A look passed between Quinton and him. I cleared my throat. "Why are you really here?"

Arius sighed. "Troy told us to stay on your heels."

"You're babysitting me?"

Quinton pulled his tie off. "No, just making sure you don't run off to hunt down Marcus on your own."

Hiking the *bodice* of the gown up, I avoided looking at either of them. "I wouldn't do that."

"Uh huh, "Quinton leaned over so I had to look at him, "and pigs spin webs and lay eggs."

I gave him my best offended look. "They could, somewhere," I mumbled.

CHAPTER THIRTY-FIVE

The next week was crazy. I bounced from one realm to the other daily, sometimes twice a day. I had no sense of time any more, or it felt like it when I would lie in my bed in Alterealm and try to tell myself it was time to sleep.

When I'd come up with the great plan to check everywhere from the alley to the club, I hadn't stopped to consider how many places that might be. The worst part was I'd lost count how many places we'd gone and a few times I thought maybe we were at a place twice. Tim was encouraging and with anyone else I might have gotten really grumpy, but he just had that way about him and knew when to talk and when not to.

Each time we came or went, Troy was present. He looked as anxious when I was leaving as when I returned. Since the dance he had been weird. I watched him during a meeting with Victor or Michael. He was standoffish with everyone, not just me.

I hadn't seen Chase since the dance, so when I called a halt to the search for a day of rest, I headed straight to Troy's office to see if he knew what was going on. The door was open, so I went right in. Troy was standing in the corner looking over the map of his side of this realm.

"Are you having any better luck on this side?"

He stiffened and turned his head. "No." Moving in my direction, he frowned. "You look exhausted."

I sighed. "I don't even know what time of day it is anymore."

Nodding, he leaned against the desk, keeping a good four feet between us. "I can relate, I've been awake for as many daylight hours as I am night ones lately."

Rubbing a hand over my face, I nodded. "Bouncing back and forth is making me dizzy."

"How much more do you have to check?"

"Enough for a couple more days, at least." He wouldn't look directly at me. "How is Chase doing looking on his side?"

He looked right at me. "You haven't spoken to him?"

"No. I've been a little busy."

Straightening, he pulled out his phone and glanced down at it. "I haven't heard directly from him; his Captain has been keeping me posted on the search."

Now I was worried. One brother was avoiding me and the other was missing. "So, where is he?"

A concerned look passed over his face. Shaking his head, strode toward the door. "Let's go find out."

I was right on his heels the entire way. Even though I knew I was technically the huntress and allowed free reign, the fastest way through any questions was to be with the large king with a certain determined look on his face.

When we were heading down the hall toward his room, Tim came around the corner. He paused with a bewildered look. "Aren't we taking today off?"

I nodded and tried to keep up with Troy. "Yes we are. Any idea where Chase is?"

With a strange look on his face, he pointed to his bedroom door. "Pretty sure he's still there."

Troy paused in his step and scowled at him. His eyes flashed red and he sighed and turned back to the door. "Stay outside, Tim, in case you're needed."

Suddenly I was the only one that didn't know what was

going on. I caught up to Troy as he went through the door and almost walked smack into him when he stopped short and stood there. Moving by him, I looked around the room until I found Chase. I know my jaw dropped when I saw him sprawled on his bed. At least most of him was on the bed, his head and one arm hung off the side.

I looked to Troy for confirmation on what I was thinking, he was already moving across the room to the table where he picked up a bottle and read it. Shaking his head, he moved over to the bed. Following, I stood beside him as he checked his twin's eyes and sighed loudly again.

"He's drunk." Probably not the most intelligent statement, but I was so surprised to see him that way.

Troy glanced at me, a worried look on his face. "And not just on alcohol." Lifting his brother's head up, he shifted him around on the pillow. "Go ask Tim to come here."

Not sure what was happening now, I went over and motioned for Tim to come in. Closing the door behind him, I stood there and watched as they sat Chase up.

Troy glanced around for me. "Can you go turn on the shower, Daxx?"

Eyebrows raising, I nodded and hurried to do it. By the time I had it ready they were at the door half dragging a limp Chase between them.

"Kitten!" He slurred. "You came."

Troy glared at me, like it was my fault his brother was wasted, but he didn't say a word.

Tim stepped in the shower. "I'll do it, Sire, no need for all of us to get soaked." I was surprised he could hold the flaccid man on his own, but he seemed to manage. Troy reached in and held his surfacing sibling's head under the spray. He reached down and twisted the tap all the way to cold, giving the sober man in the shower an apologetic look.

I stood by the door, not sure if I should stay or run back to the other side. I stayed.

When they had a sputtering, cursing king in a much more alert state glaring at them, they turned off the water and helped him get out. I hurried over and held out a towel to Tim and then Troy. Troy dried off his arms and then flung the towel over his brother's head.

With a groan, Chase pulled the towel off and held it over his face. When he lowered it, he saw me standing there. He stood there, soaking wet watching me with blood shot eyes and regret plainly visible.

Troy looked from me back to his brother before he turned to Tim. "After you change, post someone outside his door so he isn't disturbed." He looked down at me again and then turned to Chase. "We'll see you at breakfast."

Chase lowered his head and made a noise that sounded like he agreed.

Turning on his heel, Troy walked out the door. With a final look at Chase, I went out behind him. He stood outside the room waiting for me and then began walking without saying anything.

He didn't slow down or speak to me until we were almost back to his office. Pausing just inside the door, he looked down at me with a look of confusion on his face. "I was not accusing you of anything when I looked at you back there."

I had to wonder if he could actually read what I was thinking sometimes. "Okay."

Reaching over slowly, he tipped my chin up, his concerned hazel eyes moving over my face before holding my eyes with a look. "Go get some rest my queen. I'll see you at breakfast." His voice was so soft and gentle I wanted to sigh.

Backing out of his hold, I nodded and then headed anywhere but there. I was tired, but frustrated at the same time and in no way ready to rest. Stopping I considered my options, workout or snack?

Comfort food won so I headed to the kitchen and hoped Mitz would have something sweet and bad for me, better to drown out the mixed-up mess inside my brain.

****

I was digging into the bottom half of a bag of double

stuffed fudge cookies when Mitz came into the kitchen. She paused in the door and then closed it and went over to the fridge without a word.

Setting a glass of milk in front of me, she stood there with this understanding look on her face. "Want to talk about it?"

I shook my head and swallowed. "I don't even know."

"Ah." She pulled over a stool and sat across from me.

Maybe it was that she was a motherly type or just the fact that she was a female, I'm not sure but I sighed loudly. Waving a cookie around, I sighed again. "How long have you worked for the royal family?"

With a soft look on her face, she smiled. "I used to look after Victor when he was a baby."

That didn't really tell me how old she was, but it was enough to know she knew a lot more than I ever would. "I can't picture Victor as a baby."

She laughed. "He was a terror as a child, let me tell you."

That sounded more fitting than a cute cuddly baby. I glanced at her hands. "You have a husband but aren't mated?"

A look appeared on her face, that quiet one that said she knew exactly what my problem was now. "Yes, but that doesn't mean we're any less bonded."

I ate another cookie while I thought. "Your friend, the one that made my dress, she was mated." I recalled the tattoo on her arm. Mitz nodded, but didn't say anything. "Troy says finding a true mate is rare, if that's the case why am I supposed to be for either or?" I sipped the milk. "I mean shouldn't it only be one of them?" I studied a cookie and twisted it until it was separated. "I feel like a tramp, being attracted to both of them." Pushing the cookie back together I took a bite and looked back down at it. "I know they look the same but that's not why. I feel something different with both of them."

Reaching over, she steadied my hand before I could stuff

more in my mouth. I looked over at her, she had this sweet look in her eyes that made me want to hug her. Obviously, another hidden skill of hers to do that to me.

"Huntress, fate has made it so you could choose either and they know this, the buggers and are playing on it constantly." She sighed. "A little touch here, a certain look and they know the part of you that is matched to them reacts."

She pulled the bag of cookies out of my other hand and started to close it up slowly. "I think we both know that regardless of the pull between you and Chase, it wouldn't be the fit it should be." A sad look entered her eyes for a split second before it was gone. "None of this makes you a tramp." Clasping her hands together in front of her on the counter she leaned closer. "If anything, you amaze me, if I were younger and single I doubt I could resist either of them."

I grinned at her confession and then sobered. "Troy and I found Chase wasted and half passed out in his room a while ago."

She was quiet for a moment and then nodded slowly. "Good, he should beat himself up, maybe then he'll try to change for the better." With a sad smile, she shrugged. "I try to keep them all together, but at the end of the day, or start I suppose he is still over there alone while they have each other."

"We talked about it a bit at the dance and think part of the connection was enhanced because of the blood bond." I realized I had just admitted that I wasn't as drawn to Chase as I was Troy. "Troy is..."

"A little more complex than his twin, I'm afraid."

I drank the rest of the milk, wishing now I could get the taste of fudge out of my mouth. Setting the glass down I played with the rim. "So, any advice?" I shrugged. "I'd like to say all this prophecy stuff is a bunch of hooey, but I can't."

"Finally realized you fit in like you've always been here, have you?"

I nodded. "Yeah."

She grinned. "Good. As for advice, I honestly can't tell you how to sort through it all." Picking up the bag, she got up and pushed the stool in. "Things will happen as they're meant to, pushing it or fighting it will only make it more complicated in the end."

I knew she had a point, somewhere in all of that, but it didn't mean I was going to verbally agree with her. "Thanks." I stood up and stretched. "I'm going to go try to get some rest now." I turned toward the door.

"Daxx?"

I paused and looked back at her.

"I heard you were looking for the lost brother as well as hunting down Marcus."

I nodded.

She smiled at me. "Thank you."

CHAPTER THIRTY-SIX

I sat down at the table and offered a sleepy smile to all the male faces watching me. "Morning." Quinton passed me a steaming cup of coffee, I gave him an appreciative glance. While sipping it I noted the two empty chairs at the table. Neither King was present, again. I understood Chase needed some time and, I could forgive him for that, but Troy was another story. For the last three days I'd only caught a glimpse of him as he headed in the opposite direction I was as quickly as possible.

A few pairs of eyes looked at me briefly before everyone put their head down and became very interested in the food in front of them. My appetite, which never failed me, suddenly left me. Taking another sip of my coffee, I glanced around the table. "You'll have to excuse me, I have something to take care of."

"Everything alright?" Rafael asked leaning forward with a concerned look on his face. Michael sent him a deadly look making him sit back again and look embarrassed.

I nodded. "Yep, just fine. Enjoy your breakfast."

****

I knocked on the door and waited until I was told to enter. When I walked in Troy was leaning against his desk reading some papers. He paused to look me over from head to toe then turned his attention back to the papers in his hand.

"Daxx, what can I do for you?"

I was a perfectly reasonable woman, in most cases, always willing to give the benefit of the doubt. Maybe he really had pressing monarchy issues to handle. "I was just wondering if everything was alright."

He barely glanced up from the pages. "Pertaining to?"

With that tone of his voice my reasoning faded a few levels. "You. Don't you eat anymore? You haven't been to a meal or practice in three days."

He sent me another brief appraisal. "I ate earlier. I wanted to get a jump on my day."

His tone, neutral and impersonal made me feel like I was being an annoyance. I didn't like it. "Can I help with anything? I mean, it must be pressing for you to bypass on family meals."

Troy's jaw tensed, but his tone stayed even. "No, but thank you. I think I have everything under control."

I began to move around, pretending I was looking at anything but him. In truth, I saw nothing but the flicker of red. "Have you spoken to Chase in the last few days?"

"Mmm, only briefly. Perhaps he is busy with his own matters."

"Oh." I wandered over and ran my hand over the frame of a picture of all eight brothers. "I just wondered how he's doing."

There was a rustle of paper, but I didn't turn to see if I finally had his attention or not. "I thought...it seemed as if you'd patched things up at the dance."

I smiled at the picture so he couldn't see me. "Made peace is more like it."

"I see." The annoying regal tone was back.

Turning, I crossed my arms over my chest and looked at him. The pages rested on his knee, but his eyes were on me. "He asked my forgiveness and a few days grace to get his head together."

Something entered his eyes, but he lowered his lashes before I could read what it was. "I thought perhaps…"

"We were going to kiss and make up?" I supplied for him.

He cleared his throat. "Something like that."

Shaking my head, I took a few steps toward him and then chickened out and went over to the book shelf. "That's not going to happen. What inkling of attraction there was between us is gone now."

"I'm sorry to hear that." His tone was sincere.

I read a few of the titles on the spines of the books, and wanted to yawn, they were that dreary. Turning around, I leaned back against the shelf. "So, enough avoidance for one day. Is there a particular reason you're avoiding me like the plague?" Maybe not the best choice of words for a man that had been around for one or two real plagues, but I had his attention now.

His spine stiffened as he looked at me. Good for him, he could play coy until confronted. "I'm sorry, I've been busy…"

I grinned. "Don't lie to me. We can plan imminent battles and still have time for horse play in the gym, so unless there's a meteor arriving tomorrow to wipe out all living existence…you're avoiding me."

I watched his jaw clench as he thought about his next words. "Very well. I had hoped if I made myself scarce you would mend things with my brother."

"There's nothing to mend."

He raised his eyebrows and crossed his arms loosely over his chest. "I felt what he did, how can you say that was nothing?"

Damn this mind connection thing was a pain in the ass. "I'm not saying there was nothing then. With the blood bond, everything was amplified. He admitted it."

"You weren't drawn to him?"

"I didn't say that. I'd have to be blind and brain dead to not be attracted to him." My mind gave me a poke when I realized I'd pretty much admitted I was attracted to his twin, as in the look-alike whose eyes I was looking into.

A light came into his eyes. "Then maybe with a bit of time…"

I shook my head. "No. It's not the man, it's his habits…"

"He could change."

"Why should he?" Were we really having this conversation?

"If he wants you, he will."

I threw my arms up. "I'm not the toy surprise here. It can't work between Chase and I." I really didn't want to talk about this with him. Taking a deep breath, I blew it out slowly. "Look, I came here to find out why you were avoiding me."

"I'm not."

Rolling my eyes, I pushed away from the shelf and walked over to stand in front of him. The tension in his body radiated from him in damn near visible waves. "You are. It's affecting everyone and it's not right."

His eyes gave away nothing as he watched me.

"I think it would be best for everyone if I went home for a while."

"How the hell is that the best for anyone?" His tone was suddenly lethal, not a regal note in it.

I shrugged. "Chase won't come spend time here. Everyone is on edge and treating me like I'm about to burst into flames. You clearly don't want anything to do with me, which makes all of your brothers…"

He stood up so fast, I almost stumbled backwards. Leaning down so he was right in my face. "I've been staying out of the way. If you were meant for my brother than I bloody well want him to have a chance."

Well, I wanted a rise out of him but now that I had it I wasn't sure what to do with him. "If I'd been meant for Chase things would have worked out differently." I shrugged. "I'm not. Hey, we gave this prophecy thing a whirl…"

Troy pulled me by the back of my head and crushed his mouth down on mine before I even saw him move. I found myself crushed up against him with his arm wrapped around me like a steel band.

I lost all of my thought process as he quite literally plundered my mouth. By the time my body kicked in to try and catch up to his delicious brutal kiss, I was being lifted up against his body as he stumbled across the room.

When my back hit the bookshelf, I could have cared less. All I knew was that his kisses hit me like a hurricane as we both spun out of control. I gasped for air when he lifted his mouth but didn't get much as his lips quickly found mine again.

Grasping my legs, he wrapped them around his waist and roughly moved his mouth to my throat. "I stayed away…" his sharp teeth bit into my skin, the pain sent shocks of pleasure straight to my very core. "…because I want you more than my next breath." He licked over where he'd bitten and I moaned a sound I've never made in my life.

When his lips found mine again, I grabbed his hair with both hands and held on, not wanting him to move away until the lack of oxygen threatened both of our lives. As I ran my tongue over the fangs in his mouth, another rush of heat burst through me.

Growling, he pulled his mouth from mine and lowered it as he yanked my shirt free from my jeans. As his teeth scraped over my collarbone, I dropped my head back and gasped, it felt that good.

My bra snapped and it excited me even more when I realized he'd bitten through the strap with his teeth. Pulling his hair not so gently, I guided his mouth to an aching breast. I wanted his mouth all over me.

When he closed his mouth over one hard nipple and his fangs pinched together I moaned and rocked my body into his hard one, needing more of him.

He tore his head free and stood there gasping for breath,

his glowing red eyes raking over me. I shuddered with the intensity of the look. As he continued to stand there, reality slipped back into my brain. My head was spinning and body throbbing in a whole new way and I was one move away from having sex against a bookshelf in an office.

With a long shaky breath, he lowered my shirt to cover my bared skin and gently held my legs so he could lower me to the floor. Holding me so our bodies weren't touching, he let out a loud breath, "I don't..." He blew out another one, trying to slow his breathing. "I've never..."

"Yeah," I gasped. Neither of us had planned on that kind of reaction. I moved my eyes down over his body and had to fight the urge to reach out and touch.

Troy took a small step back so there was more space between us, his eyes were still red and they didn't leave my face. "I didn't mean to hurt you."

Feelings were flooding my system but pain wasn't anywhere on the list. "You didn't."

Standing with his hands on his hips, he nodded abruptly once. "That was a little intense for a first kiss."

Rubbing my hands down the legs of my jeans I could only nod. I didn't want to stand here and just look at him, I wanted to climb him like a jungle gym and play. My heart was still beating so fast that I was sure he could hear it.

His now hazel eyes, raked over me and then settle on my face, moving to my mouth more than my eyes. "I ..." The phone on his desk rang. With a curse, he shook his head at me. "I have to take this, I'm waiting on..."

I raised my hands and stepped away from the bookshelf. "I get it. I'll get out of your hair then."

Giving me another apologetic look, he went over to the desk.

Feeling confused and just a little needy, I walked to my room on wobbly legs. As I rounded the last corner near my room, Quinton was walking in my direction with two cups in his hands. He paused and looked me over slowly, his brows knitting together with a look of concern. I glanced down and figured out why, I'd been walking around with an open bra and my shirt sitting over it. Groaning, I went to the door without a word to him and went in, leaving it open behind me.

Turning I watched him set the one cup down and then focus on the liquid in the cup he still had. Without a word, he took a sip like there was nothing to say.

I snapped. Ever since I'd found out this place existed I'd been walking around feeling like a dog in heat and was sick of it. "What does a girl have to do to get laid in this realm?"

The drink he'd just taken was spewed out of his mouth in the air. He coughed and looked at the cup like it was evil and set it down beside the other one. "What?"

"What is wrong with me?" I held out my arms and watched as he looked me over again. "Am I not good enough to have sex with on this side or what?"

"I don't..." He shook his head. "I'm not..." With a loud sigh, he went over to the couch and picked up a blanket and then came over and wrapped it around me. His face was flushed red and he avoided looking at me. Heaving out a breath he stepped back and then looked at me. "What happened?"

I snorted. "Nothing!"

His eyebrows raised and then he reached over and patted my hair down. "You don't look like nothing happened."

Feeling defeated I dropped down onto the couch and slumped, holding the blanket around my shoulders. "I tracked Troy down to ask why he's avoiding me."

He looked at me with an amused look on his face.

I glared at him. "He won't come near me because he wants me to pick Chase, so I explained that's not going to happen, that it won't work." I growled. "He's so annoying when he's being all pompous and proper, it's *really* annoying..."

Quinton held up a hand to stop me. "So you want Troy?"

I gave him a duh look and glanced down at the blanket

wrapped around my chest. "I don't go around acting like that with every male."

"Thank God," he mumbled and then sat down on the table and leaned forward on his knees. "So, obviously, he's… into you, actually I knew that by the way he watches you, but what happened?"

Closing my eyes, I dropped my head back against the couch. "He just stopped and basically apologized."

When he sighed loudly, I opened my eyes and looked at him. "If I know Troy, he'll fight it every step of the way."

"Why? I thought he believed in the prophecy and everything."

Quinton nodded and sat up. "He does, but that doesn't mean he's just going to roll over and accept it all at once." Standing up, he pulled me to my feet and wrapped me in his big arms in a bear hug. "Go grab a shower and then we'll go see if we can find some of Marcus' followers to beat the crap out of."

I snuggled against his chest. "That would make me feel better." It wouldn't really, but I could at least than unload some frustration. Straightening I wrapped the blanket around me and turned toward the bathroom. "I'll be ready in ten."

"I'll be back then. And hey, don't make it easy on him, Daxx, he deserves a little hell."

Nodding, I kept walking into the bathroom and closed the door.

CHAPTER THIRTY-SEVEN

I brought us back with such enthusiasm that even Tim had to stop for a moment until things stopped spinning. When my eyes were able to focus again I was quite thrilled to see I'd landed us right where I'd meant to. Victor and Troy looked up from the map they'd been studying.

I grinned and walked over quickly. Looking over the map quickly, I stabbed my finger into the area we'd just come from. "There!"

Victor straightened. "You've found him?"

I nodded, and tried not to do the jig that was building up inside me. "We got close enough that we even have a rough idea of how many we're up against."

Troy glanced from Tim back to me. "Tim could see too?"

Bobbing my head again excitedly I glanced over to see Tim smiling. "Yeah, he went to pull me back and discovered if he's touching me he can see through the magic too."

Troy's eyes hardened and moved over me before sending a cold look in the guard's direction. "Pull you back from what?"

I shrugged. "I got a little excited and almost went barreling right into their little compound."

Raising one eyebrow at me, he straightened to look

down at me. "You aren't going to do anything on your own."

I ignored the tone that implied an order and looked back down at the map. "It used to be a hospital that was abandoned years ago when they built the new one." Pointing to the buildings on the map, I continued. "We cut their numbers down that night, but they still have at least thirty," I looked up at Victor. "Only a few are from my side."

Victor took a moment to consider what I was saying. "So he's still making the devices."

"He has to be." Looking at Troy, I tried to see what he was thinking but found him watching me instead. Warmth moved through me and I had to give myself a mental smack, now was not the time to having *those* thoughts. Blinking, I broke his stare and turned back to Victor. "Do you have some way of getting a head count on who is missing from this end?"

Going over to the desk, he picked up some papers. "It's not as exact as I'd like, some move between to be with mates, others may have just been elsewhere when we came calling…" He flipped through them briefly. "A rough guestimation, we have one hundred unaccounted for."

Troy finally stopped staring at me and looked over at his brother. "Did you add those we sent back during the fight?"

Nodding, Victor looked tired suddenly. "Yes."

"One hundred," Troy said quietly, his tone betraying the situation was dire. When he looked back at me, it was all business. "And you figure thirty are in this old hospital?"

I nodded. "That we could see. There are a lot of buildings in that area though, most have underground tunnels joining them to the main structure, so there could be a lot more than we know of."

Michael came in and glanced around at all of us. "This can't be good."

Troy turned and crossed his arms over his chest. "Daxx has found out where they are and it's not good news."

Frowning, Michael closed the door and moved over to stand in front of the map. "Why?"

I looked to Victor to explain it. He tossed the papers back on the desk and came over. Pointing to the spot I'd shown him, he looked up at his brother. "They're holed up in this area; most likely using all the buildings to keep themselves spread out and so if one group is found the rest will escape. Daxx was able to see at least thirty." He picked up the watch device off the table and turned it over in his hand. "Most are ours."

Several emotions passed over Michael's face as he stood there looking from us to the map. "We need more intel." He finally said.

Troy crossed his arms over his chest, suddenly looking all alpha. "The problem with that is only Daxx can *see* to get that." All three of the other males in the room stiffened.

I looked from Troy around at the others, and felt like I'd just missed the memo on something. "Why is that a problem?"

Tim moved a little closer, all while eyeing up Troy. "You can't just stay there around the clock." Troy sent him a look and for a second I could have sworn it was gratitude.

The idea of parking my butt in the same place for the next few days really didn't sound like something I wanted to do. "Maybe Clairee can make up some of those charms again…"

Tim shook his head. "They didn't help us see Marcus, only deflect his spell so I don't think that's going to help us this time."

"What about your friend, Huntress?"

I turned to look back at Victor. Chewing my lip, I debated on the options we had. The end result I didn't like, at all. "I'll talk to her, although she may want nothing to do with this." I looked at all four of the men for a moment, taking in how lethal they would look on first sight. "*If* she agrees, it will only be so I can rest or take a break," I held up my hand so they wouldn't say anything, "*and* only Raf or Quinton are to be with her when she does it." I motioned to all of them. "I don't want to scare the hell out of her with all of the rest of you giants."

Tim nodded, Victor and Michael did nothing to tell me if they agreed or not and Troy just stood there with his eyes roaming over me. Every nerve in my body twitched with the knowing look he was giving me. Before I could do or say anything embarrassing, I spun toward the door. "I'm going to find Quinton then go over to see Crissy."

I felt like a coward as I practically fled from him, but it was either that or make a really big heated scene right there in front of the others. He avoided being anywhere near me, and made sure we were never alone, it was *so* totally not fair that he stand there and undress me with his eyes when I couldn't do a damn thing about it.

I rounded the next corner and almost walked right into Chase's hard chest. I hadn't seen him since he was being held in the shower.

"That's what I like, kitten, you running right into my arms," he drawled but winked as he said it so I wouldn't take him too seriously. He paused and held me at arm's length studying my face. "What's wrong?"

I made an odd noise of annoyance. "Your brother is an ass!"

He smirked and rubbed the back of his neck. "I'm afraid I may need a few more specifics. I have several brothers that fit that description."

I shoved away from him and started walking. "The one that looks like you but makes no sense."

"Ah. Great seeing you, kitten. I'll catch up with you later when you're not on the war path."

I still could hear his laugh as I turned down the next hallway.

****

Crissy not only agreed, she seemed pumped to help out. For her, it confirmed all the things she had always seen. Being a part of stopping the ultimate evil, her words, was something she wanted to do. I wasn't worried about her staying hidden, as long as her new bright hair color was covered, hiding was one thing she had mastered a long time ago, and I trusted Rafael and Quinton to keep her out of harm's way but my stomach would tighten when I knew she was there.

My first watch had been the longest day of my life, there was only so much you could do while hiding out on a shed on top of a building. Tim even seemed bored and antsy, confirming that we were both people that liked action. For the second shift I brought cards, but the interest in that wore off after the first hour.

We'd only managed to discover a few things, whatever was going on down there they were keeping most of it inside. Arius, Troy and Chase were busy trying to find someone they could get set up on the inside. The problem multiplied because the plant needed to believe in Marcus' goals or he'd know.

When Criss and Quinton arrived, I was so tired from doing nothing I wasn't sure if I had the energy to get Tim and I back home. Quinton nodded to Tim and waited until Crissy filled me in on her search for the missing brother, which was an endless trail of dead ends. When she settled into the corner by the small window, he pulled me aside.

"They found someone to go in, but you're not going to like it."

Eyebrows drawn together I looked at him. Anyone on the inside was a good thing. "Who?"

"Shelby," he practically whispered.

My spine stiffened. "Shelby as in the crazy Shelby that tried to break my face?"

He nodded.

My first thought was I hoped Marcus caught her, then that was replaced with jealousy. Had Troy gone to her and asked for her help? Had she volunteered to redeem herself to him? "Well, it's not my decision."

Quinton looked at his boots more than my face. "It was Victor's idea."

That didn't make me feel any better. "They better not expect me to cover her ass when all hell breaks loose."

Rubbing a hand over his jaw, he glanced at me briefly. "When I get word that she's in, I'll take Crissy back to the apartment."

I nodded. With a quick wave to Criss I left the little shed, feeling suddenly like the walls were closing in on me. It was ridiculous, what difference did it make to me who went in and who asked them? As long as we stopped Marcus, that's all that mattered to me. Yes, I was lying to myself but that was fine too just as long as no one else knew.

By the time I reached my room, my mind was distracted by other things and I was past jealous and onto aggravated. How long was I supposed to hang back and wait for Troy to decide what he was doing? He may have millennia left, but I was a mere mortal gal and my years were numbered.

Every time we were in the same room together I smoldered. He watched me constantly, the look in his eyes made me want to climb him. I was sure he knew the effect he had on me, and he still did it anyway.

Tossing my jacket at the couch, I watched it slide to the floor. Taking a deep breath, I glanced over at the clock, there was a good chance they'd be at practice now. I should try to sleep.

Before I finished that thought, I was heading out the door to the gym, there would be no sleep for me. If I could go beat on someone and get rid of some of this frustration, I might feel just a little better.

****

I spotted Quinton as soon as I stepped through the door. Shelby must be in place inside Marcus's domain if he were here. The mere thought of Shelby started emotions churning with a desire to throttle anyone that got in my way. Most of the brothers were engaged in mock fight with a sibling, the only one not fighting was Chase.

I zeroed in on him as I went to the weapons board. His eyebrows went up and his eyes widened. Grabbing one of the wooden swords that was half my size, I swung it a few times. If it had been metal I would have fallen to the floor

319

right along with it when I'd pulled it off the rack.

Turning to Chase, I swung it a few more times. His eyes lit with understanding and he inclined his head and motioned to the mats. I had to give the guy bonus points there, letting me take my frustration out on him. When he stopped, he glanced over at his twin and sent me a daring grin. "The things I do for my siblings."

He stood ready and I swung. I felt myself pull back just before our weapons connected, but still loved the vibrations that traveled up my arms.

"Come on, kitten, you've got more than that in you," he goaded.

I came around with more force behind it this time. He deflected it without much effort.

"You know," he side stepped to throw me off, "I could always help in other ways if someone else won't man up." He gave me a cheeky grin, a glint in his eyes.

It was just the right thing to say and he knew it as he grinned widened. The frustration inside me came to a boil and I lunged at him, swinging without pause between strikes. The more I went at him, the faster the adrenalin pumped and I found strength I didn't know I had. At one point, I advanced enough to wipe his smile right off his face. Lose the goatee and it was the very face that was driving me insane.

I could hear the men around us, most cheering for me, one or two laughing at Chase's expense. I don't know how long we were actually at it, but Chase wasn't smiling at all now.

He sidestepped me twice, throwing off my balance and pissing me off all over again. Avoiding my swing, he turned and tossed the sword in the air to Troy. "I believe this is your beating I'm fending off, brother King."

Pausing with the sword in the air, I glared at Troy. A serious look crossed his face. He lifted the sword and took two steps toward me. Somewhere in the back of my mind I realized that beating on the man I wanted to kiss speechless didn't make any sense, but neither had my life lately.

I didn't even have to take the first swing, he did. Well at least he wasn't going to let me win. One of his swings connected and it rattled me up to my teeth.

I missed twice and grew more frustrated. Changing the angle of my swing I remembered the mad woman with the bat. Never let anger enter a fight.

I waited for him to swing and stepped back, rolling to the side and came up swinging. The sword connected with his hip.

With a determined look, he came at me again. I waited until he was closer and used the long piece of wood to vault myself into the air, landing a kick against his chest.

He stumbled back two steps, but before he could recover completely, I landed a blow against his hip again. His sword hit the mat as he staggered and dropped to one knee.

I stood ready, and then realized he wasn't going to get up again. When he lifted his head, and looked at me, his eyes were glowing red.

Heat shot through me. Dropping the mock weapon, I stood there fighting to catch my breath.

Troy dropped down and leaned back onto his elbows. He lay there, his chest heaving and eyes bright.

When I looked away from him I saw everyone was walking out the door. Quinton looked back long enough to grin at me. Chase stood there for a moment holding the door; he wasn't smiling but still inclined his head and gave me a reassuring look. Then he went through the door and let it swing shut.

I looked back over at the man on the floor, watching me with a heated stare. This was the first time since he'd kissed me that he wasn't walking as fast as he could in the other direction.

Hesitantly I went over to him, when I was close enough he reached up and grabbed my hand as he stood up. Without a word, he turned and pulled me along as he headed out the other door.

I almost had to run to keep up with him as he wound

through the long maze of hallways that led to his room.

CHAPTER THIRTY-EIGHT

Once inside he released my hand and closed the door, locking it before turning back to me. My heart was pounding and I wasn't sure if it was from the fast walk or the way he was devouring me with a look.

I started walking backwards even though I wanted to be closer to him. He began to stalk me, a predator hunting their prey, my blood was boiling from that look.

"You should have stayed away," his voice was low and lethal.

Stepping back to keep the few feet between us, I kept my eyes on his red ones. "I don't like being avoided."

"Even if it's for your own good?" He sidestepped around the chair.

Why was I moving away from him when all I could think of was my body against his? "According to who?"

"Me."

That was it. One word growled in his alpha tone and heat shot through my whole body. I heard myself gasp when his eyes moved slowly down my body and back up to my face. His look held me captive and I stopped moving. Swallowing, I tried to hide the way I was shaking. He didn't scare me, even though a part of my brain told me I should be running as fast as I could the other way. "Why would it be for my own good?" I asked breathlessly.

Troy stopped right in front of me, standing so close I could feel his body heat without us touching. "Because," he reached out and tucked the hair behind my ear, "I can't control myself around you."

I shivered as his fingers lightly grazed my jaw. "You'd never hurt me…" His rough finger sliding across my bottom lip stopped all thought of speaking.

"In your world I'm a demon…"

"We're not in my world." I rushed to tell him, as if he was unaware. If he didn't touch or kiss me soon I was going to vibrate right out of my own skin.

"No." He pulled me up against his body, tipping my head back with his thumb under my jaw. "We're not."

Any thought I had in my head was completely erased when his mouth covered mine and kissed me with such force my knees went weak. The fire that had been simmering ignited when his tongue plundered into my mouth.

Growling deep in his throat, he reached down and grasped the back of my thighs to boost me higher on his body. I clung to his neck, my feet hanging in the air and relished the feel of his hard body crushing mine.

When he pulled his mouth away, I gasped for air as his lips moved down over my throat. I could feel his sharp teeth grazing against my skin and it sent more heat pooling between my thighs. I moaned when he nipped my shoulder and felt the cloth from my shirt being tugged away from my shoulder.

Releasing his neck, I leaned back and pulled the shirt up my body, only to hear the material being ripped. With my arms still in the sleeves, I ran my hands down his chest tugging the material up as I went. My hands connected with the heated flesh of his stomach and I wanted to purr like a cat as the firm muscles contracted beneath my touch.

With a growl of annoyance, he released me and yanked the shirt over his head. His chest was a thing of beauty. Hard sculpted muscles under the soft skin quivered at my touch. Leaning forward, I ran my tongue over a nipple and was rewarded with a groan.

From there it was a blur of motion. Clothes being shredded by his clawed hands, if I'd had any sense at all I would have shrieked when claws appeared at the end of his fingers, but all I thought, yes more.

When he lifted me up against his naked body, I wrapped my legs around him and gasped where our bodies connected. If it weren't for his strong hands holding me in place I would have impaled myself on him and rode like a wild woman.

I was momentarily surprised to realize a soft mattress was underneath me and we weren't standing any longer. My whole being was consumed with the feelings of his hands and mouth on me and my skin against his.

As he thrust into my body he growled against my ear. "No control…"

Wrapping my legs tight around him, I gripped his hair and kept him from moving away again. "I don't want your control." I bit into the hard shoulder and found both my hands above my head held tight in one of his. Normally I'd fight this, I didn't like giving up control, but I all I could think of was more. Please.

Troy's other hand moved down and grasped my knee, pushing it against his waist as he shoved inside me again. "Can't…" his thrust was hard and fast now, "stop…"

"Don't…" I groaned against him mouth when it crushed my own.

My whole body ignited, burning for the man above me. He played my body in ways I didn't know was possible and I thought for sure I'd actually catch fire, not that I cared at the moment.

I'd had sex before, pretty good sex if the truth be told. Nothing could ever compare to what I was feeling at this moment. I didn't know where I started and he ended, we were joined from our mouths down.

I swear the whole room started to shake as I climbed higher in the ecstasy of his touch. I briefly thought I'm going to die and I can't wait. Noises I'd never made in my life were coming out of my mouth and I couldn't find the focus to care. I was being consumed. I wanted to be consumed.

I felt his teeth sink into my neck and screamed out as my whole body felt the release of my orgasm. My body convulsing around him made him speed up and join our bodies with such a force I doubted I'd ever walk again.

With an animalistic growl from his throat, he stiffened on top of me and groaned against my ear, my body spasmed again right along with him.

The room was spinning and my body felt weightless. Had I died? With a soft kiss against my throat, he lifted his weight from me. Neither of us spoke, not that I could have formed words at this moment. If I'd had the strength I would have pulled the cover over me and slept right where I was. There was no way I'd be walking back to my room, or anywhere, for that matter. Not for several hours at least. The shocking part was I really didn't care. If I had an ounce of strength left I would have climbed on top of him and purred like a contented cat.

My body was humming in the most delicious way. I was completely contented, with a satisfying burn from the exertion of the foreplay and the actual sex. Sex wasn't even the best way to describe it. I'd had sex before and what we had just done didn't even fit into the same category.

Closing my eyes, I just accepted that my brain was mush and that was okay with me. My muscles tingled, some burned and then I realized my one arm was *really* burning. My left arm.

Opening my eyes, I lifted my hand off the bed and held it in the air over my face. The sensation intensified and the dawning of what was happening hit me like ice water.

Bolting up, I watched as lines and markings appeared all down my arm. If it had been on anyone else I would have thought, nice ink, but in this case there was nothing nice about it.

"Oh my god! What…"

Troy jerked beside me and rolled to his side. "Are you…" His eyes bulged when he looked at my arm. With a curse, he shifted and sat up on the side of the bed.

I blinked over and over, refocusing on my arm, hoping it would look different if I kept doing it long enough. Grabbing the sheet, I wrapped it around me and turned to look at the man beside me.

Troy sat there looking at his hand like he couldn't believe what he saw.

"What did you do?" I struggled to my knees.

"I didn't do it," he said with doubt in his voice.

I held my palm out to him and dared him to say it again.

"Alright, I didn't *mean* to do it. I didn't know…" he looked back down at his arm.

I was up off the bed, looking around for my clothes, and then I remembered I wouldn't be putting those back on. Tripping over the sheet, I found what was left of my jeans, pulled the phone and raptor free from them. "What do you mean you didn't know? How could you not know it was happening?"

He stood up, not bothered at all by his nakedness. I even paused to admire it briefly before the burning in my arm reminded me *that* was how I got in this mess.

He looked me up and down. "I was a little preoccupied." He strode over and stood in front of me, breathing in my face. "I was having you no matter what. You didn't seem to disagree at the time," he growled in a low tone.

Throwing my arms up, I grabbed the sheet and paced around in a going nowhere circle. "Oh my god! We do it once and I'm tied to you forever."

He frowned, looking confused. "You can't say…"

"If you say one word about prophecy, I swear I will kill you right here, right now."

He held up his hands and shook his head. I felt like I was overreacting and then I spotted the matching marks along his entire arm, I was not overreacting.

With a growl, I spun around, bunching up the sheet I stomped over to the door.

"Daxx, you can't…"

I slammed the door showing him what I couldn't do. Looking around, I tried to get my bearings so I could find my way back to my own room. What I was doing once I got there I had no idea.

Walking quickly, clinging to the sheet to keep it around me and off the floor I went down the first hall that looked familiar. When I rounded the corner I almost whined in relief when I recognized it as the hallway to my room.

Quinton came out of a door and then stopped, the smile fading off his face. He rushed to me and I could see his eyes registering. I was in a sheet, probably not looking my sleekest and grasped in my hand was my raptor. His eyes widened as they looked down my arm.

"Relax," I hissed quietly. "He lives." Pulling the sheet up, I continued toward my door. "For now."

CHAPTER THIRTY-NINE

An hour later I sat on the couch pouting, which made me angry because I liked to think I wasn't the pouty type. I'd actually tried to wash the markings off my arm, it didn't work. It still burned, a constant reminder that it was there.

When someone knocked on the door, I ignored it. I was pretty sure it would be one or another of the eight males I really didn't want to see right now. They could just wait until tomorrow or longer. What I really wanted to do was go home and almost had, then I remembered that Crissy was there and explanations would be required for why I had a full sleeve tattoo. I wasn't in the mood.

My phone vibrated across the table. Grabbing it, I planned to turn it off when I saw the message notice. Troy had text me, I didn't even know he knew how. Scowling, I opened the message hoping it wasn't some stupid denial muttering. Instead it read *Open the damn door for Mitz before she threatens to castrate me again!* I had to smirk, even though I didn't want to.

A knock on the door had me scowling once more. Feeling like I had no choice, I went over and unlocked the door. Mitz peaked in and then came in and closed and locked it behind her.

She came over and just stood there, with compassion

and understanding on her face. Her eyes moved slowly over my arm. "If it's any consolation Troy feels like a heel right now."

I huffed out a breath, a non-descript sound and dropped back down on the couch. "He claims he didn't know it was happening."

Coming over she perched on the edge of the cushion and turned to look at me. "He's not lying. Fate has a way to insure mates are ..." her eyes flicked to my arm. "mated if they're in close proximity of each other."

More details no one had shared. "What do you mean?"

Clasping her hands in her lap, in a way that was so patient I wanted to growl, she smiled. "When mates are near to one another they are irresistibly attracted to each other." She shrugged. "You aren't the first to be marked without prior agreement and I dare say you won't be the last." Flicking an imaginary piece of lint off her skirt, she kept her head down. "It almost happened with Chase, but he was able to sense it happening. Troy was overcome with ..." she gave me a little smile, "well, you know more than I on that matter. What I mean is he couldn't have stopped even if he wanted to. The male is driven with the desire to claim their mate, even in some cases when they don't want to." Sighing, she leaned back against the cushions. "In history I can't even recall a male that escaped it, not even the strongest or most fierce of our kind."

My head began to throb with this new information. "What does all of this mean, really?" I caught myself rubbing my hand over the tattoo on my arm.

She smiled again and leaned forward. "It is lovely, you're very lucky to have one that looks both feminine on the woman and masculine on the male. It hasn't always been so." Clearing her throat, she gave me a serious look. "What it means is Troy will never want another, ever, even if you don't do the blood rite." She shrugged. "Many don't. You may be marked, but if you truly..." she reached over and brushed the hair back from my face. "*Truly* don't want to be his, then that too is your right."

Confusion swirled inside my mess of a brain. "But you just said he won't ever want anyone else, doesn't that go both ways?"

Another patient smile appeared on her face. "I didn't say it would be easy. You're both going to be drawn to the other constantly and there will be some discomfort." She smirked. "I used to know a woman that fought it for close to a year, she was very determined, but in the end they ended up together and have been gloriously happy for the last five decades."

I heaved out a sigh, I wanted to cry and whine, something to make me feel better. "I don't even know if I *like* Troy." I looked down at my arm. "I mean I'm certainly attracted to him, but as a person, I don't even know him."

Reaching out, she patted my arm softly. "I have no doubt you'll like him, fate isn't that cruel. Just give it some time, there's no rush, love." A tear rolled down her cheek. "I'm sorry, I've just felt like I finally have a daughter since you've come and I worry constantly those beastly boys are going to screw that up."

Well, crap. Dropping my head down, I took a deep breath. It wouldn't do any good if I started blubbering too. "I'm not going anywhere, Mitz, I may run and hide from time to time but I'm staying." She launched herself at me and hugged me so tight I thought she was going to squish all the parts inside me.

"It's been nerve wracking, the things you've going through since you found us." Straightening, she masked her face and became the strong motherly woman once more. "Now, you and Troy need to discuss this and get it out in the open. We can't have you not focusing on the present tasks."

I knew she was referring to Marcus, and she was right, but I didn't know if I could talk to him just yet. "I'll go find him later."

She smirked. "Honey, he has been camped outside your door since you took off in his bed linen."

I blushed.

"He's been growling at any brother that even enters the same hallway as your room."

I groaned, knowing I would have to talk to him now. Nodding, I sat up. "Fine."

Getting up, she took two steps toward the door and then stopped and looked back at me. "Any more questions before I leave you to tend to things?"

Closing my eyes, I sighed again. "This blood rite, what exactly is it and how do I avoid it?"

She chuckled. "It's exactly what it sounds like, you exchange each other's blood and irrevocably tie yourself to one another." She smiled. "I guess the best way to avoid it is try not to take a bite out of him."

Rubbing my hands over my face, I suddenly felt really tired. "Good to know."

"Try to get some rest, love." She went over and opened the door, Troy appeared in it before she could take another step. Craning her neck, she glared up at him and poked him in the chest. "You. Behave."

His eyes flicked to me briefly before he glanced back down at her and nodded.

CHAPTER FORTY

I sat there, my spine stiff and looked at him where he stood in front of the closed door. My last words to him were threatening to kill him, so the fact that I couldn't figure out how to start a conversation right now wasn't a surprise. Did I apologize for my behavior? I didn't feel sorry for it at all, so I wouldn't lie to him about it.

Troy stood there looking worried, tired and almost as confused as I felt, clearly he didn't know what to say either. His eyes just kept moving over me in a slow appraisal, normally I wouldn't have minded that sort of look from a male, it was very complimentary, but right now it just reminded me of what had happened to put us both in this awkward moment.

My emotions were running in about ten different directions and I tried to decide which one to go with. I was still mad as hell that I was marked but I couldn't blame him, according to what Mitz had just told me. I didn't want to forgive him too quickly either, he should suffer right along with me for a while at least. The feeling of wanting to snuggle into his arms kept flashing through my mind, which would negate pretty much everything else I was feeling. Awkward didn't even begin to cover the state we were in.

Clearing his throat, he took a few steps closer. "I seem

to be at a loss as how to proceed," he said quietly with disbelief in his tone.

I watched him carefully as he got closer, monitoring exactly how I was feeling about it. I still wanted to smack him silly, but I also wanted to forgive him. "Yeah, I'm in the same place." When he sat on the table my instinct told me to run, then my arm tingled reminding me that the opportunity to flee had long passed. I didn't want to look at his tattoo, the one that said he was mine, but my eyes moved over it despite my resolve. Mitz was right, even though it was identical to mine it looked good on him, gave him that whole bad boy aura. I mentally groaned, like he needed to look *more* appealing.

His eyes followed mine and looked down at his arm. Lifting his hand, he studied it. "It burns like a bitch."

Well at least we agreed on something. "Mine too."

With one large finger, he traced over the swirls on his palm, like he was still amazed the marks were there. "I am sorry that this happened, but I'm not at the same time." His hazel eyes caressed my face. "I am overwhelmed with pride that fate gave you to me." The look softened. "I am also fighting this very strong desire to pull you off that cushion and crush you in my arms."

I jolted, sitting further back. "My brain is mush too, if that helps." I sighed, knowing this was ridiculous behavior for two adults, one of us aged way past adulthood. "Look, Mitz explained you had no control over what happened." I looked down at my own hand. "So I'm not pissed about that anymore."

"But you're still pissed."

I nodded. "Yeah." I waved a hand around. "How does all of this exist and no one knows?" Suddenly feeling cornered, I got up to pace around. "Another realm that's been there since forever and people are just oblivious. Okay, I admit it felt different to me, but it kind of familiar too." I spun around and looked at him. "How does that happen?"

He didn't move where he sat or make any sign of

attempting to answer. Good for him, he knew to let me have my little rant.

"I've always been a fighter, I don't know when it happened or how, it was like just there one day and I went with it." I snorted. "I can't say I defended the meek and innocent, but I broke my ass to bring those to justice that deserved it." I motioned in the air. "So, all the pieces kind of clicked when I was told I was destined to be this huntress. Fine. So, I'm Alterealm's Huntress. I'll take it…" hands on my hips I glared down at the floor, "but mated? I didn't sign up for that, no offence," I glanced over at him briefly, "I mean, sure I always hoped I'd find my happily-ever-after some day but to have it forced down my throat before I can even decide if it's right for me at this point in my life…" I ran out of words, I didn't know what to say. That was a first I'm sure.

"Daxx." He stood up and took a few steps in my direction, stopping with several feet between us. Compassion bled from him as he looked at me. "I will not force this." He glanced at his arm. "Beyond what has happened. I don't want you to think I would back you into a corner," his eyes flicked to the knife on my belt, "which would undoubtedly be bad for my health." He moved closer in a cautious way until he was close enough to reach out and touch my cheek gently. "All I ask is that you give us a chance. Get to know me. No pressure." His eyes hardened. "I will not complete the blood bond until you ask me." His spin stiffened and he took on that stance of the warrior King that he was.

"And if I decide never?"

I watched several emotions go through his eyes. "Then we'll deal with it when and if the time comes."

Okay, I suddenly felt better knowing he was as big a mess with all of this, just like I was. I sighed and then nodded. "Okay." I could see him visibly relax as he continued to stand there. The look in his eyes softened with what looked like adoration and that kicked me in the gut as warmth started to spread through me. I cleared my throat and stepped back. "Now what?"

Troy's eyes moved down over me, lust very much there.

I stepped back another foot. "Besides that."

He clenched his jaw. "I'm sorry, the last week was hell as I went crazy wanting you..." he looked at me again, "*now* it seems the desire is even stronger."

I wanted to call him on it and tell him it couldn't be, but as I stood there fighting to keep my eyes on his face and not running all over his body, I couldn't. "I feel it too."

A satisfied look came into his eyes. "Mmm, well, we'll have to work on controlling it."

I nodded, even though inside my head I was saying *yeah right!* I shook my head, unable to just go along with it. "How?"

"I have no idea," he said with a grin.

"Great." I stood there with my hands clasped together just as he stood there with his hands tucked in his pockets. Neither of us moved.

"I should go so you can get some rest." He said resignedly.

I nodded again like a bobble head. "Okay."

He took one step toward me, hesitance on his face. "I ..." He huffed out an abrupt breath. "May I just," he paused looking confused. "I'd like to try something." He held out his palm and looked at it. "It won't stop tingling."

"Mine's doing it too," I said breathlessly.

His hazel eyes moved to hold mine in a look that pleaded. "I am just wondering..."

I pointed a finger at him. "You keep those teeth in your mouth."

A relieved look came over his face. "I swear."

Looking down at my hand, I lifted my head up and took the last few steps between us. When I stood right in front of him, my body started buzzing and as much as I knew where *that* was going, I still did it anyway. With slow movement, I ran my hand down the length of his arm, tracing the pattern now marking it. The achy feeling I'd been filled with eased and was replaced with calm.

The look on his face told me he felt the same. Careful to keep his movement slow and non-threatening, he lifted his hand and ran his finger-tips down over my tattoo. A heated looked filled his eyes, but he didn't do anything more than just touch me lightly.

My stomach clenched as my body tried to urge me to move closer to him. This went beyond hormonal urges, it felt more like something necessary.

Troy took a deep shaky breath, confirming that he was fighting the same urges. "I feel better but..."

"Not." I finished for him.

He moved closer, our bodies almost touching and leaned down so his face was near my head. "Keeping my teeth to myself," he whispered beside my ear, "does that include my lips?"

A shudder ran through my whole system, making me feel weak. "I don't think kissing would be a good idea." I inhaled, his scent was so good.

Moving his hand up to the back of my neck, he nuzzled his face into my hair. "Probably not, but is it allowed? I will not cross any more lines where you are concerned."

A few minutes earlier I would have said no kissing, not *any* type of kissing, but right now all I was thinking was kiss me. Turning my face towards his, our mouths touched without a single breath of time passing. His mouth was firm, but he was being very gentle as he held my head and kissed me so deeply I tingled all the way to my toes. The burning in my arm was gone, the confusion faded and all that mattered was him.

Lifting his mouth away, he pulled me in closer only to crush my mouth beneath his again. Heat moved through my body and it wasn't until I started to relax, that I realized it was exactly where we'd begun all of this a short while ago. Kissing him back like a starving woman, I pulled my face back from his and stood there trying to catch my breath.

His hold on me gentled, as he looked down at me with

bright red eyes as he eased a few inches between us. He was breathing as heavily as I was, both of us were surprised that the flames consumed us as quickly as they had. Swallowing, he took a deep breath and tried to settle. Running his hand down over my left arm in a loving way, he stepped back. "Get some rest. I'll see you at breakfast."

Through the raging hormones I groaned, dreading the moment when I'd have to walk into a room full of his siblings, knowing that they would be more than aware of what we'd done.

He sent me an amused look. "Not to worry I'll have my brothers under control by the time you get there."

I didn't know if he could sense what I'd been thinking or not, just as long as I got to eat in peace the next day. "I'll see you then."

His eyes, now almost hazel moved over me once before he inclined his head and quickly went to the door. With one last look over at me, he opened it and left.

CHAPTER FORTY-ONE

I debated for a few minutes about wearing a long sleeve shirt to breakfast. Deciding I wasn't that cowardly or ashamed of the mark on my arm, I wore my usual cut off tank top. I may not be sure I wanted to be mated, but I'd be damned if anyone would look down on me because of it. It had been feeling weird since I woke, but it wasn't burning anymore, just a tingling that I figured would either fade eventually or I'd have to get used to so I wouldn't go insane.

Tucking the raptor in its holder at my back, I grabbed my phone and headed to the door. As I walked down the hall, I was thankful I didn't run into anyone else. I wasn't feeling like small talk. My first thought upon waking was of Troy, not in a bad way, just an awareness of him in my mind. As I'd dressed I could only think about seeing him, regardless of whether his brothers would be present or not. All of this was new to me and the only thing that kept me positive was it was new territory for him too.

I skirted down the little hallway, going into the kitchen through the back rather than walk into the dining room. I stepped through the door and froze. Troy was leaning down on the counter, near Mitz, a tender look on his face as he spoke to her. Having never seen that side of him, my heart jerked in my chest.

His head snapped up and he zeroed in on me instantly. Straightening from the counter, he looked over at me with relief in his eyes.

Mitz looked from him over to me and smiled. "I'll just take this out to the table."

Neither of us acknowledged that she spoke. Our eyes were only for one another. I stepped into the room, feeling unsure if I should go over to him or not.

Tucking his hands in his pockets he stood where he was looking as undecided as I felt. "Did you rest well?"

I shrugged. "Off and on."

He nodded. "Same here." His eyes moved over my arm before going back to my face. He offered me a small, almost vulnerable smile and it was that gesture that helped me decide I wanted to go over to him. We were in this together at least and he was as lost at what to do as I was.

Moving around the island, I walked up to him and wrapped my arms around his waist. He exhaled like he'd been holding his breath and closed his arms around me. It seemed to cure the antsy feeling that had been chasing me and eased my doubts. It also felt right, and that worried me a bit, but for now.

Resting his head on top of mine, he continued to just hold me. "Is it just me or is breathing easier like this?"

I snuggled my face into the warm muscle, taking his purely male scent in. "Mitz said there would be discomfort for a while if we're apart."

He chuckled. "Slight understatement." Lifting his head, he looked down at me. "Daxx, I am two hundred and sixty years old. I thought I'd tried it all and, for the most part, I was content with life." He grinned and shook his head. "And then you come in my life and I have been spinning out of control ever since you stomped into my office." Leaning down he placed a soft kiss on my mouth, lingering only for a second. "Now you have me feeling like an awkward teenager." Stepping back, he held my waist, keeping me at arm's length. "All I ask is that you keep in mind that I am going to say and do stupid things as I blunder my way through this." He offered me a sheepish grin. "And not stab me when I'm an idiot or walk away when I'm a fool."

I didn't know what to say to that. First, he'd spoke to me like a normal man not cool and regal and second, I didn't know what to say to that so I just nodded.

With a huge sigh, he released me and motioned to the door. "The natives will be getting restless and hungry."

I looked at the door and took a deep breath, knowing that as soon as I stepped through it life would change, again. Nodding to prepare, I moved over to the door. Troy opened it and followed right behind me.

As I stepped into the room, chairs scraped the floor as seven men stood. I stopped and glanced around to see their reactions, all but Chase had a silly grin plastered on their mugs. Chase wasn't smiling, but he wasn't frowning either. Our eyes connected and he tilted his chin down slightly in a motion of acceptance.

Looking to Rafael, I wanted to groan, it looked like he was barely able to contain himself as he stood there with a foolish smile on his face. Backing up a step, I found myself against Troy's chest. All faces around the table sobered and I knew without looking that the King behind me had just issued a silent command in the form of a glare.

I moved past everyone heading to the chair I always sat in beside Quinton. Baby steps, one change at a time I was telling myself. When I sat down the chairs scraped again as the men followed my lead.

Quinton didn't miss a step as he grabbed the coffee urn and filled my cup, like he had done every morning I ate here with them. Picking up the cup, I inhaled the wonderful fragrance of coffee and took a sip. Putting it down, I looked over at Victor. "Any word?"

He paused and studied me for a moment and that was all the time he was going to spend on this new event in our lives. I knew what his look really meant was now he was going to be forced out of bachelorhood and it was all my fault. "I expect something soon."

Nodding, I accepted the platter of home fries from Quinton and heaped some onto my plate. Hesitantly, I glanced at Rafael, who still looked a little too excited, but was containing himself rather well. "Did you reach Clairee?"

Dragging his eyes away from my arm, he cleared the smile from his mouth but it continued to shine in his eyes. "I can't find a trace of her. Wanda probably has her in deep hiding again."

That wasn't the news I wanted. It meant when we did confront Marcus again we wouldn't have any protection aside from my immunity to his power. I paused with my fork in the air, waiting for Quinton to dump eggs on my plate. "That sucks. I'd hoped for a little of her help again."

Chase looked down the table at me. "We'll make it without your little protection charms, kitten, no worries." He turned to look at his twin for confirmation and then stopped.

Troy wasn't looking back at him, he hadn't even looked at the food on his plate, he just sat at the head of the table looking at me. Chase elbowed him and he jumped and finally looked at him.

"Isn't that right brother King?" The note of amusement was plain in Chase's voice.

Troy gave him a blank stare.

I watched a few of the men grin and then look down at their plates, suddenly interested in anything in the room that would keep their faces turned away from the lost man at the end of the table.

Sighing, I waved my fork around the table. "That's enough you guys. This is a whole new place Troy and I have gotten ourselves into, it's going to take a while to adjust." I stabbed a potato with my fork a little harder than required.

Troy cleared his throat and looked around the table. "Do we have numbers yet?"

Quinton glanced down at me and then to his brother. "Nothing exact, maybe forty." He set his cup down. "They stick to small groups, neither Daxx or Crissy have caught a glimpse of Marcus."

Troy glanced at me for a second, his eyes moving over me slowly before he turned to Chase. "How many guards can you spare?"

Chase finished chewing his food while he considered. "Roughly twenty," he motioned around the table, "we can use them as fall-back, most of Marcus' followers are going to run for it when they realize its over."

Nodding, Troy looked around at his brothers. "I'd like to see this compound with my own eyes before we strategize any further." Michael and Vince nodded.

"I can sketch it out," Quinton mumbled with a mouth full of food. "Crissy and I spent more than our fair share of time staring out at it."

Rafael nodded. "It's nothing special."

"Still," Troy looked from his brothers to me. "I'd like to check it out for myself, a picture is fine but I need actual visuals to plan."

Was he asking my permission? I wasn't sure what the look on his face meant. I shrugged. "I can take the three of you over, later. I have to go see someone first."

Troy's eyebrows shot up. "Who?" His tone was no longer a conversation level.

Frowning, I set my cup down and gave him a startled look. "Arius set me up a meeting with one of the higher level mages." I said in a matter a fact way, not sure why he sounded so brusque all of a sudden.

Troy gave his brother an inquisitive look.

Arius set his fork down, sent me a look saying he wasn't happy at the mention of his involvement. "Romeo, uh, Romulus has agreed to meet with *our* huntress to give her some pointers on what some of the movements Marcus might use for certain casts..." He stopped when Troy's curious look turned to anger.

"You are taking her to see *Romeo?*" Troy asked in broken words.

I glanced at Quinton, he gave me a quick look and shook

his head. Romeo, Romulus, I didn't care what they called him just as long as he could help me. I glanced from Troy's glare to Arius's scowl and felt for a moment I had missed something important. "What is the problem?" I leaned on the table and watched Troy. "I *can* see Marcus, *none* of you can. If I can get a bit of a heads up on what he's up to, then that's a bonus for us."

Troy's eyes finally flicked to me, a possessive expression on his face. "I can't..." I widened my eyes at him, daring him to use can't allow or any other form of it that meant the same thing. He took a deep breath before he spoke again. "I can't allow this."

The only sound heard was cutlery being set on the table. The men on the side of the table I sat on all sat back, giving me a clear line to their King at the other end. Chase cleared his throat and shook his head before looking at his twin with disbelief on his face.

I leaned forward in my chair and looked down the table at him. "*Allow* what exactly? My learning Marcus' moves, or going to see Romeo?" I spoke very clearly and quietly.

His jaw clenched a few times, his hazel eyes not straying from mine. "Both."

Chase rubbed a hand down over his face and then shook his head again. "Brother, I'm going to risk life and limb here to save your ass, *again*." He motioned toward me. "She has a point. If she can give us a heads up on what he's trying to do, then score one more point for us."

Troy glanced at his sibling out of the corner of his eye for a moment before they slowly moved back to me. "Very well," he said quietly. "I will accompany you for this meeting, Daxx."

I mulled it over; taking my time trying to sort out what the hell was going on. Anything we could use to find and stop Marcus had been the plan yesterday, surely Troy still saw that. I looked at Chase, who only offered me a shrug. All eyes were on me, no one moved. The tension was so thick all of sudden it was hard to think beyond it. "Fine." I said quietly.

Quinton visibly relaxed beside me. He cleared his throat. "I suggest we bypass practice today, I don't think I could watch you two try to kill each other two days in a row.

Several nods confirmed there would be no battle, mock or otherwise today. Chairs scraped the floor.

"I'll be at the cells," Michael announced.

Victor stood up. "I'll walk with you."

Rafael nodded over to Quinton. "We should go make rounds."

Nodding, Quinton gave me a brief glance. "Yeah, okay." He got up.

Sighing loudly, Chase stood up. He smirked at his twin, who continued to stare at me. Walking around the table he came up behind me and leaned around the chair to speak beside my ear. "I wish you luck, kitten, you're going to need it."

I snorted in answer. Arius glanced from his Troy over to me. "I will be in Vic's office when you're ready to leave." I nodded.

Leone offered no excuse, just pushed his chair back from the table and simply walked out of the room.

I glanced at the clock and then to the man still staring at me. "Well, you managed twenty minutes without being a jerk." I stood up and moved down to his end of the table. "What was that?"

He looked down to the untouched food in front of him. "Romulus is called Romeo for a reason..."

"Yeah, I caught that. *And?*" I stood there with my arms crossed over my chest looking down at him.

"I don't want you anywhere near him." This said in a tone that implied his word was final.

It was so not final in my mind. "Troy, you don't get to choose what I do, so you can get that notion right out of your head right now."

He stood up so quickly, the chair rocked back. Suddenly he was towering over me his face only inches from mine.

"It's not a notion, its how I *feel*." His eyes bore into mine. "I don't want you near *any* male right now," he growled.

A combination of annoyance and shock hit me, along with that was a flash of heat through my body responding to the alpha man thing. I swallowed. "Arius is coming with me," I tried to sound reassuring.

"Arius is still a male." His voice was shaking in a way that I knew he was trying to control himself.

"Arius is your brother." I reminded.

Shaking his head, he straightened, giving me a few inches of breathing space. "It doesn't matter. I watched you dance with him. He was smiling."

"We were dancing, isn't that supposed to be fun?" I was confused.

"You enjoyed dancing with all of my brothers," his tone had dropped again.

Closing my eyes, I took a deep breath and then let it out slowly before looking back up at him. "Troy, what is going on with you?"

With a strangled growl, he shook his head and paced to the other side of the room. "I don't know." Spinning, he looked at me with pain in his eyes. "I just…" he huffed out a breath, "the idea of another male, whether sibling or not anywhere near you hits me right in the gut." His voice was a mix of misery and anger.

A quiet sigh from the other side of the room had us freezing like deer in head lights. Mitz stood there, shaking her head. "You're going to be very possessive and protective of each other for a while."

"How do we fix it?" Troy asked in an exasperated tone.

She smiled and looked at him. "Hide and never be near anyone else?"

He groaned, "lovely."

"If it were meant to be easy, Troy," she scolded, "everyone would be mated."

He sighed. "I just about had a bloody fit when Arius told me he was taking Daxx to see Romeo…"

She laughed. "Don't be silly, Troy. Daxx has far better taste than a man like *that*." Her eyes moved to me. "He is a womanizer, a slimy one." She informed me in a firm tone.

"Ah." I turned and sent Troy an annoyed look. "You don't think I don't know how to deal with men like that?"

He shrugged, not committing to any comment either way.

I looked back over to Mitz. "So, what can we do to help cave man over there keep it together?" Grinning, I felt my cheeks flush slightly. "Alpha is fine behind closed doors, if you know what I mean." Mitz smirked, "but in front of others, not so cool." I glanced over my shoulder at him to see him giving me a heated look at the implication of my words.

Mitz came over and touched my cheek softly. "Something as simple as that has been known to reign in a possessive mate, a little reassuring contact."

I raised my eyebrows and then nodded. "Okay, got it." I found myself spun around by strong hands and picked up before I could react. Troy's mouth crushed mine as he held me off the floor.

I had no time to do anything, before I found myself set back down with a spinning head and weak knees.

"Something like that works too." Troy said with a glint in his eyes as he looked down at me.

Patting his chest, I shook my head. "We won't be doing *that* in the middle of breakfast or a meeting though." I turned around to see Mitz shaking her head, but smirking at the man behind me.

"You hit the nail on the head, love, a cave man for sure." With a soft chuckle, she walked back over to the door and left us alone.

CHAPTER FORTY-TWO

I stood back and watched this Romeo as he spoke to Arius, pausing often to smile over at me. Mitz had been right when she'd used the word slimy. Did he really think I was going to smile back each time he leered at me? What I wanted to do was throw my knife at him. Turning to roll my eyes at the man playing ominous bodyguard, I couldn't seriously believe he worried about my being around this 'romeo'.

Troy just continued to stand there with his arms crossed looking like an enormous statue. When he moved his eyes slowly down my body and then wandered back up to my face, I did the very same thing to him and then winked at him. He actually smirked before turning his glare back to the two men heading our way.

Arius stopped a few feet away, but the other guy moved right in and dropped to one knee in front of me. "My Lord. My Queen, I am most humbled by your presence." I lifted my hand, hovering it over his slicked back hair, glancing at Arius, his eyes flicked behind me and then he shook his head barely moving it.

"Enough, Romulus," Troy barked, "we have no time for this."

Romulus raised his head, his eyes moving up over me. I

took an automatic step back until I was leaning again Troy. His hand moved to rest on my waist, so I decided this is where I was staying.

Standing, the mage's eyes moved over my arm and then hesitantly to his King's. He inclined his head. "Of course, time is of the essence in this matter." He smiled. "I know I can be very helpful. Marcus was my mentor and taught me everything." He shook his head. "I am still troubled that this is happening." Sighing, he turned and went over to a table. "Although when one has that much power it's not surprising that it got to him." Picking up a book, he came back over to us. "This is my journal, it illustrates much of what you're looking for. To teach you would take hours, but I feel as long as you can learn some of the preludes you will be able to recognize when to bail and run and when not to." He paused and studied me. "You are really immune to him?"

I shrugged not really wanting to engage him in any sort of dialogue.

He nodded, a smile plastered to his face. "Of course, you are, prophecies don't lie." Holding out the book, he bowed his head. "If you have any questions, please don't hesitate to come and see me."

Troy reached around me and took the book out of his hands. With a nod to Arius, he placed his hand behind my back and started *guiding* me toward the door, with no room for argument.

With a helpless look to Arius, I shrugged and went where I was being lead.

Once we were outside, he paused and looked down at me. "I am sorry."

I had to wonder for which part exactly, but kept my mouth shut.

"For even considering you'd prefer him over me." He looked embarrassed.

I grinned up at him. "Oh I don't know." I sucked in a breath. "It's a tough call..." I shrieked when I found myself swung up over his shoulder.

Lifting my head, I tried to look around to see if there was something I could reach to get out of his hold. I found myself looking at an amused upside down Arius as he was closing the door.

"If I didn't know for fact you were only ten years older than I, brother, I would have to wonder if you predate the dinosaur." Arius shrugged at me and then stepped out of my sight line. "Put the huntress down, we can't walk through the village with her slung over your shoulder, despite how charming it looks." He almost sounded bored.

I would have to thank him later for that when I found myself flipped around and practically tossed up in the air before being caught in strong arms.

"Can I carry her this way?" Troy was smirking.

Arius sighed. "Perhaps you should ask your Queen if she wants to be toted around the village like a toddler, with everyone looking on."

Troy looked at me and then heaved a dramatic sigh. "I am fairly certain I know the answer to that." Gently he placed me back on my feet and smiled down at me.

Flipping the hair back from my face, I sent him a scalding glare and then turned to Arius and grinned. "Thank you."

He inclined his head and then side stepped so Troy's large body was between us. I frowned, wondering if I was going to have to always walk five feet away from everyone from now on. It could make things a little hard during a fight or even practice. Females that hung around the royal brothers were something I'd never seen yet so that would leave me on the side lines. *That* I didn't do. Shaking it off, I turned and started walking, hoping it was in the right direction. "Let's go look at the compound."

****

Being surrounded by four large men in the little steel shed on the roof was an experience I didn't want to repeat again anytime soon. Of course, I had to try to keep my distance from all of them so Troy wouldn't have another of his predatory episodes.

"How many are down there now, Daxx?" Michael asked sounding frustrated.

I made my way back to the peep hole as the men shuffled out of the way again keeping Troy closest to me. Looking out, I did a quick tally. "Fifteen." I turned and looked around Troy so I could see Michael. "They're horsing around more than practicing, but there's one group that seems to be tight and when they get the moves on it's almost beautiful to watch." I puffed out my cheeks and then sighed. "It's going to be a real shame when you guys beat on them."

Arius, who had decided he was coming at the last second, laughed. "Just remember they're going to be gunning for you too, my little huntress."

I glanced up at Troy quickly to see his jaw tense. I snorted. "Yeah good luck on them getting close enough to even get in a swing."

Troy smiled down at me confirming he wasn't going to let me get into any heavy scuffles. I didn't know how I was going to get around it, but I was not going to stand there and be the only bloody cheerleader for team Alterealm Royals.

"I've seen enough." Victor stated sounding bored. His eyes moved over me slowly and then to his sibling crowding me. "Shall we go back and do some planning? Troy?"

Troy turned and nodded.

The planning was a bunch of men leaning over a roughed-out map arguing which way would be the best. I wanted to go to my room and read through the book, not being really big on plotting out a fight. For me it was free fall and beat on anything that moved, but each to their own.

I did not get to go to my room and read the book when Troy suggested I look through it where they were. Focusing was a little difficult as I attempted to envision these arm diagrams on a body in front of me.

Sighing, I set the book down and lifted my hands again.

"Getting anywhere?" Rafael spoke from behind me.

I turned and grimaced. "No. I will never recognize any

of these from this." I pointed to the book.

He leaned over my shoulder and looked down at it. "Someone wasn't really big on art," he quipped.

I shook my head and flipped back a few pages. "This entire section is basically the beginning moves to some real whopper spells. If he's going to get down and dirty he'd have to start with these," I sighed, "if I'm even reading it right." I sounded defeated, I knew I did. It had been one hell of a day, or night so far. Troy's crowding me was starting to get on my nerves and I was trying to be patient and not rock the boat, so we could all focus on more important things.

"Maybe I can help." He smiled his player smile. "I spent a lot of time with a young mage once."

I rolled my eyes. "I'm sure you did."

He shrugged, still grinning. "I'll try to decipher these moves so you can see them in action with real arms, would that help?"

I wanted to hug him, but then glanced over at his brother that was leaning over the table with his head close to Michael bickering about something. "Yes that would be awesome."

Raf looked over at the others and winked. "Don't worry about him, he's *very* occupied right now."

I let out a deep breath. "Okay. Let's start at the beginning and see how far we get."

Picking up the book, I backed up a step and held it out so he could see it. He studied it for a moment, moving his arms a little this way or that and then nodded and looked up at me. When he went through the full motion, it was definitely different than trying to figure it out from sketches. I started to feel a little more encouraged.

He kept repeating it over and over as I watched, picking up the pattern and trying to remember it so I'd know it again. "How," he started it over once more, "are you planning to be in battle and watch which way Marcus moves his hands at the same time?"

I pouted and kept my eyes on his hands. "I really don't

know. Shit luck mostly." I grinned and then nodded at him. "Okay I've got that one." I flipped the page. "Next."

We made it through ten different moves, before they started getting more complex. A few times Raf had to start over because even looking at the book he lost his place. He sent me a sheepish grin. "I knew I should have paid more attention in school."

I laughed. "You're not the first to say that. Did any of you boys pay attention in school? Are the people being ruled by a family of drop outs?"

He placed his hand over his heart. "I'm wounded that you would think that little of us, of me. Here I am trying to wrap my brain around these chicken scratches and you're insinuating I'm a slacker."

Lowering the book, I tried to glare at him but couldn't and ended up laughing again. "You are ridiculous," I gasped out.

His deep chuckle echoed around me. "No, ridiculous would be recording me flapping my arms around like a damn bird here." He shook his head. "The things I do."

"What *are* you doing exactly?" Troy's tone silenced all movement in the room.

Rafael glanced over his shoulder at him. "Helping, Daxx try to figure these out. Did you look at this book, brother? It's like interpreting a child's drawings." He looked down at me and squeezed his eyes shut as he waited for Troy's response.

Quinton moved away from the table and strode towards us quickly. "They're that bad?"

"At least Raf can read children scratches, he's still at that level himself." Leone moved away from the others and in our direction as well, an amused look on his face.

I handed the book off to Quinton, not sure what they were up to but knew enough to know I wasn't going to take a direct part in it. When Arius smiled across at me and then edged his way around the table, I knew they were at it again.

"I didn't think to actually look in the book. I took

Romeo at his word." He came over looking very serious and held out his hand for the book. Glancing at it he shook his head. "And Raf is able to read this?" He smirked at his younger brother. "You've improved."

Michael and Victor stepped back and crossed their arms, obviously not wanting to be a part of the game when the stakes were this high.

"I think we should all help, Daxx." Raf suggested, still not facing Troy.

Leone nodded and stepped to stand beside him, blocking me from Troy's view. "I'm in."

Quinton took the book from Arius and flipped a few pages. "It could take a while, but anything to help our Huntress." He winked at me and then stood with his shoulder to Leone's.

A big grin plastered to his face, Arius stepped in line and I found myself almost surrounded by men that towered over me, blocking out anything past their bodies.

Chase's voice suddenly filled the room. "Sorry I'm late, I had to attempt some sort of sleep." His voice faded at the end. "What have I missed?" His pushed his way between Raf and Leone. "Ah, hello, kitten." He glanced around at his brother's faces as they tried not to smile. "You guys have a death wish I don't know about?" He looked over Raf's shoulder. "*That* my silly siblings is a rabid animal you're teasing." Giving me a sympathetic look when I shook my head to say I had no part of this.

I heard movement, but when I tried to look between them I couldn't see a damn thing. I was all for a little camaraderie among family, but somehow I think this was a few steps beyond considering the circumstances.

Chase sighed. "Michael and Victor have about three seconds before he breaks free. Who's the fastest runner?"

Rafael grinned and lunged toward me. "Me!" I found myself swung up over his shoulder as he ran out the door Quinton held open. I heard the door slam, but was too busy holding on tight so I wouldn't bounce off and hit the floor.

The door banged three more times before I heard thundering foot steps behind us. How was this going to look to anyone we flew past? One brother of the royal family carrying me and the rest racing after us? I wasn't a football for crying out loud.

There was a loud crashing noise that sounded like wood splintering and then some grunting before the echo of boots on the hall started again. I lifted my head, trying not to let my teeth clatter and saw Chase and Quinton trying to slow down Troy, a very determined look that said no one was keeping him from catching me. Arius was lying on the floor looking winded and possibly injured, Michael was beside him and not looking much better. Victor was bent over leaning on his knees either hurt of trying to catch his breath.

I put my head down. "Either run fast Raf or put me down and duck." I squeaked out between the jarring movements of his fast strides.

There were more grunts from behind us, and what sounded like flesh hitting flesh. "You're on your own Raf," Quinton called out.

The sound of feet behind us was now only of one pair. I squealed as Raf bolted around a corner and then almost tossed me to the ground, spinning me around so I was facing the sound of the stomping boots. Sounding winded, he steadied me so I wouldn't tip right over before his hands dropped from me and he backed away.

Troy came around the corner and came to a stop when he saw me standing there. He sent Raf a look of death and then moved toward me intention clear on his face.

I held my hands up. "I wasn't part of it."

"I know." Wrapping one big arm around my waist, he picked me up off the floor and held me tight against his body.

I held on to his neck, preferring this to hanging over a shoulder. His chest was rising and falling as he tried to breathe after the exertion and turned to head back the way we'd all just come from.

Around the corner stood Mitz shaking her head. "I

thought the days of telling you no running in the halls was over."

Troy scowled. "They started it."

Giving Mitz an exasperated glare, I tried to twist free so I could stand on my own, Troy wasn't having any of it. "How long do I have to put up with this?"

She sent the man holding me an annoyed look. "I'm not sure, until the bond is complete or…"

Troy growled something I couldn't understand and started walking back down the hall. Quinton was pulling Arius to his feet as we passed. He gave me a sympathetic look.

"Troy," I said softly, trying to sound patient. "I *can* walk."

He looked at me and then back to the next brother he stepped around. "And I *can* carry you."

"Troy," Victor caught up to us, "we really need to get back to…"

"Later." Troy said in a tone that made Victor bow his head and stop walking with us.

I glared at the man carrying me like a rag doll. "I'd like to walk, please." I said it in a way that sounded like I was asking, but I really wasn't.

He gave me a quick glance, but said nothing and we weren't slowing down so chances of him doing what I wanted seemed slim.

Chase came up beside us. He walked along in stride with his twin for several steps without saying a word. I tried to catch his eye to ask that he do something, but he looked straight ahead mimicking his brother.

"*What* do you want?" Troy asked in his lethal tone.

Shrugging, Chase finally looked at his brother. "I just wanted to be with you in your last moments."

Troy glanced at him out of the corner of his eye. "My what?"

"The way I see it," he looked me up and down in his brother's hold, "you have maybe another minute before Daxx is *really* pissed about being toted about like a puppet *or*," he grinned, "she'll keep it together until you stop and put her down and then she's going to slice you up like a loaf of bread."

Troy grunted in response but did finally look down at me. I lifted both eyebrows at him, letting him know that his sibling wasn't far off. He stopped and looked at his brother, still holding me off the floor. "I can't help it. I feel like I'm losing my mind."

"Oh, I'd say you lost it." Chase looked at his arm wrapped around me.

Sighing, Troy loosened his grip on my waist and let me slide down his body. My first thought was to step clear of him, but his hand splayed against my back ended that idea.

"Troy," I tried for understanding, but have no idea if I made it. "This is crazy. I can't live like this." I wasn't exaggerating. Here I was literally tied to a man that I'd had sex with once, spectacular as it was, and now I could barely take two steps away without him losing it.

The solution was the blood rite, but did I really want to permanently, and I mean forever and ever, *be* with him. I watched several emotions go through his eyes as he looked at me. Just the fact that he was waging an internal battle and trying to be reasonable counted for a lot more than he knew. I could feel the pull between us too, I just didn't go all predator with it.

His hold on my back loosened a little further, like he was trying to let go but his hand wasn't listening. Dropping it completely, he clenched it at his side. With a soft look in his hazel stare, he sighed again. "Go."

It almost didn't register when he said it, barely a whisper. I looked at Chase who nodded and turned and started down the hall. A few feet later, I paused and looked over my shoulder. "I'll see you at dinner."

Inclining his head, he looked back at me and then turned with a jerky movement and went back down the hall. Chase sent me a look that said he'd keep an eye on him and then followed behind him.

Heaving out a huge sigh of relief, I found my bearings and headed to my room, double time.

CHAPTER FORTY-THREE

Time away from Troy turned out to be a more difficult thing to do than I had anticipated. It had only been two hours and I was pacing around my room worrying about him, this was new. It wasn't that I'd never been anxious about anyone before, but to actually not be able to focus on anything but that person was something I'd never had happen.

Quinton had texted me to say Troy was tense but behaving as they planned and rallied the troops. I didn't worry any less, just focused on how many troops would give us the best shot for a few minutes.

Glancing at the markings on my arm I had to wonder how they could take what was a mutual attraction scenario and make him into a domineering ape and me a worry-wart. The next question was, did I like it? Feeling vulnerable and slightly lost, no I didn't like that at all.

My mind kept lingering over the bits and pieces Mitz had mentioned during our talks, how fate wouldn't put me with someone I didn't like. My question, well, more of a wondering … were Troy and I compatible enough to be together forever? In this case it was literally for*ever*. Did I even want to live that long? How was *that* managed, I wondered.

Shaking my head, I decided the details could be asked later. Mitz had said Troy would never want another woman—I looked at the swirls down my arm. How many women on my side would kill for a fidelity insurance policy like that?

I continued pacing, trying to tell myself that I had all the time in the world to figure out what I wanted. Did I want Troy? That was just silly, any woman with a pulse would want him. Whether I could live with him, especially this new territorial version was another thing all together.

Could I live without him though, began to worry my every thought. My chest started to tighten, making me pause in the middle of the room and place my hand on it. Drawing in a deep breath I tried to override the panic that was starting to fill me.

What was wrong? Something wasn't right.

My arm began to feel hot, I stared at it like the answer to why would appear. This made the tightening in my chest increase. Rubbing my hand up and down my arm, I tried to think of what would cause it to do this without warning. I hadn't tried to scrub it off since that one time, realizing it was now a permanent part of me. Waves of panic were feeding this whole lost feeling, my heart was beating an entirely different rhythm causing me to lose my breath for a few moments.

Did they have a doctor here? Surely not everyone could just magically heal themselves with one vice or another, someone with medical knowledge had to exist on this side. I knew I couldn't go to anyone on my side, where would I even begin to explain what was going on.

Closing my eyes, I took a deep breath and forced myself to exhale slowly. It didn't help, something was really wrong. Opening them I rushed over to the table to get my phone, I needed Quinton here now.

Before I could even scroll to his number, the door flew open and Troy's large form filled it.

The burning of my arm intensified as I stood there

looking at him. When my heart started to settle down, the tightness in my chest eased. Whether the emotions I had been feeling were his, or caused by being away from him I didn't know but the lost feeling was fading and I felt like I could think again.

As if synced with each other we both started walking at the same moment. His eyes moved over every inch of me in those few steps, as if he needed to see with his own eyes that I was alright.

The phone I forgot I was holding buzzed, startling me out of the almost trance like state I was in, glancing at it I saw a text from Quinton. *Troy on route – quickly!* Grinning, I tucked the phone into my pocket and looked up at the man now towering over me.

With a gentle touch, he ran his hand down my arm and the burning lessened.

"I sensed you were upset," he said in a whisper.

My next words should have been how, but instead they were, "I can't explain it."

He gave me a lopsided grin, "I don't think you need to." Palming the back of my head, he pulled me closer and began kissing me in a slow, hungry way.

All the panic inside me left and something clicked into place. A new sense of completeness filled me. Wrapping my arms around his neck, I kissed him back almost desperately, not wanting these feelings to leave.

That's all we did, kiss, drinking each other in, quenching a thirst that was never ending. In that moment, I didn't care about prophecies or fate, all I wanted was this man I was wrapped around to continue to fill my every pore with only him.

Breaking the kiss, he looked down at me, his red eyes filled with hunger. My breath was ragged and legs were weak but in that moment I would have given him anything he asked. As I pulled his head back down, he nestled me tight into his hard body.

Someone cleared their throat from the door. Troy

straightened but didn't turn to see who it was.

"I *really* hate to break this up, but Victor just got word that we better get our asses to the compound within the hour."

Both of us looked over at Rafael standing there.

With his hand against my back, Troy pulled me closer to his side and turned us so we faced him. "What's going on?"

Raf shrugged. "That's all I was told. Everyone is meeting at the weaponry in fifteen minutes."

Troy nodded. "We'll be there."

Rafael spun on his heel and left.

Serious eyes met mine. There was so much to say to each other, and somehow we silently acknowledged it. Smirking, he took my hand. "We have some ass to kick." Pulling me toward the door, he sent me a heated look. "Let's get this done so we can focus on more enjoyable things."

Ignoring the way my body responded, I shrugged. "I enjoy beating on those deserving."

His eyes flared, but he didn't comment.

****

The weaponry to me was like a shoe store to most other women. Weapons in all shapes, sizes and styles, *this* was heaven.

Chase spotted us before we got two feet in the door and came over carrying my harness for my Sais. I think I had it strapped on before it had left his hand completely. With a grin, he reached over my shoulder and put the weapons in it. Nodding to his twin, he turned and went toward the wall again.

Quinton appeared beside me holding out two knives—a six inch one with a weighted grip and a four-inch throwing knife. I'm sure I was drooling. I held out both hands, wanting all of the pretty toys. He grinned. "I'll get you the straps."

Victor came walking over, looking every bit the warrior, all black leather. He held out my little zapper box and then nodded when I clipped it to my waist. "I'm going to the shed with Michael. I'll see you when you get there."

I felt like a queen, only instead of jewels they were arming me with well-crafted weapons and accessories. Looking around, I spotted Troy, my heart doing a little flip inside my chest. Gone was his t-shirt and in its place he wore a black leather vest that left most of his upper body bare and visible. My arm tingled and then his head turned and our eyes met. I had to take a deep breath to remember what we were doing, with a small smirk he turned back to Rafael and Tim.

Mitz was suddenly standing in front of me. I must have had a shocked look on my face because she grinned. "No. I'm not going to fight." She held up a piece of leather. It looked like a restraining device crossed with a corset. "The seamstresses were hoping to have more finished before you'd need them, but with where you were injured before, I took it as an omen that this was the first piece they finished."

I felt like a little girl when she came at me and shoved it up against me rib cage. Nudging my arms out of the way, she pulled the straps around my back. "It's lined with a mesh inside, a metal one." She buckled it at my side, "but fine enough you can still move freely."

Stepping back, she gave a little nod of approval and then made a serious expression with her lips. "Bring my boys back and be careful."

With that, she turned and walked quickly through the tall bodies.

Looking down at the chunk of leather, it dawned on me what it was, covering and protecting my rib cage, sides and stomach but stopping high enough on my waist that I could still move I felt excited wearing it. I now had body armor, or at least the start of it.

When I looked up, Troy was walking toward me with a very intent look on his face. My arm tingled and I recognized now what the tingling feeling was, his desire. The rest of me caught up and heat slowly moved through me. I smiled when he was in front of me and held out my arms, waving the knives around. "What do you think?"

Nodding slowly, he stepped close enough I could feel the heat from his bare chest. Lowering his head, he nuzzled my neck. "I think, later, I'd like to see you wearing only that."

Lava replaced the blood in my veins as he leaned back and looked down at me. "We could do that," I barely managed to whisper.

"Maybe you two should stay a few feet apart." Quinton appeared beside Troy, holding out the knife straps.

Troy gave me a long intense look and then stepped back. The look changed when he sent his brother an annoyed glance. "How many of us have gone over?"

I took the first strap from Quinton and secured it to my thigh.

"Arius, Leone and Raf have most of them over there now. We'll split up and take the remaining ones with us." He handed me the other strap.

"Good." Troy motioned to Tim with his head. "Tim stays with Daxx. At *all* times," he ordered in his kingly voice.

Nodding, Quinton glanced over his shoulder at the man. "He knows."

A whistle came from behind me and I didn't have to turn to see who would be brave enough to do that with Troy standing in front of me. I busied myself securing the other strap to my calf as Chase stepped up beside his brothers.

"My, my kitten." He smirked down at me. "Once you get the full leathers you have to get some of those boots."

I knew what he was referring to, but wasn't going to play into his game.

Troy cleared his throat as I straightened up. I gave him a hesitant look only to see him smiling at his twin. "Oh she'll get boots, but you won't be seeing her in them."

Sighing dramatically, Chase held out a small wooden case to him. "I'd ask if I could have the honors, but I think I'd fight better with hands."

The smile Troy gave him was almost evil. "When did

you get brains?" Taking the case from his sibling, he opened it.

I looked in to see a large, heavy chained pendant baring Troy's symbol of the moon. It was the mate to the sun one Chase wore around his neck. Beside the man's jewelry was a smaller one like the one pendant of both symbols I'd wore to the dance, just not as fancy.

Troy took it out and leaned over to place it around my neck. The cool metal rested just below my collar bone. Placing a lingering kiss on my cheek, he straightened and then took his own out of the box. Reaching over, I took it out of his hand, noting the surprised look on his face as I did.

Moving so my body was almost touching his, I stretched up and placed the chain over his head. Following the pendant down his chest with my hand, I gave him a serious look. "If you so much as get a scratch, I'm gonna be pissed."

He grinned down at me, his eyes shining.

Turning I looked at the other men. "That goes for you guys too."

CHAPTER FORTY-FOUR

Troy, Chase and I left the others to meet up with Victor and Michael at the shed on the roof. Two men I didn't know where there as well. I gave Troy a curious look and nodded at them.

"Mages." Keeping his body between me and anyone else there, he went over and looked out the little hole. "How long will it last?"

I didn't know what he was talking about until he turned and glanced at the two men staying well away from anyone.

"Half hour, tops." The short bald one said with an uneasy tone.

"That will have to do." Troy said, looking back down at the compound. "Daxx, come and tell me what's going on down there."

Moving closer to him, I looked out. Assessing quickly, I turned and looked up at him. "They're all out in the compound, loading up trucks."

"Do you see Marcus?" Chase moved over and looked out the hole then hissed out a breath when he couldn't see anything.

I shook my head. "No." Turning I gave the bald man a hard look. "So you two can make it so everyone can see through this magic covering, but you can't stop Marcus?"

He looked as if he was going to say something unpleasant until his eyes moved over the pendant on my chest, to my arm and then to Troy that stood very close to my side. "Our powers are not that strong. We can toy with his spell and bring down the barrier, but only for a short time." His eyes darted from Troy to Chase and then he bowed his head. "Huntress," he said in a broken way as if he were nervous.

I wanted to laugh and tell the guys to knock it off, but what the hell, they liked to intimidate so who was I to stop them. I glanced at Victor. "Your call."

He nodded abruptly and then looked from brother to brother. Turning to the door, he sent the two mages a cold look. "Let us get in place and then take it down."

I was ushered out the door feeling like a sandwich between Troy and Chase's large bodies, Quinton right in front of me and Tim close enough on our heels that I could almost feel his breath on my back.

"I don't want…" Troy cleared his throat and then spoke in a softer, less demanding tone. "Don't place yourself in the direct line of fire with Marcus," his hand moved down my back in an intimate gesture, "please."

When he added it like that, I had to at least let him know I appreciated his trying without distracting either one of us. Reaching over, I gave his forearm a gentle touch and nodded. "I'll try." Gritting my teeth, I stopped there, even though I wanted to get Marcus this time.

"You stay close to Tim." Chase instructed, slowing his pace so I wouldn't have to run.

"Don't mother me, Chase. We got this." I glanced at Troy out of the corner of my eye, making sure he was alright with his brother this close to me; he seemed to be struggling but made no move toward us.

Quinton paused and looked at me over his shoulder. "Never mind trying to figure out his spells either, if his arms start moving you get your ass clear."

It was an order, but I understood he was just worrying.

"Got it." I paused and turned to look at Tim, with a daring look in my eyes. "Any orders from you?"

Glancing from one king to the other, he shrugged. "You take them down and I'll watch your back?"

I grinned, "deal."

Both men beside me tensed, but they didn't say a word, just glared at the guard.

I swatted both of them at the same time. "Relax, we all know he's only pretending to let me be in charge." I rolled my eyes up at Chase. "He'll be all over me like body armor and you know it."

Chase smiled. "He'd better."

Sighing, I grabbed Troy's hand and starting walking toward the large group that was only a few yards away now. "I missed the plotting portion of this, so you'll have to forgive me if I deviate from your carefully laid plans."

Troy squeezed my hand. "Even if you were present, I know you'd still do it your way."

I winked at him. "You are a smart man."

He jerked me to a stop and kissed me hard on the mouth. "Just remember I'm *your* man."

I nodded and stood there looking up at him, hoping he would be safe during this. "Let's do it."

****

I stood up on a crumbling balcony of an empty building about fifteen feet in the air, with Troy and Chase. I wanted to ask what the hell we were doing up here when the action was going to be on the ground, but the vibrations coming off them were serious psyching and I didn't want to mess up any of the aura that was humming through me. All I knew was that this had better not be some bogus ploy to keep me clear of the fight.

I watched the movement of those we were about to fight. They were in some kind of hurry to get everything loaded up. All of them seemed nervous and unsure, a plus for us.

"How's your landing ability, kitten?" Chase asked, a

dead serious look on his face.

I looked at the pavement below us. "As long as it's not face first, good enough."

He nodded and turned to look beyond the gates, I followed where he looked.

The darkness was just starting to fade when Victor raised his hand and glanced in the direction of the shed on the roof a few buildings over.

Four guards moved into place by the gates leading into the compound, ready to open them. The first through the gate would be the royal brothers, standing there looking like a force to be reckoned with. Tall, fierce and proud. At one end beside the brothers stood Welsley, and he looked more than ready to beat on someone. Standing at the other end was Tim, his eyes on me and not the gates like everyone else. My guess was his first priority was to get to my side when they were through the gate.

"Grab the straps crossed at our backs," Troy instructed quietly as he watched his eldest brother.

"Fight well, brother." Chase said in a distracted way.

"Well enough to beat you, brother." Troy responded automatically. "We'll hit the ground before you, Daxx, just stay between us on the way down."

Reaching, I grabbed the leather at each man's back as they crouched down. There was a loud cracking noise, followed by a breeze that washed over us. Taking a deep breath, I readied for the jump.

Heavy muscles clenched under my hands and I knew the mages had done their thing and everyone could see what I'd been seeing all along.

Before I could take another breath, the twins launched us through the air and we were free falling to the hard surface beneath us. I decided in that moment this was one hell of a rush and from now on would do this to get the juices flowing and battle ready.

Boots hit the pavement in unison and mine a second after them. Letting go, I looked at one and then the other.

"Helluva entrance, boys!"

Tim was in front of us a second later, his huge sword drawn and ready. With a nod to the kings, he grinned at me. "My Huntress."

Pulling the Sais out I held them back against my forearms, with a quick glance at the brothers, I took off with Tim into the rush of bodies. There would be no pausing to admire the action taking place all around us as three advanced on us before we could get our bearings. Tim grunted as he lunged forward and blocked the first swing.

Putting my new moves to good use, I went down under his swing and came up beside the man he was presently preventing from making a hotdog bun out of him. Stabbing the Sai into the thin man's leg to distract him, I pulled the scanner off and buzzed him before he could even howl in pain.

There was no time for praise of a smooth move as the other two growled and came at us. Flipping around again, I came up beside Tim and made sure to stay clear of the radius of his swing as he got into it with the first one to swing.

Side stepping, I cleared the blade that was swung at my head. Kicking up, I knocked the blade back to a comfortable distance, more comfortable for my health. With a twist of my wrists, I managed to score a double whammy on the guy before he could swing again. Enough fun with this one, I pulled the scanner and gave him the poof back to the holding cells.

No time to pause, I turned back to see Tim holding his guy on the ground with one well-placed foot. Ouch. No breeding for that one any time soon, I thought as I quickly moved the scanner over him.

Out of the corner of my eye I saw a blur. Spinning on my boot, I whipped the Sais out and came an inch close from dicing up Shelby. She raised one eyebrow at me, and took a step back to a safer distance. Her determined look faltered for a second as she took in the tattoo running down my arm, a longing appeared in her eyes. Shaking it off, she moved over and motioned to the last building. "Marcus is in there."

I knew her coming to me with it was the biggest suck up ever after she'd tried to relocate my face that time, but I'd take it. There was one way to stop this quickly and taking down Marcus was it. With a nod to her, I started toward the end building, skirting my way around any bodies that were scuffling in the path.

Tim was on one side of me and Shelby on the other. I wasn't going to tell her not to come, I knew she had one hell of a swing on her and if it was for me instead of against me, I'd take it.

We passed Rafael and Leone double teaming this giant of man, and I mean he made them look tiny. I paused for a step to see if they needed help, but then Victor started heading in their direction and I knew they wouldn't be needing my usefulness.

Turning, I watched Quinton take a guy down with a blow that would have stopped a Mack truck. With a satisfied grin, he turned and advanced on the next poor soul in his reach.

My boys could do the dance, of that there was no doubt. Pausing, I quickly scanned anybody that wasn't charging or swinging cutting the numbers down to a more manageable amount. Shelby and Tim had my back the whole time. I'd never had a woman fight with me before and I started to wonder if it might not be a bad idea, later on.

Just before we reached the building, a shadow appeared in the darkened doorway. A wave of something moved over me and I knew we'd just found Marcus. Slowing, I glanced to the two behind me. "Watch my back while I deal with this jerk."

Tim looked like he wanted to object, but he nodded and pointed Shelby in the direction she was to take. Shelby sent me hesitant look but moved to do it anyways.

I stood back from the door, keeping a good twenty feet between us. "Are you going to hide in the dark, Marcus? I thought you were a man." Another wave moved over me and

I knew he was trying to disable me in some way with his hoodoo junk. "Come on, Marcus, surely you know how to fight like a man, don't you?"

I chanced a few steps closer and shrugged. "You don't need magic tricks to fight one girl." That did it, he stepped out into the early dawn light, and looking pissed off like I'd never seen before.

"Do I look like a gullible child, Huntress?" He held open palms toward me.

Another wave moved over my skin, I shook it off and held my ground. "I'm too ladylike to say what you look like, dear Marcus." Motioning with my Sais all around us, I sent him an exasperated sigh. "Is this really what you want?"

"You have no idea what I want," he sneered, his eyes glowing that funky purple.

I snorted. "Gee, let me guess." I paused. "World domination."

He lifted his hands a few inches from his body and I realized I needed to keep this guy talking so he had less time to spin his little tricks.

"Come on. Whatever the problem is, I'm sure it can be resolved in a civilized manner." I remembered the last group we'd taken down. "We know about all the lies you've been feeding everyone to get them to side with you. How long do you think you can pull that off?"

A shocked look briefly crossed his face before he could mask it from me. "I don't need much longer…"

I sighed. "Let's cut the shit and get to the bottom line. It's over, take a look around you. This is the second time we've tracked your ass down and we'll just keep coming." I took a few steps in his direction and for a second I thought he was going to bolt, or worse do his disappearing thing again. "You're an intelligent man, do the math."

"I don't want to be anyone's servant ever again." He stated with a tone of determination.

I shrugged. "I hate paying taxes, but I know there's no way around it so I suck it up and do it."

When he lifted his hands with purpose, I reacted before I could even think about it. My raptor was in my hand and flying toward him. I caught him in the thigh and was momentarily shocked I'd managed to get a hit in on him.

With a snarl, he looked down at it and then it popped out and clattered to the pavement. Now, *that* I didn't see coming, it was like his body had repelled the knife. Frowning, I took several steps in his direction, hoping if I got a shot at him again I'd be able to do some real damage at a closer range.

"You're quite skilled, Huntress." He said sounding bored.

I shrugged and palmed the second Sai back into my free hand. "Ditto." The sound of clanging metal behind me started to fade as I focused solely on the lethal man in front of me. I would have felt better if he'd at least take a swing with something physical, but instead he raised his hands and began moving them in a graceful pattern. I tried to pick up something familiar in the movement, but it was nothing like any of the ones Rafael had shown me. "Come on, Marcus. I have a bit of pull with the Kings, we could discuss things in a civilized way."

His pattern faltered as he looked to me, his eyes moved over the tattoo on my arm. "As the prophecies appear to be coming true, I will have to pass on that. I too have a prophecy to avoid bringing to reality."

There was something in there that sent warning bells ringing inside my head. All of this was because of another damn prediction probably made an eon ago or longer. Jeeze, didn't this race believe in shit happens? "Maybe by doing what you're doing you're just making it happen faster."

His eyes radiated the purple hue again. "You can't possibly be naïve enough to believe that, *Huntress*."

The way he hissed huntress was really starting to grate on my nerves. Sighing, I knew talk was done and we were about to get nasty with each other. "I believe a lot of things." I stepped left, trying for a better angle to get a shot at his abdomen, hoping it wasn't as knife retardant as his leg. "I believe in justice and fair play. I believe in laws, because without them we are no better than wild animals ravishing the meek and helpless…"

"I believe," he interrupted, his hands moving again. "I've had enough conversation for today, thank you."

I spotted something I knew in the movement of his hands and braced myself for what was coming. Heat blasted over me, but it never reached the intensity he had wanted. I watched disbelief wash over him and tone down the bold brightness of his glowing violet eyes.

Before I could catch my breath, he began to move them in a jerky way with more speed. This one might hurt was all I had time to think when another wave crushed against me. I might be impervious to his powers, but the back lash still managed to grind at me. My knees began to shake as I stood there trying to keep my breathing steady. It was starting to piss me off that he had to cheat to win.

In a last attempt to get around his power, I dropped down to one knee, trying to make it look like whatever he was doing was working. Letting the Sai drop to the ground, I turned my body so he couldn't see me reach for the throwing knife.

When he laughed, I grabbed it and hurled it toward him with all the strength I could muster. It hit him just below the rib cage and he howled in pain. Lifting my head, I stumbled back to my feet, grasping the Sais in both hands again.

He had to use his hand to pull that one out and I felt a smug satisfaction knowing I'd really scored this time. With a howl of rage, he flung the knife and glared at me. All at once my head felt light and dizzy as I tried to stay on my feet and face him. I could hear someone yelling behind me, but didn't take my eyes off Marcus. It was better his attention was on me and none of the others.

I only had one knife left and knew I had to make this one count or I was in deep shit for sure. With weakening legs, I pushed forward, trying to get as close to him as possible, I stumbled twice, the second time I grasped the handle of the long blade and pulled it free.

Marcus stood there, blood flowing between his fingers of his hand as he kept the other palm aimed in my direction. A thought passed through my head and made me almost smile, I now understood Quinton's loathing of Magicians. Breathing was getting harder, but I watched him jerk and lean forward, like it was draining him too so I kept moving forward no matter how hard it was to force my legs to take steps.

Readying my power hand to grab the blade when I had the chance, it probably looked like I was holding my stomach, if it distracted him I didn't care if he saw me as weak in any way. Forcing air into my lungs, I focused on his chest and kept my gaze steady on my target.

Another wave took me by surprise and I cursed that he still had that much left in him. Someone clubbing the S.O.B. in the back of the head would have been a welcomed diversion right around now.

Taking one more step my knee almost buckled beneath me. This being my last chance I palmed the blade and took one more deep breath so I could give the toss all I had. A movement at my left side startled me and the knife missed his chest and embedded in his shoulder.

Troy crossed in front of me, the last thing I saw was him flinging his sword in the direction of Marcus, yelling a battle scream as he hit the ground. Everything faded after that.

CHAPTER FORTY-FIVE

Come on, kitten, stay with us.”

I opened my eyes and squinted against the light as Chase shook me not so gently. The first thing I saw was his relieved face as I struggled to sit up. “What the hell happened?”

“You passed out,” he said in a hushed way as his eyes roamed all over me, “Let’s not do that again.”

“Why are you always the first face I see?” I hissed out a breath, “When I come around?” He grinned at me then it dawned on me that he was way too close, Troy would be going all ape man again if he didn’t let me go. “Troy…”

“Quinton and Rafael are seeing to him.” He pulled me up slowly until I was almost sitting, my head spun faster than that stupid spinning thing at the park kids torture each other on.

Heaving out a breath, I rubbed a hand over my face. “Seeing to him?”

He nodded and motioned with his head as he sat me up completely.

My stomach lurched and then the thunder hit my brain. I was not going to battle it out with a mage ever again, this was worse than a hangover. Turning slowly, I looked in the direction he had pointed out. Quinton and Rafael were kneeling over Troy. Everything came back to me in a rush,

Troy jumping between Marcus and I. He would have been hit with whatever the spell was trying to do to me, only Troy wasn't immune to the magician's power.

Struggling to get to my feet, I gave up and crawled toward Troy. If it hadn't been for Chase keeping my face off the asphalt I would have landed on it more than once in my attempt to get to him. Rafael moved aside and helped Chase balance me as I tried to lift my hand to touch Troy.

His chest was cold and barely moving as he lay there with his eyes closed. "Is he alright?" I wobbled again and Chase steadied me once more.

The look on Quinton's face told me how serious it was. "Troy," I whispered unable to speak any louder with the pounding in my head. He didn't respond.

Panic flooded into me, what had he done? Why would he put himself in Marcus's path? "Troy?" I tried louder, leaning close to his face.

His eyelids fluttered a few times and I knew he heard me. Swallowing the nausea down I reached to touch his face. "Troy, come on. I need you to open your eyes." I was suddenly so dizzy I almost collapsed on top of him. Chase pulled me up again. "Help me," I gasped when a wave of pain stabbed through me.

Chase looked at me for a long silent moment and then sighed. "I can't, kitten. Mated to one brother and blood bonded to another would most likely land all three of us into our own personal hell." Nodding to Rafael, he leaned me into the younger man's arms and turned to glower at his twin lying there motionless. "Come on, brother. You have a mate that needs you," he spoke beside his head, "you can't leave her like this."

Troy's eyes opened to slits. He moved them around, visibly fighting to keep them open. My heart hiccupped as he looked at me. Troy turned to Chase. "Help her."

Chase shook his head. "That's for you to do now."

Troy's eyes drifted shut. "Too weak," he swallowed. "Take her home, brother."

Quinton growled a sound of annoyance. "That's for you to do, Troy. Open your damn eyes and look after your mate."

I wanted to tell them both I was fine, but I really wasn't. The dizziness was getting worse, add the tears that were threatening just seeing Troy in this condition and I was a mess.

"Need to feed," Troy mumbled.

Quinton and Arius moved around to grasp their large sibling by the arms and between them they propped him up against their bodies and held him upright.

Victor knelt down beside me. A look passed between him and Chase and then Chase nodded and turned to look at me.

Without a word, he grasped my chin lightly and held my eyes with his. Even though my head was swimming I understood what he intended and nodded my head as best I could.

Shifting me in his arms, Rafael leaned toward Troy's body. Chase helped to guide me into a better position. I felt weak and useless as he lowered me across his chest.

Leaning over Troy, Chase said clearly. "Thank me or hate me, brother but I won't see either of you suffer any longer." Lifting Troy's head, he glanced at me. "Feed, brother king and live to rule tomorrow."

I could feel Troy's ragged breath at the side of my throat as Victor knelt down and sliced into his king's muscled shoulder. I glanced at him and saw a gentle acceptance in his eyes. Placing my lips around the wound, I suckled gently as the same moment Troy's fangs bit into my neck.

Through the fog I expected the same energy to warm me that had before, but instead heat rushed into me with such intensity I stopped and gasped. A hand gently held my head in place so I wouldn't move away completely.

When Troy moved beneath me, I realized it was his hand and he was coming around. Suddenly no one was touching us or holding us up, Troy's other arm wrapped around me and he rolled us both to lie on our sides, keeping me tight against his body.

I felt his tongue slide over the bite and was going to lift my own head away, but his large hand stopped me, so I continued for a few more moments.

When he moved his hand away I looked up to see his red eyes completely open and filled with a look of love. A look I'd never seen before. "We'll discuss your stupid stunt later," he said softly against my mouth.

I only nodded and held on as he turned and lifted us both to our feet. My head was feeling a little fluffy still, but other than that I felt wonderful, inside and out. Troy held me for a few more seconds and then with a kiss to my forehead he stepped back and looked around at the men watching us. "What happened?"

Chase snorted. "Before you went all hero and jumped into the stream of magic or after?"

Troy sent his twin an exasperated look. "Both."

Chase looked at the spot we had just been on. "Well you know the after part…" He nodded to where Marcus had been standing, "he left something behind."

Running a hand down my arm gently, Troy moved over to where the magician had been. Glancing over his shoulder, he sent us an odd look. "Can the witches trace him using this?"

Leaving me standing there, my brain still lagging to catch up, I looked around the compound. Only a few guards remained behind, they were cleaning up weapons and washing down the bloodier areas. Turning back, I did a quick assessment of the boys and all seemed to be whole and well enough. Wandering over, I pushed my way between them to see what Marcus had left behind. My stomach lurched when I saw it was his foot. Troy's sword lay beside it so it wasn't hard to figure out how it was separated from its owner.

"He'll be easier to track down now," Quinton offered trying not to smirk.

Troy went over and picked up my raptor and his sword.

He motioned to the bloody foot and then looked at Michael. "Take it back and see if the witches can use it for any good."

Michael paled as he looked down at it, but he still nodded and went over to it.

Not wanting to watch him pick it up, I turned away and stood looking around the compound again. I felt Troy come up behind me and put the raptor in its case. "I can't believe we lost him."

He moved around and looked down at me, his hazel eyes filled with something entirely different then what I was talking about. "We'll get him." Reaching out he ran his hand down over my markings again. "I didn't know they were…"

I put my hand over his mouth and shook my head. "I was coherent enough, well more than you, to understand what was happening."

Kissing my hand, he pulled it away from his mouth and held it in his. "Thank you."

My heart lunged inside, almost hitting my ribs just from his simple touch. "For what?"

"Saving me. I couldn't move and when I tried after seeing you…" His eyes filled with pain as they moved over me. "Are you alright?"

I nodded, leaning into him, just wanting to feel him closer. "Yes. I can't say I was doing much better than you before your blood." I ran my finger over the pendant on his chest. "So, we're really connected now permanently?"

"Yes, you're very much stuck with me now," he lifted my chin with his finger and searched my eyes. "Can you live with that?"

The vulnerability in his eyes made my chest ache. "I think I can. You on the other hand may live to regret it. I've been told I'm a bit of a bitch at times. Think you can handle that?"

Troy chuckled. "I know I can." With a soothing motion, he ran the back of his hand up and down my tattooed arm. "And yes, we're connected permanently. Can you feel it?"

"I feel your presence inside me. It's like when you kiss me, I feel complete. Is that what I should feel?"

His eyes lit up. "Exactly that." Lowering his head, he brushed his lips across mine, lingering long enough that I wanted more.

"Can we go home now?" I asked making sure my lips brushed up against his.

"Yes." Grasping the back of my head, he kissed me roughly, enclosing me in his arms.

"I realize you've just sealed the deal, brother king, but the honeymoon will have to wait. We have prisoners to interrogate." Chase said beside us.

Troy lifted his lips from mine and straightened up but continued to look at me, his eyes were turning from hazel to red as he did. "I don't think I'm going to make it to the cells right now." He gave me a smoldering look.

My arm started to tingle but then it moved through my entire body, a sensation that took me from wanting him to needing him. Now. I sucked in a breath and began to run my hands over his bare chest.

"Troy, you can't be serious." Chase cleared his throat. "I know you're standing there with your newly mated woman, but we have…"

"Not now, Chase," I said breathlessly when Troy opened his mouth, baring his fangs. Reaching up I ran my finger over the sharp point and smiled up at him.

"Huh." Chase sighed. "Fangs do it for you then." His boots echoed on the pavement.

Biting my finger gently, Troy took my hand away from his mouth. "We need to leave. Now." I nodded.

A familiar vibration moved through me and in an instant we were standing in Troy's bedroom. Reaching up, I undid the buckle that held his sword to his back, the metal hit the floor with a loud clang. His hands were freeing me of my own harness, I paused for a split second wondering where my Sais were but the burning need began to move through me so they were quickly forgotten.

With impatient hands, he pulled the leather armor from my body and flung it to the floor, my tank top followed quickly. I was trying to get his jeans undone when his mouth closed around an aching nipple and I groaned, my knees almost folding as another wave of lust flooded me.

Grasping his head, I held on so he wouldn't stop. "Will it always be like this?" I whispered trying to breath.

Nipping me gently with his sharp teeth, then he straightened and pulled me into his body. "Hot and needy?"

I nodded, the rasping of his voice going straight to my core and robbing me of the power of speech.

Ripping the button from my pants, he had them pooled at my feet faster than I could blink. I kicked out of my boots and stepped out of them almost as fast. When he lifted me up, I wrapped my legs around his waist.

He started walking us to the bathroom, his teeth blazing a trail up my throat as he went. "No. After four or five times, I can probably slow down enough to savor you slowly."

I groaned as he sucked on my neck. "Only four or five?"

Grasping my hair, he pulled my head back so he could move his mouth up the column of my throat. "Mmm, at least."

****

My entire body was numb in the most pleasing way. I couldn't feel my feet or arms, and I'd never felt as amazing as I did right now. I looked over at the sweat-soaked man beside me lying sprawled on his back. Running my hand down over the bite marks on his chest, I wanted to purr with satisfaction. "I believe that was seven," I whispered, resting my cheek against his rib cage.

He chuckled. "Math was never my strong point." Rolling, he pulled me into his long body, fitting me tight against him. He licked the sweat from my throat leisurely for a few moments. "Are you very sore? I'm sorry I'm so rough with you. I just can't seem to help it."

He nipped my throat with sharp teeth, causing a quack of pleasure to move through me. "I'll let you know when the feeling returns."

Leaning back, he grinned at me. "You know I have healing properties in my saliva, I could *ease* your discomfort…"

Placing my hand over his lips, I smiled at him. "I fell for that on round four, or was it five? I'll just lay here and enjoy the ache for now."

"If you're sure." Pulling my head, he cradled me against his chest, his hand gently stroking down my back.

"Troy?" I inhaled the male scent of him.

"Mmm."

Tipping my head back I studied the hazel eyes moving over my face with complete adoration shining from them. "I'm not sure I want to have twins. I mean I'm all for the living a long time, I just don't think I want twins."

He chuckled. "We could get lucky and that will fall to Chase and his mate."

I sighed and rested my head over his heartbeat. "I guess we'll find out in about two hundred and forty years then."

Rolling me onto my back, his weight pushing me into the bed, he smiled down at me suggestively. "I can think of a few things to do to pass the time until then."

The exhaustion was forgotten, the hunt for Marcus pushed aside and all that mattered was the man whose lips moved over my own with aching tenderness. We'd get Marcus, later…

Much, much later.

Someone pounding on the door startled both of us. "Troy! Daxx! You need to get out here. Now!" Raf's voice was more urgent than I'd ever heard. Before we could cover up the door flew open. "It's Crissy. We have to go."

ABOUT THE AUTHOR

J. Risk is a pseudonym used by Jacqueline Paige

I wanted to write a story that would fit into new adult levels as well as adult. Something that was serious with fun elements--paranormal / fantasy that everyone could read and enjoy.

I've decided to use J. Risk as the pen name for this to separate this series from my other writing which is definitely adult reading material.

Jacqueline Paige lives in Ontario in a small town that's part of the popular Georgian Triangle area.

She began her writing career in 2006 and since her first published works in 2009 she hasn't stopped. Jacqueline describes her writing as *all things paranormal,* which she has proven is her niche with stories of witches, ghosts, physics and shifters now on the shelves.

When Jacqueline isn't lost in her writing, she spends time with her five children, most of whom are finally able to look after her instead of the other way around. Together they do random road trips, that usually end up with them lost, shopping trips where they push every button in the toy aisle, hiking when there's enough time to escape and bizarre things like creating new daring recipes in the kitchen. She's a grandmother to six (so far) and looks forward to corrupting many more in the years to come.

Jacqueline loves to hear from her readers, you can find her at

http://jacquelinepaige.com

Author note:

Did you enjoy reading one of my books?

If so, PLEASE help spread the word on social media. You can help by sharing on Facebook, tweet about it, post something on Instagram, Pinterest. Posting a review on your favorite book sites go a long way to help authors. With your help in keeping my books "out there", I can continue writing to keep those stories coming.

Writing and promoting can be very time consuming. I love talking to readers, but the hours spent on keeping so many social media outlets current can become overwhelming and time for writing pays the price. If you can take a few minutes to help, that would be awesome. Thank you!

386

www.ingramcontent.com/pod-product-compliance
Lightning Source LLC
Chambersburg PA
CBHW050857130726
47900CB00013B/117